TWIN HEIRS TO HIS THRONE

BY
OLIVIA GATES

MILLS & BOON

First Published in Great Britain 2016
By Mills & Boon, an imprint of HarperCollins*Publishers*
1 London Bridge Street, London, SE1 9GF

© 2016 Olivia Gates

ISBN: 978-0-263-91843-4

51-0116

Our policy is to use papers that are natural, renewable and recyclable products and made from wood grown in sustainable forests.The logging and manufacturing processes conform to the legal environmental regulations of the country of origin.

Printed and bound in Spain
by CPI, Barcelona

Olivia Gates has always pursued creative passions such as singing and handicrafts. She still does, but only one of her passions grew gratifying enough, consuming enough, to become an ongoing career—writing.

She is most fulfilled when she is creating worlds and conflicts for her characters, then exploring and untangling them bit by bit, sharing her protagonists' every heart-wrenching heartache and hope, their every heart-pounding doubt and trial, until she leads them to an indisputably earned and gloriously satisfying happy ending.

When she's not writing, she is a doctor, a wife to her own alpha male, and a mother to one brilliant girl and one demanding Angora cat. Visit Olivia at www.oliviagates.com.

Prologue

"Only family is allowed to visit Mr. Voronov, Ms. Stavros."

"At least…"

The nurse cut Kassandra's protest off, stonewalling her again. "Only family is allowed to learn information about his condition."

"But…"

Refusing to give concessions they both knew she wasn't allowed to grant, the nurse rushed away, dismissing her like everyone else had. For the past damned week. Since his accident.

The dread and desperation she'd been struggling to keep at bay rose until she felt her blood charring.

Leonid. Lying somewhere in this hospital, injured, out of reach, with her deprived of even knowing his condition. She wasn't family. She was nothing to him, not to the rest of the world. Nobody knew of their year-long affair.

With no one left to approach for information or reassurance, she staggered to the hectic waiting area of the highest-ranking New York City university hospital. The moment she slumped down on the first vacant seat, the tears she'd been forbidding herself to shed since she'd heard of his accident spilled right out of her soul.

Nothing could happen to him. Her vital, powerful Leonid. She couldn't live without him, could barely remember her life before she'd first laid eyes on him three years ago.

That night, she'd been the star model and one of the top designers in a charity fashion show. As she'd walked out onto the catwalk, her gaze, which normally never focused on anyone in the audience, had been dragged toward a point at the end of the massive space. Then another unprecedented thing had happened. She'd almost stumbled, had stopped for endless, breathless moments, staring at him across the distance, overwhelmed by his sheer gorgeousness and presence.

Though tycoon gods populated her Greek-American family, and she moved in the circles of the megarich and powerful, Leonid was in a league of one. Not only was he a billionaire with a sports-brand empire, but a decathlon world champion…and royalty to boot. He was a prince of Zorya, a kingdom once part of the former Soviet Union, and annexed to Belarus since its disintegration. Though the kingdom hadn't existed in over ninety years, he was still considered royalty in Asia and Europe—and sports and financial royalty in the rest of the world.

Not that any of these attributes had contributed to

his being the only man to ever get her hot and flustered with a mere look. He'd continued to scorch her with such looks for two endless years as they'd moved in the same circles. But nothing had come of it. He'd never come closer than the minimum it had taken him to keep her inflamed and in suspense, until she'd believed that the lust she'd felt blasting from him had been wishful thinking on her part.

Then had come the wedding of one of her best friends, Caliope Sarantos, to Maksim Volkov in Russia. Leonid had been one of the groom's guests. After every man but him had asked her to dance, frustrated out of her mind, she'd escaped outside to get some air. She'd found none when he'd followed her, at last, and taken away her breath completely.

She'd since relived those heart-pounding moments endless times, as he'd closed in on her, informing her that she could no longer run from him. Closing her eyes now, she could again feel his arms around her and his lips over hers as he'd dragged her into that kiss that had made her realize why she hadn't ever let another near. Because she'd been waiting for him her whole life.

But before he'd taken her on what had turned out to be a magical roller-coaster ride, he'd made his intentions clear: nothing but passion and pleasure would be on offer. And Kassandra had been perfectly okay with that. At thirty, she'd never wanted to marry, and she'd long given up on meeting a man she could want, let alone that completely. Finding Leonid had added a totally unexpected and glorious dimension to her life. Having him free from expectations had been a sure path to ecstasy and a surefire guard against disappointment.

Being with him had exhilarated and satisfied her

in ways she hadn't known existed. They'd meshed in every way, met when their hectic schedules allowed, away from the world's eyes, always starving for one another. Keeping their relationship secret from everyone, above all her conservative Greek family who'd long disapproved of her unconventional lifestyle, had made everything even more incendiary.

Then Leonid's training for his upcoming championship had intensified, and between that and running his business empire, she'd seen less and less of him. Media scrutiny had made it impossible to even visit him while he'd trained.

That was when she'd realized she was no longer content with their status quo. But before she'd had time to ponder how to demand a change in the terms of their relationship, he'd had his accident.

From the media reports that had hailed him as a hero, she'd learned that a trailer had flown over the center divider of the I-95 heading into NYC, and into the incoming traffic. Before it had managed to pulverize a car carrying a father and his daughter, Leonid had smashed into their car's side, ramming them out of the path of destruction. But the trailer had slammed into his car full force, catapulting his vehicle into a tumbling crash.

She'd almost fainted with horror at the sight of the crumpled wreck his car had become. It was a miracle he had come out alive.

Desperate to be by his side the moment she'd heard the news, the nightmare had only escalated when she hadn't been able to determine where he'd been taken. Now that she'd finally found him, she'd again been denied any information. She was being treated like the stranger everyone thought she was. He was her lover.

And the father of the baby she'd just yesterday found out she was carrying.

Suddenly, her heart boomed. Was that…?

Yes, yes it was. Ryan McFadden. Her old college friend who'd gone on to become a doctor. She'd seen him a couple of years ago, but he'd been working at another hospital at the time. Finding him here was a lifeline.

Before Ryan could express surprise at seeing her, she flung herself at him, begged him to let her see Leonid, or at least to let her know how he was.

Clearly used to dealing with frantic people, Ryan covered the hands clawing his arm. "I know that apart from his time in surgery, he's been conscious since they brought him in."

He was? And he hadn't called her?

But what if… "C-can he talk?"

"Oh, yes. None of his injuries involved vital organs, thankfully."

And he hadn't left instructions to let her in, or to even let her know how he was?

At her deepening dismay, Ryan rushed on. "He was transferred to an exclusive wing with only his medical team allowed in, to guard against media infringement. But I'll gain access to him. If he grants you permission to visit him…"

"He will." She hugged him fervently. "Thank you."

Giving her a bolstering grin, Ryan strode away.

After what felt like forever, he returned, giving her two thumbs up. She found herself flying to him, so he could take her to Leonid.

At the wing's door, Ryan stopped her. "Listen, Kass, I know it's hard for you to do in your current condition, but keep it light and short, for his sake."

Nodding, she wiped away the tears that had gathered in her eyes again. "How…how bad are his injuries?"

"I don't know details, but when he was brought in I heard he'd suffered compound fractures to both his legs."

Her heart imploded all over again. His legs.

To anyone else, it would mean months of limited mobility. To Leonid, it meant his plans for a new world record were over, who knew for how long. Maybe he'd never heal enough to compete on that elite level again. When that was a major part of his being…

Stop it. She couldn't consider worst-case scenarios. Ryan was right. She had to suppress her own anxiety. Leonid needed her support for the first time ever, and she was damned if she would fail him. Putting on a brave face, she opened the door.

He was the first thing she saw as she stepped into the exquisite suite. Only the bed with monitors surrounding it at its far end betrayed its presence in a medical facility.

Leonid, her beloved lion. He lay sprawled on his back, his perfect body swathed in a hospital gown, already diminished, both legs in full casts, arms limp at his sides, eyes closed. His almost shoulder-length hair lay tousled around a face that was unscathed, but his skin was drained of its normal vital bronze color.

Her heart lurched violently, as if to fling her across the room to him, catapulting her feet forward.

As she eagerly bent to kiss his clamped lips, he opened his eyes. Instead of the most vivid blue, they were almost black. And they slammed into her with the force of a shove. But it was what filled them that had her jackknifing up. Her nerves jangled; her balance wavered. She couldn't be reading the aversion in his expression correctly.

But what gripped his face didn't look like pain, or the effect of a drug. There was no distress or fogginess in his eyes, just clarity and…emptiness.

Telling herself it was an expected by-product of everything he'd gone through, she reached for his hand, suppressed a shudder at how cold it was. "Leonid, darling…"

He tugged his hand away, harder than necessary, from her trembling hold. "I'm fine."

Reminding herself that what she felt didn't matter, that only he did, she forced a smile. "You do look…"

His glacial look stopped her flimsy lie in its tracks. "I know how I look. But I *am* fine, considering." A beat. "I hear you kicked up quite a commotion trying to get to me."

He knew? And he hadn't told them to let her in earlier?

His expression became even more inanimate as he looked away. "I kept hoping you'd give up and just leave."

Her throat squeezed, making it nearly impossible to breathe. "I—I realize how you must feel. But there will be other championships…"

He cut her off again. "I'm sick of people placating me."

Telling herself he needed her nearness even if his current mood made him pretend he didn't, she sat down and caressed his corded forearm, trying to infuse him with her strength and let their connection bolster him. "I'm not 'people,' Leonid. I'm your woman, your lover, and you're my…"

His gaze swung to hers, this time filled with frost. "You're free to consider yourself whatever you want, but I'm certainly not your anything."

The lump in her throat grew spikes. But still convinced it was his ordeal talking, she tried again. "Leonid, darling…"

He shook off her hand, his face twisting in a snarl. "Don't you dare 'darling' me. I made my terms clear from the start. The only reason I was with you was because I thought you agreed to them."

Shocked out of her wits at his viciousness, she again told herself she must have gravely underestimated the effects of his injuries and near-death experience, that it was better to withdraw now, before he got even more worked up.

She stood up carefully so she wouldn't sway. "I only wanted to know you're okay… I shouldn't have disturbed you…"

"No, you shouldn't have. But now I'm glad you did."

"Y-you are?"

"That's the one good thing that's come out of this mess. It's giving me the chance to do what I've been trying to do."

Her heart decelerated, as if afraid to beat and let his meaning sink in. "What have you been trying to do?"

"I've been trying to end this."

Her heart stopped. "This? You mean…us?"

His stone-cold gaze slammed into her, compromising what was left of her balance. "There was never an 'us.' I thought we had an arrangement for sexual recreation, to unwind from the stresses of the pursuits that matter in our lives. But you were only pretending to abide by my terms, until I was softened enough, or maybe weakened enough, as you must believe I am now, to change the terms to what you wanted all along, weren't you? You're just another status-hunting, biological-clock-ticking woman after all, aren't you?"

Unable to breathe, she flinched away. "Please…stop…"

He pushed a button that brought him to a seated position, as if to pursue her to drive his point through her heart. "I'm not stopping until this is over, once and for all. I grabbed the opportunity of training to break it off with you naturally, but you only escalated your pursuit. And now that you think me a sitting duck, you're here to pin me down? To smother me with solicitude at my lowest ebb? You think you'll make me so grateful I'll end up offering you a commitment?"

She shook her head, shook all over, the tears she'd suppressed burning from her depths again. "You know it was never like that. Please, just calm down…"

"So now you want to make it look as if I'm raving and ranting? But you're right. I'm not calm. I'm fed up. What else can I do so you'll understand I can't bear your suffocating sweetness anymore?"

Shock seeping deeper into her marrow, she staggered back to escape his mutilating barrage. "Please… enough… I'll leave…"

"And you won't return. Ever."

His icy savagery shredded her insides. It was as if the man she loved had never existed. As if the accident had only revealed the real him, someone who relished employing cruelty to get rid of what he considered a nuisance.

She'd swayed halfway to the door before she stopped.

She couldn't bear telling him. It would only validate his accusations. But he had to know.

Teetering around, she met the baleful bleakness of his stare, and forced the admission out. "I—I'm pregnant."

Something spiked in his gaze before his thick lashes lowered, and he seemed to be contemplating something horrific.

At length, demeanor emptied of all expression, he raised his gaze to her. "Are you considering keeping it?"

Her world tilted. The Leonid she'd known would have never asked this. The real Leonid did because it was clear he'd rather she didn't.

Trying to postpone falling apart until she walked out, she choked, "I only told you because I thought you had a right to know. I guess you would have rather not known."

"Answer me."

The remaining notches of her control slipped. "Why are you asking?" she cried. "You made it clear you care nothing about what I do or about me at all."

He held her gaze, the nothingness in his eyes engulfing her.

Then he just said, "I don't."

One

Two years later...

"After his disappearance from public view over two years ago, Prince Leonid Voronov is back in the spotlight. The former decathlon world champion dropped off the radar after suffering injuries in a car crash that took him off the competitive circuits. Now the billionaire founder and CEO of Sud, named after the Slavic god of destiny and glory, one of the largest multinational corporations of sports apparel, equipment, accessories and services, could be poised to become much more. As one of three contenders for the resurrected throne of Zorya, a nation now in the final stages of seceding from Belarus, he could soon become king. With our field reporter on the scene as the former sports royalty and possible future king exited his New York headquarters..."

Kassandra fumbled for the remote, pushing every button before she managed to turn off the TV just as Leonid appeared on the screen.

But it was too late. She'd seen him. For the first time since she'd walked out of his hospital room twenty-six months ago. That had been the last time the world had seen him, too. He'd dropped off the radar completely ever since.

But he was back. Reentering the world yesterday like a meteor, making everyone gape in wonder as he hurtled out of nothingness, burning brighter than ever.

Everywhere she'd turned in the past twenty-four hours there'd been news of him. She'd avoided getting swept up in the tide of the world's curiosity about his reappearance, at least outwardly. Until now.

Now her retinas burned with the image of him striding out of his imposing Fifth Avenue headquarters. In spite of herself, she'd strained to see how much of the Leonid she'd known had survived his abrupt retirement from his life's passion.

The man she'd known had been crackling with vitality, a smile of whimsy and assurance always hovering on his lips and sparkling in the depths of his eyes. He'd perpetually looked aware of everything and everyone surrounding him, always connected and tapping in to the fabric of energy that made the world. She'd always felt as if he was always ready to break out in a run and overtake everyone as easily as he breathed. Which he'd literally done for eight years straight.

The man who'd filled the screen had appeared to be totally detached, as if he no longer was part of the world anymore. Or as if it was beneath his notice.

And there'd been another change. The stalking swagger was gone. In its place was a deliberate, almost menacing prowl. Whether this and the other changes she'd observed were sequels of the physical or psychological impact of his accident, one thing was clear, even in those fleeting moments.

This wasn't the man she'd known.

Or rather, the man she'd thought she'd known.

She'd long faced the fact that she'd known nothing of him. Not before she'd been with him, or while they'd been together, or after he'd shoved her away and vanished.

For most of that time, Kassandra had withdrawn from the world, too. After the shock of his rejection, she'd drowned in despondence as its implications and those of her pregnancy had sunk in. She'd been pathetic enough to be literally sick with worry about him, to pine for him until she'd wasted away. Until she'd almost miscarried.

That scare had finally jolted her to the one reality she'd been certain of. That she'd wanted that baby with everything in her and would never risk losing it. That day at the doctor's, she'd found out she wasn't carrying one baby, but two.

After the scare and the discovery, she'd forced everything into perspective, then had even progressed to consider what had happened a blessing. Before Leonid, she'd never thought she'd get married. She'd never considered marriage an option between them, not even when she'd wanted to demand a change in their arrangement. But she'd always wanted to be a mother. Especially after her best friends, Selene, Caliope and Naomi, had had their children. She'd known she wanted what they had, that she'd be good at it, that it would complete her life.

As he'd said, one good thing had come out of that

mess. She would be a mother without the complication of having a man around.

Not that it had been smooth sailing. Being pregnant and alone after the unbearable emotional injury of his rejection had been the hardest thing she'd ever gone through. Her family hadn't made it any easier. Their first reactions had ranged from mortification to outrage. Her mother had lamented that she'd deprived her of the traditional Greek wedding she'd planned for her from childhood, while her father had swung between wrathfully demanding the name of the bastard who'd impregnated and abandoned her to forbidding her to have a baby out of wedlock. Her siblings and other relatives had had a combination of both reactions to varying degrees, even those who'd tried to be progressive and supportive.

The only ones who'd been fully behind her from day one had been her trio of close friends. Not only had they always been there for her and vice versa, no questions asked, they'd once been in her situation. Even if *their* stories had progressed toward ecstatic endings.

But when her family realized the price for any negative stance would be never seeing her again, they'd relented. Their disappointment and misgivings had gradually melted, especially her parents', giving way to full involvement in her pregnancy and the preparation for her delivery. After the twins had arrived, they'd become everyone's favorites and considered to be the best thing that had ever happened to Kassandra. Everything had worked out for the best.

She'd reclaimed herself and her stability, had become even more successful career-wise, but most important she'd become a mother to two perfect daughters. Eva and Zoya. She'd given them both names meaning life, as they'd given *her* new life.

Then Zorya had suddenly filled the news with a declaration of its intention to reinstate the monarchy. With every rapid development, foreboding had filled her. Even when she'd had no reason to think it would make Leonid resurface.

It seemed her instincts had been correct, for here he was, back on the scene with a vengeance. In one day, he'd taken the world by storm, a mystic figure rising from the ashes of oblivion like a phoenix.

Leonid's disappearance had been the one thing left unresolved inside her. Everything she'd ever felt for or because of him had long dissipated. But wondering where he'd gone and what he'd been up to had lingered. Now explanations would be unearthed and any remaining mystique surrounding him would be gone, so she could once again resume her comforting routines, untouched by his disruption.

Leonid was a page that hadn't only been turned, but burned.

"Mama."

The tension clamping her every muscle suddenly drained at the chirping call of her eldest-by-minutes daughter, Eva. The girls had started calling her Mama two months ago. She hadn't thought it would be that big of a deal. But every time they said it, which was often now that they knew it activated her like nothing else, another surge of sheer love and indulgence flooded her. Her lips spread with delight as she strode through her spacious, cheerfully decorated Bel Air house to their room.

It had been like this for months. Eva and Zoya always woke up an hour after she put them to bed. It was as if they loathed wasting precious playtime sleeping, or thought they shouldn't leave her alone. But since she'd gone back to work after their first birthday almost six months ago, and they spent mornings with Kyria Despina, her late uncle's wife and now her nanny, she welcomed the extra time with them.

As she approached the nursery, she could hear the girls' efforts to climb out of their cribs through the ajar door. They were able to do it after a few trials now, but would soon be experts at it. She debated whether to go in or to let them complete their task and toddle their way to her in their playroom, as she'd been doing lately. It was why she'd been leaving the door ajar. She had child-proofed every inch of her home six thousand ways from Sunday after all.

Moments passed and neither toddler showed up at the end of the corridor. Heart booming with the always-hovering anxiety she'd learned was a permanent side effect of motherhood, she streaked inside and found both girls standing in their crib, literally asleep on their feet.

The tenacious tots were obeying their regular programming even though their strenuously fun weekend at Disneyland had left them wiped out.

Scooping them up, she held one in each arm in the way she'd perfected, cooing to them, letting them know as they nestled into her and made those sweet sleep sounds that she'd come, as she always would, that they hadn't missed that extra time with her they'd wanted.

Once she laid them down again, each turned to her favorite position and resumed a deep, contented sleep.

Sighing at that tremor of acute love and gratitude coursing through her, she walked out, closing the door completely now that she knew they were down for the night.

The moment she exited the room, the doorbell rang.

Frowning, she remembered that the girls' play pals, Judy and Mikey, had again left behind some toys she'd found only after a thorough tidying up. It had become a ritual for Sara, their mother and her neighbor, to come by and collect her children's articles after she'd put them to bed. They usually ended up having a cup of tea to unwind together after their hectic days.

Rushing to the door, she opened it with a ready smile. "We should establish rules about allowing only in-house toys…"

Air clogged her lungs. All her nerves fired, short-circuiting her every muscle, especially her heart.

Leonid.

Right there. On her doorstep.

She'd visualized this encounter countless times in waking trances and suffocating dreams. The perverse yearning had risen time and again for him to show up, look down at her from his prodigious height with eyes full of all he'd deprived her of, and tell her everything that had happened since his accident had been a terrible dream. She'd hoped for it until hope had turned to ashes.

And now…out of the blue, he was here…

Oh, God! He is really here.

Almost unrecognizable. Yet distressingly the same.

Observations accumulated in the white noise that filled her mind, burying her. The most obvious change was his hair. The silk that had been long enough to wind around her hands in the throes of passion was now severely cropped. It still suited him. It actually suited him better, accentuating the dominance of his bone structure.

The other major difference was his body. It hadn't been a distortion of the video or his size relative to others. He *was* bigger. Broader. More heavily muscled. The leanness of the runner had been replaced by the bulk of a supreme fitness athlete.

His every feature and nuance, familiar yet radically different, felt like a knife to the heart.

But on the whole, he looked as if everything human about him had melted away, revealing a creature of polished steel beneath. Even the way he held himself seemed…inhuman. As if he was now a being of pure intellect and purpose, like a cyborg, an animate form of artificial intelligence.

An hour could have passed as she gaped up at him and he stared blankly down at her. He'd always had that power. Time had always distorted when she'd entered his orbit.

"Invite me in, Kassandra."

His bottomless voice yanked her out of the stupor she'd stumbled in.

"I will do no such thing."

"Your porch isn't the place for what I've come to say."

Her mouth dropped open at his audacity. That he could just appear on her doorstep after what he'd done to her, and without even an attempt at apology or even civility, not only demand but expect to be invited in.

"There's no place where you can say anything to me. We have absolutely nothing to say to each other."

"After the past two years, we have plenty."

"The past two years are exactly why there's nothing to be said. Even if there was, I'm not interested in hearing it."

His eyes gave her a clinical sweep, as if assessing her

response for veracity and judging it to be false. It made her loathe her weakness for him all over again.

"I don't know what you were thinking coming here like this, what you expected, but if…"

"If you're still angry, we can discuss that, too."

If? *If?*

"Are you sure you broke only your legs in that accident? Sounds as if you'd pulverized way more. Like the components that made you human."

"I do realize showing up here must have surprised you…"

"Try *appalled* and *outraged.*"

He shifted, like the automaton she'd just accused him of becoming, as if moving into a different gear to counter her response. "That's why I showed up. I gathered if I called ahead, you would have been just as resistant to granting me an audience. So I decided to eliminate unnecessary steps."

"And this single step turned out to be as pointless. I'm not granting you an audience since we have zero things to discuss, so you might as well save us both the aggravation and go disappear again. Preferably forever this time."

"If you're concerned I might be here to exhume the past, rest assured I have no wish to resurrect anything between us. I'm not here for you at all. I'm here for my daughters."

Every word sank into her mind like a depth mine. Then the last ones exploded.

I'm here for my daughters.

My daughters.

The rage that detonated inside her, that he would dare say this, or even think it, almost rocked her on her feet.

Biting a tongue that had gone numb with fury, she gritted out, "Leave. Right this second."

Unperturbed, he gave a nonchalant shrug of his daunting shoulder. "I will leave after I've said what I came to say and when we've come to a preliminary understanding. Whether you approve or not, I am the father of your twin daughters, and I am here to—"

Red smeared her vision. "You won't be here much longer or I'm calling the police."

His searing blue gaze remained still, his pupils unmoving, indicating he had no emotional response to her threat and agitation. "I would advise against this. It would disrupt your neighborhood and bring you unneeded speculation and embarrassment. Not to mention you'd have to lie to the police to make them take action against me…"

"I won't be lying when I say you're here uninvited, harassing me and making fraudulent claims to *my* daughters."

"They're my daughters, too."

"Not according to the law, they're not. Nor to them or to the whole world. Any passing stranger they've ever briefly met is more to them than you are."

His formidable head inclined in agreement. "I know that being their biological father on its own means nothing. That's why I'm here, and I'm not going anywhere until I say my piece or until you indicate your willingness to negotiate further."

"What the hell do you mean, negotiate?"

"Over the twins, of course."

She gaped, unable to voice any of the million violent protests ricocheting in her skull and boiling her blood.

"Before you blast me off the face of the earth, I remind you that as their biological father, I do have a right to—"

"You have absolutely no right to Eva and Zoya. None. You relinquished any right to even think of them as yours way before they were born. You made it clear you didn't even want them to be born. You may have forgotten this, but I remember all too well."

"I freely admit I behaved extremely…inappropriately when you came to me after my accident. You can understand I was at my worst at the time."

"And you remained there for over two years?"

"I'm the first to admit it took me longer than acceptable to deal with everything."

Rage deepening at his dismissal of his abandonment of her, she seethed, "I care nothing about why you did what you did, and I'll be damned if I let you pretend it was forgivable and invade my life again. You're sure as hell never coming near my daughters."

"I'm not here seeking forgiveness. I don't waste my time, and I certainly won't waste yours pursuing the unattainable. But I'm here to acknowledge my responsibilities. Whatever I've done, I'm myself again."

"If you think *that* makes it any better, let me disabuse you of that notion. Being yourself is proof you know nothing of responsibility or accountability or even common courtesy and basic humanity."

Instead of stonewalling her again, he just nodded impassively. "You're right. My old self was nothing to be proud of. But the past couple of years changed me, and the man I am today is capable of at least being fully responsible and accountable, and resolved to take on his duties."

"Good for 'him.' And as long as 'he' takes his resolutions away from my family, I wish 'him' the best of luck."

"The thing is, your family is also mine. The twins are the primary duty I'm determined to take on."

She fought harder against the screams gathering at the back of her throat. "That would have been a commendable sentiment if they needed anything from you. Which they don't. And they never will. You've done your part and can now feel proud of yourself when you leave and never come back."

His azure gaze remained unwavering. "I do understand your alarm and rejection. But even if the past was rife with pain, I'm certain everything happened for a reason. Why else would I have twin girls, and now be called on to take the mantle of responsibility in the land of the twin goddesses?"

This made zero sense to her, leaving her speechless again.

Realizing she had no ready comeback, he straightened even more, seeming to grow bigger, more rigid and imposing. "I won't push for this audience tonight. I'll give you some time. Not long but enough to let it all sink in."

And a croak finally escaped her. "Let what sink in?"

"The fact that I am back to stay. That nothing will stop me from claiming my throne, and my heirs."

Two

Kassandra's entranced gaze followed Leonid as he descended the stairs of her porch, then crossed her driveway in measured strides to his parked car, a gleaming black Jaguar that looked like an extension of him.

Without looking back, he got in and drove away slowly, almost soundlessly. After the car disappeared, she remained staring at the void it had left, her mind a debris field in the wake of the havoc he'd wreaked.

Had he really been here? Or had she conjured him after seeing him earlier in that news spot? Had it all been a dream, a nightmare?

But if it had been, why couldn't she wake up, as she always did whenever his phantasm came to suffocate her at night? As much as she would have preferred an actual breakdown to him being here, she knew. He had been here. And he would be back. His last words rang in her ears in an unending loop.

Nothing will stop me from claiming my throne, and my heirs.

Legs trembling with futile rage and incipient dread, she closed the door. But it was no use. She didn't feel she'd successfully shut him out, or that she was safe anymore inside her home.

As she shakily made her way inside, one thing he'd said buzzed into her brain like an electric drill.

Why else would I have twin girls, and now be called on to take the mantle of responsibility in the land of the twin goddesses?

What had *that* meant?

She had to find out. Her first priority was to understand the motive behind his sudden interest in Eva and Zoya. Knowledge would be her best weapon against his unexpected incursion.

Still unsteady, she got some water and headed to her home office. She sat down at her desk and opened her laptop. After staring at the search engine numbly for several moments, she typed in *Zorya*.

For hours, she read all there was to read about the mythology behind that name and the land that wielded it.

It turned out Zorya was a plural name, incorporating the two guardian goddesses, Zarya and Zvezda, who represented the morning and evening stars. According to Slavic mythology, they were charged through eternity with guarding the doomsday hound, Simargi, lest he consumed the constellation Ursa Minor. They were also responsible for opening and closing the gates for the sun. Zorya, the former—and soon to be again—kingdom was said to be the only place where both stars could be perpetually seen on all clear nights. Its coat of arms depicted the blonde and dark-haired goddesses holding up stars. Though the goddesses were twins, they were quite literally night and day.

Just like her girls.

Eva had taken after her, Zoya after Leonid.

So this was what he'd meant. He considered this a sign he was meant to have both the throne and the girls.

And she'd seen it in his eyes.

He would make it all come true.

After an oppressive night spent pondering every possible distressing outcome of Leonid's reappearance, Kassandra struggled to perform her morning rituals with the girls before leaving them with Kyria Despina and heading to work. Not that she expected to get any work done, but she needed to be away from them. She'd be damned if she'd let Leonid poison their moods, too.

In half an hour, she was in her personal office on the second floor of her company, looking out the window at downtown LA but only seeing the chaos inside her mind.

What disturbed her most was that she hadn't come up with a plan of action in case Leonid *did* pursue his objectives. Which she had no doubt he would.

"I'm sorry, Kass, I tried to…"

Even before her PA's cut-short exclamation, Kassandra's senses had gone haywire.

Swinging around, hoping she was wrong but certain she wasn't, the air was still knocked out of her at the sight of him. Leonid.

He filled her doorway, dwarfing her delicate PA. Mindy was looking up at him with a mixture of mortification and all-out awe.

Kassandra understood. How she did. A god walking the earth wouldn't have looked as imposing and over-powering.

Their gazes collided, almost making her stumble against the plate glass of her wall-to-wall window. It was him who relinquished their visual lock first to look down at Mindy, who resembled a tiny herbivore that found itself in the crosshairs of a great feline.

"I apologize for overriding you, Ms. Levine. Ms. Stavros will fully understand that there was nothing you could have done to stop me. You can rest assured she'll chastise me appropriately for such high-handed behavior."

Gathering what she could of her wits, Kassandra tore her gaze off him and focused on her assistant. "It's okay, Mindy." Mindy looked back as if in a trance. Kassandra sighed. "You can go now, thanks. I'll let you know if I decide to call security."

With a ghost of a smile, Leonid stepped aside to allow Mindy to stumble out. "She won't. You can drop the red alert."

The moment the door closed, Leonid turned his focus to her. It was a good thing she'd moved to her desk so she could mask her own unsteadiness and feign a con-frontational pose.

"Don't be so sure, Leonid. My private security isn't the police and won't care if you broke any laws. The one thing that will matter to them is that I don't want you here."

"How do you know you don't want me here before you hear what I have to say?"

"I already heard it, and I not only would rather you spare me an encore, but I also wish there was some cosmic erase button to have it unsaid. If that's all you're here to say, I will cut everything short and have you removed."

"You don't need to bother. I will remove myself once I've done what I've come to do. And it's not to reiterate what I said last night. I'm here to state my terms."

"This time I will spare myself the aggravation of reacting to your terminal audacity. The answer to anything you have to say is no anyway."

"If you remember anything about me, you should know I do not take no for an answer. Now, more than ever, I won't."

Every nerve jangled as he approached, as if to emphasize that there was no stopping his invasion of her life. With every step, she felt as if he was planting a foothold that she wouldn't be able to uproot.

"My terms are the following—I want to become Eva and Zoya's father, in name and in reality. You will give me full access to them, effective immediately. You won't try to do anything to put them off me, or to put off the procedure of declaring me as their father. I will have them bear my name before the coronation. It is in just over a month's time."

Feeling she'd taken a deep breath underwater, her protest came out a gurgle. "Now, look here..."

He continued as if she hadn't interrupted. "As their mother, you can and will of course dictate your own terms and I will meet every one."

She shook her head, as if to shake off a punch to the face. "My only term is that you get the hell out of my life. You stayed out of it for two years. And that is where I demand you stay."

His face remained as hard as stone. "That is not an option. Anything else is negotiable."

"Nothing else is worth negotiating. I won't let you walk into my life, making those insane demands and expecting me to fall in with your timetable."

"I'm not walking into your life, but my daughters'."

Knowing he was powerful enough to do whatever he wished, her mind burned rubber trying to latch on to an alternative to anger or defiance to hold him at bay. Those had gotten her nowhere. Continuing to challenge him head-on would only make him more intractable. If that was even possible.

Her only way out could be to negotiate a less-damaging deal. Something other than the takeover he was bent on.

"Listen, Leonid, let's take a time-out and rewind to the beginning. Let's say, for whatever reasons, you wish to acknowledge the girls as your daughters. I can, if necessary, live with that. We can come to an agreement where you can be…included. That doesn't mean you have to be in their lives. You haven't been since before they were born and they *are* totally fine without a father. I'm not saying this to be vindictive, or because of our personal history. It's just a fact. Also consider the effort and time commitment that goes into being a parent. You can't possibly want to be a father, especially now that you're on the verge of becoming a king. You literally have far better and more important things to do."

He waited until she finished her speech, then demolished it with that vacant look. "There's nothing better or more important than becoming the father my daughters deserve. And need. No matter how adequate you are as a single parent."

Her rage seethed again. "You know nothing of how

adequate I am as a single parent, or what my daughters need."

"Like you take exception to my opinion of your life, I would appreciate you not passing judgment on mine. Being a father is exactly what I now want to be. Becoming a king only makes it more imperative I claim all my responsibilities with the utmost commitment."

"Fine, I won't presume to know what you want. I'll keep to my side of things. I need no commitment from you."

"Then, I will change your mind about what you need."

The way he'd said that… The way his gaze dropped to envelop her body before returning stonily to hers…

Did…did he mean something personal? Intimate…?

Before her thoughts caught fire, he disabused her of any ridiculous notion this was in any way about her. "No matter how strong, resourceful and successful you are, and though you've been coping exceptionally well being both a mother and a businesswoman, you will experience a huge improvement in the quality of your and the twins' lives when you have me as a fully committed partner in raising them."

She shook her head, feeling punch-drunk. "You come here…and just dictate to me…about the quality of my—"

"I came here, your territory still, but a less personal one, after your reaction to my showing up on your doorstep last night, because I thought you might feel less cornered here. It's also why I didn't have you brought to me."

That made her locate her faltering verbal skills with a vengeance. "Oh, how considerate of you. I should be grateful you didn't have me dragged to your territory, and instead chose to invade my professional space, getting my whole company abuzz with speculation, launching a hundred rumors, undermining me and generally disrupting my life?"

"I figured whatever I did, it wouldn't meet with your approval, so I did what I thought least threatening to you."

"Great rationalization, but..."

He continued speaking as if he was playing back a recording. "Starting tomorrow, I expect to be allowed in to see my daughters without resistance or ill will. I would very much prefer, for their sake and yours, if we do this on the most amicable terms possible. I hope you won't force me to resort to more drastic measures."

Having finished the speech he'd come to deliver, he turned and walked away. She could only stare after him, feeling as if she were sinking in quicksand.

Before he stepped out the door, he paused, turned. "I'll come by your house a couple of hours before the twins' bedtime."

Kassandra waited until he closed the door after him, then collapsed on her chair like a demolished building.

As everything seeped into her mind and its full impact registered, she reeled harder. Not only with the disaster in progress she could see spiraling out of control, but with how much of a stranger he'd become.

Those first hellish months after he'd kicked her out of his life, she'd been anguished by how his feelings for her had withered, then reversed. But with him so distant and clinical now, she finally believed he'd never felt anything in the first place. She didn't count at all to him, neither in the past nor in the future he had so carefully planned for them all.

The future she couldn't let come to pass.

She couldn't let this automaton near her daughters. His new programming might dictate it, but if there was anyone Eva and Zoya were better off without it was him.

But she couldn't stop him. He had the legal and personal clout to do what he wanted. She didn't have a leg to stand on, let alone a weapon to fight him off with.

But…that wasn't true. She did have weapons.

At least her best friends did. Selene, Caliope and Naomi had access to three of the most lethal weapons in the world. Their husbands. Each man was at least as powerful as Leonid was, if not more. He'd have no chance against their combined might.

Fumbling for her cell phone, she called Selene. As soon as she answered, she told her she was adding another call to Caliope, then repeated the process with her, adding another to Naomi, too, merging the calls.

The three women, once they were part of a four-way conference call with her, chorused anxiously, "What's wrong?"

"Everything," she choked. "I need Aristedes. And Maksim. And Andreas."

Six hours later, Kassandra looked around her office, her cheeks burning.

Her friends hadn't even asked her why she'd needed their husbands. After making sure she wasn't in any immediate danger, they'd all hung up. She'd expected them to get their husbands to call. They'd actually sent them over in person.

And here they all were. Aside from Leonid, the three most imposing and hard-hitting men she'd ever seen.

According to Aristedes's concise explanation, as soon as their wives had told them to drop everything and fly to her side, they'd each jumped on their jets and crossed the continent from New York to her. And they didn't seem bothered in the least by being ordered around like that to do her bidding…or rather their wives'. If she didn't love her friends so completely, she would have envied them having such unique men wrapping themselves so lovingly around their every inch. Their fairytale relationships had always emphasized how abysmal her situation with Leonid was.

Loath to impose on them more than absolutely necessary, she rushed to recount her dilemma.

But as she talked, the men looked much like three souls who'd walked into the middle of a foreign movie, clearly lost.

"Hold on a minute." That was Aristedes, shipping magnate and Selene's, her oldest friend's, husband. It had been through Selene's marriage to him that all of them had become best friends. Caliope being Aristedes's sister and Maksim's wife, and Naomi, Selene's sister-in-law and Andreas's wife. He sat forward with a spectacular frown marring his impossibly handsome face. "You're talking about Leonid Voronov?"

She'd confided in her best friends about Leonid when she'd told them of her pregnancy. Since they told their husbands everything, she'd assumed they'd told them. But it was clear, if Aristedes's reaction was any indication, that her friends considered her secrets sacrosanct.

It meant this meeting just got more agonizingly embarrassing, as she had to explain everything from the start.

After she did, Maksim, the one who used to have a personal relationship with Leonid, stood up, rage distorting his equally impressive face. "You mean you told him you were pregnant, and he didn't only kick you out of his life, but implied he'd prefer you terminated your pregnancy?" As she nodded warily, he growled, "*I'm* dealing with that scum of the earth. He's a fellow Russian and it's on me you met him at all. I invited the louse to my wedding."

"Settle down, Maksim." That was Andreas, Aristedes's younger brother and the most dangerous of the lot. "If there's punishment to be doled out, we're all getting a piece of him." He swung his icy gaze to Kassandra, making her almost regret recruiting their help. Andreas had once been involved in organized crime, and remained as lethal, if not more so, now that he'd gone legit. "But this guy says he's back to atone for his mistakes. Any reason to believe he doesn't mean it?"

"Oh, I believe he means it," she groaned. "As much as I believe the road to hell for me and the girls is paved with his good intentions."

Aristedes pursed his lips, propping an elbow on a knee. "But if he's owning up to his responsibilities, perhaps you should give him some leeway, in a limited wait-and-see fashion, without making any promises or changes in your lives?" Aristedes looked first at Maksim and then Andreas. "I think I speak for all of us when I say we were all once in more or less his same position, and we would have given anything for a second chance with the women we love and the children we fathered, or in Andreas's case, the child he was named guardian of."

Maksim's dark fury ebbed as he considered his brother-in-law's point of view. "Now that you put it that way, I can't even think what would have become of me if Caliope hadn't given me a second chance. One I didn't think I deserved and she had every right not to give me at the time."

Heart contracting at the turn in conversation, she choked out, "None of your situations was anything like mine with him."

Maksim winced. "Now that I think of it, I almost did the same thing to Caliope. I, too, abandoned her when I knew she was pregnant."

"It's not the same at all," she protested. Maksim had had the best of reasons for walking away. His father had been abusive. He'd feared he'd inherited his proclivities and had been terrified of hurting his vulnerable loved ones. "You thought you were protecting her and your baby."

Maksim sat back down, gaze gentling. "Maybe he has a valid reason, too? At least one he believed to be valid?"

Feeling cornered, she realized she couldn't get them on board without telling them *everything*. What he'd said to her in the past, and in the present, that she'd never meant a thing to him, that he was only back now for his "heirs" because he believed it was his duty and destiny, now that he was going to be king of the land of the two goddesses.

By the time she'd finished, all three men's faces were closed with so much wrath, she felt anxious about the extreme measures they might take in dealing with Leonid. In spite of everything, she found herself worried for him.

As she tried to think of a way to mitigate their outrage and their consequent actions, Maksim heaved up to his feet again, clearly bringing this meeting to an end.

"Don't worry about Leonid anymore, Kassandra," Maksim said. "I'll deal with him."

Following him up, Andreas corrected, *"We'll* deal with him."

Troubled by the respectively murderous and predatory looks in the two men's eyes, she turned to Aristedes, her oldest acquaintance among them, and ironically, since he was generally known as the devil, the one who scared her the least.

Sensing her anxiety, Aristedes gave her shoulder a bolstering squeeze. "I'll keep those two in check, and resolve this situation with the least damage possible."

As they each gave her pecks on the cheek, she was torn between being alarmed she'd let loose those hounds of hell on Leonid, and being relieved she'd soon have this nightmare over with.

By the time she leaned back on the door, panting as if she'd run a mile, she decided she should be only relieved.

Leonid had only himself to blame for whatever they did to him. If he wanted to escape those men's punishment, he should have settled for being a king, away from her and the girls.

"Yes, I understand," Kassandra said to Maksim.

She'd said almost the same thing to Andreas and Aristedes before him, just to end the calls with them, too.

For she certainly didn't understand at all. How the three predators, who'd left her office out for blood yesterday, had each come back to her less than a day later, purring a totally different tune. That of urging her to give Leonid a chance.

How had he managed to get to them all? What had he said to have them so wholeheartedly on his side?

But why was she even wondering? Didn't she already know how irresistible he could be when he put his mind to it? He'd worked the three men over but good. It was clear that their initial thoughts about having once been in Leonid's shoes and in need of clemency were back in full force. Anything she said now would be her intolerant word against Leonid's penitent one.

Putting down her cell phone, she pressed her fingers against burning eyelids.

So. She was out of options. There was no way she could stop Leonid herself. All she could do now was make sure he didn't turn their lives upside down.

Suddenly, another bolt of agitation zapped her.

The bell. Leonid. He was here. *Exactly* two hours before Eva and Zoya's bedtime, as promised.

She wouldn't even wonder how he knew at what time she put them to bed. She had a sick feeling he knew everything about her life with the girls over the past two years. And that there was far more to this whole thing than he was letting on.

Yet she could do nothing but play along, and see what exactly he wanted, and where this would lead.

Crossing from her home office past the living room, she signaled to Kyria Despina that she'd get the door.

She took her time, but Leonid didn't ring again. Stopping at the door, she could almost feel him on the other side, silently telling her he'd wait out her reluctance and wear down her resistance.

She pressed her forehead against the cool mahogany, gathering her wits and stamina. Then she straightened, filled her lungs with much-needed air and opened the door.

As always, nothing prepared her for laying eyes on him. Every time she ever had, an invisible hand wrapped around her heart and squeezed. Her senses ignited at his nearness, each time more than the time before.

Standing like a monolith on her doorstep, he was swathed in a slate-gray coat, a suit of the same color and a shirt as vivid as his eyes, radiating that inescapable magnetism that had snared her even before she'd laid eyes on him. Blood rushed to her head before flooding her body in scalding torrents.

And she cursed him, and herself, all over again. For him to still have this choke hold over her senses, when he didn't even try, didn't even want to, was the epitome of unfairness. But life was exactly that. As was he. Both did what they wanted to her, her approval irrelevant, her will overruled.

So she'd let him take his invasion to the next level. She only hoped after getting a dose of domesticity, he'd retreat to a nominal position in the girls' lives, which she could deal with without too much damage to herself.

Certain she was opening the door to a new dimension of heartache, she said, "Come in, Leonid."

Three

Leonid crossed Kassandra's threshold.

For a second, before she retreated, he almost touched her. It was the last thing he wanted to do. The one thing he couldn't bear.

If he could have done any of this without seeing her at all, he would have jumped at the chance. But it was out of the question. If he wanted his daughters, she had to be involved. Closely. Suffocatingly.

Mercifully, she'd been averse, keeping him at the distance he needed to remain, in every way. But right now he'd miscalculated his movement, and she hadn't receded fast enough. A second after he'd advanced, their clothes had whispered off each other. Just being near her caused the slow burn in his every nerve to spark into a scalding sizzle.

Before he could judge if the fleeting contact had disturbed her, too, she turned and strode away, leaving him to follow in her wake, a path filled with her sense-warping warmth and scent.

The glance she threw at him over her shoulder spoke volumes, making it even harder to breathe. The surface layer was annoyance that he'd showed up at all, and at the exact time he'd said he would. Then there was resignation that she couldn't turn him away. Beneath that lay another sort of anger he couldn't fathom. And at the core of it all, there was…a threat.

They both knew he wielded power that would give him access to the twins no matter what she did. She'd tried to recruit allies to stop him. She'd picked them well. But after he'd neutralized their threat, she must have realized there was no point in prolonging a losing fight. Being the pragmatic businesswoman that she was, she'd wasted no more time coming to the best course of action. Let him have what he wanted. For now. Until she studied the situation further and decided if she could adjust her trajectory.

But he also knew she wouldn't use the twins in her struggle against him, not even for a cause as vital as keeping him out of their lives. She'd never do anything to disturb them. So her threat didn't have any real power behind it.

Still, he couldn't let her suspect how anxious he was, how uncertain of his ability to conduct himself in any acceptable manner. For what constituted acceptable with eighteen-month-old toddlers? He knew far more about astrophysics and the latest trends in nail polish than about interacting with children. And it was almost beyond him to keep his upheaval in check.

But he had to pretend equanimity as he followed her

deeper into her exquisite home, the oasis of color, gaiety and contentment she'd built for her—for *their*—daughters, taking him to meet them for the first time. After he'd spent every day since they'd been born obsessing over their every detail.

Then she turned a corner into a great room equipped with a short plastic fence, decorative and sturdy, and just enough to keep little feet from wandering without detracting from the wide-open, welcoming feel of what must be every child's dream wonderland. And it was empty.

"Darling…"

Kassandra's breathy endearment made him stop. Suspended him in time.

She used to call him darling. Not always, just when she'd been incoherent with pleasure, which had been very frequently. The last time she'd said it to him he'd swiped at her proverbial jugular and severed it.

For heart-thudding moments, he didn't understand why she'd said it now, once, then again. Then he realized.

From what turned out to be an elaborate playhouse blended into the periphery of the room, a gleaming dark head peeked out of a tiny doorway, followed by an equally shiny golden one. She held out her arms and squeaks of glee issued from both girls as they competed to crawl out first, struggling to their feet as soon as they cleared the entrance. Two young cats, reflecting the girls' colorings, a black Angora and a golden Abyssinian, slinked out after them.

His heart contracted painfully. They were fast. He knew from his surveillance of them that their toddling had been improving every day. They were now almost running to their mother.

Kassandra went down on her haunches, preparing to receive them in her arms. But her descent only exposed him fully, bringing him into their line of vision. Their eyes rounded and their momentum slowed, both stopping just short of throwing themselves into her arms.

Knowing she was now no longer the focus of her girls' attention, Kassandra slowly stood up and slid him a sideways glance. Among the messages there was a challenge. He might have gotten what he'd demanded, but now she'd evaluate his performance and decide her consequent actions.

If he'd had any words left in him, he would have asked her to allow him a grace period without passing judgment. He'd fail her every test right now. Being face-to-face with those two tiny entities at last felt like a hurricane was uprooting everything inside him.

Before he could find his next breath, the twins rushed to stand behind Kassandra as she turned to him, each clinging to one endless jeans-clad leg and peeking up at him from the safety of their mother's barricade.

In contrast to their caution, the cats approached him, sniffing the air. Seeming to decide he didn't smell of danger, they neared him in degrees until they brushed against legs that felt as if they had grown roots. His throat tightened more as he bent without conscious thought to stroke them and receive head butts and arched backs. Then, seeming to consider this enough welcome for now, they sauntered away and jumped on shelves by the wall to watch the developing scene and groom themselves.

Unfolding with difficulty to his full height again, he found Kassandra with the miniatures of both of them staring at him. Avoiding her eyes, he focused on the girls'. Emerald eyes like Kassandra's and azure ones like his dominated faces that had occupied his thoughts since they'd been born. Two tiny sets of dewy rose lips rounded in questioning suspense.

"Vy oba...ideal'no."

It was only when chubby arms wrapped around their mother's legs tighter and those sparkling eyes widened more that he realized he'd spoken. Saying the one thing that filled his being. They were both perfect.

He waited. For Kassandra to say something. To introduce him. But she was silent, continuing to add the weight of her watchful gaze to theirs.

His mind crowded with everything he'd longed to do since they'd taken their first breaths. To swoop down and scoop them up in his arms was foremost among those urges.

But he knew there was no way this would be welcomed by Eva and Zoya, who were hanging on his every breath, bracing for his every move. They probably hadn't scurried back into their hiding place only because their mother was showing no signs of alarm, calmly facing him as if he was no threat, or at least one she was capable of protecting them from. It was as if they'd never seen anyone like him. Which was strange. He knew for a fact that their world was filled with big and imposing-looking men. The three men Kassandra had sent after him, and Kassandra's male relatives.

So why did he feel such total surprise emanating from them? Could it be they instinctively felt the bond between them?

Unable to decide, he emptied his mind, let his instincts take over. He trusted them now far more than he trusted his messed-up emotions and stalled logic.

He moved away from the trio training all their senses on him, circumventing them in a wide circle that took him to the playhouse the girls had exited. His aching gaze took in the evidence of their play session and of Kassandra's doting care. The strewn toys, coloring books and crayons, the half-built castle, the half-eaten finger foods and half-finished smoothies.

He'd missed all that. Everything, from their first day. He hadn't held them or comforted them or cleaned or served them or played with them or put them to bed. Kassandra had been alone in doing all that. Would any of them ever accept him into their lives, let him into their routines? Or even let him in any way at all? When he didn't deserve to be let in?

Feeling all eyes in the room on him, he went down on his knees, one of the hardest moves for him now. As he felt their surprise spike, he started to gather the toys and books.

Without looking back, so he'd give the girls respite from his focus, give them a sense of control and security, he started to order everything they'd knocked off onto the lushly carpeted floor on the low, sturdy plastic table. Out of the corner of his eyes, he saw Kassandra moving toward the long couch that dominated the opposite side of the space, with both girls still flocking around her legs, their gazes clinging to him.

Sampling one of the thin pineapple spears that were laid out on a cartoon-character tray among other healthy and colorful foods, he said, "That's very tasty. Can I have some more? I haven't eaten all day."

In his peripheral vision he could see the girls exchanging a glance, as if they understood his words and knew they were meant for them. Then they both looked up to their mother, as if seeking her permission to react. He stole a glance at her, found her giving them an exquisite smile. A special one he'd never seen, no doubt reserved only for them. Then she nodded, and they simultaneously let go of her legs and advanced toward him tentatively.

As they approached, he sat down on the ground, another challenging move, putting himself more at their level. This appeared to reassure them even more as their steps picked up speed. He pointed at a blunt skewer of cheese, cucumbers and strawberries, making direct eye contact with one girl, then the other. "Can I have that?"

The girls stopped on the other side of the table, eyes full of questions and curiosity. Then after what seemed to be serious consideration, Eva, the mini-Kassandra, reached out and grabbed the skewer in her dimpled hand…and leaned over to give it to him. Zoya, who'd held back, clearly more reserved like he was, took her cue from her older-by-ten-minutes sister, and repeated her action.

Throat closing, Leonid looked down on those two skewers, offered by the girls he'd fathered and hadn't been there for, until this moment. They were his life's biggest reward. And responsibility.

With hands that almost trembled out of control, he reached out and took both offerings at the same time. "That's very kind of you to share your snacks with me. *Spasiba*."

As if both recognized he'd just said a word in a language different from the one they'd been hearing and processing since birth, they looked at him questioningly.

"That is Russian. In English it means 'thank you.'" Then he repeated it a few times. "*Spasiba*…thank you."

Eyes gleaming at recognizing thank-you and clearly

making the connection between the two words, looking triumphant, Eva parroted him, "Patheba...thakyoo."

His heart thundered, its chambers just about melting at Eva's adorable lisp.

And that was before Zoya delivered the second punch of a one-two combo as she enthused, "Aseba...ankoo."

Before he could gather his wits, Eva picked up another skewer and proceeded to nibble at it, looking up at him, as if encouraging him to eat. Zoya at once did the same. When he didn't follow suit immediately, Zoya reached out and pushed his hand up, urging him to partake of their offering.

He raised the food to lips that had gone numb, unable to taste anything as he chewed. Swallowing was an even harder feat, pushing the food past the blockage in his throat. All the time he could feel Kassandra's gaze on him, scorching layers off his inflamed skin. It took what was left of his control not to turn to her, ask for her intervention.

But she didn't intervene. She didn't make a single move, as if she was trying to blend into the background to make them all forget she was there.

While that was what he'd asked her to do, now that he had the girls' full attention and interest, he would have given anything for her to dilute their focus. Which was pathetic, since this was the opportunity he'd badgered her for, what he'd been dreaming of for so long.

Inching closer now that they literally had him eating out of their hands, the two girls started handing him their favorite toys as more evidence of their acceptance, naming each one to show off their knowledge.

It became clear the second time they waited after naming something that they were waiting for him to pro-

vide the Russian equivalent. And so it started, a game
of translation.

The Russian word they loved the most was the one for
doll. They both kept giggling and reiterating, *"Kukla...
kukla!"*

They then moved on to testing him. One of them presented a coloring book and the other the crayons. When
he colored a pony in a color scheme that was different
from all the examples in the colored pages, they got more
excited, and tried to emulate him in other books. After
a while, dissatisfied with their own results compared
to his impeccable ones, they reverted to the name-and-
translate game.

Suddenly Eva seemed to realize she'd forgotten a vital
issue. Then she pointed at herself and said, with a great
sense of importance, "Eva."

Not to be outdone, Zoya immediately pointed to herself and said, "Zoya."

Then they both pointed at him, demanding he reciprocated the introduction.

He struggled to make his voice sound as normal as
possible. "Leonid."

Not expecting them to be able to say such an abrupt
name, they both surprised him by repeating accurately.
"Leonid."

Swallowing past the growing pain in his throat, he
felt the urge to complete the introduction, even when
he knew they wouldn't understand the significance. *"Ya
tvoy Papa.* This is also in Russian. It means 'I'm your
father.'"

Feeling terminally stupid for speaking in such long
sentences, and in two languages, too, when they at most
only knew a few dozen words in English and maybe also

in Greek, he smiled shakily, waiting for their attempt at the word.

This time they almost gave him a heart attack.

Getting to the heart of what he'd said, they both pointed at him and chorused, "Papa."

By now, Kassandra had gotten used to her heart's erratic function. Since Leonid had appeared on her doorstep, it had been stopping periodically before it stampeded out of control in compensation.

From the moment the girls hadn't run to welcome him as they did anyone who entered their home with her, she'd known.

They'd at once realized he wasn't just a friend or an acquaintance, but someone on a totally different level from anyone they'd seen before. Far more important than even Kassandra's family. Someone on par in importance to them with Kassandra herself.

Kassandra had bated her breath, dreading that Leonid would botch this, knowing from their instant recognition of his significance to them that it would hurt them. But Leonid had proceeded to provide one shock after another, everything he'd done and said sensitive and inventive. He'd followed no known path with the girls, and soon had them so engrossed in his presence, they'd forgotten to include her.

What had at first rattled her with chagrin and jealousy had gradually become incredibly emotional, as she watched something she'd always dreamed of but never believed would come to pass. The girls with their father, the only other person who should love them as completely as she did, behaving as if they'd known him all their lives. She couldn't have interacted with the trio had they asked.

Hours could have passed since they'd become immersed in one another. She'd lost track of self and time as she'd watched them. She'd even lost sight of her memories of the past and everything that had led to this situation. All she could see was her girls delighting in their father, and him appearing to delight in them back.

And then came their fervent proclamation that he was their "papa." Just as her stalled heart sputtered into a forced restart, Leonid stopped it again, saying so deeply and gently, "Yes, you brilliant girls, I'm your papa."

Before she could draw a breath, before she passed out and spoiled everything, the girls threw themselves at Leonid.

A surprised laugh issued from him as he hugged tight the small, robust bodies of her daughters. Kassandra reeled, trying to make sense of this.

She could only think the girls had always realized other kids had papas while they didn't. Then they had seen Leonid and simply recognized him as their own papa. Once they'd approved him through their own brand of testing, and he'd validated their belief, they'd accepted him in their own unique way.

No, they'd more than accepted him. They'd claimed him.

It was funny she'd think of this specific term, what he'd already used about them. But nothing else described what was happening in front of her eyes. It was a claiming. Declared and accepted, on both sides.

Leonid, who'd been doing everything right to put the girls at ease, from body language to expression to tone of voice, now rumbled with unfettered laughter as the girls attacked him with their zeal. But what he did next had her slumping back against the couch in a nerveless mass.

He sprawled flat on the ground, letting the girls prowl all over his great body. Thrilled by his action and the invitation it afforded them, they drowned him in hugs and kisses before launching into examining every inch of his very-different-to-hers body and clothes, acquainting themselves with the details of that new powerful entity they'd made their own.

Then she started to worry again. That this would still end badly, that Leonid would be appalled or fed up by their level of enthusiasm and attention. Would he decide he'd made a mistake coming near them and withdraw? Then she scolded herself for worrying. She should hope for that to happen so he'd leave, let them return to their contented status quo. As for the girls' psyches, they were young enough that if he disappeared now, no matter his impact on them, they'd soon forget him.

Just as she'd come to this conclusion and was pulling herself up to intervene, he looked up at her from his flat-on-his-back position on the floor, covered in toddler limbs and laughter, with a grin she'd never seen on his face before.

"Any help here?"

Okay, that didn't look like the face or attitude of a man who was regretting anything. His call for help seemed to be part of the game, maybe his way of including her in it.

Forcing her feet to function, she approached the merry mass on the ground made up of the beings who mattered most to her. Leonid once, and her girls forever.

She stopped over them, her lips quirking involuntarily at the infectious gaiety at her feet.

"What help does the unstoppable future king require?"

Eyes that had haunted her for the past five years flashed azure merriment up at her, the stiff stranger of the first two encounters gone. "I have no idea. But I can tell you that if you don't do something and they don't let me up, you may have to let me spend the night right here on the ground."

"Take heart. In a worst-case scenario, they'll keep you there until they fall asleep. Once they do, I can get them off you and you'll be free to get up."

Eva pulled his face toward her to show him another toy, a miniature lion. After he told her it was *lev* and she dutifully repeated her own version of the word, Zoya pointed to her cat Shadow, who'd come to join the fun with Goldie. After he told her both the word for *cat* and their breeds in Russian and she did the same, he swung his gaze back to Kassandra.

"Do they usually use you as a mattress or am I getting special treatment?"

"You're the one who made yourself one. But then, I'm nowhere as big and comfortable as you are."

She knew that from extensive experience. Going to sleep spread over him after long, depleting nights of excruciating pleasure.

Thankfully, he wasn't the man he'd been. That man would have latched on to that comment, teasing and provoking her. That man had been raging wildfire, while this new man was a bottomless ocean. His unexpected behavior with the girls was just another depth to him she hadn't thought could exist.

He broke eye contact when the quartet of girls and cats demanded his attention. Then one duo was climbing off him only for the other to climb on. With only the cats to contend with, he sat up, with them roaming his lap. Eva and Zoya called him to another part of their playroom, and he looked at her again, seeming to find some trouble rising to his feet.

Her heart gave a sick lurch. It appeared his injuries had never fully healed, as she'd once feared. He hid it well, but now that she was looking for evidence of it, she could see his gait wasn't normal. After sitting on the floor for so long, it was harder for him to conceal.

Not that she was about to feel bad for him. He'd never needed or even tolerated her empathy. The best she could be was civil, and it was only for the girls' sake.

After he followed the girls to their sandbox in the adjoining enclosed terrace, he looked back at her.

"So you enlisted The Savage Sarantoses and the Big Bad Russian Wolf's help to…deal with me."

Not knowing what to make of his attitude, if he was angry about her siccing them on him, or taunting her about her effort's failure, she arched an eyebrow. "Should've saved my breath. They turned out to be neither savage nor big and bad. You neutralized them as if by magic."

His lips twitched as he kneeled where the girls indicated at the edge of their sandbox, clearly unconcerned by the damages his handmade suit would certainly suffer.

With a shovel in hand, he slanted her another glance that set her insides quivering. "No spells were involved. But I applaud your effort. It was a very sound strategy. That it didn't work doesn't make it any less so."

Was he…entertained by her struggle against him? Teasing her about its futility? If he was, it was a more understated form of provocation than anything he'd ever exposed her to. And whether she was more susceptible now, or he was more potent, it was far more...unsettling.

"Join me in building a castle for our princesses?"

For several long seconds she could only stare at him. It had just dawned on her.

Eva and Zoya were actual princesses.

When one daunting eyebrow prodded a response from her, she made herself move. She came down on her knees far enough from him to keep her agitation at manageable levels, but close enough to work with him, if need be. The girls flitted between them, handing them tools, then climbing inside to make their own little molds as she and Leonid started collaborating on something intricate.

Trying to focus on what they were doing, she said, "I've never attempted anything elaborate, since their appreciation takes the form of destructive admiration. Then they're crestfallen when my creations crumble."

He shrugged those endless shoulders. "I'll try to make them realize how to preserve it, but if they level it or it's time to replace it, I'll make them understand I'll build them another. In time, I'll teach them how to build their own."

"You seem certain you can get all this across."

"I am. They're extremely intelligent and very receptive."

She almost blurted out that while they were indeed intelligent, she'd only seen this level of receptiveness directed at him. But she held her tongue. The admission would only complicate matters further.

From then on, there were stretches of silence between them as they worked, with Leonid taking the lead, creating a castle that looked like a miniature of a real one in every detail. Then, true to his conviction, he curbed the girls' appetite for destruction, encouraging them to expend their excitement in making flower and animal molds to surround it.

Then it was time for the girls' dinner, and he pounced on the chance to feed them, insisting on handling the soup part. He managed to complete the task with even less mess than she usually did. And he'd turned the whole thing into another game, pointing to kitchen articles with each spoonful, getting names in English, correcting and translating what the girls didn't know. The girls competed to provide answers, and get Papa's attention and appreciation.

An hour after dinner, two hours after their bedtime, the girls lost the fight to prolong their wakefulness to remain with Leonid. And they again did something unprecedented. Instead of turning to her, they went to him, arms raised, demanding to be picked up. At once complying, he gathered them in a secure hold, where they both promptly dozed off.

Without a word, she led him to the nursery, where he placed them, one after the other, in their cribs. She stood with bated breath, waiting to see what he'd do next as he remained standing over them, his eyes wells of mystery in the dimness.

At length, he bent and kissed them. Each girl gave a contented gurgle at his tender caress before assuming her favorite sleeping position.

Straightening, he led the way out of the room, then headed straight for the door. He didn't look her way until he'd opened it and stepped outside.

"Thank you for tonight."

With that, he turned and slowly walked down the steps. In a minute, he climbed into his car and drove away.

Closing the door, she automatically armed her security system, turned off the lights and headed to her room.

It was only after she'd gone through her nighttime routine and slipped into bed that she let it all crash on her. Everything he'd said and done all through the evening, everything about him.

Nothing made sense anymore.

For two years, the last thing she'd wanted was Leonid near again. Now, she was forced to face the truth.

She'd wanted him to come near tonight. So much that his pointed avoidance of her had felt like a knife in her gut. It still twisted there now.

She might have been able to handle it if she'd had any hope he would stay away from her altogether. But after this incredible first meeting between him and her...his... *their* daughters, she knew there was no hope for that.

Leonid would be in their lives. If everything she'd felt from him toward the girls tonight was real, and she couldn't doubt it was, she could no longer deny him, or them, that reality.

Which meant he would be in her life, too, maybe even forever.

The only man she'd ever wanted.

When he'd long stopped wanting her.

Four

A rewind button had yanked Kassandra back into her worst days—only with an even darker twist. For this time, it wasn't Leonid discarding her, leaving her desolate and then disappearing. He was now planning to stay around forever.

After she'd thought she'd been cured of any emotions she'd felt for him, she'd woken up today with her resolve to stay neutral pulverized. It had taken him exactly four hours last night to show her how self-deluding she'd been, how susceptible to his magic she remained. How pathetic she was.

If only he'd lived up to her expectations, had been the unfeeling entity he'd been with her, with the girls. It would have given her ammunition to stop him coming near them again. It would have saved her from stumbling back into the abyss of longing. But he'd been…perfect.

Worse, they'd *all* been perfect together. It had been like she'd watched scattered pieces of a vital whole finally clicking together. She of all people recognized and realized the significance of what she'd witnessed. Her very self had been built around a tight relationship with her father as much as her mother. She knew exactly how wonderful such a relationship could be, how essential a loving paternal influence was. And just by being wonderful with the girls, he'd snatched away her last weapon against him, that of his potential disruptiveness to the girls' psyches and lives. Now she had to let him be the girls' father, as she could no longer doubt he truly wanted to be. She had to let the girls have him as the other half of their world, while trying to preserve her sanity with him around. But now that she'd discovered her unilateral fixation with him had never weakened, she had no idea how she'd achieve that.

Dwelling on that terrible fate had to be postponed. Now she had work to do, far more than usual since she hadn't worked a lick since he'd reappeared. The summer line wouldn't approve itself and put itself into production.

Walking into her design house's new headquarters, she concentrated on being attentive and friendly with each and every one of her employees. She'd done it wholeheartedly so many times she could do it on autopilot now.

Reaching her office, she thought she'd escaped with her turmoil undetected, anxious to plunge into work, the only thing that would ameliorate it. But the moment she entered, she knew salvaging her schedule would have to wait. Right there in her sitting area were three of the people her staff knew to let into her private space without question.

Her best friends.

It should have been a shock to find them here, as dropping by her office on a whim was no longer something they did with her on the other side of the continent. It should have at least been a surprise. It was neither. Seemed Leonid had depleted her reserves for shock and surprise for the foreseeable future.

Bracing herself for what she knew would come, she plastered a smile back onto her face.

Selene was the first to rise to her feet, despite being the most heavily pregnant of them all. Yes, they were all pregnant. Again. Selene and Caliope were now on their third babies. Naomi, too, even if it was only her second biological one, with her first child being her late sister's.

After kissing and hugging her, Caliope and Naomi let Selene, as her oldest friend, lead the interrogation.

Selene shot her opening salvo, getting to the point at once. "What exactly is going on with Leonid?"

Kassandra's lips twisted. "You tell me. Your husbands are the ones who have answers."

Something that resembled annoyance tinged Selene's deep blue eyes. "They haven't been forthcoming, for the first time since the days they were closed-off icebergs. Each aggravating man only said it's for the best that you and Leonid work this out alone."

Kassandra flopped down on an armchair across from the couch where they sat facing her like a tribunal. "And you clearly disagree and that's why you're here."

"You scared the hell out of us when you called!" Caliope exclaimed. "We've never heard you so distressed. And when it comes to you, even our men's words aren't enough."

Naomi nodded, looking as concerned. "We had to get the final word from the source."

Kassandra huffed a mirthless chuckle. "And that's me?"

Selene's gaze softened and hardened at once. "You don't call for the big guns—who clearly didn't fire a shot—then answer our messages with more vagueness, and expect us to sit back and wait."

Kassandra squeezed her friend's hand fondly. "Vagueness is an achievement in my situation, since I'm as in the dark as any of you. Your men left this office promising me they'd leash Leonid away from me and the girls. Then each called me to cajole me into giving him a full and fair chance."

"A chance at what exactly?" Caliope sat forward, reaching for Kassandra's other hand, her smooth brow furrowing. "This is the part no one is clear on."

"At being the girls' father."

"Is that all he wants a chance at?" Naomi probed.

"Yes."

"You mean he didn't…?"

"Didn't ask for a second chance with me? No. According to him, he never wanted a first one."

"He said that?" Selene's gaze hardened to granite.

Knowing she was sealing Leonid's coffin where her friends were concerned, Kassandra sighed. "What amounted to that. When he was breaking it off, he made it clear he considered our liaison only sexual entertainment and he'd had enough long before he told me to get the hell away from him when I failed to take a hint."

Caliope, the softest heart among them, piped up. "He was at his worst when he said that. It could have been his frustration and anger at the whole world talking."

Exactly what Kassandra had thought at first. She

shrugged. "He disappeared for over two years. Too long to be at your worst."

"Maybe he realized the gravity of his mistake," Naomi offered, her newest bestie, the one clearly trying to keep emotions out of the equation. "But didn't know how to fix it."

"You mean he stayed away because he couldn't face me?" Kassandra huffed. "This is a man who has faced tens of thousands of people on the athletic field, the rest of the world when he was in the rabid spotlight of the media, not to mention the sharks of business he wrestled under the table on a regular basis. He squared off with *your* unstoppable predators and turned them into purring pussycats."

Selene exhaled heavily. "This last bit *is* something we're all beyond perplexed about. We thought only us and the kids could do this to our Triumvirate."

Kassandra gave a there-you-go gesture. "Since you know your endless power over your men, you can measure Leonid's."

Caliope's eyes shone. "Maybe *that's* your answer, since when it comes to us, our men's rules are inverted. Maybe it's the same with Leonid. The man who can make the world heel could be powerless when it comes to you."

That was the last straw. She had to put a stop to her friends' efforts to give her hope that her story could end as happily as theirs.

Sitting forward, she let any lightness she'd painted on drain from her face. "Okay, let me make one thing clear. My situation with Leonid is nothing like yours with your men. Those men were more than ninety percent in love with you when each left you or let you go or did whatever they did. Leonid never felt a thing for me, and he'd been itching to move on. He would have done so without the accident, but it gave him the opportunity to do it abruptly." And viciously. She'd never been able to bring herself to tell them just how viciously. "Now he's only back for the girls. He made this far more than clear."

Echoes of her hard tone and words rang in the silence that stretched afterward. A myriad of emotions streaked across the women's faces, each according to her character and relationship with Kassandra. What they shared seemed to be mortification, empathy...and fury.

Selene was first to gather her wits enough to ask another question. "Are you even considering giving him that chance?"

"Since I don't have a way of keeping him away, and since my reasons for wanting to do so no longer apply, I don't have the choice not to."

"So you're feeling forced into it." Naomi chewed her lip thoughtfully. "Would you have considered his return and his demand more favorably if he was back for you, too?"

"No." Kassandra paused, then had to add, "Not at first."

And *that* told them everything. That after everything he'd put her through, she still wanted him. That after her initial anger and rejection, her buried emotions had resurfaced, and she now wished he wanted her, too. Which he didn't.

Clearly realizing all that, anger set Selene's exquisite features on fire. "I don't care how he got Aris and the others on his side, I'll make them wipe him off the face of the earth. And if they don't, we three can still do a lot of damage on our own."

Caliope nodded. "You know we would do anything for you."

"Even if it means standing against your husbands?"

The three women's exclamations were simultaneous.

"Just say the word."

"Without hesitation."

"Hell, yeah."

Kassandra's eyes stung, a smile shaking her lips. "And I love you, too. But that won't be necessary. Everything changed, literally overnight. He came to visit the girls last night. And no matter what I feel, how he was with them, how they were with him, makes him deserve that full and fair chance he's convinced your men he should get."

"That man crushed your heart," Selene ground out. "And I have a feeling if he invades your life again to be with the girls, he'll hurt you again."

Kassandra sighed. "And I can't do anything about it. It's not his or the girls' fault he feels nothing for me."

Caliope threw her hands up in the air. "You should have moved on when you got the chance. *All* those chances. There were at least three men who could have been perfect for you! And they're all still waiting for your slightest signal."

"Could any of you have moved on when you were estranged from your own member of the Triumvirate?" The three women winced, lips twisting in concession. "Exactly. Same here."

"But if you know nothing would come out of it because you're feeling this way about the wrong man…"

"The problem is he isn't the wrong man," Kassandra said, interrupting Naomi. "Apart from his treatment of me and his lack of feelings for me, he remains everything I admire in a man. And though I hate it and wish it wasn't so, the fact remains that no one withstands the comparison to him in my eyes."

"But you can't just resign yourself to being miserable like this!" Selene exclaimed, her face reddening.

"As long as Eva and Zoya are happy, it's a price I have to pay. You would pay the same price and more for your kids."

"How do you know he'll make them happy?" Selene countered.

"Surely you can't tell from one meeting!" Calliope added.

Kassandra sighed. "Regretfully for me, and fortunately for them, I can. You have to see them together to understand."

Selene wouldn't give up that easily. "What if, once the novelty wears off, he becomes the son of a bitch he was with you with them?"

Kassandra set her teeth. "If he even breathes wrong around them, I'll rip out his jugular."

"That's our Kassandra!" Selene's approval was ferocious.

Caliope's face fell. "So the only thing that can make you hate him is if there's a hint of mistreatment or neglect toward Eva and Zoya. Which you don't seem to think would happen."

Naomi was as crestfallen. "*And* we can't even wish it."

"Can't we?" Selene growled protectively. "They wouldn't lose anything if he exited their lives as he entered it. They were perfectly fine without him after all."

"They were." Kassandra exhaled heavily. "But with him in their lives, they could be far more than fine. You really have to—"

"See them together to understand?" Caliope sighed. "Not really. If his effect on the girls is anything like Maksim's effect on our children, I know exactly what you're talking about."

Selene looked more horrified by the second. "So you're stuck with him? You have to suffer forever and we have to watch it and be unable to do anything about it?"

Wanting to alleviate her friend's distress on her behalf and end this debate once and for all, Kassandra decided to placate them. "Who knows? Maybe I'm just experiencing echoes of what I once felt for him, and being around him again will show me I've blown everything out of proportion, allowing me to move on at last. Maybe this will turn out to be a blessing in disguise after all."

The three women looked at her, then exchanged a look among themselves before finally nodding. It was evident they hoped so with all their hearts. But even though they let her change the subject, she knew they didn't believe this was even in the realm of possibility.

Not for a second.

At last, Selene rose to her feet, prompting the others to do so, too. As Kassandra followed suit, Selene waddled toward her, holding out both hands to pull her into a tight hug. At least as tight as her burgeoning belly allowed.

Drawing back, Selene's dark blue eyes were almost grim. "If you change your mind and you need help getting rid of him, I'll do anything."

"Ditto," the other two chorused.

Choking on a cry, Kassandra surged to envelop them in a group hug, thanking the fates for them.

Pulling back, she gave her friends a wobbly smile. "Next time I know who to run to when I need impenetrable barriers against unstoppable missiles. What was I thinking asking for your men's help when I have you?"

Selene's features relaxed into a mischievous smile. "As long as you've learned your mistake. Right, ladies?"

Caliope and Naomi expressed their enthusiastic agreement, and the meeting that had started out tense ended on a merry note.

As merry as a breather in the ongoing drama that had become her life could be.

After her friends left her office, Kassandra struggled to get any work done. But as all the lightheartedness and optimism their love and support had brought her started to dissipate, she was dragged back into the bottomless well of worries and what-ifs.

Though she'd planned to stay at work hours longer, and she'd only done a fraction of what she'd set out to do, she gave up. At least at home she wouldn't have to make decisions that had millions of dollars and hundreds of jobs riding on them. Decisions she was starting to doubt she'd be able to make again.

Half an hour later, as she entered her home, a shroud of premonition descended around her heart. Though there was no car parked outside, and there were no sounds coming from inside, all her senses rioted with certainty.

Leonid was in there. She could scent him in the air, sense his presence in her every cell.

Trying to curb her stampeding reactions, she leaned on the wall, only to feel it tilt beneath her. Struggling with the wave of dizziness, she shrugged out of her suddenly suffocating coat, was trying to hang it when Kyria

Despina came rushing toward her, her expression the very definition of awe.

"Kassandra, dearest, I'm so glad you're home early!" The woman's voice buzzed with excitement as she took Kassandra's coat and hung it in the foyer's closet. "Prince Voronov has been here for two hours."

So he was here. Seemed her extrasensory abilities where he was concerned remained infallible.

Dark brown eyes gleaming with curiosity and pleasure, Despina linked their arms as she hurried Kassandra to the living room. "He came thinking you'd be back home at your usual time. The girls were beside themselves with delight to see him."

Feeling her legs about to buckle as the quietly prattling Despina led her to him, her mind was a battlefield of suspense, aversion and resignation. Confusion soon took precedence over the absolute silence emanating from the living room.

Then they reached it and it all made sense.

At the end of the room, Leonid was propped up against the playhouse. The girls were asleep on top of him. The cats were also snoozing, one on his legs, the other against his thigh.

"He played with them nonstop, games I'm sure he invented just for them," Despina whispered. "The darlings laughed and bounced around like I've never seen them. Then about fifteen minutes before you arrived, they climbed on his lap and turned off. The dear man made them comfortable, even crooned what must be a Russian nursery rhyme."

They'd slept on top of him. They hadn't fallen asleep in her arms since they were six months old.

"He hasn't moved or made a sound since, even when

I assured him nothing would wake them up again. You should go save him before he cramps something." Despina patted her on the back. "Now, since you're home and he's here to help you put the girls to bed, I may yet catch a bit of the ladies' poker night I had to miss to stay late tonight."

As if from the depths of a dream, Kassandra thought she nodded her agreement. Then everything fell off her radar but the sight Leonid and the girls made, a majestic lion with his cubs curled in slumber over him, totally content and secure in their father's presence and protection.

His eyes remained closed, but she knew he wasn't asleep. She could sense it. He was savoring the texture of the new experience, soaking in the girls' feel and closeness and trust. She also knew he was aware of her standing there. Like her, he'd always had an uncanny ability to sense her presence. She'd once thought he'd been so attuned to her, he felt her before he had reason to think she was near. That had been before she'd realized she'd never been special or even worthwhile to him.

Swallowing the lump that seemed to have taken permanent residence in her throat, she approached the pile. He let her come within less than a foot of them before he opened his eyes, connecting with hers, and almost compromised her precarious balance. Then he lowered his gaze to the girls in his arms again.

Forcing air into her shut-down lungs, she attempted nonchalance. "You can flip the girls in the air and they still wouldn't wake. Not now anyway. They only wake up around an hour after I put them in bed."

"Did they wake up last night after I left?"

"No."

She'd told herself they hadn't because he'd kept them way beyond their bedtime. But apart from logic, another theory explained the unusual occurrence. She believed that they always woke up out of some sense of uncertainty. But after he'd appeared, and they'd sensed his intention of being here to stay, that anxiety that woke them up was gone.

She exhaled. "My point is, you can move if you want."

"I don't want. There's no place I'd rather be."

What felt like acid welled behind her eyes. "Well, though you do look as if you make them very comfortable, I don't think they should start considering you a substitute for their bed."

His lips twisted as he kept gazing at the shiny heads nestled into his chest. "Though I would fully welcome that, I can appreciate the repercussions of such a development."

Sighing as he secured them both, he sat up. She again almost winced at the difficulty he had in adjusting his position, of rising to his feet. It had nothing to do with the girls being in his arms, since their weight had to be negligible to him. That knot behind her sternum, the same one that had formed when she'd realized the extent of his injuries and their consequences, tightened to an ache again.

Taking her eyes off him, so she wouldn't focus on his stiff gait and the fact that he was looking everywhere but at her, she led the way to the nursery, her mind racing.

Though the competition circuits were certainly out, had it been possible for him to practice his sports on any level? Being extremely fit but bulkier than before, it was clear he maintained his fitness with exercise that didn't rely on the speed and agility of his former specialties. So how much did he resent being forced to relinquish what he'd considered the epitome of his personal achievement? How much did he miss what had once been the main pillar of his existence?

Giving herself the mental equivalent of a smack upside the head as they put the girls in the cribs, she reminded herself how pointless and pathetic it was to wonder. Whatever his trials to adjust his path, and whatever he'd suffered or now felt about it all was none of her concern. He'd made that clear in the past. He was making it clearer now. This was all about Eva and Zoya. Beyond what she represented to them, she, and anything she thought and felt, mattered nothing to him.

As they exited the room, he finally looked at her. "I hope it's not your habit to sleep as soon as they do. I have a few things I need to discuss with you."

She stifled the urge to hiss that she'd lost the habit of sleeping altogether since him, that she had to exhaust herself on a daily basis only so she could turn off and hope for the oppressive silence and darkness of dreamlessness.

Managing to reach her living room without blasting his thick hide off, she sat down carefully instead of flinging herself on the couch. She also refrained from hurling a remote at him as he remained towering over her.

"How would you like to go about declaring me the girls' father?"

Blinking, her mind emptied. Had she heard him right? He wasn't dictating a course of action, but asking her preference?

Suddenly her blood tumbled in a boil. "How about you spare me the pretense that you care about what I want?"

"I do care. As Eva's and Zoya's mother you are—"

"Entitled to dictate my own terms. Yeah, I heard it the first time. And I already told you, my only term is to have the life I built for myself and the girls. But since this isn't going to happen, just do what you wish, and don't bother pretending that my preferences matter."

Those winged eyebrows she'd once luxuriated in tracing with fingertips and lips knotted as he seemed to examine every fiber in her lush carpet. The way he kept avoiding making eye contact with her at crucial moments was driving her up the wall.

He finally exhaled, his gaze once again on her and maddening her with its opacity. "That first night I came, I had to drive it home that I wasn't taking *go away* for an answer. But ever since I met the twins, and we interacted as their parents, many things have changed. I do want this arrangement to work for you, not only for them."

She never thought he'd say those words—and he actually seemed to mean them. It made everything even worse. Anger was her only defense against him, her last shield. If he made her let that go, what would become of her?

But that was a consideration for another time. For the rest of her lifetime. Now she had to give him an answer.

The truth was the only thing she had. "I haven't given any thought to how I'll break the news about you being the girls' father. I suppose I'll just tell the people I care about. Anyone else doesn't matter. Even if I am a public figure, I'm not in the spotlight nearly as much as you and my importance to the media is nothing compared to yours. You're also the one with a kingdom to consider in your public statements from now on. I'll leave it up to you to announce this as you see fit."

"In that case, I'll move on to the major reason I came." Suddenly, she wished she hadn't resented his lack of eye contact as his gaze transfixed hers, paralyzing her with a bolt of blue lightning. And that was before he said, "I came to ask you to marry me."

Five

"**M**arry you?"

Kassandra wasn't even sure she'd said that out loud. From the way her voice sounded, as if issuing from beneath a ton of rubble, maybe it was in her head. All of it. Including what he'd just said, so earnestly, asking her to…

"*Marry* you?"

This time she was sure she'd said it, judging by the urgency that surged in his eyes.

"I'm only asking this for Eva and Zoya."

Of course. None of it was or had ever been for her.

"It's the only way to secure their legitimacy."

"Legitimacy…" She parroted him again, her shock deepening.

She hadn't even thought of this aspect of things before. But he had said he'd *claim* them, and she'd vaguely realized he meant giving them his name. Yet the significance of that, that it would make them "legitimate," had escaped her. Now, knowing the implications, it felt so…offensive.

Fury flooded her, drowning her shock. "Legitimacy is an outdated concept. My daughters aren't and won't ever be defined or even affected by it. In this day and age, it's not a stigma anymore to have children out of wedlock." Suddenly, the room spun, making her slouch back on the couch. "And will you quit looming over me like this?"

He sat down at once, still careful to keep her at arm's length. His eyes took on a hypnotic edge, as if trying to compel her to succumb to his demand.

"Legitimacy wouldn't have mattered to me if I was anyone else. I would have become their father in all ways that matter and left it up to you when or if you let them have my name on official papers. But as you just pointed out, with my future role, bowing to the social and political mores of my kingdom has become imperative. Eva and Zoya aren't only my daughters, they're my heirs. They have to carry my name."

"And marrying me is the only way to have them carry your name instead of mine?"

"Not instead, with yours. I want them to have both our family names. They would be Eva and Zoya Stavros Voronov."

Her heart kicked her ribs so hard she almost keeled over. Those names. They sounded so…right.

But still… "We can do that without getting—"

He shook his majestic head, cutting her off.

"Getting married is also an unquestionable necessity. Consider that not even in recent history has the president of a progressive country had children out of wedlock. It isn't even a possibility for a king in Zorya. Our marriage isn't only a must for social acceptance and political stability in this case, it's also the only guarantee of the twins' rights and privileges as my heirs."

"*And* the restrictions and responsibilities, maybe even dangers. Even if you prove to be a great father to them, and that would be in their best interests, being heirs to the precarious throne of such a stuck-in-time kingdom isn't."

The azure of his eyes darkened to cobalt. "While your worries are logical, I pledge I will protect them from anything in this world, starting with any drawbacks of their title and my position. It's part of the reason why I'm taking the crown in Zorya. To see to it that it retains its useful traditions, but discards any backward practices. It must fully join the modern world where it matters on every level, be it social or political or economical. I will make Zorya a land I would be proud to raise our daughters in."

His fervent convictions and assured intentions seeped into her thoughts, suppressing misgivings and painting an enchanted future she'd certainly want for Eva and Zoya. Then his last words sank in with a thud, jogging her out of the trance.

"You mean you expect us to move there?"

"It's the only way for me to be in the twins' lives constantly, but it's you who'll dictate how to divide your time between Zorya and the United States. Of course, it would be ideal if you move to Zorya now."

She gaped at him, feeling as if she was watching a movie playing so fast everything had ceased to make sense.

"If you fear being in Zorya would interrupt the normal flow of your life, don't. I'll have every resource constantly at your disposal. You'll be able to travel anywhere in the world at a moment's notice. And when you have to be somewhere for any length of time, or even return here for an extended period, of course the girls will be with you, and I'll arrange my affairs so that I may join you as much as possible."

His assurances again underlined the extent of his power and wealth. But only one thing kept screeching like a siren in her mind.

"You expect me—us—to live with you in Zorya, and when we're back here…?"

His hand rose in a placating gesture. "You'll have your own quarters in the royal palace with the twins. I will visit them there according to the schedule you set, or have them with me within the parameters you approve. When you return here for visits or for longer stretches and I join you, I will arrange my own accommodations. I'm ready to provide all of these terms and any others you specify in a legally binding format."

This nightmare was getting darker with his every word. Though he was insisting she'd retain control of all decisions that shaped the girls' daily lives and futures, his every promise made her more heartsick. It all reinforced the simple fact that they were adversaries forced to come to an understanding. He'd progressed from bulldozing her to drawing legal lines to protect her share of rights, and no doubt his own. The only interactions they would have would be with the girls and through them, with them playing the part of polite partners in their presence and in front of others. Or would he ask her to play the part of a loving bride in front of the latter…?

Then he answered her uncertainties. "You have nothing to worry about when it comes to my presence in your life. In front of the girls, you need only keep doing what you have. In front of others, it's accepted for royal couples to be reserved in public, so you don't need to worry about putting on a facade of intimacy. In both private and public, our relationship would remain as it is."

In other words, nonexistent.

"I expect you'll have your own demands and modifications and I intend to fully accommodate your every wish."

Feeling the quicksand dragging her down into its depths even harder, she choked out, "You're talking as if I've already accepted, as if the only thing to do now is vet out details."

He stilled. "Why wouldn't you accept?"

"Why?" She huffed in incredulity. "Are you for real? This is my *life* you're turning upside down."

"I gave you my pledge your life won't be affected in any adverse way, but only enhanced. You'd be a queen…"

The word *queen* went off like a gong inside her head.

She found herself on her feet, staring down at him, shaking from head to toe. "You think I care about that title or could even want it? I never wanted *anything* but to raise my daughters in privacy and peace, and with you in our lives, there will never be either of those things ever again!"

He rose slowly to his feet, and even in her distress her muscles contracted in empathy at the difficulty he found in rising from her too-low couch. As he straightened, his balance wavered, and for seconds, he came so close, heat flaring from his body, in his eyes, and she thought he'd reach for her…touch her. All her nerves tangled, firing in unison.

Then he regained his stability and stepped back, leaving a cold draft in his wake. The blaze in his eyes was gone, as if she'd imagined it. Perhaps she had.

Turning, he walked to the opposite armchair, picked up the coat he'd draped over its back and put it on in measured movements. Then he came back to her where she stood ramrod tense.

He stopped even farther away than usual, his expression as impassive as ever. "I know this is too much to take in, so I'll leave you to think. I didn't expect you to give me an answer right away."

Trying to suppress her tremors, she failed to stem the shaking in her voice. "Are you even expecting any answer but yes? Would you accept any other answer?"

The perfect mask that had replaced his previously animated face became even harder to read. "Any other answer would be no. So no, I can't accept that."

Her lips twisted in bitterness. "So why are you pretending you'd give me time to think? Think of what? How to say yes? Or to reach the conclusion that it's pointless to say anything at all from now on, since you'll always do what you want anyway, using the girls' and your kingdom's best interests to silence my protests and misgivings and make me fall in line with your plans?"

His eyes dimmed even more. And she realized.

What she'd thought was meticulous impassiveness was something else altogether. Bleakness.

This epiphany silenced the rest of the tirade that had been brewing inside her. His despondency dug into her chest, snatching at her heart.

Was he distraught because he had to tie himself to

her? Was he feeling as hopeless as she was, sacrificing his freedom and what remained of his ambitions of pursuing what fulfilled *him*, for the girls' and his kingdom's sakes? Would being near her, to have access to his daughters, be too harsh a sentence to bear?

When she couldn't say anything more, he exhaled. "I didn't expect you'd welcome my proposition, but I do want you to take some time to think. Contrary to what you believe, there's a lot to consider, practical details that you need to sort out, questions you need to ask, demands you will want to make. I regret this is unavoidable but I pledge I will comply with any measures you specify to make everything as painless as possible."

As painless as possible.

The words ricocheted in Kassandra's head until she felt they'd pulped her brain.

He didn't even realize he'd already done the most painful thing he could have. Proposing marriage, for everyone's and everything's sake but hers.

What made it all worse was admitting she would have jumped at his proposal if there'd been any hope they could have rekindled a fraction of what they'd once had. His offer would have even been somewhat acceptable, for all other considerations, if he wasn't as averse to her being a constant part of his life.

But with both of them feeling they'd be imprisoned for life, there was no way she could accept.

Forcing her focus back on him, now that she saw through his expressionlessness, it battered her heart to feel the gloom gripping his stance, the dejection that blasted from him.

She struggled not to sound as shredded as she felt. "Even if I believe you'd keep every word, and though I understand the need for this step, I *can't* say yes. But I have an alternative. We can tell everyone we are already married but estranged, and that we decided to get back together. I would play my part for as long as you need to 'claim' the girls to fulfill your kingdom's traditional requirements, solving all your problems without creating a bigger one...for both of us."

His gaze dropped to the ground he now seemed to find so fascinating. Then without even a nod, he turned away.

Feeling him recede, she stared into nothingness, struggling to stem the bottled-up misery he'd stirred up.

The moment she heard him closing the front door with the softest thud, she broke down, let the storm overtake her.

Each time he'd gone to Kassandra, Leonid had sent away his driver and bodyguards.

The latter, fellow patriotic Zoryans who'd volunteered for the job and considered guarding him a sacred duty and ultimate honor, had always objected. There was no doubt in their minds anymore he'd become king, and his safety was no longer his personal concern, but a matter of national security and what the future of their kingdom rested on.

He'd still been adamant. He hadn't wanted anyone to know about Kassandra and the girls until he'd resolved everything with her. As he'd gone to her tonight bent on doing.

He'd parked miles away. He still found it hard to walk, always ended up in varying levels of discomfort after being on his feet and moving for a considerable length of time. And that was exactly what he'd needed tonight.

He'd needed the pain of exertion to dissipate some of the storm frying his system, the bite of cold to chill a measure of the inferno that had been raging higher every time he'd seen her.

He'd arrived at her home earlier to find the girls with only their nanny. Kassandra had picked today to swerve from her unchanging timetable to catch up on the schedule he'd disrupted.

He'd been dismayed by her absence for about ten seconds. Then the girls had come running to meet him, making him glad instead that she wasn't there. He could have some time with them alone, savoring their unbridled eagerness for his presence without the searing upheaval of hers.

The nanny, who'd instantly recognized him from the constant media exposure he'd been suffering recently, had delightedly invited him in. Though it had been to his advantage, he'd at first been disturbed she had without consulting the lady of the house. However, his thorough research, which he subjected anyone who came near Kassandra and the twins to, had indicated she was impeccably trustworthy. Though in her case, Kassandra's implicit trust in her would have been enough to put his mind at ease.

But besides judging someone in his exalted position to be safe, the lady must have taken one look at him with Zoya and worked out with 100 percent certainty who he really was. Yet even if she'd let him in for all the right reasons, he still needed to have an aside with her about never assuming anything, always checking first with Kassandra. He had zero tolerance when it came to the security of this household.

Only one thing had made him lenient with her. The

girls' fervent welcome. He still couldn't believe its extent. It had been as if they'd been waiting for him all their lives. As he had been for them.

The only pursuit that had kept him sane had been monitoring their every breath, along with Kassandra's, in those endless months after his accident. He hadn't allowed himself to imagine, let alone hope, for anything like that. He hadn't even tried to extrapolate his own reactions to seeing and feeling them in the flesh.

To have them respond so…miraculously to him had been beyond belief. As for his own feelings, they were… beyond description. At times, beyond endurance. From that moment they'd so unbelievably given him their trust, he'd known. He wouldn't be able to live another day without either of them.

Tonight had been further proof the magic he'd experienced with them the night before hadn't been a fluke. By the time they'd climbed over him and fallen asleep in perfect synchronicity, as if they shared an off switch and had telepathically agreed to flip it simultaneously, he'd been beyond enchanted and overwhelmed. Then he'd felt Kassandra's approach. Long before he heard her garage door opening.

He'd been suddenly loath to face her, yet unable to do anything but clasp the girls and wait for her to initiate the confrontation. His heart now thundered in his chest like it had then. In tandem, his hip joint started to throb with a red-hot warning that he'd pay the price of these miles in shoes unfit for walking for days to come.

He would welcome the physical discomfort. If only it were potent enough to counter his emotional turmoil. But no amount of pain could do so.

He'd expected being near Kassandra again would be

hard. Horrible, even. It wasn't. It was unbearable. With every passing moment in her company, the corrosive longing he'd suffered since he'd pushed her out of his life had been escalating to all-consuming need.

After her initial rejection, she'd been evidently shocked at the twins' reaction to him, and at his handling of them. She'd surrendered to the necessity of putting up with him, for her—their—daughters' sake. But it was clear this was the extent of her concession. She wanted nothing more to do with him.

As she shouldn't. Even if she weren't so averse, he'd be the one to keep away. As he'd been exhausting himself trying to. Then he'd asked her to marry him.

He'd thought he'd braced himself for any response. But her horror had been so deep, so total, he'd scrambled to pledge every guarantee, offer every incentive to make the union worth her while. But it had only made things worse. Her desperation as she'd offered to lie to the whole world for as long as it took had made clear the depth of her abhorrence of him. Of anything that bound her to him, even a marriage in name only. Even if it made her a queen.

But how could he have expected any less? After the way he'd rejected and abandoned her? In the cruelest way, at the worst time?

And he'd only come back to add more injuries. He'd forced his way back into the life she'd struggled long and hard to make into an oasis of peace and stability for their daughters.

That moment she'd stepped back and told him to come into her home, into her life, he'd felt as if he'd been taken in after being out in the freezing cold forever. But that had only been an illusion. As it should be.

He didn't want her to take him back.

But though her extreme reaction to his proposal had proved she never would accept him, even for show, she hadn't moved on. She hadn't found another man to bless. She hadn't even let any near. During his painstaking surveillance, many, many men had approached her. Three had offered her everything a man could offer a woman, starting with their hearts. It pained him to admit it, but she wouldn't have gone wrong accepting any of them.

So why hadn't she?

Had she been so busy with work and the twins she'd had nothing left to offer, or want? Or was he responsible for her being unable to move on, for becoming defensive and distant, even with the people closest to her, when she'd been the most emotionally generous and approachable person he'd had the undeserved privilege to know?

Pushing her away after the accident, he'd known he'd hurt her. But he'd thought her pain would soon become anger, helping her get over it. Over him. He hadn't suspected she'd linger in perpetual purgatory. Like he had.

But if she couldn't move on, then he hadn't just hurt her. He'd crippled her. And this had only one explanation: her feelings for him had been much deeper than he'd suspected.

Now she'd distilled her entire existence to being the twins' mother. Even her business seemed to have become a means to financial independence for their sake. Success and achievement were by-products, not the goals they'd once been.

He couldn't bear to think he'd damaged her irrevocably. That just by being near her again, he'd cause her even more harm.

But…maybe he didn't have to. Maybe instead of being

a disruption to her peace and a threat to her psyche, he could instead be her support, her ally. Maybe in time, he could heal her. Enough so she could move on, find love and build a life for herself, as a woman, with another man.

Even if it would finish him off.

When Leonid arrived at Kassandra's office the next day, her PA didn't intercept him, only fumblingly gave her boss the heads-up she'd failed to give her at his first incursion.

This time Kassandra opened her office door herself, and stepped silently aside to let him in, making no eye contact.

As she turned to him, he began at once. "I know how inconvenient and unfair to you the whole situation is, and if it was up to me, I'd accept your alternative proposition without qualifications. I will, as soon as I make certain it would satisfy the twins' legal legitimacy requirements in my kingdom."

Pushing a swathe of hair that seemed to encompass a thousand golden hues behind her ear, her emerald gaze regarded him steadily. "Then, it's as good as accepted. I'm sure you can achieve anything."

He tried not to wince at the cold resentment in her eyes, and the hot pain in his hip. "If only that was true. But I'll need your help to authenticate our fictitious marriage."

Everything about her stilled. "What am I supposed to do?"

"You have to come to my homeland."

A dozen conflicting emotions raced across her face before she shrugged. "Once you 'legitimize' the girls and become king, if I have to sign or swear anything in front of kingdom officials, I'll come."

He shook his head in frustration at his inability to make this easier on her. "I need you there before the coronation."

That wary watchfulness gripped her again. "When is that?"

"If all goes well, in a month's time now."

Her lips fell open. "You mean you want me to go to Zorya in less than a month?"

"No, I don't mean that." Before she could relax her clenched muscles, he exhaled. "We have to leave tomorrow."

Six

By the time the limo stopped at the private airfield, Eva and Zoya were sound asleep. Kyria Despina had also nodded off. Kassandra's alertness and agitation had only intensified with every passing second.

They reached a screaming pitch when Leonid got out and came around to hand her out. His smile, more than the coldness of the night after the warmth of the limo, sprouted goose bumps all over her. Oblivious to his effect on her, he got busy releasing the girls' car seat harnesses, insisting on carrying both.

After gesturing for those awaiting them on the tarmac to take her and the groggy Despina's hand luggage and the cats' carriers, he led them up into the giant silver jet.

With many of her family and friends being billionaires, she'd been on private jets before. But she'd never been on one of Leonid's. That fact underlined the superficiality of their liaison. She'd been the one who'd made the fatal mistake of becoming deeply involved, breaking the rules they'd agreed on, as he'd accused her of.

But all the other jets were nothing compared to this one. It felt…royal. So was it Zorya's equivalent of Air Force One? That made sense. From the news, Zorya no longer considered Leonid a candidate, but the future king, the man who'd resurrect their kingdom and restore its grandeur. It was a fitting ride for a man of his stature and importance.

With his staff and the jet's crew hovering in the background, Leonid led them through many compartments to a spiral staircase to the upper deck. Once there, he walked them across an ultrachic foyer, then through an automatic door that he opened using a fingerprint recognition module. So no one was allowed past this point except him, and those he let in.

The door whirred shut behind them as he guided them to a bedroom with two double beds, two special cribs and a huge pet enclosure for the cats. He'd prepared the jet for them!

After she helped him secure the girls and cats, he showed Despina the suite's amenities and assured her she should settle down for a full night's sleep.

As he led Kassandra back outside, it dawned on her that, with the transcontinental flight, they'd be traveling all through the night. Alone together.

Even if she convinced him to sleep himself, so she'd be spared the turmoil of his company, she wouldn't be able to even close her eyes knowing he was so close by. But she doubted he'd sleep and leave her. Apart from that one time he'd been beyond observing decorum and had told her what he'd really felt, he'd always been terminally gallant. And since she'd agreed to go to Zorya, he'd been more courteous than ever. It was enough to make her want to scream.

Resigned to a night in the hell of his nearness, she sagged down on a cream leather couch. Forcing her attention off him, she looked around the grand lounge.

Dominated by Slavic designs, the room was drenched in golden lights and earth tones, embodying the serenity of sumptuousness and seclusion. At the far end of the space that occupied the breadth of the massive jet, a screen of complementing colors and designs obscured another area behind it.

"This—" he gestured to a door "—is the lavatory." Another gesture. "And those buttons access all functions and services in this compartment. Please order refreshments or whatever you wish for until I come back."

She almost blurted out that he *didn't* need to come back, that he should go tend to matters of state or something. But she remained silent as he paused at the lounge's door, his fathomless voice caressing every starved cell in her.

"I'll only be a few minutes."

Once he disappeared, she headed to the lavatory, just for something to do, and stayed inside for as long as she could bear.

Once she came out, she did a double take, and faltered, gulping air. He'd come back, and he'd taken off his...jacket!

Had he been naked, he probably wouldn't have affected her more. Okay, he would have, but it was bad enough now. And his clothes weren't even that fitted, just a loose and simple white shirt and black pants. If anything about him or what he provoked in her could be called simple.

He smiled that slow, searing smile he'd been bestowing on her again since yesterday. Unable to smile back, she approached him, her stamina tank running lower by the second.

He'd been supremely fit before, but the added bulk of his new lifestyle suited him endlessly. The breadth of his chest and shoulders that had never owed their perfection to tailoring felt magnified now that only a layer of finest silk covered them. They, and his arms, bulged with strength and symmetry. Yet his abdomen was as hard as ever, his waist and hips as narrow, making his upper body look even more formidable. She didn't dare pause on the area at the juncture of his powerful thighs.

And that was only his body. The body that had enslaved her every sense, owned her every response, had possessed and pleasured her for a whole year. The body whose essence had mingled with hers and created their twin miracles. Then came the rest. The regal shape of his head, the deep, dark gloss of his hair, the hewn sculpture of his face, the seductiveness of his lips, the hypnosis of his eyes.

If he'd been Hermes before, he was now Ares. If ever a man was born to lead, to be king, it was him.

He extended one of those perfect, powerful hands that had once treated her to unimaginable intimacies and ecstasies.

"Come sit down, Kassandra. We're about to take off."

She sat down where the tranquil sweep of his hand indicated. Before she collapsed. No longer the stiff stranger he'd been with her, the way he moved, sounded, smelled, breathed, the way he just *was*…

It was all too much.

Unaware that just being near, just being him, was causing her unbearable pain, he sat down on the seat opposite her couch. His descent was smoother than her flop, yet a frown shadowed his leonine brow. She could feel frustration radiating from him at his inability to move as effortlessly as before. After his previous preternatural litheness, it must be indescribably disconcerting to him to no longer have total control over his every move, to orchestrate them in that symphony of grace that he used to.

Getting his irritation under control with obvious difficulty, he secured his seat belt and pressed a button in his armrest. The engines revved higher and the jet started moving.

To escape the gaze he pinned on her again, she fastened her seat belt and examined the panel in her own armrest. She didn't get most of the functions. But then, in her condition, she wouldn't have recognized a neon exit sign.

If only this situation came with one. It didn't, not for the foreseeable future. If one ever became available, it wouldn't be called an exit, but an escape, with whatever could be saved. If anything remained salvageable this time.

For now, she couldn't even figure out what had happened since Leonid had said they had to go to Zorya in a day's time.

That statement had been met with her finest snort. But he'd been as serious as a tidal wave, inundating her objections. And as she continued to discover, resistance with him was indeed futile.

After he'd left, she'd done what he'd made her agree

to, called every person, agency and organization she'd made prior plans, signed contracts or had delivery dates with, to request extensions. Not expecting to get any, she'd felt secure that these commitments would be her excuse not to comply with his timetable.

But they'd all come back to her within hours, *offering* her all the time she wanted. Sans penalty. Some with an increase in compensation for her "extra time and effort."

Not only was she burning to know how he'd done that, but she was getting more anxious about what he'd done to achieve these unbelievable results.

But now that she was sentenced to a night of sleepless torture in his company, she was bent on getting some answers. She wouldn't let him escape her questioning again as he had so far, on account of being too busy preparing their departure.

She raised her gaze to him, found him studying her with yet another inscrutable expression in his incredible eyes.

Suppressing tremors of longing, she cocked her head at him. "Now that you have nowhere to go for the next fourteen hours, you will tell me."

His eyes maintained that enigmatic cast. "Who says I have nowhere to go? This jet has a depressurizing compartment in the rear so I can make a dash for it in extreme emergencies."

"And you consider this one? You'd skydive from forty thousand feet, at six hundred miles an hour, into the big unknown below, to escape telling me how you got all those multibillion-dollar enterprises to postpone my multimillion-dollar deals with a smile and a bonus on top?"

His eyes crinkled, filling with what she thought she'd

never see there again. Bedevilment. "If you saw the look in your eyes, you'd categorize this as a jump-worthy situation."

Pursing her lips to suppress the moronic urge to grin at him, when for the past two years plus he'd certainly caused her nothing to grin about, she plastered her best attempt at severity on her face. "What did you do, Leonid?"

His lips mimicked hers in earnestness, but the smile kept attempting to escape. "What do you think I did?"

"I have theories, and fears. Not in your best interests to keep me in suspense with that combustible mix."

A revving chuckle erupted deep in his endless chest. "I did mean it when I said I'd tell you when I had the time and presence of mind. But now that I realize you have all those theories and fears, I must hear them first. So you tell me what you think I did, and if it's close, I'll tell you the exact details."

Was he...teasing her? What had gotten into him? Where was the automaton who'd stood on her doorstep playing back what had sounded like a recorded script and programmed responses?

Was he practicing the ease they'd display as newly reconciled husband and wife? He had said polite formality would be fine in public, but what if he'd decided it was more effective to give his adoring subjects a doting couple to moon over?

In other modern kingdoms, the alleged love stories between royal couples counted as a major asset for the monarchy, contributing to its political and social stability. It was also a huge source of economic prosperity via revenues for the media and tourism machines.

So now that she'd accommodated all his demands and

he was no longer anxious about his plans, was he relaxing and rehearsing in preparation for giving the public a convincing performance?

Or was it even worse? Had he decided to enslave the world by reverting to his previous self, the one she'd fallen fathoms deep for, and hadn't been able to kick her way to the surface since?

Unable to even think of the ramifications to herself if this was the case, she focused on his current challenge, knowing he wouldn't reveal anything if she didn't meet it.

"It's not what I think as much as what I hope you did. For the future of my business, I hope there was no coercion or intimidation on your part, but that as a former world champion, current mogul and future king, you have endless strings to pull, gently, and that you binged on using all the favors you could."

Those perfectly arched eyebrows shot up. "And leave myself in a favor deficit as I embark on ruling a historically contested land with a nascent independence amidst a turbulent sea of cranky killer-whale and bloodthirsty-shark nations?"

When he put it that way, her worries didn't even seem relevant.

Shoulders drooping, she flopped back on the couch. "So my business was too small a fry for you to spend favors on, huh?"

He unbuckled himself, rose and came down beside her, much closer than his usual very long arm's length. "Actually, your business is a huge enough fish I didn't need to."

Her wits scattering at his action, his nearness, she tried to focus on the meaning of his words. And failed.

Giving up, she croaked, "What's that supposed to mean?"

"It means the only good my calls did was explain the time-sensitive nature of your request, since you didn't."

"What exactly did you tell them?"

"The truth, but I requested their discretion until we made a public announcement. But they were already falling over themselves to adjust their plans to accommodate your needs. I just told them you needed their response ASAP for your peace of mind before our trip and subsequent major events. All I did was make them call you sooner with their acceptance."

When she could only gape at him in disbelief, his lips crooked with what very dangerously resembled indulgent pride.

"I already knew how respected and valued you are, but today I discovered your popularity is phenomenal. You've built such a massive reserve of goodwill, such need for your name, products and collaboration, everyone said and proved they'd do whatever they had to for the opportunity to keep on working with you."

Finding this revelation too much to accept, she shook her head. "They must have hoped it would be a big favor to you. Who wouldn't want to be in your good graces?"

His pout was all gentle chastisement. "You don't know your own influence on people at all, do you?"

I used to have a pretty good idea. Until you pulverized my belief in my own judgment and my self-esteem.

But it wasn't time now, or ever, to voice that grievance.

"Even if some were willing to accommodate me, you have to be exaggerating such a sweeping response. It had to be *your* influence. They must have calculated that a point with you would appreciate astronomically. No advantage gained by rejecting my request would be worth being in your bad books."

Without saying anything further, he got out his phone, dialed a number. In seconds, the line opened.

"Signor Bernatelli…" He paused for a second as an exclamation carried to her ears from the other side.

Sergio Bernatelli, the top Italian designer she was collaborating with in her biggest project to date, had recognized his voice, or saved his number. Probably both.

"…yes, it's indeed fortunate to be talking to you again. Yes, we are on our way to Zorya." Another pause as the man bubbled over on the other side. "That would be totally up to Kassandra. Why don't you ask her? And can you please also repeat to her what you said to me when I called you earlier? Thank you, Signor Bernatelli, and look for our invitation to the coronation in the mail in a couple of weeks."

After she numbly took the phone from him, she barely got a hello in before the flamboyant man submerged her in his excitement about her upgrade to royal status, and his hopes she would consider him for a creation designed for her to wear to the coronation, or any royal function at all. Before she could express her gratitude for such a gift—though it would mean huge publicity for him—he repeated everything Leonid had told her, in his far more over-the-top language, which he usually reserved for blistering complaints and demolishing critique.

After she ended the call, she kept staring at Leonid, tingling with the incredible praise Bernatelli had lavished on her. Not only where it pertained to him and his design empire, but to the whole field.

"I trust you believe me now?" Leonid smiled expectantly.

She started to nod, but stopped. "Maybe not. Maybe knowing I'd ask, you put him up to this so he'd back your story."

Incredulity widened his eyes. "Following that reasoning, shouldn't I have picked an accomplice you'd be more inclined to believe would have such a glowing opinion of you? Why pick that cantankerous scrooge when praises from him would be the most suspicious?"

"Maybe that's exactly why you chose him, because it would have been too obvious to pick someone agreeable, and such a famed grouch's vote would carry more weight and credibility."

Leonid threw his hands up in the air, *"Bozhe moy*, Kassandra! That's too convoluted for even me. My brain is now starting to ache trying to contort around that pretzeled piece of logic."

She opened her mouth to confront him with another suspicion, but closed it. That was real bewilderment in his eyes. Worse, the levity that had been present all day, that she'd delighted in in spite of herself, was gone. She'd weirded him out because of her attack of dogged insecurity.

At her prolonged silence, he exhaled. "Did you only run out of arguments, but still believe in my deceit?"

Grimacing at how unreasonable she must have sounded, she sighed. "No, I believe you. But even if your calls only made a difference in timing, that's still a big thing. I would have been beside myself with worry if we left without hearing back from them. And because of your calls I learned something I wouldn't have on my own. People find it hard to say their opinions to someone's face, even if it's glowing praise. Or especially when it is. It's good to know I'm in such universal favor."

A relieved smile dawned on his heartbreakingly handsome face. "Which isn't a favor at all, but your due." He sat up, eagerness entering his pose. "And now that you realize your power, I'll counsel you on how to exercise it more effectively, to your benefit and that of the whole industry."

Her first instinct was to decline his offer. Then her mind did a one-eighty.

Why refuse? What made more sense than for her to accept the advantages of his invaluable insight and enormous experience, when it would be for everyone's benefit?

Suddenly, what she'd thought would never come to pass happened. She exchanged a smile with him, devoid of tension and shadows. Then the door to the bedroom opened.

Tousled and half-asleep on her feet, Despina stood in the door, carrying a very awake Eva and Zoya.

Leonid pushed to his feet before she could, his delight at seeing the girls blatant and unreserved. Their equal glee at finding him again manifested in excited shrieks as both of them flung themselves into his open arms.

Resigned that she was the old news they'd forgo until Leonid's novelty wore off, Kassandra sighed. "Sorry, Kyria Despina. I really thought they'd sleep through the night since they haven't woken up the past few days. Wonder if they're back to their habit, or if it's only today's different pattern and strange cribs that roused them."

"Why do you think they wake up?" Leonid asked.

"They seemed to hate letting go of all the fun they

were having before they sleep, wanting a few more hugs or another song or anything they were enjoying before they turned off."

Squeezing the girls tighter into his chest until their squeals became piercing, he laughed...*laughed.* "And there's plenty more of all of those things for *moy zvezdochky.*"

His starlets. This was his favorite endearment for them already. His morning and evening stars.

He used to have endearments for her, too. Mostly while in the throes of pleasure. *Moya dorogaya krasavista... moya zolotoya krasota... My beautiful darling...my golden beauty.*

She would never hear them from him again.

Now all his attention was diverted to the girls, and he looked as if he'd been given an unexpected second chance at something irreplaceable. Then he grimaced, turning his gaze to Despina.

"Kyria Despina, please go back to sleep. We'll keep them with us if they fall asleep again, so as not to disturb you."

Shaking off her dimming mood, Kassandra had to intervene. "Uh, I actually never let them wake up to find themselves outside their cribs. They're notorious for picking up bad habits once I break a pattern and it's a struggle going back to any sort of order."

Nodding his deference to her decree at once, he strode toward Despina. "Let me take you to another bedroom. I'm sorry to move you, but from now on your sleep will be uninterrupted when the twins wake up at night."

Despina rushed beside him, assuring him she didn't mind at all, her cheeks flushed by the pleasure of having a royal god like Leonid fussing over her.

Within moments, Leonid marched back with the girls, one straddling his shoulders, the other his waist. They babbled as he cooed to them. "Papa" was repeated profusely as both swamped him in hugs and kisses, with him looking utterly blissful as he reciprocated.

They looked agonizingly beautiful together.

But that agony dissipated as they joined her, and she was infected by their gaiety and pleasure at being together.

An hour later, long after they should have gone back to sleep, as they all sat playing in the sandbox that had been ingeniously hidden until Leonid had unveiled it, the toddlers started gnawing their fists and drooling.

Concern coated Leonid's magnificent face as they both rushed to clean the twins' hands, even if what passed for sand was totally safe. He looked at her. "They're in the molar eruption phase now, right?"

She was impressed. "Give the new daddy a star. You've done your homework, I see."

"Of course. But since they didn't display any of the usual signs of teething before, I almost forgot about it."

"Well, health-wise, the girls have been a dream. Even teething has been progressing without signs of discomfort."

"But they're almost gnawing their little hands off and drooling up a storm!"

She chuckled at his growing agitation, content to be the wise, experienced parent who kept a cool head. "Don't ask me why, but it's their current method of letting me know they're hungry. No, let me correct that. Starving."

His eyes lit up in relief. "Of course they are. I thought they ate so much less than usual during their dinner."

"They were too excited with all the preparations to eat."

"And it turned out to be the best thing they did. So they'd wake up and play with their papa, and let him feed them their first Zoryan meal. I'm ordering you a feast!"

His enthusiasm widened her grin as he reached for the panel in his chair. He'd explained he'd given that jet to Zorya, not the other way around, to be the monarch's jet, long before he knew it would be him.

Though she'd thought she wasn't hungry, by the time he opened the door to waiters holding trays high, her stomach rumbled. Loudly. The food aromas were distressingly delicious, and even the fussy girls were smacking their lips.

Grinning at their demonstration of hunger, he rose, held his hand down to her. She took it, but along with her own upward momentum, she ended up falling against him. For a moment, it felt as if a thousand-volt lash had flayed her where their bodies touched, from chest to hip.

It was he who pulled back first, almost anxiously, his eyes once more unfathomable. The moment passed as the girls scampered around, pulling at them to get on with feeding them.

Getting back into the flow of talking with Eva and Zoya with their system of English, Zoryan Russian and baby talk, he led them behind the screen she'd noticed before. Turned out there was a full dining area there, with gold-and-black silk-upholstered chairs. In the center stood an elaborate table decorated with Zorya's magnificently rendered and detailed emblem of the two goddesses.

As they sat down, Leonid explained to the girls that they were like those two goddesses, night and day twins. Zorya would consider them the symbol of its rebirth, just like the goddesses were responsible for its original birth. He enlisted Kassandra's help in simplifying the concept, and it all turned into a game as the girls caught on to the resemblance and imitated the goddesses' poses.

The food, which Leonid explained in detail, was beyond delicious. Even the usually picky girls devoured anything Leonid offered them. Kassandra insisted it had more to do with him doing the offering than the tastiness of the food itself.

Midmeal, the girls asked to sit in the place of the goddesses in the emblem. Getting her okay, Leonid improvised a new game, placing plates on the symbols surrounding the goddesses, offering them all forkfuls, and making Eva and Zoya laugh all the harder each time he theatrically dipped a fork in a plate and zoomed it toward a wide-open mouth, sometimes even Kassandra's.

She kept wondering how this had become the last thing she'd expected it to be—a delightful family trip. His new approachability and the girls' enthusiasm and spontaneity had dissolved the artifice and distance the past had imposed on them, revealing Leonid as he was now. He'd told the truth. He was no longer the man she'd loved, but far better, warmer, endlessly patient and accommodating, the perfect companion and the best father-in-training she could have imagined.

After they finished eating and the waiters had removed all signs of their meal, Leonid got the girls off the table and clapped. "How about some Zoryan music, *moy zvezdochky*?"

As if they understood, and maybe they truly did, the girls yelled in agreement. Once Leonid had the infectiously joyous music filling their cocoon of luxury, he started teaching the girls the steps of a Zoryan folk dance. Noticing how hard it was for him to execute even those simple steps, she studied them quickly and took over teaching them as best she could. Soon they were all dancing with Leonid watching them, keeping the tempo with powerful claps, singing along, his rich bass deepening the spell.

Whenever one song ended and another started, Leonid would urge them on. *"Tantsevat', moy prekrasnyye damy.* Dance!"

This time, he'd included her when he'd said "my beautiful ladies." At least she thought he'd included her.

But why should she doubt it? The whole day he'd gone above and beyond doting on both the girls and her. He'd given her the gift of showing her how important she was to her colleagues in her field. He'd been exemplary in recognizing her superior knowledge of the girls, had showed them in no uncertain terms that, though he was their papa who would do anything for them, it was mama who was the boss. He'd been plain magnificent to her.

When she said no more, he invited her down on the carpeted floor. They sat with their backs to the couch, with the girls climbing on and off them, bringing them toys and asking them to name them in their respective languages. Then she and Leonid quizzed them. To all their excitement, the girls remembered almost everything and said the words as accurately as possible in the three languages.

The games continued for hours. Then the girls suddenly lay down across his and her side-by-side bodies, making a bridge between them with theirs, and promptly fell asleep.

They remained sitting like this, sharing the connection their daughters had spontaneously created between them in serene silence for what could have been another hour, alternating caressing the girls' silky heads.

Suddenly, his black-velvet voice spread over her like a caress. *"Oni ideal'ny."*

She nodded, heart swelling with sudden, overwhelming gratitude. For them. And for him. "Yes. They are perfect." At length, she added, "Let's put them to bed."

Without objection, even when she could see he wanted to savor them for far longer, he gathered one girl after the other and rose with them in his arms.

On the way to their bedroom, she had to voice her wonder. "You'll have to show me how you keep them stuck to you like this when they're asleep. Either you're a literal babe magnet, or you three share some Voronov Vacuum quality."

A surprised huff of mirth escaped him before he suppressed it. Then he seemed to remember nothing could disturb them, and let it all out.

As they went back to the lounge, he was still chuckling as he put on a different kind of music, still Zoryan, but perfect for setting a soothing mood.

Sitting down on the couch, he suddenly guffawed again. "Voronov Vacuum. I should patent this."

She grinned her pleasure at his appreciation of her quip. "You should. That brand name is just meant to be."

He sighed, still smiling. "I wanted to ask you to let them sleep like that between us, as if laying claim to both of us. You know I lost my parents when I was not much older than they are, was raised by indulgent relatives. What you don't know is that I struggled to cultivate the discipline my parents would have instilled in me, had they lived. So I know how important it is to have structure in one's life, and I truly admire your ability to provide and maintain it. I will happily follow your lead and reinforce your methods." He signed even more exaggeratedly. "Even if the new papa in me wants to mindlessly indulge them to thorough and decadent rottenness."

She chuckled at his mock-mournful complaint. "You have a lifetime to indulge them, *and* discipline them, *and* the rest of the roller coaster of unimaginable ups and downs of parenthood to look forward to. Pace yourself. I'm trying to."

His eyes glittered with such poignancy, as if it was the first time he dared to let himself look forward that far. "I do have a lifetime, don't I? I am their father forever."

Throat sealing with emotion, she nodded. "If you want to be."

His azure eyes flared with such elation and entreaty. Then he only said a hoarse "Please."

The word rolled through her every cell like thunder. And everything inside her snapped.

Then she was pressing all she could of herself into what she could of him, lips blindly seeking every part of him she'd starved for, all her suppressed longing bursting out in a reiteration so ragged it was a prayer.

"Yes, Leonid, yes, please...*please*..."

Seven

Among the cacophony of her thundering heart and strident breathing, Kassandra heard a piece of music ending and a more evocative one starting. And she was pleading. Pleading. Pleading. For what, she didn't know.

But she *did* know. She was pleading for him. For them. For an explanation. A reconnection. A resurrection.

Just touching him again felt like coming back to life. If only he'd touch her back.

But he had frozen from the moment she'd obliterated the distance between them, had done what she'd been suffocating for since that moment she'd seen his crumpled car in the news. To touch him, feel him, reassure herself he was here and whole, that she hadn't lost him.

But she had lost him. He'd imposed his loss on her. But she now realized that through all the pain, there had remained the consolation that he still existed, that she hadn't lost him that way. In the depths of her soul, hidden from her pain and pride, there had always been the hope that maybe, one day, this meant she could have him back.

Now nothing mattered to her anymore but the fact that he was the only man she'd ever want, that he was her girls' father and he loved them. That he'd come back for them had shown her a glimpse of the perfection they could have.

Now all she wanted was for him to end her exile.

Her hands and lips roaming his solid vitality, singed by his heat, tapping into his life, she begged for his response.

Please. Please. Please.

Then he moved…away.

Her lips stilled on his chest, mortification welling inside her like lava. He was rejecting her again.

But…maybe not. With the debris of the past between them, he wouldn't presume to take what she was offering when he didn't know what it was, or how it would affect their sensitive situation and fragile new harmony.

But this wasn't the past. This was now. It could be their tomorrows. She had to risk new injury for the slightest possibility this new man he'd become had changed toward her, too, and might now want her as she wanted him. He had wanted her once, before he'd stopped. Maybe this time he wouldn't stop.

Pulling back to look up at him through eyes filling with tears, she found his face clenched as hard as the muscles that had turned to rock beneath her fingers, buzzed like live wires. He was shocked. And aroused as hell.

His hunger buffeted her, left her in no doubt. It wasn't lack of desire that made him pull back, but uncertainty.

Attempting to erase any doubts he had, she pressed against him, sobbed into his hot neck against his bounding pulse, "Take me, Leonid, just take me, *please*…"

"Kassandra…" His rumble of her name reverberated inside her as he heaved up, tugging her with him. In the past, he would have scooped her up, but she knew he couldn't now.

Her legs still almost gave out as he rushed her through compartments, past the dining area to another closed door. Behind it was a bedroom as big as the lounge, dominated by a king-size bed covered in gold-and-black satin. His bedroom.

Before she could use what was left of her coordination to stumble to the bed, he closed the door and pressed her against it, taking her face in both hands. In the pervasive golden light, his face was supernatural in beauty, reflecting the hurricane building up inside him. His blue-fire gaze was explicit with one question: Did she know what she'd be getting into when he let it break over her?

Feeling she'd crumble into ashes if it didn't, she cried out, "Leonid, I want it all with you…"

With a groan that sounded as if something had ripped inside him, his head swooped down and blocked out existence.

Then he was swallowing her moans of his name, giving her his breath, reanimating her as he growled hers inside her.

"Kassandra…"

It was like opening a floodgate. To the past. To that first kiss that had been exactly like that. A conquering; a claiming. Her breath fractured inside her chest as she drowned in his feel and scent and taste. As she had that first time, and for a whole year afterward. She'd only drowned in desolation, alone, after he'd cast her out.

But she *was* drowning again now. In kisses that tantalized her with only glimpses of the ferocity she needed from him. His hands added to her torment, gliding all over her, never pausing long enough to appease, until she writhed against him, whimpering for what she'd never and could never stop wanting. Everything with and from him.

But he wasn't giving her everything, as if still testing her, not sure how total her surrender was.

She dug her fingers into his shoulders. "Leonid… *please*, give me *everything* you've got."

His head rose for one suspended moment, long enough for her to see his shackles snapping, then at last, he clamped his lips down on hers, hard, hot branding. His tongue thrust deep, singeing her with pleasure, breaching her with need, draining her of moans and reason.

She took it all, too lost to pleasure him in turn. His absence had left a void that had been growing larger every day until she'd feared it would hollow her out, leaving only a shell. Now he was here again, filling the emptiness.

Pressure built in her eyes, chest and core. Her hands convulsed on his arms until he relented, pushed her blouse up and over her head, pulled her bra strap down, setting her swollen breasts free.

She keened with relief, with the spike in arousal. He had her exposed, vulnerable. Desperate with arousal. Shaking hands pressed her breasts together to mitigate their aching as everything inside her surged, gushed, needing anything he would do to her. His fingers and tongue and teeth exploiting her every secret, his body all over hers, his manhood filling her core, thrusting her to oblivion…reclaiming her from the void.

Tears flooded down her cheeks. "Don't go slow, Leonid… I can't wait, I can't…"

Leonid had to be dreaming.

It had to be one of those tormenting figments that had hunted him mercilessly every moment since he'd watched her stumble out of his hospital room. Kassandra couldn't be pressing into him, all that glorious passion and flesh, sobbing for him to take her. He couldn't be scenting her arousal, feeling it vibrating in his loins, hearing it thundering in his cells.

She couldn't want him still, after what he'd done to her.

Her teeth sank into his bottom lip, hard, breaking his flesh. The taste of his blood mixing with her taste, inflamed his every nerve. Her distress felt so real.

It *was* real, a firebomb of madness detonating inside him, blowing away the last of his disbelief, and his control.

He smashed his lips harder into hers, and her cry of relief, of exultation tore through him. The need to ram into her, ride her, spill himself inside her, with no finesse, no restraint, drove him. Her flesh buzzed with her distress beneath his burning hands. Her incessant moans filled his head.

She wanted an invasion. And he would deliver.

It had been so long without her…so agonizingly long. He'd thought it would be for the rest of his miserable life. But his banishment was suddenly over. She was taking him back when he'd thought it an impossibility.

And he would take her as she needed him to, binge on her, perish inside her.

He swept her off her feet and she arched deep against the door, making a desperate offering of her core, her breasts, her hands behind his head sinking further into his sanity, speeding his descent into delirium.

He fell on her engorged breasts, starving, took what he could of her ripened femininity, where his daughters had suckled, insane with regret that he hadn't been there to witness it. Tearing her skirt farther up in rough, un-coordinated moves, he spread her thighs wide around his hips. She thrashed, clamped him with her legs and need, her sobs sharpening. His distress just as deep, he held her with one arm, reached between her legs, pushed aside her soaked panties, opened her folds and shuddered, on the brink of release just gliding his fingers through her fluid heat.

Drawing harder on one nipple, then the other, he rubbed two fingers in shaking circles over the knot of flesh where her nerves converged. Once, twice, then he felt her stiffen, that soon. He gritted his teeth, anxious for the music of her release, even if he suffered permanent damage hearing it.

She came apart in his arms, magnificent, abandoned, her cries fueling his arousal to the point of agony. His hands shook out of control as he freed himself, the anticipation so brutal his grip on consciousness was slipping.

Fighting to focus, he snatched her thighs back around him, groaned as her wet heat singed his erection, even as her heavy-lidded gaze scalded the rest of him. Growling something not even he understood, driven, wild, his fingers dug into her buttocks. Her breasts swelled more at his roughness, her hardened nipples branding his raw flesh even through his clothes.

His vision distorted over lips swollen from his ferocity, quivering from a taut-with-need face. "Come inside me n—"

He drove up into her, roaring her name. But though molten for him, she was as tight as ever, her flesh resisting his invasion as he stretched her beyond her limits. But knowing their impossible fit only drove her beyond coherence with pleasure, he pulled out only to thrust back, again, then again, again, again, to the rhythm of her piercing screams as she consumed him in her velvet inferno, until he'd embedded himself inside her to the hilt.

Then he stilled in her depths, surrendered to her clenching hunger as it wrung him, razed him. At last. *At last.*

He rested his forehead against hers, overwhelmed, transported, listening to her delirium, to his. Her graceful back was a deep arch, granting him total freedom with her body.

Then it was no longer enough. The need to conquer her, finish her, end inside her rose like a tidal wave, as it always had, crashing and destroying everything, before building again as if it had never dissipated.

Blind, out of his mind, he lifted her, filled his mouth and hands with her flesh. He had to leave no fiber of her being unsaturated with pleasure. He withdrew all the way out of her then thrust back, harder, then harder still, until he was hammering inside her to the cadence he knew would overload her, until she convulsed in orgasm, her satin screams echoing his roars as he followed her into the abyss of pleasure.

Her convulsions spiked in intensity at the first splash of his seed against her womb, and he felt her heart spiraling out of control with his as a sustained seizure of release destroyed the world around them.

Then it was another life, where nothing existed except being merged with her, riding the aftershocks, savoring the plateau of ecstasy, sharing the descent.

It had been beyond control or description. Everything.

Yet it wasn't enough. Would anything with Kassandra ever be?

He knew the answer to that. Nothing ever would. He'd never had enough of her. He'd been hers alone since that first time he'd laid eyes on her. He would have remained hers even if he'd never had her again. Even if she'd hated him forever.

But defying comprehension, she didn't. Not only didn't she hate him, not only did she still want him, she seemed to have forgiven him. She'd given him her body again, her acceptance, her support with the twins, her ease. Her laughter. How was it even possible?

And he realized. *He'd* done that. When he hadn't meant to.

All he'd meant when he'd let go of the act of stiffness and distance had been to end her fears toward him, neutralize her hostility, for her own peace of mind. He hadn't dreamed she would not only relinquish her rightful hatred of him but seek his intimacy again, and with this unstoppable urgency.

And he realized something else. Even though she'd completed her descent from the peak of pleasure, she wasn't pulling away.

He withdrew a bit, keeping them merged as he looked down at her. She seemed disoriented, her eyes slumberous, fathomless as they gazed up at him. A goddess of temptation and fulfillment, something every man dreamed of but never really expected to find. And he'd found her, not only once, but against all odds, twice.

Unable to stop himself, his hands dug into her buttocks, gathering her tighter to him.

Her eyes scorched him to the bone with the amalgam of pleasure and pain that transfigured her amazing beauty as he expanded even more inside her. Her core, molten with their combined pleasure, contracted around him, making him thrust deeper into her, wrenching moans from both their depths. Then slowly, her lids slid down.

In seconds her breathing evened. She'd fallen asleep.

Overwhelming pride that he'd pleasured her so completely, as he'd used to, it had literally knocked her out, burgeoned inside him. He hardened even more, that first explosive encounter only serving to whet his appetite. As it always had, during their past extended sessions of delirium. Visions assailed him, of taking her to bed, making love to her again as she slept, until she woke up on another orgasm.

But he couldn't do that. He had to let her sleep.

Cursing his shoddy coordination, he gathered her in his arms and walked slowly with her precious weight. She'd left it all to his power in lax trust, testing his precarious balance. The trek to the bed felt endless. Placing her under the covers and adjusting her clothes, she stirred only to touch what she could of him with sleepy kisses and caresses, murmuring wonderful little incoherencies in appreciation of his caresses and coddling. He struggled up, heart thundering, brow covered in cold sweat. His control had one last notch before it slipped again.

One thing pulled him back from the temptation. The sheer regret and despair that pulverized the heart he'd thought had shriveled the day he'd pushed her away all over again.

This had been a terrible mistake.

For her sake, from now on, he had to leave her alone.

He couldn't succumb to her need, or his weakness, ever again.

Kassandra woke up from an inferno of eroticism, on fire.

Gasping as her dream about Leonid evaporated and with it the impending orgasm he'd been about to give her, it took her a disoriented minute to realize where she was. In Leonid's luxurious jet bedroom, fully clothed and tucked beneath covers that felt alive with silky touches and sighs.

Leonid had knocked her out with pleasure. As he'd always done. So even this hadn't changed.

Barely able to move, she turned her head to squint at the digital clock pinned down on the bedside table... and gasped. It was seven hours since she'd shut down in his arms. They must be about to land. And he must have had things to attend to. Which was a good thing. She didn't know how she would have faced him after what she'd done.

She'd almost attacked him in her arousal!

But once he'd made sure he knew what she'd been asking for, how far she'd wanted him to go, he'd...devastated her. She felt...ravished. Every inch of her felt fully exploited, delightfully sore and was screaming for an encore. Pushing away the covers that suddenly felt filled with hot thorns, she teetered barefoot to the adjoining bathroom.

It turned out to have a whirlpool tub, which she couldn't rush to fast enough, taking her clothes off to sink in.

As the warm currents bombarded her ultrasensitive flesh, her condition worsened as the memories of her encounter with Leonid boiled over in her blood. If he'd been here, she would have lost her mind all over again, and again.

When she couldn't take it anymore, she heaved out of the water and headed on trembling legs for the mirror, in front of which she shakily dried herself. She looked exactly like what she was. A woman who'd been possessed and pleasured within an inch of her sanity, and was now looking wild with her need for more.

But…would there be more? What would he say and do when she next saw…

"We are now approaching Zvaria, and will be landing in ten minutes. Please fasten your seat belts."

The pilot's announcement pulled her out of her feverish musings. But before she could head for the door, it opened. And she found herself face-to-face with Leonid.

Before her next heartbeat, he smiled, but it was detached, impersonal.

"Good, you're awake." Before she could respond, he opened the door wider. "Let's join the twins and share this historic event of landing in the Zoryan capital for the first time together."

As she approached him, he receded to let her pass. She tried to meet his eyes, read in them his response to what had happened between them, where he thought they'd go from there.

But he turned his gaze away in what seemed like a natural move as he invited her to lead the way.

Heart thudding to the rhythm of uncertainty and mortification, she walked ahead, her thoughts tangling.

Did he have too much on his mind, with the resolution of their situation and his looming responsibilities? Or was he just regretting what had happened?

Trying to project the ease she'd perfected for the girls' sake, she pinned a brittle smile on her face as they joined the others. As usual, Eva and Zoya demanded his attention, and hers to a lesser degree, leaving no room to focus on anything but them until they landed.

By the time they did, she'd decided she wouldn't torment herself with conjectures, that she'd let Leonid tell her what he thought and wanted when he had time for her alone again.

The moment she stepped out of the jet behind Leonid, who was carrying the girls, frosty air flayed her face and filled her lungs, so crisp and clean it made her gasp. The winter-wonderland vista beyond what was clearly another private airfield, with the imposing Carpathian Mountains in the distance, was so different from anywhere she'd ever lived, or even visited, that it reinforced again that she was a world away from her normal life in every sense.

She didn't have time to marvel at the awe-inspiring surroundings, or to linger over the realization that this rugged land must be responsible in part for Leonid's uncompromising distinctiveness. Her attention was drawn instead to the multitude of reporters and photographers who came literally out of left field to gather around the bottom of the stairs.

Her every hair stood on end as Leonid, who'd secured both girls in one arm, reached for her with the other one, posing for their first-ever family picture.

Then, as they resumed descending the stairs, the girls clung to him, burying their faces in his chest, eyeing the dozens of strangers calling out a cacophony of questions. Feeling his heat and power surrounding her, she found herself instinctively seeking his protection, too, dimly realizing what a sight they must make. The proud lion king, literally, with his pride of clinging females.

Leonid paused at the last step of the stairs and addressed the crowd. "Thank you for coming to meet my family, but you will understand that after the long flight, my only priority is their comfort. Each of you will get invitations to the press conference I will hold to answer all your questions as soon as my family is settled in their new home."

The reporters still tried to get him to say more, their voices rising with dozens of queries.

Leonid chose to answer one. "I do believe my daughters, Eva and Zoya, represent new life for our kingdom. They are literally that for me."

Brooking no further interruptions, he strode ahead and even the most dogged reporters parted before him as if unable to stand being in the path of his power.

Within minutes, they were seated inside a gleaming black stretch limo with the Zoryan flag flapping at the front.

She sat beside Leonid with the girls in their car seats facing them and Despina beside them. Leonid focused almost exclusively on the girls all the way to the palace, pointing out landmarks on the way and explaining their significance and history, with the girls appearing to take absolute interest in everything he brought to their attention and gleefully repeating the words he emphasized. Kassandra just kept telling herself to stick to her decision not to analyze his behavior, to stop thinking altogether.

Then they entered the palace complex grounds and all thought became impossible as she plunged ever deeper into the unreality of it all.

She'd been to the world's grandest palaces, as a tourist. Entering this place as a future resident, if things went according to Leonid's plan, was something else altogether. With the massive grounds populated by only those who worked there, it felt totally different from all the other palaces that had been crawling with visitors.

"This place was first laid out on the orders of Esfir the First, Zorya's founder and first queen." Her gaze swung to Leonid, and he gestured to her to look back at their surroundings as he continued narrating its history. "Her name, the Russian variant of Esther, also means *star*. This complex of palaces and gardens are sometimes referred to as the Zoryan Versailles. The central palace ensemble had been recognized as a UNESCO World Heritage Site since the fall of the Soviet Union and its return to the Zoryan state."

As she took in the information, he pointed toward another landmark. "The dominant natural feature is this sixteen-meter-high bluff lying less than a hundred meters from the shore of the Sea of Azov, which is part of the Black Sea. The Lower Gardens, or *Nizhny Sad*, encompassing over a square kilometer, are confined between this bluff and the shore. The majority of the complex's fountains are there, as are several small palaces and outbuildings. Atop the bluff, near the middle of the Lower Gardens, stands the Grand Palace, or *Bolshoi*

Dvorets, where the monarch historically resided…which I'm now repairing and renovating, so I hope you'll excuse any mess. Ah, here is one of my favorite features of the place…"

Kassandra's head swung to where he was pointing, the most glorious cascade and fountain she'd ever seen, situated right on the bluff's face below the body of a palace so grand it looked right out of a fairy tale.

"That's the Grand Cascade, or *Bolshoi Kaskad*, with the Grand Palace forming the centerpiece of the entire complex, and it's one of the most extensive waterworks of the Baroque period."

Leonid kept explaining and describing what they were passing through, with all of them, including the girls, hanging on his every word. Apart from realizing he was telling them important things he wanted them to learn, the girls, like every other living being, she suspected, just loved listening to his voice and were hypnotized by the way he spoke.

The hypnosis only deepened as Leonid took them inside what he kept referring to as their "new home."

In her jumbled state, Kassandra's mind couldn't assimilate the details her eyes were registering, just the major strokes. From beneath the scaffoldings of in-progress renovations clearly close to being finished, she could see an entrance, staggering in size and grandeur, under hundred-foot, painted dome ceilings, halls with soaring arches with dozens of paintings depicting naval battles, atmospheric landscapes and royal ancestry, and chambers displaying countless ethnic influences in their art and decor.

What made her focus sharpen were an inner garden and pool that, while they had elements of the rest of the place, were evidently new, and the most incredible parts of the palace to her. Somehow she had no doubt they were Leonid's idea and taste.

Throughout the tour, the girls, who'd never been in an edifice of that size, ran around squealing and pointing out their discoveries to interrogate Leonid about before another thing distracted them.

"And here are your quarters, for now."

They entered through white-painted, gold-paneled double doors to the most exquisite, expansive living area she'd ever seen. Though the dimensions and architecture echoed the rest of the palace, the furnishings and decor were more modern, comfort inducing and closely resembling the style and color scheme of her own living room in LA. And it was also outfitted and proofed for toddlers, clearly with Eva and Zoya in mind.

She wouldn't even ask how and when he'd had such personalized furnishings installed. He was powerful and rich enough he could have anything realized as soon as he thought of it.

But one thing didn't make sense. "For now?"

His smile didn't reach his eyes. "This is my effort at anticipating your needs and preferences. But you may decide you'd prefer some other place in the palace, or want something built on the grounds from scratch to your demands. So this will do until then."

"You can't seriously think I wouldn't find this perfect? It's actually...too much. This living *room* is as big as my whole place, which is big to start with. And I see glimpses of more tennis court–size rooms beyond."

He shrugged dismissively. "Everything is built on a grand scale in Zorya, even peasant's houses. You'll get used to it."

Will I? Will I also get used to you blowing searing then arctic, to never knowing where I really stand with you?

She only tossed her head toward Despina and the girls, who were rushing about exclaiming at all the delights he'd layered the place with. "Even if this magnificent place for some inexplicable reason didn't suit my taste, the girls and their nanny have given it their fervent seal of approval."

His lips twisted fondly before his eyes returned to hers earnestly. "I hope I thought of everything you might need, but you already met Fedor and Anya during our tour, my valet and his wife. Anya will be at your service for any domestic needs, and Fedor for anything else. Always call *me* first, with anything serious, even if I'm occupied with state emergencies. But Anya and Fedor are always ready for immediate and trivial matters." She nodded and he walked away. Midway to the door, he turned again. "You promise you *will* call me if you need anything?"

Heart expanding at his solicitude, shriveling at his withdrawal, she knew he'd wait until she said, "I promise."

Once he was gone, she rushed to the nearest bathroom and locked herself in. And let the tears flow. For she'd just promised she'd call him if she needed anything.

Anything but him. When he was all she needed.

Eight

Leonid stared at his reflection in the bathroom mirror.

He looked like hell. Much like he had in those days after he'd sent Kassandra away. He'd been keeping her away since they'd come to Zvaria three days ago. Every hour, every minute, every *second* had been sheer torture. Total chaos.

Every moment had been dedicated to concocting legitimate ways to escape being alone with her, so he wouldn't be forced to clarify his position. It had been getting progressively harder, with him perpetually on the precipice of doing something totally insane or irrevocably damaging. Or both. Like taking her against the nearest vertical surface, as he'd done back on the jet.

And he'd run out of excuses, could no longer run from a confrontation. Doing so could cause the very damage he'd been trying to avoid.

So he hadn't disappeared after they'd put the twins to bed. He was sure she would come after him. He could feel her drawing nearer, his every cell rioting with her proximity.

And he had no idea about what to say or do. None.

Severing the visual clash with his own bloodshot eyes, he stiffly moved away from the mirror, shuffled back to his reception area and sank down on an armchair facing the door. Counted down the heartbeats that would bring her to him with an infallible certainty. The soft knock on the door came as his countdown ran out. Though expected, it still juddered through him. His nerves were shot, his resistance depleted. At any point in this encounter, if she touched him, he would devour her.

Unable to rise again, he called out thickly, "Come in."

She'd realize he knew it was her. Who else would his guards allow to walk up to his quarters at this hour, or at all?

Bracing himself, his nerves still fired in unison when he saw her. That magnificent creature that had occupied his every waking and sleeping thought since he'd first laid eyes on her. In that deep burgundy floor-length dress she'd worn earlier tonight for dinner, which accentuated her complexion and curves. With her thousand-shade golden waterfall of silk and green-meadow eyes, she looked as magical as always. And as haggard as he did.

Without closing the door behind her, she approached, her gaze stripping away what was left of his tatters of control.

Thankfully, she didn't come close enough to test his nonexistent resolve. She started without preamble.

"I could pretend I didn't still want you when I was

angry with you, when I was afraid of you. But even before I quit being either, I admitted it to myself first, then to you on that jet. I do want you, more than ever."

He stared at her. He'd expected outrage, scolding, blame, anything but this confession.

She went on, "I know we agreed on a plan, and I haven't changed my mind about it. You tell everyone whatever would be best for you, the girls and your kingdom, and I'll back it up. I know you'd prefer to be together only for the girls, and I realize you haven't said a word about what happened between us on the jet because you're uncertain how to handle it. But I'm here to tell you that you don't need to overthink it or feel anxious about it. If your response to me wasn't just a random male one, if you want *me*, I am asking you not to hold back out of worry for your other considerations. Let's have this. Let's be together. No strings, no expectations. Just like in the past."

Then she fell silent, the brittle hope in her gaze shattering what remained of his sanity, and his heart. He struggled to force himself to remain still, expressionless, but inside him, a hurricane raged.

How was it possible she could offer him this? Not knowing his reasons for taking everything she had, in the past and recently, then throwing it in her face, she would be a masochist, a victim, to offer him a second, and now a third chance. Which she wasn't.

So did she want him so much that she was convincing herself his reasons were justifiable? Or was it even worse? Did she love him? In the past, and still now? Was she, after this magical trip to Zorya, and their explosive episode of passion, ready to expose herself to further injury for the chance of resurrecting something she shouldn't believe had ever been real?

It overwhelmed him, agonized him, that her feelings for him could be so fierce and profound they'd survived his humiliation, his desertion. When he had to let her down, again. And for the last time.

Even though it would leave him bloodied and extinguished.

But he was still unable to rebuff her, hurt her like that again. He had to try to soften the blow any way he could.

Feeling he'd be cutting off a vital part of himself with a jagged blade all over again, he started, "I doesn't matter what I want…"

Her stepping closer stopped him, and her tremulous objection twisted the knife hacking his guts. "It's all that matters. This isn't the past. Things have changed. You have. I have, too, along with things between us and everything else. We should be together for the sole reason that we want each other."

Feeling he was drowning, a breath away from heaving up and crushing her in his arms, begging for anything for as long as she would give it, come what may, he shook his head.

"You're right, this isn't the past. It's far worse. In the past, when I messed up, I hurt only you. Not that that was any less significant, or any more forgivable, but it remains a fact the damages I caused were limited to you. You've contained any repercussions for the twins so far with your strength and resourcefulness, aided by their young age. But now the situation is exceedingly more complicated. Personal considerations are the last thing to feature in my worries, and any damages would ripple out into widespread destruction."

Another urgent step brought her closer, her incredible beauty alight with passion. "That's what I meant by no expectations. There would be no repercussions to your kingdom or your relationship with the girls no matter what happens between us."

Destroyed by her offer of carte blanche, hating himself and the whole world even more for being forced to do this, her next words cleaved the remaining tatters keeping his heart in place.

"I've been thinking back to the time of your accident. Just before it happened, I was starting to feel restless. You were right when you thought I wanted to change the rules of our liaison. Though it wasn't premeditated, as you had believed. And contrary to what you thought, I wanted to negotiate, not for strings, but for more freedom. Our secrecy imposed too many barriers and limitations, and I wanted to be free of those, not to suggest different shackles. But when I saw your crumpled car, I knew then I only wanted you alive and well. That if I could only have you again, any way at all, I'd never want anything more. That feeling came back to me on the way here, made me face that I prefer the way it ended a million times to having it end...*that* way. And now I can't bear the possibility of missing out on being with you because I didn't let you know how I feel."

He looked away, unable to bear her baring everything inside her to him like that. He wasn't worthy of her courage and generosity, deserved none of her pure and magnificent emotions.

But escaping her gaze only brought her closer, until she touched him. Burned him to the marrow with one gentle, trembling caress on his shoulder.

"All that time, after you said you didn't want me anymore, what hurt most was the confusion, the disbelief. I couldn't imagine that what I felt from you, and so powerfully, didn't exist. Now everything inside me tells me what I felt from you back on the jet wasn't just sex. So please, Leonid..." Her cold, trembling hand cupped his jaw. It clenched so hard he was worried he'd grind his teeth to dust. "Tell me the truth. If you tell me you don't want me now, I'll walk away and this time I'll keep my distance and will never bring it up again. Just tell me, and I promise you, it won't change anything for you."

Tell her you don't want her. Set her free.

But he couldn't look at her and tell another such terrible lie. He couldn't watch the last embers go out in her eyes, and be replaced by the darkness of his final letdown.

Unable to breathe, praying he'd suffocate, cease to exist, he escaped the brutality of her gossamer touch, pitched forward, elbows crashing on his knees and head in his hands.

"Was this my mistake, then and now? Showing you how I feel? Was that what put you off?" And there they were. The tears she'd been holding at bay, soaking her voice as she entreated him one last time. "Leonid?"

He shook his head. Shook, period.

She made no sound, no gasp or whimper or sob. Even her steps were soundless. Yet her anguish as she silently left him was deafening, almost rupturing his head.

He'd hurt her irreparably and unforgivably again.

But now more than ever, now that he knew the sheer extent of her emotions, he knew he'd made the right decision. In the past and now. It was better to push her away, have her hate him, hurt her temporarily...than to do so permanently.

* * *

Kassandra walked through the majestic halls and corridors of the palace, afraid she'd scatter apart if she went any faster.

But she had to hold it together until she reached her quarters. Apart from the eyes that she felt were looking at her disapprovingly and pityingly from those lofty portraits, other hidden ones were monitoring her progress. Leonid's invisible security detail.

Not that they should be worried about him. Their future king was impervious. And lethal. As he should be, as he'd just explained he had to be, to be king.

The distance to her quarters seemed to have doubled. And they weren't her quarters. They were just the place Leonid had exiled her to across the massive palace. Now she knew beyond a doubt why. She had known since the first night he'd avoided her, but just had to make him stab any hope she'd been wrong to death.

Not that she could blame him this time. She'd taken a gamble that there was something between them, something old to resurrect or new to nurture, and she'd lost. She'd thought the slightest possibility she was right had been worth any price she'd have to pay if she turned out to be totally wrong. As she had been.

Leonid didn't want her. That incendiary encounter had been an unspecific response of an overendowed male to a female in heat. And he was clearly disgusted with himself for succumbing to a base urge he feared would jeopardize his priorities: his relationship with the girls, and his position as a king reestablishing a struggling monarchy.

And though it devastated her that she wasn't one of the things he cared about, she understood. He couldn't help how he felt, and how she felt wasn't his problem. He owed her nothing, but owed the girls and his kingdom everything.

So now she had to live up to her promises. Live close to him for her girls' sake, for his kingdom's, playing her expected role for the world, while showing him nothing but neutrality and pleasantness. Even as she withered with futile yearning for him forever. As she would.

In spite of everything, she'd never stopped loving him. No. It was far worse that that.

Inexplicably, she loved him now more than ever.

"You were married all this time, let us suffer through the scandal of your pregnancy, and you want me to calm down?"

Kassandra winced. Her father's booming voice was loud enough it actually made the phone vibrate in her hand. Not to mention her brain shudder in her skull.

"Hush, Loukas, as if this is important anymore." That was her mother on the other line of a five-way video call.

It had taken Kassandra four days after her last confrontation with Leonid to call her family, who mainly lived in New York but for two exceptions, to explain the whole situation and invite them to the coronation in three weeks' time.

Only four out of the seven who made up her immediate family had been available. Her other two older brothers and another older sister texted to say they'd call as soon as they could. Now she was talking to her parents and two of her siblings.

"But Leonid Voronov... Now, *that's* the relevant thing here!" her mother exclaimed. "How were you even able to hide your relationship? Hide *him*?"

Kassandra sighed. Leave it to her parents to each fixate on what they considered the issue here. Her father felt she'd shamed him socially for nothing, and would now make him look like the oblivious father his daughter had ignored in choosing a husband, and her mother was questioning her gossiping network and her own secret-divining prowess.

"What's not making sense to me is that your breakup clearly happened after his accident." That was her oldest sister, Salome, married with four kids and living in Greece since her marriage. "The Kassandra we all know wouldn't have left the man she loved, at least loved enough to marry and submit to those convoluted cloak-and-dagger shenanigans to accommodate his desire for secrecy, when he'd just had a major accident."

"Can't you see you just answered your own question?" That was Aleksander, her year-younger brother, and almost her twin. "Voronov was the one who broke it off."

"But why, for God's sake?" Salome exclaimed as she rushed to stop her youngest, a four-year-old tornado by the name of Tomas, from dragging her laptop off the countertop. "At the time when he must have needed you most, when you needed to be with him…!" She put her son on the ground and focused back on her. "Say, it was around that time you discovered you were pregnant with the girls, wasn't it?"

She'd already resigned to spending this conversation answering questions, and sighing. As she was now. "I found out just before his accident."

"So he broke it off before you told him?" That was her father again, his voice like rumbling thunder. When she hesitated, he exploded. "He *knew* and still broke it off? And he's back now expecting you to forgive him and give him every right to the girls? I don't care who he is or who he's going to be, this man doesn't deserve to come near my daughter or granddaughters, and I'll see to it that he doesn't! I'll kill him first!"

"Baba…" Kassandra parroted her siblings' similar groans.

"Loukas!" her mother intervened. "You will calm down right this second. You're not going to kill anyone, starting with yourself. I forbid you to have another coronary!"

Kassandra's heart kicked. "Coronary! When was that?"

"See what you did, Rhea?" her father grumbled, looking like a petulant grizzly. "We agreed we wouldn't tell her. Now she'll worry herself silly when it was just a minor thing."

"Minor?" her mother huffed furiously. "You call multiple balloon catheters and stents minor? How about keeping me on my feet and dashing around for days as you whined and grouched and made impossible demands until I literally dropped? Still minor?"

"Don't mind them, Kass." Aleks chuckled, the mellowest male in their pureblood-Greek clan, and the one who'd been fully Americanized. Almost. "They're both back to peak condition, as you can see *and* hear, so don't even start asking what happened. Their tempers have been more hair-trigger than usual since that hospital stay and we won't be able to get them to stop if they start another episode in their Greek-tragedy love affair."

Aleks had always joked that their parents' dramatic fights were their way of spicing up a forty-plus-year marriage.

Looking positively murderous, her father glared at

his son, then turned to her. "I'm bringing your uncles and cousins, even those from your maternal side, to take care of this man."

"Whoa, you're deeming to enlist my brothers' and their progeny's help?" Her mother scoffed. "After forty-three years, they're finally good for something, in your opinion?"

Ignoring his wife, her father focused his wrath on Kassandra. "Russian king or billionaire or mobster or whatever that Voronov guy is…"

"He's actually Zoryan, not Russian," Aleks piped up.

"*Whatever* he is," their father shouted to drown out his youngest son's bedeviling, "we're teaching him a lesson about being a man, one he won't forget in this lifetime."

Kassandra's sigh was her deepest yet. "Congratulations, Baba. Now that you've detailed your plan to cause an international incident, you just made me revoke your invitation to the coronation."

Paternal thunder broke over her again, making everyone grimace and groan. "You're protecting him? He came back to you with puppy-dog eyes and all is forgiven? Not in my book. He needs to know the kind of consequences he faces when he messes with the Stavroses and their own."

"So you're drafting the Papagiannis in your war, but they don't even get mentioned in the credits?" Her mother snorted.

Salome raised her hand like a student seeking to be heard in a raucous class. "Didn't you notice the little detail that he came back with something more than a wagging tail? He's making your granddaughters princesses and your daughter a queen, for God's sake." She turned her eyes to Kassandra, the implication clearly just sinking in. "Oh, God, I can't wait to tell everyone here we're going to be European royalty!"

"Is Zorya a European kingdom, or is it counted as Asian?" Aleks mused the pragmatic curiosity on purpose, Kassandra was sure, to amplify her father's fury.

Ignoring him, Loukas Stavros leveled a glare at his firstborn, as if Salome had just called him a dirty name to his face. "I care nothing about what he offers. My granddaughters and daughter are already princesses and a queen without him."

Aleks chuckled. "As are all girls to their fathers, especially Greek fossils. Lighten up, Baba, this is the twenty-first century and your daughter is a world-renowned celebrity and businesswoman. She can take care of herself."

"And I *don't* care what she is to the world. To me, she is and will remain my little girl and I'll take care of her as long as there's breath in my body."

"You won't have many of those left if you keep hollering like that," her mother grumbled.

Kassandra raised her hand. "I knew I'd regret telling you anything, so thanks, everyone, for proving me right." She turned her gaze to her father. "If taking care of me means bringing the Stavros and Papagianni testosterone mob to Zorya to ambush Leonid, I'll have immigration revoke your visas at the airport and send you back on the first flight home."

Eyes widening at her threat, knowing she didn't make them lightly, her father pretended to laugh. "You're worried we're going to rough him up or something, *nariy kyria*? Nah, we'll just take him aside and…convince him of the error of his ways. I'm sure he'll be a better husband and father after our talk. This is men's stuff, so leave it to the men."

"Fine." As her father's face started relaxing, macho triumph coating his ruggedly handsome face, Kassandra added, "I'll have them send you home with heavily armed escorts from the CIA and its Zoryan equivalent."

Before her father went off again, she raised her voice, looking at her mother and sister. "About the estrogen posse... I'll leave instructions that the authorities are to sift you from your male components and let you through. But *only* if you promise you won't ambush Leonid yourselves, if for other purposes."

Salome burst out laughing. "After seeing the latest footage of him on the news today? No promises."

Her mother chuckled in agreement. "Don't be stingy. Let the women have some crumbs of your fairy-tale king. You're going to have, *and* eat, his whole cake, forever."

After that overt innuendo, her parents left the conference call to continue their argument in private. Her siblings had dozens of questions for her, each according to his or her interests.

She detailed the hectic preparations for the coronation, and the sweeping changes Leonid was implementing as he transitioned Zorya back to a sovereign state and kingdom. But whenever Salome asked about their relationship, she steered the conversation to Leonid's blossoming relationship with the girls. She wasn't about to tell her sister she'd resigned herself to a lifetime of co-parenting the girls with Leonid as polite strangers.

Not that that was accurate. He wasn't one. She had no idea what he was, had been going insane, constantly exposed to the suppressed emotions and hunger that blasted out of him.

Either she was imagining it, or what she sensed was real. But even if it was, by now she knew he had made up his mind never to act on those feelings, had zero hope he ever would.

For now, she managed to end the call without letting her siblings suspect this whole thing was the furthest thing from a fairy tale, or even an actual reconciliation. Or that she'd never been more miserable, hopeless and confused in her life.

She'd resigned herself to being so for the rest of her life. For the girls, and for the larger-than-life destiny she by now believed was their birthright.

Later that night, after disappearing all day, Leonid materialized like clockwork to have dinner with her and the girls, and to share in all their nightly rituals.

After they put their daughters to bed, he headed out of the wing, saying little, seeming anxious to leave her, alone and unappeased on every level, for another endlessly bleak night.

As he reached the door, she cried out, "Leonid!"

He stiffened, as if her voice was an arrow that had hit him between the shoulder blades. Then he turned, his movement reluctant, his gaze apprehensive.

"I thought I could go on like this," she choked. "But I can't. You never gave me a straight answer and I have to have one. However terrible it is, it will be far better than never knowing for sure where we stand and why, and going nuts forever wondering."

In response, there it was again, that corrosive, devouring longing in his eyes.

"You can't keep looking at me like that! Not when you never let me know what it means!"

He only squeezed his eyes shut. But it was too late. She'd seen that look, could no longer doubt what it was.

Her voice rose to a shriek. "If you want your daughters to have a mother and not a wreck, you must put me out of my misery. Tell me what the *hell* is going on."

His gaze lowered, and she thought he'd escape her again, leaving her to go insane with speculation.

Then he raised his gaze and she saw it. The severe aversion to coming clean. And his intention to do it. At last.

Still saying nothing, he walked toward her. But instead of stopping, he bypassed her. Feeling like a marionette, she followed him until he reached the master bedroom.

After closing the door behind them, he half turned to her. "There's something I need to…show you."

Then he started to strip.

Her stupefaction wavered into deeper bewilderment when she realized he wasn't exactly stripping. Turning sideways, brow knotted, face darkened with pain-laced consternation, he left his shirt on, took off his shoes, his belt, undid his zipper, let his pants drop before kicking them away.

Straightening, he finally turned to face her.

But long before he had, with each inch he exposed, her confusion had turned to shock, then to horror.

One of his legs was a map of livid, hideous scars, where massive tissue had been lost, where fractured bones had torn through muscles and shredded skin, and surgeries had put it all back in a horribly disfigured whole.

His other leg was…gone.

Nine

His leg.

Leonid had lost his leg.

In its place, there was a midthigh prosthesis with a facade that resembled his previously normal leg, looking even more macabre than his remaining, mutilated one for it.

All the instances she'd noticed his difficulties in moving, his discomfort, his pain, came crashing back, burying her in an avalanche of details. Then the wheel of memory was yanked to a stop before spooling back at a dizzying speed to that time in his hospital room. New explanations to his every word and glance, making such perfect sense now with hindsight, thudded into place, decimating everything she'd thought she'd known, until she felt everything in her brain falling in a domino effect.

The wheel shot forward through time again, to

the moment he'd reappeared in her life. The way he'd avoided coming near. Stepped away every time she had. Their time on the jet, undoing his clothes only enough to release himself. Not lying down with her, so she wouldn't find out.

But she should have.

Nausea welled, the bile of recriminations filling her up to her eyes. That she hadn't even suspected the significance of what she'd noticed, what she'd felt from him, that she'd been so disconnected from him, so wrapped up in her own suffering and loss, she hadn't felt his.

Every thought and feeling she'd had, toward him, about him, built on that obliviousness, came back to lodge in her brain like an ax, shame hacking at her.

But it wasn't only because he'd lost a limb. Leonid's loss cut so much deeper than that. His legs, both of them, had been more than a vital part of his body. He'd used them like so few on the planet ever had, turning them through discipline and persistence into supreme instruments, catapulting himself to an almost superhuman level of physical prowess and achievement.

But—oh, God—he hadn't only lost his supremacy, he'd lost the ability to walk and run like any other average human being.

And she hadn't been there for him. He'd been alone through the loss and the struggle back to his feet. Such as they were.

Now he was reversing the painfully stilted process of exposing his loss to her, putting his pants and shoes back on, the difficulty with which he found something so simple shredding her heart to smaller pieces. And that was when she was still shell-shocked. When it all sank in, it would tear her apart.

Not that what she felt mattered. Only he did.

Numb with agony, mind and soul in an uproar, she watched him as he walked to the room's sitting area, his every step now taking on a whole new meaning and dimension. Reaching the couch by the balcony with her favorite view of the grounds and the sea, he sank down as if he could no longer stand.

When he finally raised his eyes to her, they were totally empty, like they'd been when he'd first come back.

"That's your answer, Kassandra. From the look on your face, it's even more terrible than anything you've imagined."

Fighting the muteness to contradict his catastrophically inaccurate analysis, she choked, "It's...not...not..."

"Not terrible?" His subdued voice cut across her failed efforts to put what raged inside her into words. "There's no need to placate me, Kassandra. I know exactly how my legs...my *leg*...and the prosthesis look. They're both right out of a horror movie, one from a Frankenstein-like one, the other a Terminator-like one. It's perfectly normal you're appalled."

Objections burst out of her, her anguish at the way he perceived his injuries, her indignation that he thought the way they looked was what horrified her. But they only sounded in her mind. Out loud, she couldn't say one word.

Keeping his dejected gaze fixed on her no doubt stricken one, he exhaled as he heaved up again. "Now you've had your answer, I hope everything is settled."

Her muteness shattered. "Settled? Settled how? You think showing me this answered anything?"

His teeth made a terrible sound. He said nothing.

More realizations bombarded her. "Was that why?

Why you broke it off with me in the past, why you didn't take me up on my offer now? For God's sake, Leonid, why?"

"What do you mean, why? I just showed you."

"I see no answers here. Absolutely none. What do your injuries and loss have to do with anything between us?"

He looked away, as if to hide his response to her feverish response. She teetered up to her feet, approached him. Her heart broke into tinier pieces as he pulled farther away, as if unable to bear her proximity, guarding against her possible touch.

She stopped advancing, stood trembling from head to toe. "If you think you've given me an answer, *the* answer, all you've done is give me more maddening questions. So just tell me, Leonid. Everything since the accident. *Please*."

He appeared about to evade her again, then she sensed something crumbling inside him. That…dread of laying everything inside him bare before her.

Heading back to the couch, he sat down heavily. Wincing, supersensitive to his every move more than ever, she followed him, sat far enough away to give him the space he needed.

Then he talked. "Everything started *before* the accident. While I was training, I realized our arrangement had only been satisfactory because we were together almost every day. Being apart from you made me realize I wanted to be with you, all the time, all my life. I wasn't sure if you felt the same, but I was going to risk it. I was going to propose."

She'd thought she was now prepared for anything he'd say, would hold it together no matter what he threw at her. But this confession made her collapse back on the couch in a nerveless heap.

His expression blipping momentarily at her reaction, he went on. "Even if you'd said no, I'd have waited until you one day wanted me enough or trusted me enough, if that was the issue, to change your mind. But before I could, the accident happened. Then you came to me.

"I'd just been told my legs were beyond salvaging. I also had a spinal injury, and they thought I'd suffer severe erectile dysfunction or even total impotence."

Falling deeper into shock, every second brought her more proof the past two years had been built on misconceptions and ignorance. She'd known nothing of the life-uprooting blows he'd suffered, and he had chosen to suffer alone.

Oh, God, Leonid.

"I was agonized I'd never be a competitive athlete again, would at best rehabilitate enough to walk with a minimum of pain. But what devastated me most was knowing I'd never be the man you'd wanted so fiercely, and had taken such pleasure in."

Before she could cry out that she would want him whatever happened, his next words made her see how he would have never believed it, how he'd convinced himself of the opposite.

"But I knew you were noble, and if you knew, even when it repulsed and horrified you, you wouldn't leave me. I couldn't have you stay with me out of pity. I couldn't saddle you with an impotent cripple. I would have been worse than useless to you, a constant source of unhappiness. I knew even if I was selfish and terrified enough that I clung to you, I'd lose you anyway, when the reality of my situation drove you away in disgust or crushed you in despair.

"I decided to drive you away, without letting you even doubt my prognosis, thought it better to do it at once, rather than in a slow and far more mutilating ordeal. But I didn't expect you to make it that hard. You forced me to push you away as viciously as it took for you to leave me, to save yourself.

"Just as I thought I succeeded in setting you free, you told me you were pregnant. I asked if you'd keep the baby, vaguely wishing your pregnancy wouldn't continue somehow, or that you'd maybe consider giving the baby up for adoption, so you'd sever every tie you had to me, so you could restart your life unburdened again."

This. This was it. What she'd gone insane for, the explanation for his sudden cruelty and coldness, what she'd felt had to exist, but had to accept didn't, to her deepening heartache. But it existed. It explained everything and rewrote history. He'd forced himself to hurt her, fearing he'd destroy her if he didn't. He'd loved her so much, he couldn't let her share the bleak fate he'd thought awaited him.

His gaze swept downward, as if he was looking into his darkest days. "The next months were a worse hell than even I'd imagined they would be. The least of it was the anxiety over my impending physical losses. The memory of hurting you became more suffocating as time went by. My sanity became more compromised as I lived in dread that what I'd hoped for you, that you'd move on, would come to pass, and *then* feeling even worse when it didn't, when you had Eva and Zoya and confined your whole life to them.

"After many setbacks, they managed to save one of

my legs, if in the condition you saw. My spinal injury healed without any neurological deficit, and they hoped I wouldn't be impotent. Not that I could test that. All I could do was struggle to heal, physically and psychologically, and cope with my new, severe limitations. And all that time, I watched you and the twins obsessively from afar as you went through everything I should have been there for, alone.

"Then I was back on my feet, real and prosthetic, just in time for Zorya to call me to duty. And though I never dreamed of having anything with you again, I was no longer going to let anything keep me from being there for you, and from serving the family you gave me, the family I never had, and my country.

"But the moment I saw you again, I knew. My potency was more than intact, and the separation and suffering had only left me perpetually, ferociously starving for you. Yet I had to stay away. You deserve better than the disfigured wreck I am now. I...I would have rather had my remaining leg cut off than let you see me this way, and see that look of horror in your eyes. But your anguish and confusion cornered me into showing you. Now you can at least understand, if not forgive, everything I did."

He fell silent, breathing strident, eyes reddened, face clenched as if with fighting against unbearable pain.

She stared at him, paralyzed.

The enormity of what he'd suffered and lost overwhelmed her. And through it all, he'd selflessly, if mistakenly, thought only of her needs, and not his own.

But his last words had been the worst. Along with his irrevocable losses, his self-worth had been shattered.

The tears finally came, pouring out of her very soul as if under pressure.

Grimacing as if she'd stabbed him, he groaned. "*Bozhe moy*, Kassandra, I can't bear your pain, or your pity."

"Pity? *Pity?*"

Finding nothing that could express her outrage at how totally he'd misconstrued her reaction, she charged him, knocking him back on the couch and climbing all over him, trembling hands groping every inch of him, real and replacement. Inert with shock, he lay beneath her as she smothered him in hugs and kisses and drowned him in tears.

"How dare you… How *dare* you think anything you suffered could have burdened me or put me off? How *could* you make that decision for me, deprive me of being there for you through your ordeal? Didn't you realize I would have given anything to be with you at all, let alone in your darkest time? Didn't you realize that whatever you lost only makes every inch of you even more precious to me? If I could give you a limb to restore yours, I wouldn't think twice."

Looking dazed by her fervor, this last bit made him shudder. "Don't say that, *Bozhe moy*, Kassandra, don't…"

"I'll say it because it's true. Because I love you. You are the only man I loved or would ever love."

He looked even more flabbergasted. "How can you love me after what I put you through, no matter the reasons?"

She grabbed his face, forced him to look at her, as if to drive her conviction into his mind. "I now know I must have always felt what's in your heart, never believed what you said in mine. It was what agonized me most, that what I felt and what I thought I knew were such opposites. Your reasons would have been more than enough to forgive you if you'd done much worse that just pushed me away, and thinking it was for my own good."

His breathing, which usually never quickened due to his supreme fitness, came in rapid, ragged wheezes beneath her burning chest. "Kassandra, you don't know what you're saying, you're shocked by what you saw and heard, feeling sorry for me..."

"Oh, my beloved Leo, I do feel sorry, but not only for you, for me, for us. I am crushed with regret, because I wasn't there for you through it all, because you deprived me of you, throwing us both in hell apart. I feel as if my heart is splintering because you deprived yourself of me and my love and support, of our daughters, missed out on having them bless your life and heal your heart during your darkest time, as they would have even before they were born. But I'm not letting you deprive us of each other anymore. Marry me, Leonid, my love, my only love, for real and forever."

His eyes had been reddening more with her every word. But with her last words, his face contorted and air rushed into his chest, as if he'd been drowning and was drawing a lifesaving breath after breaking the surface.

His eyes glittered, but not with the tears she rained over his face. With what she'd thought she'd never see. *His* tears.

"Don't decide anything now, take time to think, wait..."

Her trembling lips silenced his working ones. "You've been making me wait since I first laid eyes on you. Before you let us be together, while we were together, since you pushed me away and since you came back. And I can't wait anymore. I won't, ever again. I will never waste another moment waiting or worrying or doing anything but loving you and being with you."

And his tears flowed. His body shook beneath hers as she cried out, moved beyond endurance, sobs rocking her.

Straining over him, as if she wanted to slip beneath his skin, to hide him under hers, she moaned into his gasping lips, "Stop thinking, stop assuming what's best for me. You are what's best for me. You are everything I ever wanted for myself. Will you give me everything I want? Will you give me yourself?"

His tears flowing faster, his body beneath hers easing toward impending surrender, he said, "But I'm not the man you once loved anymore…"

She pulled back, let him see himself in her eyes, willing everything she felt for him to restore his faith in himself. "You're not. You're better. Far better. Your ordeals have tempered you into the purest, strongest, best form of yourself. I loved the man you were, but when forced to, I could live without him. I can't live without the man you are now."

"It was the inferno of yearning for you." She gazed in confusion down at him and he elaborated. "What tempered me."

"Then, say yes, Leonid. Marry me, be with me, love me and never leave me alone again."

Tears froze in his eyes as his gaze deepened, as if trying to probe her soul, filling with so much vulnerability, disbelief and hesitation she felt she'd burst with it all.

Slowly, conviction seeped in, followed by dawning elation. Then it was as if he was letting her see into *his* soul for the first time, and all she saw there was…love.

God, *so* much love. Adoration.

"Kassandra, *moya lyubov*, my love, if you'll have me, if you'll let me love you for the rest of my life…yes. Yes to anything and everything you want or will ever want."

Flinging herself at him with all her strength, she bombarded him with tear-drenched kisses, reiterating her supplication. "You. You're all I ever wanted or will ever want."

"And you are everything," he pledged as he surrendered to her fervor, his voice as deep as the sea, and as turbulent with fathoms-deep emotion, mirroring what his eyes detailed. "From the moment I first saw you, I was always yours. Even when I believed you'd never be mine again, I remained yours. I would have remained yours forever."

Suddenly everything inside her exploded into a devastating blaze of lust. After this beyond-belief declaration, she felt she'd crumble if he didn't merge them in every way, right now, hard and long and completely.

Shuddering with need, she scrambled off him, tugging him up with her. He followed her silently as she stumbled to bed, stood watching her as she flung herself onto it, searing her with his hunger.

"Love me, Leonid." Her voice was a husky tremolo that fractured with the desperation of her passion. "Now that I know you love me, *show* me."

Groaning, he came down over her, filled her arms, his hands trembling all over her, as if afraid she wasn't real. Her hands shook in turn over his stubble-covered jawline, up the chiseled planes of his divine face until they dipped into his raven-hued hair. Pulling him closer, her desperate lips clamped over his, her tongue restlessly searching their seam. A pained rumble escaped him as his tongue lashed out to snare hers, duel with it.

His rumbles deepened, filling her, shaking her apart; his hands owned her every inch, setting it ablaze. Reaching her buttocks, he squeezed hard, as if trying to bring himself under control.

Needing him to unleash everything inside him, devastate her with it, her thighs fell apart for him, begging his invasion. "Since you took me again, needing you has become agony. Please, do everything to me again."

Groaning, he nodded, snatching her clothes off her burning body. But as she undid his pants, tried to push them down, his teeth clenched, like his hands over hers.

"Don't. I don't want you to see me like that."

She freed her hands from his convulsive grip, grabbed his face, needing him to believe her once and for all. "I already saw you, and it did horrify me, but only to realize the extent of your injury, what you lost, what you're suffering. But for me, the scars and prosthesis are now part of you, and I love and crave all of you. I'll forever feel thankful whenever I look at them and see a reminder that I still have you, that fate didn't take you from me and granted me the miracle of being able to love you and share our daughters and everything I am with you."

Groaning as if in searing pain, he buried kisses in her palms mixed with tears and a litany of her name and *lyublyu tebya*. It was the first time he'd said it. *I love you.*

She drowned him with her reciprocation.

Getting rid of her last shred of clothes, he freed himself and brought her to his daunting hardness. Shaking with the need to impale herself on it, she threw herself over his chest, pushing his jacket off, teeth undoing his shirt, needing his flesh on hers. But he stopped her again.

"Let me pleasure you like that. I did on the jet, didn't I?"

He meant without exposing himself, at all. He didn't want her to see any part of him, probably was concealing other scars.

He was teetering on the edge of control between her thighs, everything about him promising her the explosive pleasure he'd given her before. She only had to say yes and his hot, throbbing girth and length would slam inside her, in that rough, frenzied tempo that had made her orgasm around him repeatedly on the jet before he'd made her come one last time as he'd climaxed deep inside her.

But… "I want you to *love* me this time. With all of you. I want to make love to all of you."

He held her gaze for one last second before capitulating.

Laying her back on the bed, he rose on his knees, started to take off his clothes. She whimpered as each button, each shrug revealed more to her starving eyes.

She'd been wrong. He hadn't just been upgraded; he'd metamorphosed. This was what the next step of evolution had to look like. And there *were* more scars, crisscrossing his chest, running down his arms and abdomen, interrupting the dark, silky patterns adorning his magnificence. And to her, they looked like arcane patterns, bestowed by destiny, marking him as chosen for glory and uniqueness, and were as beautiful and arousing as everything else about him.

Surging up, she traced the scars with worshiping hands and lips, making him shudder harder with every touch and nip. Delighted to discover they were even more sensitive than the rest of him, would amplify his pleasure, she got bolder.

"Kassandra, you're driving me past insanity."

"Just like you do to me. Stop tormenting me and let me see all of you. Now, Leonid."

Naked from the waist up, eyes averted, he stood up and exposed the rest, his movements so reluctant it squeezed her heart with anguish. He hated doing this, was sick with self-consciousness, still unable to believe she wouldn't cringe at his physical damage and deficit. It would have been easier to let him hide from her. But she couldn't. It would only become a barrier.

She was done letting anything come between them.

She lay back, spread herself, gaze devouring him. "Look at me, my love. See how much more arousing I find you now. Every inch of you is stamped with maturity and power, more than ever. The marks of your suffering tell me incredible stories of endurance and persistence. They're like brands of triumph and they only make you more unique to me. Give me everything you are, my darling Leonid."

Exhaling raggedly, he nodded, growled something ferocious at the sight of her spread in surrender before him. Coming down on the bed, he prowled over her like a ravenous tiger, fully exposed, dauntingly engorged. His hands sought her secrets, her triggers. He took her mouth in a rough kiss before he withdrew, his eyes flaring and subsiding like blue infernos.

"Every single inch of you, every word you say, every breath and look—you are an aphrodisiac I could dilute and dispense to the world and cure all sexual dysfunction. Had I suffered from any, you would have cured me."

Unable to hold back anymore, she writhed beneath him, twisted over him. Realizing what she wanted, he reversed their positions, spread himself for her, letting her have his mind-blowing potency where she craved it, in her watering mouth. He let her do everything she wanted to him, explore him with darting tongue and trembling hands, growling his enjoyment of her homage.

"Own me, *moya dorogaya*, take what's always been yours."

Unable to bear the joy of knowing it had been the same for him, that it had to be her and only her, she took it all, roaming his leg, his prosthesis, his potency, all of him.

She wanted to ask him to take his prosthesis off, let her touch what remained of his leg without barriers. But he'd already crossed too many lines to accommodate her need. That had to wait until he had no lingering doubts of how she'd react, or discomforts in exposing the rest of his vulnerabilities to her.

She was lapping his arousal, more rushes of molten agony flooding her core as she wondered how she would accommodate that much demand, when his hands on her shoulders stopped her. She cried out in frustration, only to find herself on her back again. She held out her arms, hurrying him, hands flailing over whatever she could reach of him. Chuckling his gratification at her urgency, he drowned her in a luxurious, tongue-mating embrace, before he suddenly started extricating himself from her clinging limbs. She whimpered, tried to drag him back, but he restrained her hands.

"Patience. This time, I'm doing this right."

She tried to drag him back with her legs. "You did it right the first time and every time. Just do it again."

He bit into one of the thighs clinging to him. "I will do it, again and again. But I want to do something first."

Getting off the bed, he strode out of sight, then suddenly the chamber was plunged in total darkness.

Her heart thudded. Was he still loath to make love to her while she saw all of him? Or maybe now that he *had* let her see all of him, he needed the respite of darkness?

Suddenly silver light engulfed the whole bed. It took her several stunned heartbeats to realize he'd thrown the drapes and inner shutters of the enclosed balcony open to the night sky. The full moon was framed in the middle of the paneled windows. The moonlight was so intense, she could see nothing outside its domain, didn't know where Leonid was now.

"This is how you should be showcased…" She lurched at his bass rasp as he seemed to materialize before her moonstruck eyes, a colossal shadow detaching from the darkness, made of mystery and magic. "A goddess of wanton desires, of rampant pleasures, waiting for worshippers to come pay homage, glowing, ripe, voracious, spellbinding."

She was all that?

She could only murmur, "Look who's talking."

He came into the moon's spotlight, the stark illumination casting harsh shadows over the noble sculpture of his face, turning it from regal to supernatural. His skin and hair glimmered with highlights as he pushed her back on the bed, loomed over her, the full moon blazing at his back, turning him into a magnificent silhouette. Only his eyes caught its silver beams, glowing like incandescent sapphires. She went limp beneath him with the power of it all, the sheer brutal beauty of him, of these moments.

Her chest tightened one last time over the jagged pieces of the past, the terrible memories, before it let them go, then swelled with the new and uncontainable hopes and expectations. Those of having him again. This time, forever.

Crying out, her desperation shattered the last shackle holding him back. He lunged between her eagerly spreading thighs, letting her feel his dominance for a fraught moment.

"Moya boginya..." Gazing into her streaming eyes, calling her his goddess, he plunged inside her with one long, hard thrust.

Her body jerked beneath him as the hot, vital glide of his thick, rigid shaft in her core drove her into profound sensual shock. She clamped her legs around him, high over his back, giving him full surrender, delirious with witnessing the pleasure of possessing her seizing his face. He ground deeper into her until his whole length was buried inside her, filling her beyond capacity. Sensation sharpened, shattering her. She cried out again, tears flowing faster.

He started moving, severing eye contact only to run fevered appreciation over her body, watching her every quake and grimace of pleasure, all the while growling driven, tormenting things.

"How could there be wanting like this...pleasure like *this*?"

She keened as he accentuated every word with a harder thrust. He devoured the explicit sounds, his tongue invading her mouth, mimicking his body's movements inside her.

Her sanity burned with the friction and fullness of his flesh in hers, the fusion, the totality of it, now that she knew it was indeed total, and would never end.

Her cries grew louder as his plunges grew longer,

until she clawed at him for the jarring rhythm that would finish her. Only then did he build to it, his eyes burning, his face taut, savage with need, sublime in beauty. She fought back her own ecstasy, greedy for the moment his seized him.

Realizing she was holding back, he growled, "Come for me, *moya koroleva*, let me see what I do to you."

Her body almost erupted hearing him call her *my queen*.

But she held on, thrashed her head. "Come with me…"

Roaring, he thrust deeper, destroying her restraint. Release buffeted her, razing her body in convulsions. Those peaked to agony when he succumbed to her demand, gave her what she always craved. Him, at the mercy of the ecstasy of union with her, pleasure racking him, his seed filling her in hard jets. She felt it all, and shattered.

Time and space vanished as he melted into her, grounded the magic into reality, eased her back into her body.

Everything came back into jarring focus when he tried to move off her. She caught him. His weight should have been crushing, but it had always been only anchoring, necessary. Like he was.

But he'd never let her have his weight as long as she wished, insisting it burdened her. He now rose on outstretched arms, his eyes gleaming satisfaction over her ravished state.

"Koroleva moyey zhizhni." He trailed a gently abrasive hand over her, eyes worshipping. "Queen of my life."

A vast thankfulness expanded inside her so hard,

she could barely speak. "How do you say 'king of my world'?"

His whole face blazed with pleasure and pride, his drawl painfully sexy and harsh with emotion. *"Korol' moy mir."*

"Korol' moy mir."

Whispering the pledge against his lips, she could say no more as perfect peace, for the first time in her life, dragged her into a well of contentment where nothing else existed…

Live classic Zoryan music woke Kassandra from a delicious dream filled with Leonid.

The royal band was rehearsing in the seafront gardens again for the coming ceremonies.

Though the drapes were securely drawn, and the chamber was dark, she just knew. The sun was shining today.

It had been shining the past two weeks. Everyone she met insisted it was the blessing of the new king and his twin stars. Kassandra was ready to believe it. If happiness like this was possible, then maybe it bent the very laws of nature to itself, too.

It had changed *her* on a fundamental level. Her heart beat to a different rhythm, her skin had a richer texture, colors had magical hues and life tasted and smelled of him.

Leonid.

Even if she was back in her quarters, and he hadn't been sleeping beside her this past week, practically had no time for her at all in his consuming preoccupation with preparations, she felt him all around her.

And as if he hadn't been insanely busy enough, he

was now preparing living quarters for *them*, not his or the ones she was currently staying in, but something totally new and theirs, now that their marriage would be real.

She'd refused to even see where it would be, wanted him to surprise her. Even as a designer, her imagination could never match what his love would bestow on her.

Now he was running against time so it would be ready on the day of the combined rituals: his coronation, and their wedding.

God…their wedding!

She still couldn't believe any of this was happening.

When she'd asked him to marry her, she'd thought they'd elope, since they'd told everyone they were already married. But Zorya's newly reformed royal council wouldn't sanction an undocumented marriage as proof of the twins' legitimacy. Leonid had said if she hadn't proposed that night, he would have the next morning. Zorya was demanding a wedding to fix their lack of documentation. And from what she was seeing, it was going to be the royal wedding of the century. Her family, who would come two days before the rituals, were all beside themselves with excitement. Yes, even her father.

Everything felt like a fantasy. Far better than one. She constantly found herself wondering if she was having a ridiculously extravagant wish-fulfillment dream and would wake up to the bleak reality of two weeks ago.

Could everything really be this perfect?

Suddenly, her heart contracted with foreboding.

Pausing until the spasm passed, she wondered at the far stronger than usual attack. Seemed the approaching ceremonies and the superstitious bent of this land had her spooked.

Pushing the ridiculous and unfounded anxieties away, she rose and rushed through getting ready.

Hurrying to the girls first, her mood soared again as they concluded their morning rituals. Afterward, she left them with Despina and Anya and went in search of Leonid. Though she'd been leaving him alone to take care of his endless details, she had to see him today. Just touch and kiss him, before leaving him to his urgent affairs.

As she reached his stateroom, Fedor informed her that Leonid had a surprise visit from an important royal family member.

Before she told Fedor to ask Leonid to touch base with her when he could as she didn't want to call and disturb him, the door opened, and what she thought a Valkyrie would look like walked out. And it was clear she was not happy.

Suddenly, Leonid appeared after the woman, and the expression on his face froze her heart. He looked… pained.

The woman turned to him and they shared a charged moment. She was clearly angry. He appeared to be doing all he could to placate her.

Refusing his efforts, the mystery statuesque blonde turned away, leaving him looking more distressed. In a minute she passed Kassandra as she stood in the shadows. Surprise flickered in the woman's eyes before she impaled her on a glance of hostility and walked away.

Leonid just then noticed her and rushed to her, his expression trying to warm, and failing.

Heart thudding, she asked, "Anything wrong?"

He waved. "A trivial dispute. Olga already doesn't approve of my policy making. She'll come around."

Then, kissing her, he promised he'd be there for dinner as usual, excused himself and rushed away.

After watching him until he disappeared, she walked back slowly, wrestling with tremors all the way back to her quarters. It had to be that time of the month making her morose, making her find normal things distressing.

But...if this was normal, why had Leonid lied?

For she had no doubt that he had.

Was there anything else he could have lied about? Like the reason he hadn't been sleeping with her since they'd announced their coming wedding ten days ago?

Had her intuition that nothing could be this perfect been right?

As the girls received her with their usual fanfare, she tried to shake those insidious, malignant doubts.

But they'd already taken root.

Ten

"I so hope Princess Olga will get over her disappointment soon."

Kassandra's hands froze over the gold-and-black costumes she'd designed for Eva and Zoya for the ceremonies.

Anya's words brought images of the incredibly beautiful and regal Olga assailing her. Standing toe-to-toe with Leonid, looking like his female counterpart, every line in her majestic body taut with emotion.

Did Olga's disappointment have to do with Leonid's impending wedding to her? Was that why she'd shot her that antagonistic look? Was she what stood between Olga and the man she wanted?

Forcing herself to sound normal, she asked, "Disappointment over what?"

"That she won't be queen."

That was the first time she'd heard that. No one around here, including Leonid, had told her the details of what had led to him being announced the future king. Even in the news, when other candidates were said to exist, they were never named, since Leonid was the only one who mattered, the one with the global fame and clout.

"So she was one of the candidates for the throne?"

Anya, who Leonid had appointed as her lady-in-waiting, nodded. "She was actually the preferred one. Not only has Zorya always preferred female monarchs, since its birth at the hands of a queen and under the mantle of two goddesses, but Olga is the spitting image of Esfir, Zorya's founder and first queen. Many believe she's her reincarnation."

Kassandra's heart started to thud. "So what happened?"

Oblivious to her condition, Anya handed her another needle threaded with the last color Kassandra needed to finish embroidering Zorya's emblem on Eva's skirt.

"Prince Leonid was always the better candidate, logically speaking, outstripping Olga, and anyone in Zorya for that matter, in wealth and influence by light years. But everyone in Zorya would have overlooked all that because of Olga answering Zorya's specific criteria better. We are a land steeped in tradition and legend, and our beliefs in what makes us Zoryan rule supreme. Olga was an omen, representing our founding queen, a return to the glory days, a rebirth. But *then* Prince Leonid produced something even better. Nonidentical twin daughters, the very personification of our patron goddesses. That made the scale crash in his favor. The representatives of the people and the new royal council were unanimous that it was a sign from the fates. You, my lady, naming them both names meaning *life*, heralding a new life for the kingdom, was, as you Americans say, the cherry on top."

Kassandra tried not to stare at Anya as if she'd just shot her. But the woman's next words felt like more bullets.

"Before Prince Leonid announced the existence of the royal twins and his marriage to you, Princess Olga's supporters advised her to marry him, so Zorya would have him and his power as the queen's consort. So you can understand her disappointment that she not only won't have the title, but won't have the best man on earth as a husband. I only hope she gets over her displeasure and starts collaborating with Prince Leonid. Zorya needs them both."

Three hours and endless details later, Anya left her only when the girls' costumes were done.

Still in an uproar over the revelations, which Leonid hadn't once hinted at, Kassandra continued her efforts to distract herself, now having the girls try on the costumes they'd just finished.

Looking at her daughters in the ornate dresses she'd designed to reflect their new home's history, their new roles as the kingdom's icons, she couldn't help but believe they were born to wear them, to be princesses, with a legacy rooted in tradition and legend.

No wonder the people whose beliefs were based on the lore of the two goddesses thought them a sign from the fates.

But those same people bowed to tradition so much, they'd still refused to sanction such signs' legitimacy based on an undocumented marriage, and had demanded a new wedding. That had been what Kassandra wanted most in life. To marry her beloved Leonid on the same day he became king.

At least, it was what she'd wanted until a few hours ago.

But now…now…she didn't know what to think.

Actually, she did know. And it was…terrible.

If Leonid had needed Eva and Zoya to win the race for the crown, if this is why he'd come for them, it changed everything.

It meant he hadn't come back for them as his daughters. He'd only needed them as his ace, which would trump anyone else's claim, even the preferred heir. But what about her?

Had everything that had happened between them been second to attaining his goal? Was he now marrying her because it was the one way to seal the deal? Or was it far worse than that?

Could it be Olga had always been his preferred choice, but he wouldn't accept anything less than being king himself, with her by his side as his queen consort? Could Kassandra be simply the more convenient choice, a means to make the best of a terrible situation, since he adamantly believed that he and the girls were what was best for the kingdom?

Could he be that driven to become king, over anybody's hearts and lives, including his own? Could it be all that passion, all those emotions, all the things he'd told her, had all been him doing whatever it took to fulfill his duty, to claim his destiny?

From then on her projections grew even more morbid. Maybe he was biding his time until after the coronation and the wedding, when his need for her would end, so he could leave her for the woman he wanted for real.

If so, was what he'd told her that day in his hospital room the truth after all? That he'd never cared for her, hated her clinging and couldn't wait to be rid of her?

It all made sense in a macabre way. For if it didn't, why had he come back for the girls, and according to him for her, too, only when Zorya had announced its secession and its revival of the monarchy? Why hadn't he told her anything about Olga or his need for the girls to secure the throne before? Was he really as preoccupied as he appeared, or was he only unable to feign desire for her anymore?

If *any* of that was real, how could she go through with the wedding? How could she give him every right to the girls?

If any of those horrible suspicions were true, it made him a monster.

"Yes, sir, I understand."

This statement, or variations of it, had been all that Leonid got to say for the past half hour, as Kassandra's father gave him a winded lecture, liberally peppered with ill-veiled threats, about manhood, marriage and family life.

At least it seemed his total submission to the man's badgering and his unqualified acceptance of his menacing directives appeased the proud and forceful Greek man. Now Leonid decided to put his mind to rest completely.

"I assure you, Kyrie Stavros, I left Kassandra only because I thought my life was over after the accident, and I believed it was for the best not to tie her life, and the twins', to someone as damaged as I was. But I've since been restored more than I dreamed possible, and Kassandra, and Eva and Zoya, have completed my healing. Kassandra is my heart, my everything, and I'd give my life without a second thought to never hurt her again. I *will* give my life to make her happy."

Loukas Stavros's eyes had widened with every word, seemingly impressed by Leonid's impassioned declaration, which he clearly hadn't expected.

Reeling back his surprise, Stavros tried to pin austerity back on his face. "As long as we understand each other."

Fiercely glad that Kassandra, and the twins, had such a man, such a family to love and protect them so fiercely, Leonid's lips spread in a grin. "We certainly do. And thanks for your restraint. If it was me talking to the man who left either Eva or Zoya pregnant and heartbroken, I would have taken him apart first, *then* given him the lecture."

The man flung his arms at him in a see-what-I-mean gesture. "I told her that! But she threatened she'd ban me from ever entering Zorya if I didn't give my word to take it easy on you!"

Leonid laughed, his gaze seeking Kassandra. His golden goddess was fierce in her protectiveness of him.

Finding her nowhere, he turned his attention to Stavros. "That sounds very much like our indomitable Kassandra. I'm only glad you complied so you can attend the wedding, and give her away as is your, and her, right. But if you want to discipline me afterward, I'm at your service."

The man gave him an excited wolflike grin. "It seems you and me are going to get along, boy."

Leonid grinned back at him as widely. "I have no doubt we will. I would get along with the devil if he loved and cherished Kassandra. But as my father-in-law, and my daughters' grandfather, you automatically commanded privileges few in this world do. Now after meeting you, you've just moved to the top of my list."

Stavros laughed. "The list of devils?"

Leonid winked at him. "I do have a weakness for my kind."

Stavros guffawed louder and thumped him on the back so hard he almost knocked him off his unsteady feet.

By the time Stavros moved on, the demonstrative man had inundated him with enough physical gestures to tell him he was already family to him.

Relieved that he'd won over the most important man in Kassandra's life, Leonid turned to the other people who sought his attention at the reception, all the while seeking Kassandra, to no avail.

The coronation, and more important, the wedding, was tomorrow, and her whole family, all two-hundred-plus members of it, had arrived in Zorya the day before. She'd been lost in their sea ever since. Not that she'd been easily found before that. In the two weeks after they'd come together, he'd almost killed himself to wrap a million things up so he could rush back into her arms. But once he could, there had always been something stopping her from taking him there. For the past week she'd either been busy, sleeping, out or just unavailable when he'd sought her.

Even when he did see her, he couldn't help but notice she'd...changed. She was subdued, as if all her fire had gone out. She'd only told him she had her period, and it was a particularly distressing one, what with all the preceding events.

But when he'd thought they'd go to meet her arriving family members together, and she'd gone alone, all his past doubts had crashed back on him.

For what if, after the first rush of sympathy for what had happened to him, it had all sunk in, that she'd be tying herself to a man who wasn't only damaged, and who in spite of her protestations, she found revolting, but who would be the king of a country passing through turbulent times for the foreseeable future? What if she dreaded all the tension and trouble he would bring into her own life by association?

But though it agonized him to think any of that could be true, he dreaded saying anything to her even more, in case she validated his suspicions. So he'd chosen to convince himself she'd been having wedding jitters, that whatever it was, it was a passing thing that had nothing to do with him, or their impending marriage.

But when the reception ended, and she'd reappeared only to entertain her guests while keeping dozens of feet and people between them, he could no longer fool himself.

Something was wrong. Horribly wrong.

Three hours before the coronation and wedding ceremonies, Leonid stood before the full-length mirror in the quarters he'd relinquish forever tonight to move with Kassandra to the ones he'd slaved over realizing for her, her perfect wonderland.

His traditional Zoryan regal costume fit him perfectly. And weighed down on him absolutely. But he realized it wasn't the lifelong responsibility it represented that was getting him down, but the hovering dread that he wouldn't be bearing its burdens with a happy Kassandra by his side.

Then, as if he'd summoned her with his anxiety, Kassandra entered his quarters.

Just one look into her extinguished eyes told him.

His worst fears were about to be realized.

Forcing himself to ignore his trepidations, he rushed to take her in his arms. His heart almost ruptured when the woman who'd dissolved with passion in his arms a couple of weeks ago turned to stone there now. When she was supposed to walk down the aisle with him to a lifetime together in mere hours.

Before he could choke out his anguish, she whispered, "In spite of everything that happened, and how you came back into our lives, I believe you now love our daughters."

Confused beyond words at hers, he again tried to reach for her. "Kassandra, *moya lyubov'*…"

Her hand rose, a feeble move without any energy. It still stopped him in his tracks. "I also do believe you'd make Zorya the best king. So for our daughters and for your kingdom, I'll walk out there in three hours and marry you, Leonid. But for myself, I want things to go back to what you intended before. A marriage in name only, with separate lives."

Feeling his world coming to an end, he couldn't even breathe for long moments until he thought he might suffocate.

It was finally uncontainable agony that forced the choking question from his lips. "What changed?"

"Nothing changed. Things only became clear."

He squeezed his eyes, his whole left side going numb.

Things were clear to her now. When he'd been trying to cling to the hope that she'd never come to her senses.

"It's too much for you, isn't it?" he rasped. "You tried to pretend my mutilation doesn't appall you, but it does, doesn't it? You can't face a lifetime of curbing your revulsion at the sight of my stump, to the feel of my scars, can you?"

Her gaze deadened even more. "You can pick whatever reason you want. I'll back up any story you decide on."

"Story?"

"If you ever need grounds for divorce."

With that, she turned and walked out, looking like an automaton.

But somewhere in the tornado that was uprooting everything inside him, he knew. She was now going to put on her wedding dress, then she'd walk with him to the altar, pledge to be his wife and queen, and instead of love and joy, he'd see in her eyes that she no longer wanted him. But out of duty to her daughters and their kingdom, she would still walk into the prison of being with him forever.

He couldn't let her do this to herself.

He had to set her free, forever this time.

Shattered by her brief yet annihilating confrontation with Leonid, Kassandra had gone back to her quarters, where all the women of her family had gathered. In a fugue, she surrendered to their fussing as they dressed her in the fairy-tale dress Signor Bernatelli had designed for her. She thought she'd talked, smiled, even laughed, putting on a show for her family's sake, for Eva's and Zoya's, for Zorya's.

After her suspicions about Leonid's intentions had

erupted, wiping out her sanity, they'd receded enough to make her see the facts. That Leonid did love Eva and Zoya, with everything in him, and they loved him back. He was everything they could have hoped for in a father. Also undeniable was the fact that he was a formidable force for good, and as Zorya's king, he would not only save the kingdom, but he'd stabilize the whole region.

As for his feelings for her, whatever he'd felt before, she now believed he was trying sincerely to be as attentive and loving as he could be. In the past week, he'd resumed seeking her, yet it had been as if it hurt him to do so.

Whatever it was, it wasn't as sinister as she'd thought in that first wave of insanity. He was trying to do his best for all of them. It was she who was too greedy, too damaged. She couldn't take what he was offering, when it was far more than what most women could dream of. Because it wasn't everything. She'd either have all of him, or none of him at all.

In keeping with tradition, everyone left her for one last hour of solitude before the wedding. As the minutes counted down to zero, she waited to be called when the ceremonies began.

Then Anya walked in, looking stricken.

"My lady, it's terrible. An absolute shock!"

Kassandra shot to her feet, her blood not following her up, making her sway. "What happened?"

"Prince Leonid has left the palace. After calling Princess Olga and relinquishing the crown to her!"

Among the total mayhem Leonid's departure had caused, Kassandra clung to one thing.

The letter he'd left her.

Not that she'd even tried to read it. His actions had spoken far louder than anything he could ever say. That she'd catastrophically and unforgivably misjudged his feelings and misread his intentions. Again.

She'd exploded from the palace in search of him five hours ago. She'd taken Fedor and he'd driven her to every single place he could think of where Leonid might be. Leonid had turned off his phone, hadn't been anywhere they'd searched. There'd been no sighting of him anywhere. Yet there was no evidence that he'd left the kingdom.

After the last failed attempt, she broke down and wept until she felt she'd come apart. But she got out his letter, hoping it would give her a clue where he'd gone.

Shaking so hard, eyes so swollen, it was almost impossible to read it. But she kept trying.

And every word killed her all over again.

Kassandra,

I will never be able to beg your forgiveness enough or atone enough for everything I cost you, every heartache I caused you, but I'll make sure you never again sacrifice your well-being and desires for anything, starting with me. I will always love you, and our daughters. You will all, always, have everything that I have. But I only want you to be free and happy. While I will always be infinitely grateful for all the happiness and blessings you've given me, I only wish I could take back the suffering I've inflicted on you. But since I can't, I can only cause you no more.

The letter ended, no signature, no closing, just this ominous pledge. The whole message sounded like... like a...

No. No. *No.*

Then it erupted in her mind. A memory. A realization. Of the only place he could be. *Had* to be. One with significance only to him, where he'd taken her and the girls, saying it had been his favorite spot when he'd been a child. The one memory he had of his parents, where they'd taken him right before they died.

Crying out for Fedor to find it, knowing just a name and a description, it felt like forever before Fedor found out where it was. All that time terror hacked at her, that she might have pushed him into doing something drastic.

Then they were there...and...so was Leonid.

He stood in the distance, looking over the frozen lake where his parents had taken him skating for the first, and last, time. A colossus among the snow, looking desolate, defeated.

"Leonid!"

He jerked so hard at her shriek. He must have been so lost in thought that he hadn't heard the car's approach. He almost lost his balance as he swung around. Then he gaped.

She knew how she must look to him. Maniacal, her elaborate wedding gown tearing in places, hair falling all over out of its chignon, eyes reddened and bleeding mascara, the rest of her makeup streaked down her swollen face.

She only cared that she'd found him. That she'd give her life to make it up to him, that she still had the chance to.

When she was a few dozen feet away, he started talking, voice hoarse and even deeper than usual with bleakness. "You shouldn't have come, Kassandra. I meant every word, that only your happiness and peace of mind matter to me."

She would have closed those final feet between them in a flying leap that landed her against him. The old Leonid would have caught her midair as easily as a pro basketball player caught a ball. But as it was, she could knock him off his feet or even injure him. She'd done enough of that, and she'd die before she hurt him again.

"I don't want you to feel bad," he choked. "It's not your fault..."

And she wrapped her arms around as much of his bulk as she could, squeezed him until she felt her arms would break off.

Stiffening as if with insupportable pain in her arms, he groaned in protest again. "Don't, Kassandra. Don't let your tender heart overrule your best interests again. I don't matter..."

"Only you *ever* mattered." She shut him up when he attempted to protest, surging for his precious lips, taking them in wrenching kisses, pouring her love and agony into him. Then she told him what she'd learned that day from Anya, and how it had set off the chain reaction of uncertainty.

"I've lived with the demons of doubt tormenting me for so long," she sobbed in between desperate kisses. "And they overwhelmed my reason. I was terrified you couldn't possibly love me as totally as I love you, that I couldn't be your one and only choice, and that you were only struggling to accommodate my emotions to make the best of a less-than-ideal situation for all involved. And once I thought that, I couldn't do this to you, couldn't bear having you on those terms." Tears poured thicker, sobs coming harder as she mashed her lips against his. "Please forgive me, my love, forgive me for letting malignant insecurity drive me insane enough to commit the unforgivable crime of doubting you again."

As he started to push away, to get a word in, she clung harder, sobs dismantling her soul as she rushed on to confess her original sin.

"I should have *never* walked away when you asked me to. I *knew* you were at your lowest, *knew* you couldn't be in your right mind. Your decision to push me away for my own good was wrong. But the blame for everything that happened is mine, for not insisting on staying, taking anything from you, until you realized I'd a million times rather be miserable with you than at peace without you. I'm the one who made us all suffer."

"Now, wait a minute here…"

She cut across his protest. "No more waiting. And no more doubts or distance of any sort, ever again. I'm never leaving your side again. And I'm *not* letting you relinquish the crown."

"Kassandra, listen to me…"

"No, you listen. I'm not letting you even think of abandoning something this enormous and imperative, your duty to the land only you can rule."

"If you'll just let me get a word in here…"

"What word would that be? If it's not yes to everything I've just said, don't bother. Zorya needs you as much as I and the girls do." She stopped, grimaced. Every cell hurt with loving him so much, finding him so damned beautiful. "Okay, so that's not true. Anyone else, even the girls, can live without you. I can't. And I never will. I need you to believe this, my love, and understand it as a fundamental fact of my being. For the girls, my family and work, I can exist, appear to be functioning, for a lifetime if need be. But to *live*, to know joy and ecstasy and peace, I need you. Only you."

Anguish and insecurity evaporating slowly in his eyes under the flames of her fervor, he caressed her face with trembling hands, the love in his gaze so fierce it seared her to her soul, the raggedness in his deep, velvet voice heart wrenching.

"It was so easy to fall prey to my own demons as soon as I felt your withdrawal. They convinced me I repelled you, and the kingdom's duties and dangers oppressed you. And I would rather die a thousand deaths than inflict a moment's unhappiness on you. But without you fueling my will to be, nothing else mattered. Leaving everything behind became the only thing I could do, and my one desire."

Before she could lament a protest, his lips shook in a smile of reassurance. "But Olga will make a fine queen. And with you by my side again, I can again function, can serve Zorya as her advisor, as a businessman and politician. But it is better for our family that I step down now."

"If you're referring to those moronic fears I had at the start, please forget I ever said anything so stupid. Whatever hardships will be involved in reestablishing the monarchy, this is your *destiny*. I will eagerly and proudly share in all its tests and burdens, and be the happiest woman on earth, because I will do it all with you, and will have the honor and delight of being your succor and support through it all."

And she felt it, the exact moment he let go of the last traces of reluctance and doubt and hesitation. Then she was in the only home she ever wanted, his embrace, crushed and cherished and contained.

"You've got one thing wrong, *dorogaya*. The crown isn't my destiny. You are. You and our girls." Suddenly he groaned. "But how can I now go back and demand to be crowned? After I left the whole kingdom in the lurch?"

Caressing his chiseled cheek dreamily, she sighed. "Don't you worry. Everything about you is the stuff of fairy tales, and when I'm finished playing the media, the whole world will be raving about the king who started his rule with a romantic gesture for the ages. Bet you will go down history as a legend to rival that of the goddesses or even Cinderella and Prince Charming."

His breathtaking smile singed her to her toes. "You mean *we* will. Even though the roles were embarrassingly reversed here, and it was the big, lethal hero who ran away."

A laugh bubbled from her depths. "Leaving me a priceless letter instead of a glass slipper."

His eyes glowed with so much love it caused a literal pain in her gut. "And you didn't send people to look for me, but cast out your love like a net to find me."

Suddenly a storm of honking erupted, jogging them out of their complete absorption with one another.

Swinging around in shock, they found their whole wedding party, six-hundred-plus strong, descending from a fleet of limos. Fedor must have reported their position. Or her testosterone tribe had followed her GPS signal. Or her friends had had their Triumvirate comb the planet for them.

Whatever had really happened, they'd found them and were advancing on them en masse. In the first line of the approaching army were her parents, each with a girl yelling for Kassandra and Leonid in their arms.

Before they reached them, she looked up at Leonid, her soul in human form, the source of every towering emotion she'd ever experienced and the fuel for every ambition and passion and delight for the rest of her life. He was looking back at her, so hungrily, so adoringly, she again wondered how she could have ever doubted his feelings. But never again.

Heart soaring with all the endless possibilities and promises of a lifetime with him, she suddenly grinned at him.

"How about you demonstrate one of your unique abilities to the good people who came trudging through the snow after us?"

His eyes filled with the mischief that had started appearing in his eyes in those short days of bliss, the bliss that would now be their status quo.

"The Voronov Vacuum Maneuver?"

Devouring his lips once again, she caressed his chiseled cheek. "Right the first time."

Laughing, the most delightful sound in heaven or on earth, he opened his arms wide.

The girls launched themselves there, and stuck.

As she explained the property he and the girls, the pieces of her soul, shared, everyone laughed. Then their interrupted wedding guests inundated them with a hundred questions about what was going on.

As they tried to escape answering any, her friends, their Triumvirate and her siblings came to their rescue.

Selene, hooking her arm around her own Greek god, grinned. "You people just have to get used to having a very unconventional, unpredictable king and queen. Don't bother trying to figure them out."

Aristedes grinned adoringly at his wife and corroborated her words. "There's no doubt that under Leonid and Kassandra's rule Zorya will rise to unprecedented prosperity, but it won't be in any way you people would expect. So just sit back and enjoy their reign."

Maksim nodded, grinning, too, as he hugged Caliope to his side. "Now you'll add a new legend to your impressive arsenal, that of The King Who Ran."

Caliope smiled from ear to ear. "And The Queen Who Brought Him Back."

Naomi chuckled. "With yours being a femalecentric culture, that gender-reversal twist on Cinderella and Prince Charming is right up your alley."

Andreas kissed the top of Naomi's head, clearly loving the wit of his wife's remark. "One thing is certain. With those two and their twin stars, I assure you, you'll be forever entertained."

Aleks chuckled. "Indeed. I have a feeling those two will treat us all to lifelong episodes of an epic Greek *and* Slavic–in-one drama. I, for one, can't wait to watch it unfold."

As everyone laughed, Kassandra's eldest brother, Dimitri, who'd spent last night's reception wrapped around Olga, cleared his throat importantly.

"And now I interrupt today's episode with a news bulletin. A message for you, Leonid, from HRH Princess Olga."

As everyone turned to Dimitri, all ears, he smirked.

"The lady is telling you, quote, she'll be your spare heir, until your real ones grow up, but that would be it. You have to get back where you belong, that lofty palace you spent bazillions renovating, put that crown on your head and take the weight of this messed-up kingdom on your endless shoulders. And if you think every time she pinches your ear over some state policy you can flounce away and say you're not playing, you have another think coming, unquote."

Dimitri turned his bedeviling gaze to Kassandra. "*And* she thought you were the reason Leonid was being so uncharacteristically lenient as to approve that policy that made her blast him. But I assured her you're a shark, and that as soon as you knew he didn't use his many rows of teeth when he should have, you'll straighten him, and those teeth, out. And that if she ever needs anything at all done to him, including twisting him into a pretzel, you're the girl to call." He winked broadly at her. "She thinks you'll be her new best friend."

Leonid again laughed along with everyone, unable to believe what a difference an hour made. A minute. A word. Even a breath from Kassandra turned his world upside down, then right side up again.

And she'd given him everything he'd never dared dream of having, dissipating the darkness of despair and insecurity and guilt forever. She'd given him certainty, stability, permanence. She'd taken him and would keep him, no matter what—scars, fake parts, burdens and obsessions and all.

And he finally knew what happiness felt like. And boundless hope. What he'd been scared to even wish for since he'd lost her that first time.

She'd given him everything. And more.

As everyone's voices rose in side conversations and questions and proddings, he was unable to go on another second without another kiss.

Everyone hooted and said they should have brought the minister with them and completed the wedding right here.

Whispering to Kassandra, she just nodded delightedly and said, "Anything you want, always."

He addressed the crowd. "I apologize for the drama I
caused, though it seems you all enjoyed the mystery and
the exercise. But my queen and bride has decreed we go
back and resume the interrupted ceremonies, even if by
now they'll be concluded long after the sun of the new
day rises. I hope you're all game."

As everyone's voices rose in approval, he squeezed
his little princesses, who were beside themselves with
the excitement of the unusual circumstances.

"And now it's time your papa took you back to your
new home, where you will always be the earthbound
Zoryan stars that will guide me with their bright light,
and the blessing of our kingdom."

As everyone walked back to the limos, Kassandra,
whose tears of joy had been flowing freely, reached for
his lips, her voice thick with emotion, sultry with hunger.

"I've got news for you, my liege. After all the odds
you've beaten, how you've survived and become far
more than you've been, how you've come back for us,
how you love us and how you make our lives far better
than any dream, the real blessing is you."

He hugged the twins tighter, hugged his Kassandra
until he felt her under his skin, inside his heart, coursing through his veins and pledged, "And I am all yours
totally, irrevocably…and forever."

* * * * *

"I should have just slept with him," she murmured, the declaration sounding unbearably loud in the silent house.

Then at least she'd have a good reason to regret her actions.

"It's not too late to change your mind," a low male voice said from the doorway.

Startled, Hadley whirled in Liam's direction. Heat seared her cheeks. "I thought you went out."

"I did, but it wasn't any fun without you." He advanced toward her, his intent all too clear.

When his arms went around her, pulling her tight against his strong body, Hadley stopped resisting. This was what she wanted. Why fight against something that felt this right?

"Kiss me quick before I change my mind," she told him, her head falling back so she could meet his gaze. "And don't stop."

* * *

Nanny Makes Three
is part of the series Texas Cattleman's Club:
Lies and Lullabies—Baby secrets
and a scheming sheikh rock Royal, Texas.

NANNY MAKES THREE

BY
CAT SCHIELD

First Published in Great Britain 2016
By Mills & Boon, an imprint of HarperCollins*Publishers*
1 London Bridge Street, London, SE1 9GF

© 2016 Harlequin Books S.A.

ISBN: 978-0-263-91843-4

Special thanks and acknowledgement are given to Cat Schield for her contribution to the Texas Cattleman's Club: Lies and Lullabies series.

51-0116

Our policy is to use papers that are natural, renewable and recyclable products and made from wood grown in sustainable forests.The logging and manufacturing processes conform to the legal environmental regulations of the country of origin.

Printed and bound in Spain
by CPI, Barcelona

Cat Schield has been reading and writing romance since high school. Although she graduated from college with a BA in business, her idea of a perfect career was writing books for Mills & Boon. And now, after winning the Romance Writers of America 2010 Golden Heart® Award for series contemporary romance, that dream has come true. Cat lives in Minnesota with her daughter, Emily and their Burmese cat. When she's not writing sexy, romantic stories for Mills & Boon Desire, she can be found sailing with friends on the St. Croix River, or in more exotic locales, like the Caribbean and Europe. She loves to hear from readers. Find her at www.catschield.com. Follow her on Twitter @catschield.

For Jeff and Roxanne Schall of Shada Arabians

One

Shortly after the 6:00 a.m. feeding, Liam Wade strode through the barn housing the yearling colts and fillies, enjoying the peaceful crunching of hay and the occasional equine snort. It was January 1, and because of the way horses were classified for racing and showing purposes, regardless of their calendar age, every horse in every stall on the ranch was now officially a year older.

Dawn of New Year's Day had never been a time of reflection for Liam. Usually he was facedown in a beautiful woman's bed, sleeping like the dead after an evening of partying and great sex. Last year that had changed. He'd left the New Year's Eve party alone.

His cell phone buzzed in his back pocket, and he pulled it out. The message from his housekeeper made him frown.

There's a woman at the house who needs to speak to you.

Liam couldn't imagine what sort of trouble had come knocking on his door this morning. He texted back that he was on his way and retraced his steps to his Range Rover.

As he drove up, he saw an unfamiliar gray Ford Fusion in the driveway near the large Victorian house Liam's great-great-grandfather had built during the last days of the nineteenth century. Liam and his twin brother, Kyle, had grown up in this seven-bedroom home, raised by their grandfather after their mother headed to Dallas to create her real estate empire.

Liam parked and turned off the engine. A sense of foreboding raised the hair on his arms, and he wondered at his reluctance to get out of the truck. He'd enjoyed how peaceful the last year had been. A strange woman showing up at the crack of dawn could only mean trouble.

Slipping from behind the wheel, Liam trotted across the drought-dry lawn and up the five steps that led to the wraparound porch. The stained glass windows set into the double doors allowed light to filter into the wide entry hall, but prevented him from seeing inside. Thus, it wasn't until Liam pushed open the door that he saw the infant car seat off to one side of the hall. As that was registering, a baby began to wail from the direction of the living room.

The tableau awaiting him in the high-ceilinged room was definitely the last thing he'd expected. Candace, his housekeeper, held a squalling infant and was obviously trying to block the departure of a stylish woman in her late fifties.

"Liam will be here any second," Candace was saying. With her focus split between the child and the blonde woman in the plum wool coat, his housekeeper hadn't noticed his arrival.

"What's going on?" Liam questioned, raising his voice slightly to be heard above the unhappy baby.

The relief on Candace's face was clear. "This is Diane Garner. She's here about her granddaughter."

"You're Liam Wade?" the woman demanded, her tone an accusation.

"Yes." Liam was completely bewildered by her hostility. He didn't recognize her name or her face.

"My daughter is dead."

"I'm very sorry to hear that."

"She was on her way to see you when she went into

labor and lost control of her car. The doctors were unable to save her."

"That's very tragic." Liam wasn't sure what else to say. The name Garner rang no bells. "Did she and I have an appointment about something?"

Diane stiffened. "An appointment?"

"What was your daughter's name?"

"Margaret Garner. You met her in San Antonio." Diane grew more agitated with each word she uttered. "You can't expect me to believe you don't remember."

"I'm sorry," Liam said, pitching his voice to calm the woman. She reminded him of a high-strung mare. "It's been a while since I've been there."

"It's been eight months," Diane said. "Surely you couldn't have forgotten my daughter in such a short period of time."

Liam opened his mouth to explain that he wasn't anywhere near San Antonio eight months ago when it hit him what the woman was implying. He turned and stared at the baby Candace held.

"You think the baby's mine?"

"Her name is Maggie and I know she's yours."

Liam almost laughed. This was one child he knew without question wasn't his. He'd been celibate since last New Year's Eve. "I assure you that's not true."

Diane pursed her lips. "I came here thinking you'd do the right thing by Maggie. She's your child. There's no question that you had an affair with my daughter."

He wasn't proud of the fact that during his twenties, he'd probably slept with a few women without knowing their last name or much more about them other than that they were sexy and willing. But he'd been careful, and not one of them had shown up on his doorstep pregnant.

"If I had an affair with your daughter, it was a long time ago, and this child is not mine."

"I have pictures that prove otherwise." Diane pulled a

phone out of her purse and swiped at the screen. "These are you and my daughter. The date stamp puts them at eight months ago in San Antonio. Are you going to deny that's you?"

The screen showed a very pretty woman with blond hair and bright blue eyes, laughing as she kissed the cheek of a very familiar-looking face. Kyle's. A baseball cap hid his short hair, but the lack of a scar on his chin left no doubt it was Kyle and not Liam in the picture.

"I realize that looks like me, but I have a twin brother." Liam was still grappling with seeing his brother looking so happy when Diane Garner slipped past him and headed toward the entry. "But even so, that doesn't mean the baby is a Wade."

Diane paused with her hand on the front doorknob. Her eyes blazed. "Margaret dated very infrequently, and she certainly didn't sleep around. I can tell from the pictures that she really fell for you."

Either Diane hadn't heard Liam when he explained that he had a twin or she saw this as an excuse. While he grappled for a way to get through to the woman, she yanked the door open and exited the house.

Stunned, Liam stared after her. He was ready to concede that the child might be a Wade. A DNA test would confirm that quickly enough, but then what? Kyle was on active duty in the military and not in a position to take on the responsibility of an infant.

The baby's cries escalated, interrupting his train of thought. He turned to where Candace rocked the baby in an effort to calm her and realized Diane Garner intended to leave her granddaughter behind. Liam chased after the older woman and caught her car door before she could close it.

"Are you leaving the baby?"

"Margaret was on her way to see you. I think she meant

to either give you Maggie or get your permission to give her up. There were blank forms to that effect in her car."

"Why?"

"She never wanted to have children of her own." Diane's voice shook. "And I know she wouldn't have been able to raise one by herself."

"What happens if I refuse?"

"I'll turn her over to child services."

"But you're the child's grandmother. Couldn't you just take care of her until we can get a DNA test performed and…"

"Because of health issues, I'm not in a position to take care of her. You're Maggie's father," Diane insisted. "She belongs with you."

She belonged with her father. Unfortunately, with Kyle on active duty, could he care for a baby? Did he even want to? Liam had no idea—it had been two years since he'd last spoken with Kyle. But if the child was a Wade—and Liam wasn't going to turn the child out until he knew one way or another—that meant she belonged here.

"How do I get in contact with you?" Liam asked. Surely the woman would want some news of her grandchild?

"I gave my contact info to your housekeeper." The older woman looked both shaken and determined. "Take good care of Maggie. She's all I have left." And with more haste than grace, Diane pulled her car door shut and started the engine.

As the gray car backed down the driveway, Liam considered the decision his own mother had made, leaving him and Kyle with her father to raise while she went off to the life she wanted in Dallas. He'd never really felt a hole in his life at her absence. Their grandfather had been an ideal blend of tough and affectionate. No reason to think that Maggie wouldn't do just as well without her mother.

He returned to the house. Candace was in the kitchen

warming a bottle of formula. The baby continued to show-case an impressive set of lungs. His housekeeper shot him a concerned glance.

"You let her go?" Candace rocked the baby.

"What was I supposed to do?"

"Convince her to take the baby with her?" She didn't sound all that certain. "You and I both know she isn't yours."

"You sound pretty sure about that."

Liam gave her a crooked smile. Candace had started working for him seven years ago when the former house-keeper retired. Diane Garner wasn't the first woman to show up unexpected and uninvited on his doorstep, al-though she was the first one to arrive with a baby.

"You've been different this last year." Candace eyed him. "More settled."

She'd never asked what had prompted his overnight transformation from carefree playboy to responsible busi-nessman. Maybe she figured with his thirtieth birthday he'd decided to leave his freewheeling days behind him. That was part of the truth, but not all.

"I've been living like a monk."

She grinned. "That, too."

"What am I supposed to do with a baby?" He eyed the red-faced infant with her wispy blond hair and unfocused blue eyes. "Why won't she stop crying?"

"She's not wet so I'm assuming she's hungry." Or maybe she just wants her mother. Candace didn't say the words, but the thought was written all over her face. "Can you hold her while I get her bottle ready?"

"I'd rather not."

"She won't break."

The child looked impossibly small in Candace's arms. Liam shook his head. "Tell me what to do to get a bottle ready."

The noise in the kitchen abated while the baby sucked greedily at her bottle. Liam made the most of this respite and contacted a local company that specialized in placing nannies. Since it wasn't quite seven in the morning, he was forced to leave a message and could only hope that he'd impressed the owners with the urgency of his need. That done, he set about creating a list of things that baby Maggie would need.

Hadley Stratton took her foot off the accelerator and let her SUV coast down the last thirty feet of driveway. An enormous Victorian mansion loomed before her, white siding and navy trim giving it the look of a graceful dowager in the rugged West Texas landscape.

The drive from her apartment in Royal had taken her fifteen minutes. Although a much shorter commute than her last job in Pine Valley, Hadley had reservations about taking the nanny position. Liam Wade had a playboy reputation, which made this the exact sort of situation she avoided. If he hadn't offered a salary at the top of her range and promised a sizable bonus if she started immediately, she would have refused when the agency called. But with student loans hanging over her head and the completion of her master's degree six short months away, Hadley knew she'd be a fool to turn down the money.

Besides, she'd learned her lesson when it came to attractive, eligible bosses. There would be no repeat of the mistake she'd made with Noah Heston, the divorced father of three who'd gone back to his ex-wife after enticing Hadley to fall in love with him.

Parking her SUV, Hadley headed for the front door and rang the bell. Inside a baby cried, and Hadley's agitation rose. She knew very little about the situation she was walking into. Only that Liam Wade had a sudden and urgent need for someone to care for an infant.

A shadow darkened the stained glass inset in the double door. When Hadley's pulse quickened, she suspected this was a mistake. For the last hour she'd been telling herself that Liam Wade was just like any other employer. Sure, the man was a world-class horseman and sexy as hell. Yes, she'd had a crush on him ten years ago, but so had most of the other teenage girls who barrel raced.

A decade had gone by. She was no longer a silly fangirl, but a mature, intelligent, *professional* nanny who knew the risks of getting emotionally wrapped up in her charges or their handsome fathers.

"Good morning, Mr. Wade." She spoke crisply as the door began to open. "Royal Nannies sent me. My name is—"

"Hadley..." His bottle-green eyes scanned her face.

"Hadley Stratton." Had he remembered her? No, of course not. "Stratton." She cleared her throat and tried not to sound as if her heart was racing. Of course he knew who she was; obviously the agency had let him know who they were sending. "I'm Hadley Stratton." She clamped her lips together and stopped repeating her name.

"You're a nanny?" He executed a quick but thorough assessment of her and frowned.

"Well, yes." Maybe he expected someone older. "I have my résumé and references if you'd like to look them over." She reached into her tote and pulled out a file.

"No need." He stepped back and gestured her inside. "Maggie's in the living room." He shut the door behind her and grimaced. "Just follow the noise."

Hadley didn't realize that she'd expected the baby's mother to be ridiculously young, beautiful and disinterested in motherhood until she spied the woman holding the child. In her late forties, she was wearing jeans, a flannel shirt and sneakers, her disheveled dark hair in a messy bun.

"Hadley Stratton. Candace Tolliver, my housekeeper."

Liam cast a fond grin at the older woman. "Who is very glad you've come so quickly."

Candace had the worn look of a first-time mother with a fussy baby. Even before the introductions were completed, she extended the baby toward Hadley. "I've fed her and changed her. She won't stop crying."

"What is her normal routine?" Hadley rocked and studied the tiny infant, wondering what had become of the child's mother. Smaller than the average newborn by a few pounds. Was that due to her mother's unhealthy nutritional habits while pregnant or something more serious?

"We don't know." Candace glanced toward Liam. "She only just arrived. Excuse me." She exited the room as if there were something burning in the kitchen.

"These are her medical records." Liam gestured toward a file on the coffee table. "Although she was premature, she checked out fine."

"How premature?" She slipped her pinkie between the infant's lips, hoping the little girl would try sucking and calm down. "Does she have a pacifier?"

Liam spoke up. "No."

Hadley glanced at him. He'd set one hand on his hip. The other was buried in his thick hair. He needed a haircut, she noted absently before sweeping her gaze around the room in search of the normal clutter that came with a child. Other than a car seat and a plastic bag from the local drugstore, the elegant but comfortable room looked like it belonged in a decorating magazine. Pale gray walls, woodwork painted a clean white. The furniture had accents of dusty blue, lime green and cranberry, relieving the monochrome palette.

"Where are her things?"

"Things?" The rugged horseman looked completely lost.

"Diapers, a blanket, clothes? Are they in her room?"

"She doesn't have a room."

"Then where does she sleep?"

"We have yet to figure that out."

Hadley marshaled her patience. Obviously there was a story here. "Perhaps you could tell me what's going on? Starting with where her mother is."

"She died a few days ago in a traffic accident."

"Oh, I'm sorry for your loss." Hadley's heart clenched as she gazed down at the infant who had grown calmer as she sucked on Hadley's finger. "The poor child never to know her mother."

Liam cleared his throat. "Actually, I didn't know her."

"You had to have..." Hadley trailed off. Chances were Liam Wade just didn't remember which one-night stand had produced his daughter. "What's your name, sweetheart?" she crooned, glad to see the infant's eyes closing.

"Maggie. Her mother was Margaret."

"Hello, little Maggie."

Humming a random tune, Hadley rocked Maggie. The combination of soothing noise and swaying motion put the baby to sleep, and Hadley placed her in the car seat.

"You are incredibly good at that."

Hadley looked up from tucking in the baby and found Liam Wade standing too close and peering over her shoulder at Maggie. The man smelled like pure temptation. If pure temptation smelled like soap and mouthwash. He wore jeans and a beige henley beneath his brown-and-cream plaid shirt. His boots were scuffed and well worn. He might be worth a pile of money, but he'd never acted as though it made him better than anyone else. He'd fit in at the horse shows he'd attended, ambling around with the rest of the guys, showing off his reining skills by snagging the flirts who stalked him and talking horses with men who'd been in the business longer than he'd been alive. His cockiness came from what he achieved on the back of a horse.

"This is the first time she's been quiet since she got here." His strained expression melted into a smile of devastating charm. "You've worked a miracle."

"Obviously not. She was just stressed. I suspect your tension communicated itself to her. How long has she been here?"

"Since about seven." Liam gestured her toward the black leather couch, but Hadley positioned herself in a black-and-white armchair not far from the sleeping child. "Her grandmother dropped her off and left."

"And you weren't expecting her?"

Liam shook his head and began to pace. "Perhaps I should start at the beginning."

"That might be best."

Before he could begin, his housekeeper arrived with a pot of coffee and two cups. After pouring for both, she glanced at the now-sleeping child, gave Hadley a thumbs-up and exited the room once more. Liam added sugar to his coffee and resumed his march around the room, mug in hand.

"Here's what I know. A woman arrived this morning with Maggie, said her name was Diane Garner and that her daughter had died after being in a car accident. Apparently she went into labor and lost control of the vehicle."

Hadley glanced at the sleeping baby and again sorrow overtook her. "That's just tragic. So where is her grandmother now?"

"On her way back to Houston, I'm sure."

"She left you with the baby?"

"I got the impression she couldn't handle the child or didn't want the responsibility."

"I imagine she thought the child was better off with her father."

"Maggie isn't mine." Liam's firm tone and resolute

expression encouraged no rebuttal. "She's my brother's child."

At first Hadley didn't know how to respond. Why would he have taken the child in if she wasn't his?

"I see. So I'll be working for your brother?" She knew little of the second Wade brother. Unlike Liam, he hadn't been active in reining or showing quarter horses.

"No, you'll be working for me. Kyle is in the military and lives on the East Coast."

"He's giving you guardianship of the child?"

Liam stared out the large picture window that overlooked the front lawn. "He's unreachable at the moment so I haven't been able to talk to him about what's going on. I'm not even sure Maggie is his."

This whole thing sounded too convoluted for Hadley's comfort. Was Liam Maggie's father and blaming his absent brother because he couldn't face the consequences of his actions? He wouldn't be the first man who struggled against facing up to his responsibilities. Her opinion of Liam Wade the professional horseman had always been high. But he was a charming scoundrel who was capable of seducing a woman without ever catching her name or collecting her phone number.

"I'm not sure I'm the right nanny for you," she began, her protest trailing off as Liam whirled from the window and advanced toward her.

"You are exactly what Maggie needs. Look at how peaceful she is. Candace spent two hours trying to calm her down, and you weren't here more than ten minutes and she fell asleep. Please stay. She lost her mother and obviously has taken to you."

"What you need is someone who can be with Maggie full-time. The clients I work with only need daytime help."

"The agency said you go to school."

"I'm finishing up my master's in child development."

"But you're off until the beginning of February when classes resume."

"Yes." She felt a trap closing in around her.

"That's four weeks away. I imagine we can get our situation sorted out by then, so we'd only need you during the day while I'm at the barn."

"And until then?"

"Would you be willing to move in here? We have more than enough room."

Hadley shook her head. She'd feel safer sleeping in her own bed. The thought popped into her mind unbidden. What made her think that she was in danger from Liam Wade? From what she knew of him, she was hardly his type.

"I won't move in, but I'll come early and stay late to give you as much time as you need during the month of January. In the meantime, you may want to consider hiring someone permanent."

Despite what Liam had said about Maggie being his brother's child, Hadley suspected the baby wasn't going anywhere once the DNA tests came back. With the child's mother dead and her grandmother unwilling to be responsible for her, Liam should just accept that he was going to need a full-time caregiver.

"That's fair."

Liam put out his hand, and Hadley automatically accepted the handshake. Tingles sped up her arm and raised the hair on the back of her neck as his firm grip lingered a few seconds longer than was professionally acceptable.

"Perhaps we could talk about the things that Maggie will need," Hadley said, hoping Liam didn't notice the odd squeak in her voice.

"Candace started a list. She said she'd get what we needed as soon as you arrived." His lips curved in a wry grin. "She didn't want to leave me alone with the baby."

"Why not?"

"It might seem strange to you, but I've never actually held a baby before."

Hadley tore her gaze away from the likable sparkle in Liam's arresting eyes. She absolutely could not find the man attractive. Hadley clasped her hands in her lap.

"Once you've held her for the first time, you'll see how easy it is." Seeing how deeply the baby was sleeping, Hadley decided this might be a great opportunity for him to begin. "And there's no time like the present."

Liam started to protest, but whatever he'd been about to say died beneath her steady gaze. "Very well." His jaw muscles bunched and released. "What do I do?"

Two

Going balls-out on a twelve-hundred-pound horse to chase down a fleeing cow required steady hands and a calm mind in the midst of a massive adrenaline rush. As a world-class trainer and exhibitor of reining and cutting horses, Liam prided himself on being the eye of the storm. But today, he was the rookie at his first rodeo and Hadley the seasoned competitor.

"It's important that you support her head." Hadley picked up the sleeping baby, demonstrating as she narrated. "Some babies don't like to be held on their backs, so if she gets fussy you could try holding her on her stomach or on her side."

Hadley came toward him and held out Maggie. He was assailed by the dual fragrances of the two females, baby powder and lavender. The scents filled his lungs and slowed his heartbeat. Feeling moderately calmer, Liam stood very still while Hadley settled Maggie into his arms.

"There." She peered at the sleeping child for a moment before lifting her eyes to meet Liam's gaze. Flecks of gold floated in her lapis-blue eyes, mesmerizing him with their sparkle. "See, that wasn't hard."

"You smell like lavender." The words passed his lips without conscious thought.

"Lavender and chamomile." She stepped back until her path was blocked by an end table. "It's a calming fragrance."

"It's working."

As he adjusted to the feel of Maggie's tiny body in his arms, he cast surreptitious glances Hadley's way. Did she remember him from her days of barrel racing? He hadn't seen her in ten years and often looked for her at the events he attended, half expecting her name to pop up among the winners. At eighteen she'd been poised to break out as a star in the barrel-racing circuit. And then she'd sold her mare and disappeared. Much to the delight of many of her competitors, chief among them Liam's on-again, off-again girlfriend.

"I almost didn't recognize you this morning," he said, shifting Maggie so he could free his right arm.

Hadley looked up at him warily. "You recognized me?"

How could she think otherwise? She'd been the one who'd gotten away. "Sure. You took my advice and won that sweepstakes class. You and I were supposed to have dinner afterward." He could tell she remembered that, even though she was shaking her head. "Only I never saw you again."

"I vaguely remember you trying to tell me what I was doing wrong."

"You had a nice mare. Lolita Slide. When you put her up for sale I told Shannon Tinger to buy her. She went on to make over a hundred thousand riding barrels with her."

"She was a terrific horse," Hadley said with a polite smile. "I'm glad Shannon did so well with her."

Liam remembered Hadley as a lanky girl in battered jeans and a worn cowboy hat, her blond hair streaming like a victory banner as her chestnut mare raced for the finish line. This tranquil woman before him, while lovely in gray dress pants and a black turtleneck sweater, pale hair pulled back in a neat ponytail, lacked the fire that had snagged his interest ten years earlier.

"We have a three-year-old son of Lolita's out in the barn.

You should come see him. I think he's going to make a first-class reining horse."

"I don't think there will be time. Infants require a lot of attention."

Her refusal surprised him. He'd expected her to jump at the chance to see what her former mount had produced. The Hadley he remembered had been crazy about horses.

"Why'd you quit?"

Hadley stared at the landscape painting over the fireplace while she answered Liam's blunt question. "My parents wanted me to go to college, and there wasn't money to do that and keep my horse. What I got for Lolita paid for my first year's tuition."

Liam considered her words. When was the last time he'd been faced with an either-or situation? Usually he got everything he wanted. Once in a while a deal didn't go his way, but more often than not, that left him open for something better.

Maggie began to stir, and Liam refocused his attention on the baby. Her lips parted in a broad yawn that accompanied a fluttering of her long lashes.

"I think she's waking up." He took a step toward Hadley, baby extended.

"You did very well for your first time."

Unsure if her tiny smile meant she was patronizing him, Liam decided he'd try harder to get comfortable with his niece. Strange as it was to admit it, he wanted Hadley's approval.

"Would you like a tour of the house?" Liam gestured toward the hallway. "I'd like your opinion on where to put the baby's room."

"Sure."

He led the way across the hall to the dining room. A long mahogany table, capable of seating twelve, sat on a black-and-gold Oriental rug. When he'd overhauled the house six years ago, bringing the plumbing and wiring up to code, this was the one room he'd left in its original state.

"It's just me living here these days, and I haven't entertained much in the last year." The reason remained a sore spot, but Liam brushed it aside. "When my grandfather was alive, he loved to host dinner parties. Several members of Congress as well as a couple governors have eaten here."

"When did you lose him?"

"A year and a half ago. He had a heart condition and died peacefully in his sleep." Grandfather had been the only parent he and Kyle had ever known, and his death had shaken Liam. How the loss had hit Kyle, Liam didn't know. Despite inheriting half the ranch when their grandfather died, his brother never came home and Liam dealt with him only once or twice a year on business matters.

"I remember your grandfather at the shows," Hadley said. "He always seemed larger than life."

Liam ushered her into the large modern kitchen. Her words lightened Liam's mood somewhat. "He loved the horse business. His father had been a cattleman. Our herd of Black Angus descends from the 1880s rush to bring Angus from Scotland."

"So you have both cattle and horses?"

"We have a Black Angus breeding program. Last year we sold two hundred two-year-olds."

"Sounds like you're doing very well."

After a quick peek in the den, they finished their tour of the first floor and climbed the stairs.

"Business has been growing steadily." So much so that Liam wasn't able to do what he really loved: train horses.

"You don't sound all that excited about your success."

He'd thought the abrupt cessation of his personal life would provide more time to focus on the ranch, but he'd discovered the more he was around, the more his staff came to him with ideas for expanding.

"I didn't realize how focused my grandfather had been on the horse side of the business until after his heart problems forced him into semiretirement. Apparently he'd been keeping things going out of respect for his father, but his heart wasn't really in it."

"And once he semiretired?"

"I hired someone who knew what he was doing and gave him a little capital. In three years he'd increased our profits by fifty percent." Liam led Hadley on a tour of three different bedrooms. "This one is mine."

"I think it would be best if Maggie is across the hall from you." Hadley had chosen a cheerful room with large windows overlooking the backyard and soft green paint on the walls. "That way when she wakes up at night you'll be close by."

While Liam wasn't worried about being up and down all night with the infant, he preferred not to be left alone in case something went wrong. "Are you sure I can't convince you to live in?"

"You'll do fine. I promise not to leave until I'm sure Maggie is well settled."

That was something, Liam thought. "If you have things under control for the moment, I need to get back to the barn. I have several calls to make and an owner stopping by to look at his crop of yearlings."

"Maggie and I will be fine."

"Candace should be back with supplies soon, and hopefully we'll have some baby furniture delivered later today. I'll have a couple of the grooms empty this room so it can be readied for Maggie."

Hadley nodded her approval. In her arms, the baby began to fuss. "I think it's time for a change and a little something to eat."

"Here's my cell and office numbers." Liam handed her his business card. "Let me know if you need anything."

"Thank you, I will."

The short drive back to the barn gave Liam a couple minutes to get his equilibrium back. Kyle was a father. That was going to shock the hell out of his brother.

And Liam had received a shock of his own today in the form of Hadley Stratton. Was it crazy that she was the one who stuck out in his mind when he contemplated past regrets? Granted, they'd been kids. He'd been twenty. She'd barely graduated high school the first time she'd made an impression on him. And it had been her riding that had caught his attention. On horseback she'd been a dynamo. Out of the saddle, she'd been quiet and gawky in a way he found very appealing.

He'd often regretted never getting the chance to know anything about her beyond her love of horses, and now fate had put her back in his life. Second chances didn't come often, and Liam intended to make the most of this one.

The grandfather clock in the entry hall chimed once as Hadley slipped through the front door into the cold night air. Shivering at the abrupt change in temperature, she trotted toward her SUV and slid behind the wheel. An enormous yawn cracked her jaw as she started the car and navigated the circular drive.

In order for Hadley to leave Liam in charge of Maggie, she'd had to fight her instincts. The baby was fussier than most, probably because she was premature, and only just went to sleep a little while ago. Although Liam had gained confidence as he'd taken his turn soothing the frazzled infant, Hadley had already grown too attached to the motherless baby and felt compelled to hover. But he needed to learn to cope by himself.

Weariness pulled at her as she turned the SUV on to the deserted highway and headed for Royal. Her last few assignments had involved school-age children, and she'd forgotten how exhausting a newborn could be. No doubt Liam would be weary beyond words by the time she returned at seven o'clock tomorrow morning.

This child, his daughter, was going to turn his world upside down. Already the house had a more lived-in feeling, less like a decorator's showplace and more like a family home. She wondered how it had been when Liam and his brother were young. No doubt the old Victorian had quaked with the noisy jubilance of two active boys.

Twenty minutes after leaving the Wade house, Hadley let herself into her one-bedroom apartment. Waldo sat on the front entry rug, appearing as if he'd been patiently awaiting her arrival for hours when in fact, the cat had probably been snoozing on her bed seconds earlier. As she shut the front door, the big gray tabby stretched grandly before trotting ahead of her toward the kitchen and his half-empty food bowl. Once it was filled to his satisfaction, Waldo sat down and began cleaning his face.

The drive had revived her somewhat. Hadley fixed herself a cup of Sleepytime tea and sipped at it as she checked the contents of the bags a good friend of hers had dropped off this afternoon. After seeing what Candace had bought for the baby, Hadley had contacted Kori to purchase additional supplies. She would owe her friend lunch once Maggie was settled in. Kori had shown horses when she was young and would get a kick out of hearing that Liam Wade was Hadley's new employer.

Hadley had a hard time falling asleep and barely felt as if she'd dozed for half an hour when her alarm went off at five. Usually she liked to work out in the morning and eat a healthy breakfast while watching morning news, but today she was anxious about how things had gone with Liam and Maggie.

Grabbing a granola bar and her to-go mug filled with coffee, Maggie retraced the drive she'd made a mere five hours earlier. The Victorian's second-floor windows blazed with light, and Hadley gave a huge sigh before shifting the SUV into Park and shutting off the engine.

The wail of a very unhappy baby greeted Hadley as she let herself in the front door. From the harried expression on Liam's face, the infant had been crying for some time.

"It doesn't sound as if things are going too well," she commented, striding into the room and holding out her arms for the baby. "Did you get any sleep?"

"A couple hours."

Liam was still dressed for bed in a pair of pajama bottoms that clung to his narrow hips and a snug T-shirt that highlighted a torso sculpted by physical labor. Hadley was glad to have the fussy baby to concentrate on. Liam's helplessness made him approachable, and that was dangerous. Even without his usual swagger, his raw masculinity was no less potent.

"Why don't you go back to bed and see if you can get a little more sleep?"

The instant she made the suggestion, Hadley wished the words back. She never told an employer what to do. Or she hadn't made that mistake since her first nanny job. She'd felt comfortable enough with Noah to step across the line that separated boss and friend. For a couple months that hadn't been a problem, but then she'd been pulled in too deep and had her heart broken.

"It's time I headed to the barn," Liam said, his voice muffled by the large hands he rubbed over his face. "There are a dozen things I didn't get to yesterday."

His cheeks and jaw were softened by a day's growth of beard, enhancing his sexy, just-got-out-of-bed look. Despite the distraction of a squirming, protesting child in her arms, Hadley registered a significant spike in her hormone levels. She wanted to run her palms over his broad shoulders and feel for herself the ripple of ab muscles that flexed as he scrubbed his fingers through his hair before settling his hands on his hips.

Light-headed, she sat down in the newly purchased rocking chair. Liam's effect on her didn't come as a surprise. She'd had plenty of giddy moments around him as a teenager. Once, after she'd had a particularly fantastic run, he'd even looked straight at her and smiled.

Hadley tightened her attention on Maggie and wrestled her foolishness into submission. Even if Liam was still that cocky boy every girl wanted to be with, she was no longer a susceptible innocent prone to bouts of hero worship. More important, he'd hired her to care for this baby, a child who was probably his daughter.

"Do you think she's okay?" Liam squatted down by the rocker. He gripped the arm of the chair to steady himself, his fingers brushing Hadley's elbow and sending ripples of sensation up her arm.

"You mean because she's been crying so much?" Hadley shot a glance at him and felt her resolve melting beneath the concern he showered on the baby. "I think she's just fussy. We haven't figured out exactly what she likes yet. It might take swaddling her tight or a certain sound that calms her. I used to take care of a baby boy who liked to fall asleep listening to the dishwasher."

"I know we talked about this yesterday," Liam began, his gaze capturing hers. "But can you make an exception for a few weeks and move in here?"

"I can't." The thought filled her with a mixture of excitement and panic. "I have a cat—"

"There's always plenty of mice in the barn."

Hadley's lips twitched as she imagined Waldo's horror at being cut off from the comforts of her bed and his favorite sunny spot where he watched the birds. "He's not that sort of cat."

"Oh." Liam gazed down at Maggie, who'd calmed

enough to accept a pacifier. "Then he can move in here with you."

Hadley sensed this was quite a compromise for Liam, but she still wasn't comfortable agreeing to stay in the house. "I think Maggie is going to be fine once she settles in a bit. She's been through a lot in the last few days."

"Look at her. She's been crying for three hours and you calm her down within five minutes. I can't go through another night like this one. You have to help me out. Ten days."

"A week." Hadley couldn't believe it when she heard herself bargaining.

Triumph blazed in Liam's eyes, igniting a broad smile. "Done." He got to his feet, showing more energy now that he'd gotten his way.

After a quick shower and a cup of coffee, Liam felt a little more coherent as he entered his bookkeeper/office manager's office. Ivy had been with Wade Ranch for nine years. She was a first cousin twice removed, and Grandfather had hired her as his assistant, and in a few short years her organizational skills had made her invaluable to the smooth running of the ranch.

"Tough night?" Ivy smirked at him over the rim of her coffee cup. She looked disgustingly chipper for seven in the morning. "Used to be a time when you could charm a female into doing your bidding."

Liam poured himself a cup of her wickedly strong brew and slumped onto her couch. "I'm rusty." Although he'd persuaded Hadley to move in for a week. Maybe it was just babies that were immune.

"Have you considered what you're going to do if the baby isn't Kyle's?"

As Ivy voiced what had filtered through Liam's mind several times during the last twenty-four hours, he knew

CAT SCHIELD   31

he'd better contact a lawyer today. Technically, unless he claimed the child as his, he had no legal rights to her.

"I really believe Kyle is her father," Liam said. "I'm heading to a clinic Hadley recommended to have a DNA test run. I figured since Kyle and I are identical twins, the results should come back looking like Maggie is my daughter."

And then what? Margaret was dead. With Kyle estranged from his family, it wasn't likely he or Maggie would spend much time at Wade Ranch. And if Liam was wrong about his brother being Maggie's father, Diane Garner might give her up to strangers.

Liam was surprised how fast he'd grown attached to the precious infant; the idea of not being in her life bothered him. But was he ready to take on the challenge of fatherhood? Sure, he and Kyle had done okay raised by their grandfather, but could a little girl be raised by a man alone? Wouldn't she miss a mother snuggling her, brushing her hair and teaching her all the intricacies of being a woman? And yet it wasn't as if Liam would stay single forever.

An image of Hadley flashed through his thoughts. Beautiful, nurturing and just stubborn enough to be interesting. A year ago he might not have given her a second thought. Hadley was built for steady, long-term relationships, not the sort of fun and games that defined Liam's private life. She'd probably be good for him, but would he be good for her? After a year of celibacy, his libido was like an overwound spring, ready to explode at the least provocation.

"Liam, are you listening to me?" Ivy's sharp tone shattered his thoughts.

"No. Sorry. I was thinking about Maggie and the future."

Her expression shifted to understanding. "Why don't we

talk later this afternoon. You have a fund-raising meeting at the club today, don't you?"

He'd forgotten all about it. Liam had been involved with the Texas Cattleman's Club fund-raising efforts for Royal Memorial's west wing ever since it had been damaged by a tornado more than a year ago. The grand reopening was three weeks away, but there remained several unfinished projects to discuss.

"I'll be back around three."

"See you then."

Fearing if he sat down in his large office, he might doze off, Liam headed into the attached barn where twelve champion American quarter horse stallions stood at stud. Three of them belonged to Wade Ranch; the other nine belonged to clients.

Liam was proud of all they'd accomplished and wished that his grandfather had lived to see their annual auction reach a record million dollars for 145 horses. Each fall they joined with three other ranches to offer aged geldings, sought after for their proven ranch performance, as well as some promising young colts and fillies with top bloodlines.

At the far end of the barn, double doors opened into a medium-sized indoor arena used primarily for showing clients' horses. One wall held twenty feet of glass windows. On the other side was a spacious, comfortable lounge used for entertaining the frequent visitors to the ranch. A large television played videos of his stallions in action as well as highlights from the current show and racing seasons.

Liam went through the arena and entered the show barn. Here is where he spent the majority of his time away from ranch business. He'd grown up riding and training reining horses and had won dozens of national titles as well as over a million dollars in prize money before he'd turned twenty-five.

Not realizing his destination until he stood in front of

the colt's stall, Liam slid open the door and regarded WR Electric Slide, son of Hadley's former mount, Lolita. The three-year-old chestnut shifted in the stall and pushed his nose against Liam's chest. Chuckling, he scratched the colt's cheek, and his mind returned to Hadley.

While he understood that college and grad school hadn't left her the time or the money to own a horse any longer, it didn't make sense the way she'd shot down his suggestion that she visit this son of her former mount. And he didn't believe that she'd lost interest in horses. Something more was going on, and he wasn't going to let it go.

Three

Hadley sat in the nursery's comfortable rocking chair with Maggie on her lap, lightly tapping her back to encourage the release of whatever air she'd swallowed while feeding. It was 3:00 a.m., and Hadley fended off the house's heavy silence by quietly humming. The noise soothed the baby and gave Hadley's happiness a voice.

She'd been living in the Wade house for three days, and each morning dawned a little brighter than the last. The baby fussed less. Liam smiled more. And Hadley got to enjoy Candace's terrific cooking as well as a sense of accomplishment.

Often the agency sent her to handle the most difficult situations, knowing that she had a knack for creating cooperation in the most tumultuous of households. She attributed her success to patience, techniques she'd learned in her child development classes and determination. Preaching boundaries and cooperation, she'd teach new habits to the children and demonstrate to the parents how consistency made their lives easier.

Feeling more than hearing Maggie burp, Hadley resettled the baby on her back and picked up the bottle once more. Her appetite had increased after her pediatrician diagnosed acid reflux, probably due to her immature digestive system, and prescribed medication to neutralize her stomach acids. Now a week old, Maggie had stopped losing weight and was almost back to where she'd started.

In addition to the reflux problem, Maggie had symptoms of jaundice. Dr. Stringer had taken blood samples to run for DNA, and the bilirubinometer that tested jaundice levels had shown a higher-than-average reading. To Liam's dismay, the doctor had suggested they wait a couple weeks to see if the jaundice went away on its own. He'd only relaxed after the pediatrician suggested they'd look at conventional phototherapy when the blood tests came back.

By the time Hadley settled Maggie back into her crib, it was almost four in the morning. With the late-night feedings taking longer than average because of Maggie's reflux problem, Hadley had gotten in the habit of napping during the day when the baby slept. The abbreviated sleep patterns were beginning to wear on her, but in four short days she would be back spending the night in her tiny apartment once more.

Yawning into her pajama sleeve, Hadley shuffled down the hall to her room. Seeing that her door was open brought her back to wakefulness. In her haste to reach Maggie before she awakened Liam, Hadley hadn't pulled her door fully shut, and after a quick check under the bed and behind the chair, she conceded that the cat was missing. Damn. She didn't want to tiptoe around the quiet house in search of a feline who enjoyed playing hide-and-seek. Given the size of the place, she could be at it for hours.

Silently cursing, Hadley picked up a pouch of kitty treats and slipped out of her room. The floorboards squeaked beneath her. Moving with as much stealth as possible, she stole past Liam's room and headed toward the stairs.

Once on the first floor, Hadley began shaking the treat bag and calling Waldo's name in a stage whisper. She began in the living room, peering under furniture and trying not to sound as frustrated as she felt. No cat. Next, she

moved on to the den. That, too, was feline free. After a
quick and fruitless sweep of the dining room, she headed
into the kitchen, praying Waldo had found himself a perch
on top of the refrigerator or made a nest in the basket of
dirty clothes in the laundry room. She found no sign of
the gray tabby anywhere.

Hadley returned to the second floor, resigned to let
the cat find his own way back, hoping he did before Liam
woke up. But as she retraced her steps down the dim corridor, she noticed something that had eluded her earlier.
Liam's door was open just wide enough for a cat to slip
inside. She paused in the hall and stared at the gap. Had
it been like that when she'd passed by earlier? It would be
just like Waldo to gravitate toward the one person in the
house who didn't like him.

She gave the pouch of cat treats a little shake. The sound
was barely above a whisper, but Waldo had fantastic hearing, and while he might disregard her calls, he never ignored his stomach. Hadley held her breath for a few tense,
silent seconds and listened for the patter of cat paws on the
wood floor, but heard nothing but Liam's deep, rhythmic
breathing. Confident that he was sound asleep, she eased
open his door until she could slip inside.

Her first step into Liam's bedroom sent alarm bells
shrilling in her head. Had she lost her mind? She was
sneaking into her employer's room in the middle of the
night while he slept. How would she explain herself if
he woke? Would he believe that she was in search of her
missing cat or would he assume she was just another op-
portunistic female? As the absurdity of the situation hit
her, Hadley pressed her face into the crook of her arm and
smothered a giggle. Several deep breaths later she had
herself mostly back under control and advanced another
careful step into Liam's room.

Her eyes had long ago grown accustomed to the darkness, and the light of a three-quarter moon spilled through the large window, so it was easy for her to make out the modern-looking king-size bed and the large man sprawled beneath the pale comforter. And there was Waldo, lying on top of Liam's stomach looking for all the world as if he'd found the most comfortable place on earth. He stared at Hadley, the tip of his tail sweeping across Liam's chin in a subtle taunt.

This could not be happening.

Hadley shook the pouch gently and Waldo's gold eyes narrowed, but he showed no intention of moving. Afraid that Liam would wake if she called the cat, Hadley risked approaching the bed. He simply had to move on his own. In order to pick him up, she'd have to slide her hand between Waldo's belly and Liam's stomach. Surely that would wake the sleeping man.

Pulling out a treat, she waved it in front of the cat's nose. Waldo's nose twitched with interest, but he displayed typical catlike disdain for doing anything expected of him. He merely blinked and glanced away. Could she snatch up the cat and make it to the door before Liam knew what had happened? Her mind ran through the possibilities and saw nothing but disaster.

Maybe she could nudge the cat off Liam. She poked the cat's shoulder. Waldo might have been glued where he lay. Working carefully, she slid her finger into his armpit and prodded upward, hoping to annoy him into a sitting position. He resisted by turning his body to stone.

Crossing her fingers that Liam was as sound a sleeper as he appeared, Hadley tried one last gambit. She scratched Waldo's head and was rewarded by a soft purr. Now that he was relaxed, she slid her nails down his spine and was rewarded when he pushed to his feet, the better to enjoy the caress. Leaning farther over the mattress, she slid one hand behind his front legs and cupped his butt in her other palm when she felt the air stir the fabric of her pajama top against her skin.

Hadley almost yelped as a large hand skimmed beneath the hem of her top and traced upward over her rib cage to the lower curve of her breast. Awkwardly looming over Liam's bed, her hands wrapped around an increasingly unhappy feline, she glanced at Liam's face and noticed that while his eyes remained closed, one corner of his lips had lifted into a half smile.

Liam was having an amazing dream. He lay on a couch in front of a roaring fire with a woman draped across him. Her long hair tickled his chin as his hands swept under her shirt, fingers tracing her ribs. Her bare skin was warm and soft beneath his caress and smelled like lavender and vanilla.

It was then he realized whom he held. He whispered her name as his palm discovered the swell of her breast. His fingertips grazed across her tight nipple and her body quivered in reaction, He smiled. A temptress lurked beneath her professional reserve and he was eager to draw her out. Before he could caress further, however, something landed on his chest with a thump.

The dream didn't so much dissolve as shatter. One second he was inches away from heaven, the next he was sputtering after having his breath knocked out. His eyes shot open. Darkness greeted him. His senses adjusted as wakefulness returned.

The silken skin from his dream was oh so real against his fingers. As was the disturbed breathing that disrupted the room's silence.

"Hadley?"

She was looming over his bed, frozen in place, her arms extended several inches above his body. "Waldo got out of my room and came in here. I was trying to lift him off you when you…" Her voice trailed off. She gathered the large gray cat against her chest and buried her face in his fur.

Liam realized his hand was still up her pajama top, palm resting against her side, thumb just below the swell of her breast. The willpower it took to disengage from the compromising position surprised him.

"I was dreaming…" He sat up in bed and rubbed his face to clear the lingering fog of sleep. "Somehow you got tangled up in it."

"You were dreaming of me?" She sounded more dismayed than annoyed.

He reached for the fading dream and confirmed that she had been the object of his passion. "No." She'd already pegged him as a womanizer; no need to add fuel to the fire. "The woman in my dream wasn't anyone I knew."

"Perhaps it was Margaret Garner."

It frustrated him that she continued to believe Maggie was his daughter. "That's possible, since I never met her." His tone must have reflected his frustration because Hadley stepped away from his bed.

"I should get back to my room. Sorry we woke you."

"No problem." Liam waited until the door closed behind her before he toppled backward onto the mattress.

The sheer insanity of the past few moments made him grin. Had she really sneaked into his room to fetch the cat? Picturing what must have happened while he slept made him chuckle. He wished he could have seen her face. He'd bet she'd blushed from her hairline to her toes. Hadley didn't have the brazen sensuality of the women who usually caught his interest. She'd never show up half dressed in his hotel room and pout because he'd rather watch a football game than fool around. Nor would she stir up gossip in an attempt to capture his attention. She was such a straight arrow. Her honesty both captivated and alarmed him.

Rather than stare sleepless at the ceiling, Liam laid his

forearm over his eyes and tried to put Hadley out of his mind. However, vivid emotions had been stirred while he'd been unconscious. Plus, he was having a hard time forgetting the oh-so-memorable feel of her soft skin. With his body in such a heightened state of awareness, there was no way Liam was going to just fall back asleep. Cursing, he rolled out of bed and headed for the shower. Might as well head to the barn and catch up on paperwork.

Three hours later he'd completed the most pressing items and headed out to the barn to watch the trainers work the two-year-olds. At any time, there were between twenty and thirty horses in various stages of training.

They held classes and hosted clinics. For the last few years, Liam had taught a group of kids under ten years old who wanted to learn the ins and outs of competitive reining. They were a steely-eyed bunch of enthusiasts who were more serious about the sport than many adults. At the end of every class, he thanked heaven it would be a decade before he had to compete against them.

"Hey, boss. How're the colts looking?" Jacob Stevens, Liam's head trainer, had joined him near the railing.

"Promising." Liam had been watching for about an hour. "That bay colt by Blue is looking better all the time."

"His full brother earned over a quarter of a million. No reason to think Cielo can't do just as well." Jacob shot his boss a wry grin. "Think you're going to hold on to him?"

Liam laughed. "I don't know. I've been trying to limit myself to keeping only five in my name. At the moment, I own eight."

Until Hadley had shown up, he'd been seriously contemplating selling Electric Slide. The colt was going to be a champion, but Liam had more horses than he had time for. If only he could convince Hadley to get back in the saddle. He knew she'd balk at being given the horse, but maybe she'd be willing to work him as much as time permitted.

"Thing is," Jacob began, "you've got a good eye, and the ranch keeps producing winners."

Liam nodded. "It's definitely a quality problem. I've had a couple of good offers recently. Maybe I need to stop turning people down."

"Or just wait for the right owner."

"Speaking of that. Can you get one of the guys to put Electric Slide through his paces? I want to get some video for a friend of mine."

"Sure."

As he recorded the chestnut colt, Liam wasn't sure if he'd have any luck persuading Hadley to come check out the horse, but he really wanted to get to the bottom of her resistance.

Lunchtime rolled around, and Liam headed back to the house. He hadn't realized how eager he was to spend some time with Maggie and Hadley until he stopped his truck on the empty driveway and realized Hadley's SUV was absent.

Candace was pulling a pie out of the oven as he entered the kitchen. Her broad smile faded as she read the expression on his face. "What's wrong?"

"Where's Hadley?"

"Shopping for clothes and things for Maggie." Candace set a roast beef sandwich on the center island and went to the refrigerator for a soda. "The poor girl hasn't been out of here in days."

"She took Maggie with her?"

"I offered to watch her while she was gone, but the weather is warm, and Hadley thought the outing would do her some good."

"How long have they been gone?"

"About fifteen minutes." Candace set her hands on her hips and regarded him squarely. "Is there some reason for all the questions?"

"No."

Liam wondered at his edginess. He trusted Maggie was in good hands with Hadley, but for some reason, the thought of both of them leaving the ranch had sparked his anxiety. What was wrong with him? It wasn't as if they weren't ever coming back.

The thought caught him by surprise. Is that what was in the back of his mind? The notion that people he cared about left the ranch and didn't come back? Ridiculous. Sure, his mother had left him and Kyle. And then Kyle had gone off to join the navy, but people needed to live their lives. It had nothing to do with him or the ranch. Still, the sense of uneasiness lingered.

Royal Diner was humming with lunchtime activity when Hadley pushed through the glass door in search of a tuna melt and a chance to catch up with Kori. To her relief, her best friend had already snagged one of the booths. Hadley crossed the black-and-white checkerboard floor and slid onto the red faux-leather seat with a grateful sigh.

"I'm so glad you were able to meet me last-minute," Hadley said, settling Maggie's carrier beside her and checking on the sleeping infant.

She'd already fed and changed the baby at Priceless, Raina Patterson's antiques store and craft studio. Hadley had taken a candle-making class there last month and wanted to see what else Raina might be offering.

"Thanks for calling. This time of year is both a blessing and a curse." Kori was a CPA who did a lot of tax work, making January one of her slower months. "I love Scott, but his obsessive need to be busy at all times gets on my nerves." Kori and her husband had started their accounting company two years ago, and despite what she'd just said, the decision had been perfect for them.

"You're the one doing me a favor. I really need your

advice." Hadley trailed off as the waitress brought two Diet Cokes.

They put in their lunch order and when the waitress departed, Kori leaned her forearms on the table and fixed Hadley with an eager stare.

"This is fantastic. You never need my help with anything."

Her friend's statement caught Hadley off guard. "That's not true. I'm always asking for favors."

"Little things, sure, like when you asked me to pick up baby stuff for Miss Maggie or help with your taxes, but when it comes to life stuff you're so self-sufficient." Kori paused. "And I'm always boring you with the stuff that I'm going through."

Hadley considered. "I guess I've been focused on finishing my degree and haven't thought much beyond that. Plus, it's not like I have a social life to speak of."

Kori waved her hands. "Forget all that. Tell me what's going on."

Embarrassment over her early-morning encounter with Liam hadn't faded one bit. Her skin continued to tingle in the aftermath of his touch while other parts of her pulsed with insistent urgency. The only thing that kept her from quitting on the spot was that he'd been asleep when he'd slid his hand beneath her clothes.

"Oh my goodness," Kori exclaimed in awe. "You're blushing."

Hadley clapped her hands over her cheeks. "Am I?"

"What happened?"

"Waldo got out of my room last night when I got up for Maggie's feeding, and when I tracked him down, he was in Liam's room, curled up right here." Hadley indicated where her cat had been on Liam's anatomy.

"You said he isn't a cat person. Was he mad?"

"He was asleep."

Kori began to laugh. "So what happened?"

"I tried to lure him off with a treat, but Waldo being Waldo wouldn't budge. As I was picking him up..." Swept by mortification, Hadley closed her eyes for a span of two heartbeats.

"Yes?" Kori's voice vibrated with anticipation. "You picked him up and what?"

"I was leaning over the bed and Liam was sleeping. And dreaming." Hadley shuddered. "About having sex with some woman, I think."

"And?" Kori's delighted tone prompted Hadley to spill the next part of her tale.

"The next thing I knew, his hand was up my shirt and he—" she mimed a gesture "—my breast." Her voice trailed off in dismay.

"No way. And you're sure he was asleep?"

"Positive. Unfortunately, I was so shocked that I didn't keep a good hold of Waldo and he jumped onto Liam's chest, waking him. I don't think he knew what hit him."

"What did he say?"

"I honestly don't remember. I think I mumbled an apology for waking him. He retrieved his hand from beneath my pajama top and I bolted with Waldo."

"Did you talk to him later?"

"He was gone before Maggie woke up again, and then I took off before he came home for lunch." Hadley glanced at her charge to make sure the baby was sleeping soundly. "What am I supposed to say or do the next time I see him?"

"You could thank him for giving you the best sex you've had in years."

"We didn't have sex." Hadley lowered her voice and hissed the last word, scowling at her friend.

"It's the closest thing you've had to a physical encounter in way too long." Kori fluffed her red hair and gazed in disgust at her friend. "I don't know how you've gone so long without going crazy. If Scott and I go three days without sex we become vile, miserable people."

Hadley rolled her eyes at her friend. "I'm not in a committed, monogamous relationship. You and Scott have been together for seven years. You've forgotten how challenging being single is. And if you recall, the last time I fell in love it didn't work out so well."

"Noah was an ass. He led you on while he was still working through things with his ex-wife."

"She wanted him back," Hadley reminded her friend. "He'd never stopped loving her even after finding out she'd cheated on him. And he was thinking about his kids."

"He still hedged his bets with you. At the very least, he should have told you where things stood between them."

On that, Hadley agreed. Five years earlier, she'd been a blind fool to fall in love with Noah. Not only had he been her employer, but also things had moved too fast between them. Almost immediately he'd made her feel like a part of the family. Because it was her first time being a nanny, she hadn't understood that his behavior had crossed a line. She'd merely felt accepted and loved.

"That was a long time ago." Thinking about Noah made her sad and angry. He'd damaged her ability to trust and opened a hole in her heart that had never healed. "Can we get back to my more immediate problem? Do I quit?"

"Because your boss sleep–felt you up?" Kori shook her head, "Chalk it up to an embarrassing mistake and forget about it."

"You're right." Only she was having a hard time forgetting how much she enjoyed his hands on her skin. In fact, she wanted him to run his hands all over her body and make her come for him over and over.

Kori broke into her thoughts. "You're thinking about him right now, aren't you?"

"What?" Hadley sipped at her cold drink, feeling overly warm. "No. Why would you think that?"

"You've got the hots for him. Good for you."

"No. Not good for me. He's my boss, for one thing. For another, he's a major player. I knew him when I used to race barrels. He had girls chasing after him all the time, and he enjoyed every second of it."

"So he's a playboy. You don't need to fall in love with him, just scratch an itch."

"I can't." Hadley gave her head a vehement shake to dispel the temptation of Kori's matter-of-fact advice. "Besides, I'm not his type. He was asleep during most of what happened this morning."

"Wait. Most?"

Hadley waved to dismiss her friend's query. "It might have taken him a couple extra seconds to move his hand."

Kori began to laugh again. "Oh, he must have really been thrown for a loop. You in his bedroom in the middle of the night with the cat."

The picture Kori painted was funny, and Hadley let herself laugh. "Thank you for putting the whole thing in perspective. I don't know why I was so stressed about it."

"Maybe because despite your best intentions, you like the guy more than you think you should."

Hadley didn't even bother to deny it. "Maybe I do," she said. "But it doesn't matter, because no matter how attractive I may find him, he's my boss, and you know I'm never going there again."

Four

After missing Maggie and Hadley at lunchtime, Liam made sure he was home, showered and changed early enough to spend some time with his niece before dinner. She was in her crib and just beginning to wake up when he entered her room. Hadley wasn't there, but he noticed the red light on the baby monitor and suspected she was in her room or downstairs, keeping one ear tuned to the receiver.

Before Maggie could start to fuss, Liam scooped her out of the crib and settled her on the changing table. Already he was becoming an expert with the snaps and Velcro fastenings of Maggie's Onesies and diapers. Before the baby came fully awake, he had her changed and nestled in his arm on the way downstairs.

The domestic life suited him, he decided, entering the kitchen to see what Candace had made for dinner. The large room smelled amazing, and his mouth began to water as soon as he crossed the threshold. He sneaked up behind Candace and gave her a quick hug.

"What's on the menu tonight?"

"I made a roast. There's garlic mashed potatoes, green beans and apple pie for dessert."

"And your wonderful gravy."

"Of course."

"Is Jacob joining us?"

"Actually, we're going to have dinner in town. It's the seventh anniversary of our first date."

Candace and Jacob had been married for the last six years. They'd met when Candace had come to work at Wade Ranch and fell in love almost at first sight. They had the sort of solid relationship that Liam had never had the chance to see as he was growing up.

"You keep track of that sort of thing?" Liam teased, watching as Candace began fixing Maggie's bottle.

"It's keeping track of that sort of thing that keeps our relationship healthy."

Liam accepted the bottle Candace handed him, his thoughts wrapped around what she'd said. "What else keeps your relationship healthy?"

If the seriousness of his tone surprised her, the housekeeper didn't let on. "Trust and honesty. Jacob and I agreed not to let things fester. It's not always easy to talk about what bugs us, especially big issues like his sister's negative attitude toward me and the fact that I hate holding hands in public. Thank goodness we're both morning people and like the same television shows, or we'd never have made it this far."

As Liam watched Maggie suck down the formula, he let Candace's words wash over him. He'd never actually been in a relationship, healthy or otherwise. Oh, he dated a lot of women, some of them for long periods of time, but as he'd realized a year ago, not one of them wanted more than to have a good time.

At first he'd been shocked to discover that he'd let his personal life remain so shallow. Surely a thirty-year-old man should have had at least one serious relationship he could look back on. Liam hadn't been able to point to a single woman who'd impacted his life in any way.

He didn't even have mommy issues, because he'd never gotten to know her. She was a distracted, preoccupied guest at Christmas or when she showed up for his birthday. When she couldn't make it, expensive presents arrived and were dutifully opened. The most up-to-date electronics, gift cards, eventually big checks. For Liam, their mother had been the beautiful young woman in the photo framed by silver that sat on Grandfather's desk. According to him, she'd loved her career more than anything else and wasn't cut out to live on a ranch.

"...and of course, great sex."

The last word caught his attention. Liam grinned. "Of course."

Candace laughed. "I wondered if you were listening to me. Turns out you weren't."

"I was thinking about my past relationships or lack thereof."

"You just haven't found the right girl." Candace patted him on the arm, adopting the persona of wise old aunt. "Once she shows up, you'll have all the relationship you can handle. Just remember to think about her happiness before your own and you'll be all right."

Liam thought about his past girlfriends and knew that advice would have bankrupted him. His former lovers wanted the best things money could buy. Expensive clothes, exotic trips, to be pampered and spoiled. Living such an affluent lifestyle had been fine for short periods of time, but at heart, Liam loved the ranch and his horses. None of his lady friends wanted to live in Royal permanently. It was too far from the rapid pace of city life.

"I'm out of here," Candace said, slipping her coat off the hook near the kitchen door. "You and Hadley should be able to handle things from here. See you tomorrow." She winked. "Probably for lunch. You'll have your choice of cereal or Pop-Tarts for breakfast."

Grimacing, Liam wished her a good night and returned his attention to Maggie. The greedy child had consumed almost the entire bottle while he'd been talking to Candace. Knowing he should have burped her halfway through, he slung a towel over his shoulder and settled her atop it. Hadley's simple ways of handling Maggie's reflux issues had made a huge difference in the baby's manner. She was much less fussy.

Liam walked around the kitchen, swaying with each stride to soothe the infant. He'd been at this for ten minutes when Hadley entered the room. She'd left her hair down tonight, and the pale gold waves cascaded over the shoulders of her earth-tone blanket coat. The weather had turned chilly and wet in the early evening, and Hadley had dressed accordingly in jeans and a dark brown turtleneck sweater.

"Have you already fed her?" Hadley approached and held her hands out for the baby. She avoided meeting his gaze as she said, "I can take her while you eat."

"Maggie and I are doing fine." The baby gave a little burp as if in agreement. "Why don't you fix yourself a plate while I give her the rest of her bottle? I can eat after you're done."

Hadley looked as if she wanted to argue with him, but at last gave a little nod. "Sure."

While he pretended to be absorbed in feeding Maggie, Liam watched Hadley, thinking about their early-morning encounter and wondering if that accounted for her skittishness. Had he done more while asleep than she'd let on? The thought brought with it a rush of heat. He bit back a smile. Obviously his subconscious had been working overtime.

"Look, about this morning—" he began, compelled to clear the air.

"You were sleeping." Hadley's shoulders drooped. "I intruded. I swear I won't let Waldo get out again."

"Maybe it's not good for him to be cooped up all the time."

"My apartment is pretty small. Besides, you don't like cats."

"What makes you say that?" Liam had no real opinion either way.

Hadley crossed her arms over her chest and gave him the sort of stern look he imagined she'd give a disobedient child. "You suggested I put him in the barn."

"My grandfather never wanted animals in the house, so that's what I'm used to."

"The only time Waldo has been outside was after the house where he lived was destroyed by the tornado. He spent a month on his own before someone brought him to Royal Haven, where I adopted him. He gets upset if I leave him alone too long. That's why I couldn't stay here without bringing him."

Talking about her cat had relaxed Hadley. She'd let down her guard as professional caretaker, and Liam found himself charmed by her fond smile and soft eyes. No wonder she had such a magical effect on Maggie. She manifested a serenity that made him long to nestle her body against his and...

Desire flowed through him, brought on by a year of celibacy and Hadley's beauty. But was that all there was to it? Over the last year, he hadn't been a hermit. Promoting the ranch meant he'd attended several horse shows, toured numerous farms. Every public appearance provided opportunities to test his resolve, but not one of the women he'd met had tempted him like Hadley.

Liam cleared his throat, but the tightness remained. "Why don't you bring him down after dinner so he and I can meet properly and then let him have the run of the house?"

"Are you sure?"

He'd made the suggestion impulsively, distracted by

the direction his thoughts had taken, but it was too late to change his mind now. "Absolutely."

The exchange seemed to banish the last of her uneasiness. Unfortunately, his discomfort had only just begun. Maggie had gone still in his arms, and Liam realized she was on the verge of sleep. Knowing her reflux required her to remain upright for half an hour, he shifted her onto his shoulder and followed Hadley to the kitchen table where he ate most of his meals since his grandfather had died.

"Is something the matter?" Hadley asked. She'd carried both their plates to the table.

"No, why?"

"You're frowning." She sat down across from him. "Do you want me to take Maggie?"

"No, she's fine." In less than a week he'd mastered the ability to hold the baby and do other things at the same time. He picked up his fork. "I was just thinking that I haven't used the dining room much since my grandfather died. Every meal he ate in this house was in there. I find it too big and lonely to use by myself."

"You could eat there with Maggie."

"*We* could eat there with Maggie."

Her eyes widened briefly before she gave a reluctant nod. "Of course, I would be there to take care of Maggie."

Liam didn't think they were on the same page. He'd been thinking of her in terms of companionship. She'd obviously assumed he'd want her as Maggie's caretaker. Or was she deliberately reminding him of their different roles in the household?

"I promised I'd bring Maggie down to the barn tomorrow for a visit. I'd like you to come with us." Now that the DNA results had come back indicating that Maggie was Kyle's daughter, he was eager to introduce her to everyone.

"Of course." Hadley didn't sound overly enthusiastic.

"She's a Wade, which means she's going to be spending a lot of time there."

"Or she may take after…my mother. She left the ranch to pursue a career in real estate and rarely visits." He had no idea what had prompted him to share this about his mother.

"Not everyone is cut out for this life, I suppose."

Or for motherhood. She'd left her sons in the care of their grandfather and hadn't returned more than a handful of times during their childhood. Liam knew it had bothered Grandfather that his only child didn't want anything to do with her family's legacy. As for how Kyle felt, Liam and his brother rarely discussed her.

"You mentioned that you're finishing up your degree. What are your plans for after graduation?"

Hadley smiled. "I've submitted my résumé to several school districts in Houston. That's where my parents live."

"You're not planning on staying in Royal then?"

"I like it here. My best friend and her husband run an accounting firm in town. I'm just not sure there are enough job opportunities in the area for someone just starting out in my field. And I'm an only child. My parents hate that I live so far away."

"What sort of a job are you looking for?" Liam found himself wanting to talk her into remaining in the area.

"School counseling. My undergraduate degree is in teaching, but after a couple years, I decided it wasn't my cup of tea and went back for my master's."

"You're certainly good with children," Liam said. "Any school would be lucky to have you."

While they spoke, Hadley had finished eating. She took charge of Maggie, settling her into the nearby infant seat while Liam finished his dinner. He made short work of Candace's excellent cooking and set both of their plates in the sink.

"Can I interest you in a piece of caramel apple pie? Candace makes the best around."

"Sure." Hadley laughed. "I have a weakness for dessert."

Liam heated both pieces in the microwave and added a scoop of ice cream to each. With Maggie sound asleep, she no longer provided any sort of distraction, and Liam was able to focus his full attention on Hadley.

"I took some video of Electric Slide being worked today. Thought you might be interested in seeing him in action." He pulled up the footage he'd taken with his phone and extended it her way. "Even though he's young, I can already tell he has his mother's work ethic and athleticism. I'd love your opinion on him."

"You're the expert," she reminded him, cupping the phone in her hands.

"Yes, but as I was discussing with my head trainer today, I have too many horses, and I need to figure out which ones I should let go."

"You're thinking of selling him?" She looked up from the phone's screen, her expression concerned.

And with that, Liam knew he'd struck the right chord at last.

Knowing she shouldn't care one way or another what Liam did with his horses, Hadley let her gaze be drawn back to the video of the big chestnut colt racing across the arena only to drop his hindquarters and execute a somewhat sloppy sliding stop. His inexperience showed, but she liked his balance and his willingness.

Lolita had been a dream horse. For two years she and Hadley had dominated as barrel racers and scored several championships in the show ring. During that time she'd had several offers to purchase the mare but couldn't imagine being parted from her.

Until Anna's accident, when everything changed.

"He's a nice colt," she said, making an effort to keep her reply noncommittal. She replayed the video, paying close attention to the horse's action. He looked so much like his mother. Same three white socks. Same shoulder and hip. Same nose-out gesture when he moved from a lope into a gallop. How many classes had she lost before that little quirk had been addressed?

"Maybe you can give him a try when you come to the barn tomorrow."

Her stomach tightened as she contemplated how much fun it would be to ride Lolita's son. But Hadley hadn't been on a horse in ten years, not since Anna had ended up in a wheelchair. Remorse over her role in what happened to her friend had burdened Hadley for a decade. The only thing that kept her from being overwhelmed by guilt was her vow never to ride again. And that was a small sacrifice compared with what Anna was living with.

"I'm afraid I don't ride anymore."

"I'm sure you haven't lost any of your skills."

Hadley found dark amusement in his confidence. She was pretty sure any attempt to swing into a saddle would demonstrate just how rusty she was.

"The truth is I don't want to ride." She didn't think Liam would understand her real reason for turning him down.

"But you might enjoy it if only you got back in the saddle."

The man was as stubborn as he was persuasive, and Hadley wasn't sure how to discourage him without being rude. "I assure you I wouldn't. I was pretty crazy about horses when I was young, but it no longer interests me."

"That's a shame. You were a really talented rider."

Her heart gave a little jump. "I really loved it."

"And it showed. Shannon used to complain about you all the time." Liam's intent gaze intensified his allure. "That's when I started watching you ride, and I figured out why all the other girls lost to you."

"Lolita."

"She was a big part of it, but you rode the hell out of her."

Hadley shook her head. "You said it yourself. Shannon won a lot on Lolita."

"Yeah, but her times never matched yours."

The temptation to bask in Liam's warm regard almost derailed Hadley's professionalism. The man had such a knack for making a woman feel attractive and desirable. But was he sincere? She'd labeled him a player, but maybe she'd done that to keep from being sucked in by his charm. The way he cared about Maggie made Hadley want to give him the benefit of the doubt. And yet he hadn't known he'd gotten her mother pregnant. That didn't exactly illustrate his accountability.

"Does Shannon still own her?" Parting with the mare had been one of the hardest things Hadley had ever done.

"No. She sold her after a couple years."

"How did you end up with one of her foals?"

"A client of mine in California had him."

"And Lolita?" For someone who claimed she was no longer interested in anything horse-related, Hadley was asking a lot of questions. But Lolita had been special, and she wanted to hear that the mare had ended up in a good home.

"I don't know." Her disappointment must have shown because Liam offered, "I can find out."

Hadley waved off his concern. "Oh, please don't bother. I was just…curious."

"It's no problem. Jack is a good friend."

"Really, don't trouble yourself. I'm sure she's doing great." A wave of nostalgia swept over Hadley. She wished she could say she hadn't thought about Lolita for years, but that wasn't at all the case.

Hadley didn't realize she was still holding Liam's phone until it began to ring. The image of a stunning brunette appeared on the screen. The name attached to the beautiful face: Andi. She handed Liam back his phone and rose.

"I'll take Maggie upstairs."

Andi looked like the sort of woman he'd want privacy to talk to. Hadley was halfway up the back stairs before she heard him say hello. She didn't notice the disappointment dampening her mood until she reached the nursery and settled into the rocking chair that overlooked the enormous backyard. What did she have to be down about? Of course Liam had a girlfriend. He'd always had a girlfriend, or probably several girls that he kept on ice for when he found himself with a free night.

And yet he hadn't gone out once since she'd moved into the house. He spent his evenings watching sports in the large den, laptop open, pedigrees scattered on the sofa beside him. Back when she'd been a teenager, she'd spent a fair amount of time poring over horse magazines and evaluating one stallion over another. Although it was a hobby, she liked to think her hours of study had been instrumental in how well she'd done in selecting Lolita.

Until coming to Wade Ranch, Hadley hadn't realized how much she missed everything having to do with horses. The familiar scents of the barn that clung to the jacket that Liam hung up in the entry roused emotions she'd suppressed for a long time. She missed riding. Barrel racing was in turns exhilarating and terrifying. Competing in a Western pleasure class might not be an adrenaline rush, but it presented different challenges. And no matter the outcome, a clean ride was its own reward.

Tomorrow when she took Maggie to the barn to visit Liam, she needed to keep a handle on her emotions. Liam was a persuasive salesman. He would have her butt in a saddle before she knew what was happening. Hadley shook her head, bemused and unable to comprehend why he was so determined to revive her interest in horses.

Could it be that his own passion was so strong that he wanted everyone to share in what he enjoyed? Hadley made a mental note to feel Candace out on the subject tomorrow. That settled, she picked up the book she'd been reading and settled back into the story.

A half hour later, Liam appeared in the doorway. He'd donned a warm jacket and was holding his hat.

"I have to head back to the barn. One of the yearlings got cut up in the paddock today and I need to go check on him." Liam's bright green gaze swept over her before settling on Maggie snuggled in her arms. "You two going to be okay in the house by yourselves?"

Hadley had to smile at his earnest concern. "I think we'll be fine."

"It occurs to me that I've been taking advantage of you." His words recalled their early morning encounter, and Hadley's pulse accelerated.

"How so?" she replied, as calmly as her jittery nerves allowed.

"You haven't had any time off since that first night, and I don't think you were gone more than five hours today."

"I don't mind. Maggie isn't a lot of trouble when she's sleeping, and she does a lot of that. I've been catching up on my reading. I don't have a lot of time for that when I'm in school. Although, I do have my last candle-making class at Priceless tomorrow. We're working with molds. I'd like to make it to that."

"Of course."

Almost as soon as Liam left the old Victorian, Hadley wished him back. Swaddled tight in a blanket, Maggie slept contentedly while Hadley paced from parlor to den to library to kitchen and listened to the wind howl outside. The mournful wail made her shiver, but she was too restless to snuggle on the couch in the den and let the television drown out the forlorn sounds.

Although she hadn't shared an apartment in five years, she never thought of herself as lonely. Something about living in town and knowing there was a coffee shop, library or restaurant within walking distance of her apartment was reassuring. Out here, half an hour from town, being on her own in this big old house wasn't the least bit comfortable.

Or maybe she just wanted Liam to come back.

Five

Promptly at ten o'clock the next morning, Hadley parked her SUV in front of the barn's grand entrance and shut off the engine. She'd presumed the Wade Ranch setup would be impressive, but she'd underestimated the cleverness of whoever had designed the entry. During warmer months, the grass on either side of the flagstone walkway would be a welcoming green. Large pots filled with Christmas boughs flanked the glass double doors. If Hadley hadn't been told she was about to enter a barn, she would have mistaken her destination for a showcase mansion.

Icy wind probed beneath the hem of Hadley's warm coat and pinched her cheeks when she emerged from the vehicle's warmth and fetched Maggie from the backseat. Secure in her carrier, a blanket over the retractable hood to protect her from the elements, the infant wouldn't feel the effects of the chilly air, but Hadley rushed to the barn anyway.

Slipping through the door, Hadley found herself in a forty-foot-long rectangular room with windows running the length of the space on both sides. To her right she glimpsed an indoor arena, empty at the moment. On her left, the windows overlooked a stretch of grass broken up into three paddock areas where a half-dozen horses grazed. That side of the room held a wet bar, a refrigerator and a few bar stools.

On the far end of the lounge, a brown leather couch

flanked by two matching chairs formed a seating area in front of the floor-to-ceiling fieldstone fireplace. Beside it was a doorway that Hadley guessed led to the ranch offices.

Her rubber-soled shoes made no sound on the dark wood floor, and she was glad. The room's peaked ceiling magnified even the slightest noise. She imagined when a group gathered here the volume could rattle the windows.

A woman in her early fifties appeared while Hadley was gawking at the wrought iron chandeliers. They had a Western feel without being cliché. In fact, the whole room was masculine, rugged, but at the same time had an expensive vibe that Hadley knew would appeal to a clientele accustomed to the finer things.

"Hello. You must be Hadley." The woman extended her hand and Hadley grasped it. "I'm Ivy. Liam told me you'd be coming today."

"Nice to meet you." Hadley set the baby carrier on the table in the center of the room and swept the blanket away. "And this is Maggie."

"She's beautiful." Ivy peered at the baby, who yawned expansively. "Liam talks about her nonstop."

"I imagine he does. Having her around has been a huge change for him." Hadley unfastened the straps holding the baby in the carrier and lifted her out. Maggie screwed up her face and made the cranky sounds that were a warm-up for all-out wailing. "She didn't eat very well this morning, so she's probably hungry. Would you hold her for me while I get her bottle ready?"

"I'd be happy to." Ivy didn't hesitate to snuggle Maggie despite the infant's increasing distress. "Liam has been worthless since this little one appeared on his doorstep."

Hadley had filled a bottle with premeasured powdered formula and now added warm water from the thermos she carried. "I think discovering he's a father has thrown him for a loop, but he's doing a fantastic job with Maggie."

"You think he's Maggie's father?"

Something about Ivy's neutral voice and the way she asked her question caught Hadley's attention. "Of course. Why else would Maggie's grandmother have brought her here?" She shook Maggie's bottle to mix the formula and water.

"It's not like Liam to be so careless. May I?" Ivy indicated the bottle Hadley held. "With someone as good-looking and wealthy as Liam, if he wasn't careful, a girl would have figured out how to trap him before this."

"You think Kyle is Maggie's father?"

"That would be my guess."

"But I thought he was based on the East Coast and never came home. Candace told me Maggie's mom was from San Antonio."

Hadley was uncomfortable gossiping about her employer, but reminded herself that Ivy was his family and she'd asked a direct question.

Ivy smiled down at the baby. "She's Kyle's daughter. I'm sure of it."

Any further comment Hadley might have made was forestalled by Liam's arrival. His cheeks were reddened by cold, and he carried a chill on his clothes. Hadley's pulse tripped as his penetrating gaze slid over her. The brief look was far from sexual, yet her body awakened as if he'd caressed her.

"Here are my girls," he said, stopping between Ivy and Hadley. After greeting Maggie with a knuckle to her soft cheek, he shifted his attention to Hadley. "Sorry I wasn't here to greet you, but I was delayed on a call. What do you think of the place so far?"

"Impressive." Warmth poured through her at the inconsequential brush of his arm against hers. "I never expected a ranch to have a barn like this." She indicated the stone fireplace and the windows that overlooked the arena. Staring around the large lounge kept her gaze from lingering on Liam's infectious grin and admiring the breadth of his shoulders encased in a rugged brown work jacket.

"It's been a work in progress for a while." He winked at Ivy, who rolled her eyes at him.

The obvious affection between the cousins didn't surprise Hadley. Liam had an easy charisma that tranquilized those around him. She'd wager that Liam had never once had to enforce an order he'd given. Why bully when charm got the job done faster and easier?

"I imagine a setup like this takes years to build."

"And a lot of convincing the old man," Ivy put in. "Calvin was old-school when it came to horses. He bred and sold quality horses for ranch work. And then this one came along with his love of reining and his big ideas about turning Wade Ranch into a breeding farm."

Liam tossed one of Maggie's burp rags on his shoulder and eased the infant out of Ivy's arms. "And it worked out pretty well," he said, setting the baby on his shoulder. "Come on, let's go introduce this little lady around."

With Liam leading the way through the offices, his smile broad, every inch the proud parent, he introduced Hadley to two sales associates, the breeding coordinator, the barn manager and a girl who helped Ivy three mornings a week.

Hadley expected that her role as Maggie's nanny would relegate her to the background, but Liam made her an active part of the conversation. He further startled her by bringing up her former successes at barrel racing and in the show ring. She'd forgotten how small the horse business could be when one of the salespeople, Poppy Gertz, confessed to rejoicing when Hadley had retired.

"Do you still compete?" Hadley questioned, already anticipating what the answer would be.

"Every chance I get." The brunette was in her midthirties with the steady eye and swagger of a winner. "Thinking about getting back into the game?"

At Hadley's head shake, Poppy's posture relaxed.

"We're going to get her into reining," Liam said, shifting Maggie so she faced forward.

Hadley shook her head. "I'm going to finish getting my masters and find a job as a guidance counselor." She reached out for the infant, but Liam turned away.

"Maggie and I are going to check out some horses." His easy smile was meant to lure her after them. "Why don't you join us." It was a command pitched as a suggestion.

Dutifully she did as he wanted. And in truth, it wasn't a hardship. In fact, her heartbeat increased at the opportunity to see what Wade Ranch had to offer. She'd done a little reading up about Liam and the ranch on the internet and wasn't surprised at the quality of the horses coming out of Liam's program.

They started with the stallions, since their barn was right outside the barn lounge. While Liam spoke in depth about each horse, Hadley let her thoughts drift. She'd already done her research and was far more interested in the way her body resonated with the deep, rich tone of Liam's voice. He paused in front of one stall and opened the door.

"This is WR Dakota Blue." Pride shone in Liam's voice and body language.

"He's beautiful," Hadley murmured.

The stallion stepped up to the door and nuzzled Liam's arm, nostrils flaring as he caught Maggie's scent. An infant her age couldn't clearly see objects more than eight to ten inches away, so Hadley had to wonder what Maggie made of the stallion.

"She isn't crying," Liam said as the horse lipped at Maggie's blanket. "I guess that's a good sign."

"I don't think she knows what to make of him."

"He likes her."

The stallion's gentleness and curiosity reminded her a lot of how Liam had first approached Maggie. Watching horse and owner interact with the infant, something unlocked inside Hadley. The abrupt release of the constriction left her reeling. How long had she been binding her emotions? Probably since she'd shouldered a portion of responsibility for Anna's accident.

"Hadley?" Liam's low voice brought her back to the present. He'd closed the door to the stallion's stall and stood regarding her with concern. "Is everything okay?"

"Yes. I was just thinking how lucky Maggie is to grow up in this world of horses." And she meant that with all her heart. As a kid Hadley had been such a nut about horses. She would have moved into the barn if her parents let her.

"I hope she agrees with you. My brother doesn't share my love of horses." Liam turned from the stall, and they continued down the aisle. "You miss it, don't you?"

What was the point in denying it? "I didn't think I did until I came to Wade Ranch. Horses were everything until I went off to college. I was remembering how much I missed riding and what I did to cope."

"What did you do?"

"I focused on the future, on the career I would have once I finished school."

"I'm not sure I could give up what I do."

Hadley shrugged. "You've never had to." She considered his expression as he guided her through the doors that led into the arena and wondered what it would be like to be him, to never give up something because of circumstances. "Have you ever considered what would happen if you lost Wade Ranch?"

His grin was a cocky masterpiece. "I'd start over somewhere else."

And that summed up the differences between them. Hadley let life's disappointments batter her. Liam shrugged off the hits and lived to fight another day. Which is exactly what drew her to him. She admired his confidence. His swagger. What if she hadn't let guilt overwhelm her after Anna's accident? What if she'd stood up to her parents about selling Lolita and changed her major when she realized teaching wasn't her cup of tea?

"I wish I'd gotten to know you better back when I was racing barrels," she said, letting him guide her toward a narrow wooden observation deck that ran the length of the arena.

He handed over Maggie. "You could have if you hadn't disappeared after my advice helped you win the sweepstakes. You were supposed to thank me by taking me to dinner."

"I thought you were kidding about that." Only she hadn't. She'd been thrilled that he'd wanted to go out with her. But Anna's accident had happened before she had the chance to find out if his interest in her was real. "Besides, I wasn't your type."

"What sort of type was that?"

She fussed with Maggie's sweater and didn't look at him. "Experienced."

Liam took the hit without an outward flinch. Inside he raged with frustration. "I'm not sure any woman has a worse opinion of me than you do." It was an effort to keep his voice neutral.

"My opinion isn't bad. It's realistic. And I don't know why you'd care."

Women didn't usually judge him. He was the fun guy to have around. Uncomplicated. Charming. With expensive taste and a willing attitude. But Hadley wanted more than an amiable companion who took her to spendy restaurants and exclusive clubs. Glib phrases and seduction wouldn't work on her. He'd have to demonstrate substance, and Liam wasn't sure how to go about that.

"I care because I like you." He paused a beat before adding, "And I want you to like me."

Without waiting to see her reaction, he strode across the arena toward the horse being led in by one of the grooms. He'd selected four young horses to show Hadley in the hopes of enticing her to get back in the saddle. Why it was so important to see her ride again eluded him. As always he was just going with his gut.

Liam swung up into the saddle and walked the gelding toward the raised viewing deck. "This is a Blue son. Cielo is three. I think he has a great future in reining. At the moment I personally own eight horses and I need to pare that down to five. I'm going to put him and three others through their paces, and I want you to tell me which you think I should keep and which should go."

Hadley looked appalled. "You can't ask me to do that. I'm no judge."

"When I'm done riding all four you will tell me what you think of each." He bared his teeth at her in a challenging smile. "I value your opinion."

He then spent ten minutes working Cielo through his paces all the while staying aware of Hadley's body language and expression. With Maggie asleep in her arms, Hadley had never looked so beautiful, and Liam had a hard time concentrating on his mounts. After he rode all four horses, he had a special one brought out.

"You might recognize Electric Slide from his video."

Hadley's color was high and her eyes were dancing with delight, but her smile dimmed as he approached with the colt her former mare had produced. "I can't get over how much he looks like his mother."

"Want to give him a try?"

She shook her head. "It's been too long since I've ridden, and I'm not dressed for it."

He recognized a lame excuse when he heard one. She'd worn jeans and boots to the barn and didn't want to admit the real reason for her reluctance.

"Next time." Liam swung into the saddle and pivoted the colt away.

Disappointment roared through him, unfamiliar and unpleasant. He couldn't recall the last time he'd invested so much in a project only to have it fall flat. Was that because he didn't throw himself wholly into anything, or because he rarely failed at things he did? His grandfather would say that if he was consistently successful, he wasn't challenging himself.

Isn't that why he'd quit dating a year ago and refocused on Wade Ranch? He'd grown complacent. The horse business was growing at a steady pace. He enjoyed the companionship of several beautiful women. And he was bored.

Liam's mind was only half on what he was doing as he rode Electric Slide. The pleasure had gone out of the exhibition after Hadley turned down a chance to ride. After a little while, he handed the colt off and strode across the arena toward her.

"It's almost noon," he said. "Let's go back to the house and you can tell me which horses I should keep over lunch."

"Sure."

As they ate bowls of beef stew and crusty French bread, Hadley spelled out her take on each of the horses he'd shown her.

"Cielo is a keeper. But I don't think you'd part with him no matter what anyone said to you."

"You're probably right." He missed talking horses with someone. Since his grandfather died, Liam hadn't had anyone to share his passion with. "What did you think of the bay filly?"

"Nice, but the roan mare is better, and bred to Blue you'd get a really nice foal." Hadley's gaze turned thoughtful as she stirred the stew with her spoon. "I also think you'd be fine letting the buckskin go. He's terrific, but Cielo will be a better reining horse." Her lips curved. "But I'm not telling you anything you hadn't already decided."

"I appreciate your feedback. And you're right. Of the four I showed you, I'd selected three to sell. But your suggestion that I breed Tilda to Blue was something I hadn't considered."

Her smile warmed up the already-cozy kitchen. "Glad I could help. It was fun talking horses. It was something my friends and I did all the time when I was younger. I always imagined myself living on a ranch after I finished school, breeding and training horses."

Liam's chest tightened. Hadley possessed the qualities he'd spent the last year deciding his perfect woman must have. Beautiful, loving, maternal and passionate about horses.

"Of course, that wasn't a practical dream," Hadley continued. "My parents were right to insist I put my education first. I figured that out not long after I started college."

"But what if you could have figured out a way to make it work? Start small, build something."

"Maybe ten years ago I could have." Her voice held a hint of wistfulness. A moment later, all nostalgia vanished. "These days it's no longer what I want."

Her declaration put an end to the topic. Liam held his gaze steady on her for a moment longer, wondering if he'd imagined her overselling her point. Or was he simply wishing she'd consider giving up her future plans and sticking around Royal? He'd grown attached to her in a very short period of time and wanted to see more of her. And not as his niece's nanny.

Liam pushed back from the table. "I have a meeting late this afternoon at the Texas Cattleman's Club, but I'll be back in time for you to make your class at seven."

"Thank you. I really enjoy the class as much for the company as the candle making." She carried their bowls to the sink and began rinsing them. "When I'm in school, I don't have a lot of free time."

"Sounds like you don't make enough time for fun," he said.

"I keep telling myself that I'll have plenty of time to enjoy myself once I'm done with school. In the meantime, I make the most of the free hours I have."

Liam was mulling Hadley's attitude as he strode into the Texas Cattleman's Club later that day. Originally built as a men's club around 1910, the club opened its doors to women members as well a few years ago. Liam and his grandfather had been all for the change and had even supported the addition of a child care center. For the most part, though, the decor of the original building had been left intact. The wood floors, paneled walls and hunting trophies created a decidedly masculine atmosphere.

As Liam entered the lounge and approached the bar, he overheard one table discussing the Samson Oil land purchases. This had been going on for months. Several ranchers had gone bankrupt on the heels of the destructive tornado that had swept through Royal and the surrounding ranches. Many of those who'd survived near financial ruin had then had to face the challenge of the drought that reduced lakes and creeks and made sustaining even limited herds difficult. Some without established systems of watering tanks and pumps had been forced to sell early on. Others were holding out for a miracle that wouldn't come.

"I guess I know what's on the agenda for the meeting

today," Liam mentioned as he slid into the space between his best friend, David "Mac" McCallum, and Case Baxter, current president of the Texas Cattleman's Club. "Has anybody heard what's up with all the purchases?"

Mac shook his head. "Maybe they think there are shale deposits."

"Fracking?" The man on the other side of Mac growled. "As if this damned drought isn't bad enough. What sort of poison is that process going to spill into our groundwater? I've got two thousand heads relying on well water."

Liam had heard similar complaints every time he set foot in the clubhouse. The drought was wearing on everyone. Wade Ranch relied on both wells and a spring-fed lake to keep its livestock watered. He couldn't imagine the stress of a situation where he only had one ever-dwindling source to count on.

"Mellie tells me the property lawyer who's been buying up all the land for Samson Oil quit," Case said. His fiancée's family owned several properties the oil company had tried to buy. "She's gotten friendly with one of her tenants, the woman who owns the antiques store in the Courtyard. Apparently she and Nolan Dane are involved."

"Howard Dane's son?"

"Yes, and Nolan's going back to work with him doing family law."

Liam missed who asked the question, but Case's answer got him thinking about Kyle. That his brother was still out of touch reinforced Liam's growing conviction that Maggie deserved a parent who was there for her 24/7. Obviously as long as he was on active duty, Kyle couldn't be counted on. Perhaps Liam should reach out to an attorney familiar with family law and see what his options might be for taking over custody of his niece. He made a mental note to give the man a call the next morning and set up an appointment.

"Maybe we should invite him to join the club," Liam suggested, thinking how their numbers had dwindled over the last year as more and more ranchers sold off their land.

"I think we could use some powerful allies against Samson Oil," Case said. "Nolan might not be able to give us any information on his former client, but he still has a background in property law that could be useful."

The men gathered in the bar began to move toward the boardroom where that night's meeting was to be held.

"How are things going for you at home?" Mac asked. "Is fatherhood all it's cracked up to be?"

"Maggie is not my daughter," Liam replied, wearying of everyone assuming he'd been foolhardy. "But I'm enjoying having her around. She's really quite sweet when she's not crying."

Mac laughed. "I never thought I'd see you settling down."

"A year ago I decided I wanted one good relationship rather than a dozen mediocre ones." Liam was rather impressed with how enlightened he sounded.

"And yet you've buried yourself at the ranch. How are you any closer to a good relationship when you don't get out and meet women?"

"I've heard that when you're ready, the right one comes along." An image of Hadley flashed through his mind.

Mac's hand settled forcefully on Liam's shoulder. "You're talking like an idiot. Is it sleep deprivation?"

"I have a newborn living with me. What do you think?"

But Liam knew that what was keeping him awake at night wasn't Maggie, but her nanny and the persistent hope that Waldo might sneak into Liam's bedroom and Hadley would be forced to rescue him a second time. Because if that happened, Liam had prepared a very different end to that encounter.

Six

Ivy entered Liam's office with her tablet in hand and sat down. The back of the chair thumped against the wall, and her knees bumped his desk. She growled in annoyance and rubbed her legs. Unbefitting his status as half owner of the ranch, Liam had one of the tiniest offices in the complex. He preferred to spend his days out and about and left paperwork for evenings. When he met with clients, he had an informal way of handling the meetings and usually entertained in the large lounge area or brought them into the barns.

"I'm finalizing your plans for Colorado this weekend," she said, her finger moving across the tablet screen. "The caterer is confirmed. A Suburban will be waiting for you at the airport. Give Hannah Lake a call when you land, and she will meet you at the house."

Ivy kept talking, but Liam had stopped listening. He'd forgotten all about the skiing weekend he was hosting for five of his clients. The tradition had begun several years ago. They looked forward to the event for months, and it was far too late to cancel.

"Liam?" Ivy regarded him with a steady gaze. "You seem worried. I assure you everything is ready."

"It's not that. I forgot that I was supposed to be heading to Colorado in a couple days. What am I going to do about Maggie?"

"Take her along." She jotted a note on the tablet with a stylus. "I'll see if they can set up a crib in one of the rooms."

"Have you forgotten this is supposed to be a guys' weekend? A chance for everyone to get away from their wives and families so they can smoke cigars, drink too much scotch, ski and play poker?"

"Sounds lovely." Ivy rolled her eyes.

Liam pointed at Ivy's expression. "And that is exactly what they want to get away from."

"I don't know what you're worrying about. Bring Hadley along to take care of Maggie. The house is big enough for a dozen people. No one will even know they're there."

Ivy's suggestion made sense, but Liam's instincts rebelled at her assumption that no one would realize they were present. He would know. Just like every other night when she slept down the hall.

"That's true enough, and Maggie is doing better at night. She barely fusses at all before going back to sleep." Liam wondered how much of a fight Hadley would make about flying to Colorado. He got to his feet. It was late enough in the afternoon for him to knock off. He'd been looking forward to spending a little time with Maggie before dinner. "I'd better give Hadley a heads-up."

"Let me know if she has anything special to arrange for Maggie." With that, Ivy exited the office.

Liam scooped his hat off the desk and settled it on his head. As he drove the ten minutes between barns and house, Liam considered the arguments for and against taking Maggie with him to Colorado. In the ten days since his niece had become a part of his life, he'd grown very attached to her. When his brother contacted him, Liam intended to convince him to give the baby up. With the dangerous line of work his brother was in, Maggie would be better off with the sort of stable home environment found here on Wade Ranch.

Liam entered the house and followed the scent of wood smoke to the den. Hadley looked up from her book as Liam entered. "You're home early."

"I came home to spend some time with Maggie." And with her. Had he imagined the way her eyes had lit up upon seeing him? They'd spent a great deal of time together in the last few days. All under the guise of caring for Maggie, but Liam knew his own motives weren't as pure as he'd let on.

"She had a rough afternoon."

She glanced down at the sleeping infant nestled in her arms. Hadley's fond expression hit Liam in the gut.

"She looks peaceful now."

"I only got her to sleep half an hour ago." Hadley began shifting the baby in her arms. "Do you want to hold her?"

"Not yet. I spent most of the day in the saddle. I'm going to grab a shower first."

He rushed through his cleanup and ran a comb through his damp hair. Dressed in brown corduroy pants and a denim shirt, he headed back to the den. The afternoon light had faded until it was too dark for Hadley to read, but instead of turning on the lamps, she was relying on the flickering glow of the fire. Outside, the wind howled, and she shivered.

"Is it as chilly as it sounds?"

"I suspect the windchill will be below freezing tonight."

He eased down on the couch beside her and took the baby. Their bodies pressed against each other hip to knee during the exchange, and Liam smiled as her scent tickled his nose. They'd become a well-oiled machine in the last few days, trading off Maggie's care like a couple in sync with each other and their child's needs. It had given him a glimpse of what life would be like with a family. Liam enjoyed Hadley's undemanding company. She'd demonstrated an impish sense of humor when sharing stories of her fellow nannies' adventures in caretaking, and he was wearing down her resistance to talking about horses by sharing tales of people she used to compete against.

"I have a business trip scheduled in a couple days," Liam began, eyeing Hadley as he spoke. Her gaze was on the baby in his arms.

"How long will you be gone?"

"I rented a house in Colorado for a week, but usually I'm only gone for four days." He paused, thinking how he'd prefer to stay in this cozy triangle with Hadley and Maggie rather than flying off to entertain a group of men. "It's a ski weekend for five of my best clients."

"Are you worried about leaving Maggie here?"

"Yes. I want to bring her along." He paused a beat before adding, "I want you to come, as well." He saw the arguments building in her blue eyes. He already had the answer to her first one. "Candace has offered to take Waldo, so you don't have to worry about him."

"I've never traveled with a client before." She wasn't demonstrating the resistance he'd expected. "Are you sure there will be room for us?"

"The house is quite large. There are seven bedrooms. Ivy is coordinating the trip and said you should let her know about anything you think Maggie might need. She is already making arrangements for a crib."

"When would we leave?"

"We'll fly up in two days. I like to get in a day early to make sure everything is in place. Is that enough time for you to get what you'll need?"

"Sure." But she was frowning as she said it.

"Is something wrong?"

She laughed self-consciously. "I've never seen snow before. What will I need to buy besides a warm coat?"

"You've never seen snow?" Liam was excited at the

thought of being there when Hadley experienced the beauty of a winter day in the mountains.

"For someone as well traveled as you are, that must seem pretty unsophisticated."

Liam considered her comment. "You said you'd never traveled with your clients. Is that because you didn't want to?"

"It's mostly been due to school and timing. I always figured there'd be plenty of time to travel after I graduated and settled into a job with regular hours and paid vacation time."

Her wistful smile gave him some notion of how long and arduous a journey it had been toward finishing her master's degree.

He felt a little hesitant to ask his next question. "Have you flown in a small plane before?"

"No." She drew the word out, her gaze finding and holding his. Anxiety and eagerness pulled at the corners of her mouth. "How small is small?"

Small turned out to be forty feet in length with a forty-three-foot wingspan. Hadley's heart gave a little bump as she approached the elegant six-seat jet with three tiny oval windows. She didn't know what she'd been expecting, maybe a single-prop plane with fixed wheels like the ones used by desperate movie heroes to escape or chase bad guys.

"This doesn't look so scary, does it?" She whispered the question to a sleepy Maggie.

Hadley stopped at the steps leading up to the plane. Liam had gone ahead with her luggage and overnight bag carrying all of Maggie's things. Now he emerged from the plane and reached down to take Maggie's carrier.

"Come on in." Liam's irresistible grin pulled Hadley forward.

She almost floated up the stairs. His charm banished her nervousness, allowing her to focus only on the excitement of visiting Colorado for the first time. Not that she'd see much of it. Her job was to take care of Maggie. But even to glimpse the town of Vail covered in snow as they drove past would be thrill enough.

The plane's interior was luxurious, with room enough for a pilot and five passengers. There were six beige leather seats, two facing forward and two backward as well as the two in the cockpit. She knew nothing about aviation equipment, but the instrument panel placed in front of the pilot and copilot seats had three large screens filled with data as well as an abundance of switches and buttons and looked very sophisticated.

"I set up Maggie's car seat here because I thought you'd prefer to face forward. You'll find bottles of water and ice over there." He pointed to the narrow cabinet behind the cockpit. "There's also a thermos of hot water to make Maggie's bottle."

"Thank you. I made one before we left because it helps babies to adjust to altitudes if they're sucking on something."

"Great. We should be set then."

Hadley settled into her seat and buckled herself in. She looked up in time to see Liam closing the airplane's door.

"Wait," she called. "What about the pilot?"

The grin he turned on her was wolfish. "I am the pilot." With a wink, he slid into the left cockpit seat and began going through a preflight check.

Surprise held her immobile for several minutes before her skin heated and her breath rushed out. For almost two weeks now his actions and the things he'd revealed about himself kept knocking askew her preconceived notions about him. It was distracting. And dangerous.

To avoid fretting over her deepening attraction to Liam,

Hadley pulled out Maggie's bottle and a bib. As the plane taxied she had a hard time ignoring the man at the controls, and surrendered to the anxiety rising in her.

What was she doing? Falling for Liam was a stupid thing to do. The man charmed everyone without even trying.

As the plane lifted off, her stomach dipped and her adrenaline surged. Hadley offered Maggie the bottle and the infant sucked greedily at it. Out the window, land fell away, and the small craft bounced a little on the air currents. To keep her nervousness at bay, Hadley focused all her attention on Maggie. The baby was not the least bit disturbed by the plane's movements. In fact, her eyes were wide and staring as if it was one big adventure.

After what felt like an endless climb, the plane leveled off. Hadley freed Maggie from her car seat so she could burp her. Peering out the window, she saw nothing but clouds below them. With Liam occupied in the cockpit and Maggie falling asleep in her arms, Hadley let her thoughts roam free.

Several hours later, after Liam landed the plane at a small airport outside Vail, their rental car sped toward their destination. When she'd stepped off the plane, Hadley had been disappointed to discover that very little snow covered the ground. She'd imagined that in the middle of January there would be piles and piles of the white stuff everywhere she looked. But now, as they neared the mountains, her excitement began to build once more.

Framed against an ice-blue sky, the snow-covered peaks surrounding the town of Vail seemed impossibly high. But she could see the ski runs that started near the summit and carved through the pine-covered face of each mountain. Liam drove the winding roads without checking the navigation, obviously knowing where he was headed.

"What do you think?"

"It's beautiful."

"Wait until you see the views from the house. They're incredible."

"Do you rent this house every year?"

"A longtime friend of my grandfather owns it."

"I didn't realize you like to ski."

"I had a lot more free time when I was younger, but these days I try to get out a couple times a year. I go to New Mexico when I can get away for a weekend because it's close."

"It must be nice having your own plane so you can take off whenever you want."

"I'm afraid it's been pretty idle lately. I've spent almost ninety percent of my time at the ranch this year."

And the other ten percent meeting Maggie's mother and spending the night with her. Hadley glanced into the backseat where the baby was batting at one of the toys clipped to her car seat.

"You said that's been good for your business," Hadley said, "but don't you miss showing?"

"All the time."

"So why'd you give it up?" From the way Liam's expression turned to stone, she could tell her question had touched on something distasteful. "I'm sorry. I didn't mean to pry. Forget I said anything."

"No, it's okay. A lot of people have asked me that question. I'll tell you what I tell them. After my grandfather died, I discovered how much time it takes to run Wade Ranch."

She suspected that was only half of the reason, but she didn't pry anymore. "Any chance your brother, Kyle, will come back to Texas to help you?"

"No." Liam's answer was a clipped single syllable and discouraged further questions. "I'm finding a balance between ranch business as a whole and the horse side that I love. Last summer I hired a sales manager for the cattle division. I think you met Emma Jane. She's been a terrific asset."

She *had* terrific assets, Hadley thought wryly. The beautiful blonde was memorable for many reasons, not the least of which was the way her eyes and her body language communicated her interest in Liam. That he'd seemed oblivious had surprised Hadley. Since when did a man who enjoyed having beautiful women around not notice one right beneath his nose?

Maybe becoming a father had affected him more than Hadley had given him credit for.

Liam continued, "But it's not like having someone I could put in charge of the entire operation."

Obviously Liam was stretched thin. Maybe that's why he'd been looking so lighthearted these last few days. The break from responsibility would do him good.

Forty minutes after they'd left the airport, Liam drove up a steep driveway and approached a sprawling home right at the base of the mountain.

"We're staying here?" Hadley gawked at the enormous house.

"I told you there was enough room for you and Maggie." He stopped the SUV beside a truck and shot her a broad smile. "Let's get settled in and then head into town for dinner. It's a quarter mile walk if you think Maggie would be okay."

"We can bundle her up. The fresh air sounds lovely." The temperature hovered just above freezing, but it was sunny and there wasn't any wind, so Hadley was comfortable in her brand-new ski jacket and winter boots.

A tall man in his midsixties with an athletic bounce to his stride emerged from the house and headed straight for Liam. "Mr. Wade, how good to have you with us again."

"Hello, Ben." The two men shook hands, and Liam turned to gesture to Hadley, who'd unfastened Maggie from her car seat and now walked around to the driver's side. "This is Ms. Stratton and Maggie."

"Ivy mentioned you were bringing family with you this year. How nice."

The vague reference to family disturbed Hadley. Why couldn't Liam just admit that he had a daughter? He obviously loved Maggie. What blocked him from acknowledging her as his? This flaw in his character bothered Hadley more than it should. But it was none of her business. And it wasn't fair that she expected more of him. Liam was her employer. She had no right to judge.

"Nice to meet you, Ben," she said.

While Liam and Ben emptied the SUV of luggage and ski equipment, Hadley carried Maggie inside and passed through the two-story foyer to the large living room. The whole front of the house that faced the mountain was made up of tall windows.

"There's a nice room upstairs for you and Maggie." Liam came over to where she stood staring at the mountain range. "Ben said he was able to get a crib set up in there."

Hadley followed Liam up a broad staircase. At the top he turned right. The home sprawled across the hillside, providing each bedroom with a fantastic view. The room Hadley and Maggie were to share was at the back of the house and looked west, offering views of both mountains and the town. At four in the afternoon, the sun was sliding toward the horizon, gilding the snow.

"Is this okay?"

"It's amazing." The room was large by Hadley's standards, but she guessed it was probably the smallest the house offered. Still, it boasted a queen-size bed, plush seating for two before the enormous picture window and a stone fireplace that took up most of the wall the bed faced. The crib had been set up in the corner nearest to the door that led to the hall.

"I'm next door in case you need me."

Her nerves trumpeted a warning at his proximity. Not that there was any cause for alarm. She and Liam had been sleeping down the hall from each other for almost two weeks.

Plus, it wasn't as though they would be alone. Tomorrow, five others would be joining them, and from the way Liam described past years, the men would be occupied with cards, drinking and conversation late into the night.

"What time should I be ready to leave for dinner?"

"I think we won't want to have Maggie out late. What if we leave here in an hour?"

"I'll have both of us ready."

With Maggie snug in her new winter clothes and Hadley dressed for the cold night air in a turtleneck sweater and black cords, they came downstairs to find Liam waiting in the entry. He held Hadley's insulated jacket while she slid her feet into warm boots and then helped her into the coat. The brush of his knuckles against her shoulders caused butterflies to dance in her stomach. The longing to lean backward against his strong chest was so poignant, Hadley stopped breathing.

Because she'd had her back to him, Liam had no idea how the simple act of chivalry had rocked her equilibrium. Thank goodness she'd learned to master her facial expressions during her last five years of being a nanny. By the time Liam picked up Maggie's carrier, set his hand on the front door latch and turned an expectant gaze upon her, she was ready to offer him a polite smile.

Liam closed and locked the door behind them and then offered his arm to help Hadley negotiate the driveway's steep slope.

"You have Maggie," she told him, considering how lovely it would be to snuggle against his side during the half-mile walk. "Don't worry about me." She might have convinced him if her boots hadn't picked that second to skid on an icy patch.

"I think I can handle a girl on each arm," he said, his voice rich with laughter.

Hadley slipped her arm through Liam's and let him draw her close. The supporting strength of his muscular arm was supposed to steady her, not weaken her knees, but Hadley couldn't prevent her body from reveling in her escort's irresistible masculinity.

At the bottom of the driveway, Hadley expected Liam to release her, but he showed no inclination to set her free. Their boots crunched against the snow-covered pavement as they headed toward town. Sunset was still a little ways off, but clouds had moved in to blanket the sky and speed up the shift to evening. With her heart hammering a distracting tattoo against Hadley's breastbone, she was at a loss for conversation. Liam seemed okay with the silence as he walked beside her.

The restaurant Liam chose was a cute bistro in the heart of Vail Village. "It's my favorite place to eat when I come here," he explained, holding open the door and gesturing her inside.

The early hour meant the tables were only a third full. The hostess led them to a cozy corner table beside the windows that ran along the street front and offered a wonderful view of the trees adorned with white lights. Above their heads, small halogen lights hung from a rustic beam ceiling. A double-sided stone fireplace split the large room into two cozy spaces. White table linens, candlelight and crystal goblets etched with the restaurant's logo added to the romantic ambience.

"I hope the food is half as good as the decor," Hadley commented, bending over Maggie's carrier to remove the infant from her warm nest before she overheated.

"I assure you it's much better. Chef Mongillo is a culinary genius."

Since becoming Maggie's nanny, Hadley had grown accustomed to the rugged rancher Liam was at home and forgot that his alter ego was sophisticated and well traveled. And by extension, his preferred choice of female companionship was worldly and stylish. This abrupt return to reality jarred her out of her dreamy mood, and she chastised herself for forgetting her role in Liam's life.

Taking refuge behind the tall menu, she scanned the delicious selection of entrees and settled on an ahi tuna dish with artichoke, black radish and egg confit potato. The description made her mouth water. Liam suggested the blue crab appetizer and ordered a bottle of sauvignon blanc to accompany it.

She considered the wisdom of drinking while on duty, but deliberated only a few seconds before her first sip. The crisp white burst on her taste buds and her gaze sought Liam. The glint lighting his eyes was a cross between amusement and appreciation. Heat collected in her cheeks and spread downward.

She spoke to distract herself from the longing his scrutiny awakened. "This is delicious."

"Glad you like it." His deep voice pierced her chest and spurred her heart to race. "I'm really glad you were willing to come along this weekend."

This is not a date.

"Are you kidding? You had me at snow." She tried to sound lighthearted and casual, but ended up coming across breathless and silly. Embarrassed, she glanced away. The view out the window seemed the best place for her attention. What she saw made her catch her breath. "And speaking of snow…"

Enormous white flakes drifted past the window. It was

so thick that it was almost impossible to see the storefronts across the cobblestoned street.

"It's really beautiful. I can see why you come here."

"I arranged the weather just for you." As lines went, it wasn't original, but it made her laugh.

Hadley slanted a wry glance his way. "That was very nice of you."

"And I'm sure the guys will be happy to have fresh powder to ski."

When the waiter brought their appetizer, Liam asked about the weather. "How many inches are you expecting?"

"I've heard anywhere from eight to twelve inches here. More elsewhere. It's a pretty huge system moving across the Midwest."

"That's not going to be good for people trying to get in or out of here."

"No. From what I've heard, the Denver airport is expecting to cancel most if not all of their flights tomorrow. I don't know about Eagle County." Which was where they'd landed a few hours earlier.

"Sounds like we're going to be snowed in," Liam said, not appearing particularly concerned.

Hadley didn't share his nonchalance. "What does that mean for your guests?"

"I'll have to check in with them tonight. They might be delayed for a couple days or decide to cancel altogether depending on how long the storm persists."

"But…" What did she plan to say? If the storm moving in made inbound travel impossible, they certainly couldn't fly out. Which meant she, Maggie and Liam were going to be stuck in Vail for the foreseeable future. Alone.

Hadley focused on the food in front of her, annoyed by her heart's irregular beat. What did she think was going to happen in the next few days? Obviously her hormones thought she and Liam would engage in some sort of passionate affair.

The idiocy of the notion made her smile.

Seven

Liam knew he'd concealed his delight at being snowed in with Hadley, so why was she so distracted all of a sudden? And what was with the smile that curved her luscious lips?

He cleared his throat to alleviate the sudden tightness. "I take it you like blue crab?"

Hadley glanced up, and her eyes widened as she met his gaze. "Yes. It's delicious." Her attention strayed toward the window and the swiftly falling flakes. "It's really magical."

Her dreamy expression startled him. He'd become accustomed to her practicality and was excited that her professional mask might be slipping.

With the snow piling up outside, they didn't linger over dinner. As much as Liam would have enjoyed several more hours of gazing into her eyes and telling stories that made her laugh, they needed to get Maggie home and tucked in for the night. His disappointment faded as he considered that they could continue the conversation side by side on the living room sofa. Without the barrier of a table between them, things could get interesting.

"Ready?" he asked, as he settled the check and stood.

"Sure."

Helping her into her coat gave him the excuse to move close enough to inhale her scent and give her shoulders a friendly squeeze. He hoped he hadn't imagined the slight hitch of her breath as he touched her.

Liam gestured for Hadley to go ahead of him out of the restaurant. They retraced their steps through town, navigating the slippery sidewalk past trees strung with white lights and shop windows displaying their wares. Liam insisted Hadley take his arm. He'd enjoyed the feel of her snuggled against him during the walk into town.

Once the commercial center of the town was behind them, the mountain once again dominated the view. As they strolled along, boots sinking into an inch of fresh snow, Liam was convinced he couldn't have planned a more romantic walk home. The gently falling snow captured them in a world all their own, isolating them from obligations and interruptions.

Hadley laughed in delight as fat flakes melted on her cheeks and eyelashes. He wanted to kiss each one away and had a hard time resisting the urge to take her in his arms to do just that. If not for the weight of Maggie's carrier in his hand, he doubted if he could have resisted.

The strength of his desire for Hadley gave him pause. It wasn't just sexual attraction, although heaven knew his lust flared every time she came within arm's reach. No, it was something more profound that made him want her. The way she took care of Maggie, not as if she was being paid to look after her but with affection and genuine concern for her welfare.

He could picture them as partners in the ranch. She had a great eye when it came to seeing the potential in horses, and he had no doubt if she would just remember how much she enjoyed her days of showing that she would relish being involved with the ranch's future.

Yet she'd demonstrated complete disinterest in the horses, and he had yet to figure out why, when it was obviously something she'd been passionate about ten years earlier. Maybe he should accept that she was planning to leave Royal after she graduated. Plus, she'd invested five years getting a graduate degree in guidance counseling. Would she be willing to put that aside?

"You're awfully quiet all of a sudden," Hadley commented. "Cat got your tongue?"

He snorted at her. "I was just thinking about the girl I met ten years ago."

"Which one? There must have been hundreds." An undercurrent of insecurity ran beneath her teasing.

Liam decided to play it straight. "The only one that got away."

His declaration was met with silence, and for a moment the companionable mood between them grew taut with anticipation. He walked on, curious how she'd respond.

"You can't really mean me," she said at last. "You must have met dozens of girls who interested you where the circumstances or the timing weren't right."

"Probably. But only one sticks out in my mind. You. I truly regret never getting a chance to know you better."

While she absorbed this, they reached the driveway of the house where they were staying and began to climb. In minutes he was going to lose her to Maggie's bedtime ritual.

"Why did you sell Lolita and disappear?"

She tensed at his question. "You asked me before why I was no longer interested in horses. It's the same reason I stopped showing. At that sweepstakes show, my best friend fell during her run. She wanted really badly to beat me, so she pushed too hard and her horse lost his footing. He went down with her under him. She broke her back and was paralyzed."

"I remember hearing that someone had been hurt, but I didn't realize how serious it was."

"After that I just couldn't race anymore. It was my fault that she rode the way she did. If I hadn't... She really wanted to beat me." Hadley let out a shaky sigh. "After it happened she refused to talk to me or see me."

Liam sensed there was more to the story he wasn't getting, but didn't want to push deeper into a sensitive issue. "I don't want to downplay your guilt over what was obviously a tragedy, but don't you think it's time you forgave yourself for what happened?"

Hadley gave a bitter laugh. "My best friend is constantly getting on my case for not letting go of mistakes I've made in the past. She's more of a learn-something-and-move-on sort of a girl."

"Maybe if you start riding again you could put it behind you?"

"I'll think about it."

Which sounded like a big fat *no* to Liam's ears. As soon as they entered the front door, Hadley took Maggie's carrier.

"Thank you for dinner."

"You're welcome."

"I'd better get this one into bed." She paused as if having more to say.

"It's still early. I'm going to bet there's some seriously decadent desserts in the kitchen. Ivy knows my guest John Barr has quite a sweet tooth, and she always makes sure it's satisfied."

"It's been a long day, and I'm dying to finish the mystery I started on the plane. I'll see you in the morning."

Liam watched her ascend the stairs and considered following, but decided if she refused to have dessert with him, she was probably not in the mood for his company. He'd ruined what had been a promising evening by asking about matters that were still painful to her. Well, he'd wanted to get to know her better, and he'd succeeded in that.

Pouring himself a scotch, Liam sat down in front of the enormous television and turned on a hockey game. As he watched the players move about the rink, his thoughts ran to the woman upstairs. Getting to know her was not going to be without its ups and downs. She was complicated and enigmatic.

But Liam hadn't won all his reining titles because he lacked finesse and patience. He thrived on the challenge of figuring out what each horse needed to excel. No reason he couldn't put those same talents to use with Hadley.

He intended to figure out what this filly was all about, and if he was lucky—the news reports were already talking about airport shutdowns all over the Midwest—it looked as though he'd have four uninterrupted days and nights to do so.

After a restless night pondering how some inexplicable thing had changed in her interaction with Liam, Hadley got up early and went to explore the gourmet kitchen. Up until last night she'd characterized her relationship with him as boss and employee. Maybe it had grown to friendship of a sort. They enjoyed each other's company, but except for that time she'd gone to retrieve Waldo from his bedroom—which didn't count—he'd never given her any indication that the physical desire she felt for him was reciprocal.

Because of that, Hadley had been confident she could come on this trip and keep Liam from seeing her growing attraction for him. That was before they'd had a romantic dinner together and then walked home in the snow. Now a major storm system had stalled over the Midwest, stranding them alone in this snowy paradise, and she was in trouble.

"I'm sorry your clients won't make the skiing weekend," she said, her gaze glued to the pan of bacon she was fixing. Nearby a carton of eggs sat on the granite counter; she was making omelets.

"I'm not." Liam's deep voice sounded far too close behind her for comfort. "I'm actually looking forward to spending the time with you."

She should ignore the lure of his words and the invitation she'd glimpsed in his eyes the night before. Hadn't she learned her lesson with Noah? Getting emotionally involved with clients was never smart. She couldn't lie to herself and pretend the only thing she felt for Liam was sexual attraction. Granted, there was a great deal of lust interfering with her clear thinking, but she wasn't the type to lose her mind over a hot guy.

What Liam inspired in her was a complicated mixture of physical desire, admiration and wariness. The last was due to how she wanted to trust his word when he claimed he wasn't Maggie's father. Obviously the man had a knack for making women come around to his point of view. She was back to pondering his apparent sincerity and her susceptibility. What other outrageous lie could he tell her that she would believe?

Liam had propped his hip against the counter beside her and was watching her through narrowed eyes. "What can I help you with?"

"You never offer to help Candace." The statement came out sounding like an accusation.

"I've given up trying. Haven't you noticed she doesn't like anyone interfering in her kitchen?" He reached across her to snag a piece of cooked bacon off the plate where it cooled. His gaze snagged hers as he broke the piece in half and offered part to her. "I'm completely at your disposal. What would you like me to do?"

Hadley told herself there was no subtext beneath his question, but her body had a completely different interpretation. She wanted to turn off the stove and find a use for the kitchen that had nothing to do with cooking.

"I'm going to make omelets. Can you get the ingredients you want in yours from the fridge?"

Liam's lazy smile suggested that he'd heard the uneven-ness of her tone and had an idea he'd put it there. But he didn't push his advantage. Instead, he did as she asked, and Hadley was left with space to breathe and a moment to cool off. Almost immediately she discovered how this had back-fired. The gap between them didn't bring relief from her cravings, but increased her longing for him. She was in a great deal of trouble.

Without asking, he pulled out a cutting board and began chopping onion and tomatoes. Engrossed in the task, he didn't notice her stare. Or that's what she thought until he spoke.

"Candace doesn't work 24/7," he commented, setting a second pan on the six-burner stove and adding olive oil. "I have been known to cook for myself from time to time."

"Sorry for misjudging you."

"You do that a lot."

"Apologize?"

"Jump to negative conclusions about me."

"That's not true."

"Isn't it?" He dumped the diced onions into the pan and stirred them. "From the moment you walked into my house you pegged me as a womanizing jerk who slept with some random woman, got her pregnant and never contacted her again."

She couldn't deny his statement. "I don't think you're a jerk."

"But you think I treat women like playthings."

"It's none of my business what you do."

Liam's breath gusted out. "For the rest of this trip I give you a pass to speak your mind with me. I'm not going to dance around topics while you keep the truth bottled up."

"Fine." Hadley couldn't understand why she was so an-noyed all of a sudden. "Back when I used to show, you had a reputation for going through girls like chewing gum."

"Sure, I dated a lot, and I know that not every girl was happy when I broke things off, but I never treated any of them like they were disposable."

"What do you call sleeping with them once and then never calling again?"

"I never did that. Who said I did?"

"A friend of mine knew someone..." Hadley trailed off. Why hadn't she ever questioned whether what Anna had said about him was true?

Anger faded from Liam's green eyes. "And because she was your friend, you believed her."

Liam shook his head and went back to stirring the onions. While Hadley searched for answers in his expression, he added raw spinach to the pan and set a lid on it.

"We have cheddar and Cojack cheese," Liam said. "Which would you prefer?"

"Cojack." Hadley had finished with the bacon while they'd been talking and began cracking eggs for their omelets. She moved mechanically, burdened by the notion that she'd done Liam a great injustice. "I'll pour some orange juice. Do you want toast? There's some honey wheat that looks good."

"That's fine. I'll finish up the omelets." His neutral tone gave away none of his thoughts, but Hadley moved around the large kitchen with the sense that she was in the wrong.

Instead of eating in the formal dining room, Hadley set the small kitchen table. She paused to stare out the window at the new blanket of snow covering the mountains and gave a small thank-you to the weather gods for giving her and Liam this weekend alone. He was a far more complicated man than she'd given him credit for, and she welcomed the opportunity to get inside his head between now and when they returned to Royal.

A few minutes later, Hadley carried Maggie's carrier to the table and Liam followed her with plates of omelets and the bacon. Awkward silence had replaced their companionable chatter from the previous evening. It was her fault. She'd wounded him with Anna's tale. But whom was she supposed to believe? Her best friend at the time or a man who admitted to *dating* a lot of women?

The delicious omelet was like a mouthful of sand. Hadley washed the bite down with orange juice and wondered what she was supposed to believe. For ten years she'd lived with guilt over the pain her actions had caused Anna. What if none of it had been as her friend said?

"I know you haven't had any reason to believe I've left my playboy ways behind me," Liam began, his own food untouched. "And perhaps I deserve your skepticism, but I'd like to point out that nothing has happened between you and me, despite my strong attraction to you."

"Strong…attraction?" Hadley fumbled out the words, her heart hammering hard against her ribs.

His gaze was direct and intense as he regarded her. "Very. Strong."

What could she say to that? She looked to Maggie for help, but the baby had her attention locked on the string of stuffed bugs strapped to the handle of her carrier and was too content to provide a convenient distraction.

"I wish you weren't," she said at last, the statement allowing her to retreat from a very dangerous precipice.

"That makes two of us. And I have no intention of worsening your opinion of me by doing anything that makes you uncomfortable. I wouldn't bring it up at all except that I wanted to illustrate that I'm done with casual relationships." He picked up his fork and began breaking up his omelet.

"When you say casual relationships…"

"Ones that are primarily sexual in nature." His head bobbed in a decisive nod.

"So you're not…"

"Having sex? No." He gave her a rueful grin. "I haven't been with anyone in a year."

That wasn't possible. "But Maggie…"

"Isn't mine. She's my brother's daughter."

Hadley stared at him, saw that this wasn't a come-on or a ploy. He was completely serious. And she wanted to believe him. Because if he hadn't been with anyone in a year, that meant he might not be the player she'd taken him for. Suddenly, the speed at which she was falling for him was a little less scary than it had been five minutes ago.

"Why haven't you…?"

He took pity on her and answered her half-asked question. "When Grandfather died and I inherited half of Wade Ranch, it suddenly became apparent that the women I'd been involved with saw me as a good time and nothing more."

"And you wanted to be more?" She couldn't imagine Liam being anything less than completely satisfied with who he was, and this glimpse into his doubts made him more interesting than ever.

"Not to be taken seriously bothered me a great deal."

Hadley was starting to see his problem. "Maybe it was just the women in your sphere who felt that way. If you found some serious women, maybe then you'd be taken seriously."

"You're a serious woman." His green eyes hardened. "And you've been giving me back-off vibes from the moment we met."

"But that's because I work for you and what sort of professional would I be if I let myself get involved with my employer?" *Again.* She clung to the final thought. This conversation had strayed too deep into personal territory.

"You won't be working for me forever. What happens then? Does a serious girl like you give me a chance?"

* * *

Liam watched Hadley's face for some sign of her thoughts. Sharing the details of his recent personal crisis had been a risk. She could decide he was playing her. Building up sympathy to wear down her defenses. Or she might write him off as a sentimental fool in desperate need of a strong woman. The thought of that amused him.

"I…don't know."

He refused to be disappointed by her answer. "Then obviously I have my work cut out for me."

"What does that mean?"

"You need to be convinced I'm sincere. I'm up for the challenge."

"Is that what you think? That I need to be convinced I'm wrong about you?" She shook her head in disgust. "I can make up my own mind, thank you."

Torn between admiration and frustration, Liam debated his next words. "I seem to be saying everything wrong today." To his amazement, she smiled.

"I might be harder on you than you deserve. It's really not for me to offer an opinion on your past behavior or judge the decisions you've made." She glanced at Maggie and then fastened serious blue eyes on him. "You're wonderful with Maggie, and that's the man I'd like to get to know better."

In business and horses, this would be the sort of breakthrough he'd capitalize on. But her next words deflated his optimism.

"Unfortunately, you are also my boss, and that's a line I can't cross."

But she wanted to. He recognized regret in her downcast eyes and the tight line of her lips. With the snow still falling, he would have plenty of time to turn her to his way of thinking. The chemistry between them was worth exploring. As were the emotions she roused in him. She wouldn't react well to being rushed, but it appeared he'd have several days with which to nudge her along.

"Any idea how you'd like to spend the day?" he asked. "It's unlikely we'll be dug out any time soon,"

She gestured to the mountain. "I thought you'd be dying to go skiing. Isn't all this new powder a skier's dream?"

How to explain his reluctance to leave her behind? "It's not as much fun alone."

"That makes sense." But her expression didn't match her words.

"You don't look convinced."

"You've never struck me as a man who sits still for long. I can't imagine you'll be happier here than out on the slopes."

"Are you trying to get rid of me for some reason?"

"No. Nothing like that."

"I don't want to leave you and Maggie alone."

"We'd have been alone if your guests showed up. No reason anything has to be different."

Except that it was. This was no longer a business trip. It had morphed into a vacation. And Liam had very different expectations for how he'd like to spend his time.

That night's dinner had been arranged for six, but since it was beef medallions in a red wine sauce with mushrooms, herb-roasted potatoes and creamed spinach, it had been a simple matter for the chef to make only two portions.

With the chandelier lights dimmed and flickering candlelight setting a romantic scene, the tension kept rising between them. Liam had dated enough women to recognize when a woman was attracted to him, but he'd never known one as miserable about it as Hadley.

"You are obviously uncomfortable about something," he commented, breaking the silence that had grown heavier since the chef had presented them with dessert and left for the night.

"Why would you say that?"

"Because you are as jumpy as a filly being stalked by a mountain lion."

Her brows drew together. "That's ridiculous."

"What's on your mind?" he persisted, ignoring her protest. When she pressed her lips together and shook her head, he decided to talk for her. "Let me guess. Since you started acting all skittish shortly after learning we were going to be snowed in alone together, you think I'm going to seduce you." Liam sipped his wine and observed her reaction.

"I don't think that."

He could see that was true. So what gave her cause for concern? "Oh," he drew the word out, "then you're worried you're going to try to seduce me."

One corner of her mouth lifted in a self-deprecating grin. "As if I could do that." She had visibly relaxed thanks to his bluntness.

"You aren't giving yourself enough credit."

She rolled her eyes, but refrained from arguing. "I thought you'd given up casual sex."

"I have. Which should make you feel more relaxed about our circumstances." He set his elbows on the table and leaned forward.

"Okay, maybe I'm a little on edge."

"What can I do to put you at ease?"

"Nothing. It's my problem."

"But I don't want there to be a problem."

"You really aren't going to let this go, are you?"

He shook his head. "What if I promise that whatever you say will not be held against you after we leave here?" He spread his arms wide. "Go ahead, give me your best shot."

"It's awkward and embarrassing."

She paused as if hoping he'd jump in and reassure her again. Liam held his tongue and tapped his chest to remind her he could take whatever she had to dish out.

"I'm attracted to you, and that's making me uncomfortable, because you're my boss and I shouldn't be having those sorts of feelings for you."

He'd been expecting something along those lines and wished she wasn't so damned miserable about feeling that way. "See, that wasn't so hard. I like you. You like me."

"And nothing can happen between us."

"If that's what you really want." If that was the case, he would respect her decision. But nothing would convince him to like it.

"It is." Her expression closed down. "I made a mistake once, and I promised myself I'd never do anything like that ever again."

"You are too hard on yourself. Everyone screws up. You shouldn't beat yourself up about it."

"That's what my best friend tells me."

"Sounds like a smart friend." Liam dropped the subject. Asking her to confide in him would only cause her to shut down, and he didn't want that to happen. "What should we do after dinner? We could watch a movie. Or there's board games stored in the front closet if you think you can best me at Monopoly or backgammon."

"You don't really want to play either of those, do you?"

"Not really."

"I suppose if you were entertaining clients, you'd go out to a bar, or if you didn't have the energy for that after a full day of skiing, you'd sit around drinking scotch and smoking cigars."

"Something like that." Neither of those activities sounded like much fun while his thoughts were filled with Hadley's soft lips yielding beneath his and the wonders of her generous curves pressed against his body. Gripped by a fit of restlessness, Liam pushed back from the table. "You know, I think I'll head into town and grab a drink. Don't wait up. It'll probably be a late night. I'll see you tomorrow."

Eight

Hadley sat in miserable silence for several minutes after the front door closed behind Liam, cursing her decision to push him away. Was it fair that doing the right thing made her unhappy? Shouldn't she be feeling wretched only after acting against her principles?

With a disgusted snort, Hadley cleared the dessert dishes from the table and set them in the sink. With a lonely evening stretched out before her, she puttered in the kitchen, washing the plates and wineglasses, wiping down the already-immaculate counters and unloading the dishwasher.

None of these tasks kept her thoughts occupied, and she ran her conversation with Liam over and over in her head, wishing she'd explained about Noah so Liam would understand why it was so important that she maintain a professional distance.

After half an hour she'd run out of tasks to occupy her in the kitchen and carried Maggie upstairs. The baby was almost half-asleep and showed no signs of rousing as Hadley settled her into the crib. For a long time she stared down at the motherless child, her heart aching as she contemplated how fond she'd become of the baby and realized that the end of January was fast approaching.

Soon she wouldn't have to worry over Maggie's welfare. Liam would find another nanny. It shouldn't make her heart ache, and yet it did. Hadley began to pace the comfortable guest room. Once again she'd let her heart lead instead of her head. Nor was it only her charge who had slipped beneath her skin. Liam had skirted her defenses as well. Earlier that day she'd accepted that Liam wasn't Maggie's father, but yet he'd demonstrated a willingness to step up and raise his niece, and that said a lot about his character.

Hadley stopped to peer out the window but could see nothing but fat white flakes falling past the glass. The day she'd driven up the driveway to the ranch house, she'd never dreamed that the crush she'd developed on him a decade earlier might have been lying dormant all these years. Born of hero worship and adolescent fantasies, it shouldn't have survived all the life lessons Hadley had learned. Her guilt over the role she'd played in Anna's accident, her poor judgment with Noah, the financial consequences of choosing the wrong career. All of these should have made her incapable of acting foolishly.

So far they had.

But that was before Liam Wade reentered her life. Before, she couldn't think about the man without longing to fall into bed with him, ignoring all consequences for the chance to be wildly happy for a few hours.

The baby made a sound, and Hadley went to make sure she was still asleep. Over the past week, Maggie had grown more vocal as she slept.

Hadley settled a light blanket over the baby, knowing she was fussing for no good reason. She still couldn't calm the agitation that zinged along her nerves in the aftermath of turning aside Liam's advances during dinner.

"I should have just slept with him," she murmured, the declaration sounding unbearably loud in the silent house. Then at least she'd have a good reason to regret her actions.

"It's not too late to change your mind," a low male voice said from the doorway.

Startled, Hadley whirled in Liam's direction. Heat seared her cheeks as she spotted him lounging against the door jam, an intense gleam in his half-lidded eyes. "I thought you went out."

"I did, but it wasn't any fun without you." He advanced toward her, his intent all too clear.

When his arms went around her, pulling her tight against his strong body, Hadley stopped resisting. This is what she wanted. Why fight against something that felt this right?

"Kiss me quick before I change my mind," she told him, her head falling back so she could meet his gaze. "And don't stop."

She laced her fingers through his hair as his mouth seized hers. Nerve endings writhing like live electric wires, she lost all concept of gravity. Up. Down. Left. Right. Without Liam's arms anchoring her to him, she would have shot into space like an overheated bottle rocket.

After the first hard press of his lips to hers, Liam's kiss gentled and slowed. He took his time ravishing her mouth with a bit of pressure here and a flick of his tongue there. Hadley panted in a mix of excitement and frustration. He'd been so greedy for that first kiss. She'd expected what followed would be equally fast and demanding.

"Your lips are amazing," he murmured, nipping at her lower lip. "Soft. Pliant. I could spend all night just kissing you."

Pleasure speared downward as his tongue dipped into the shallow indents left behind by his tender bite. "Other parts of me are just as interesting." She arched her back and rubbed her breasts against his chest, hoping he'd take the hint and relieve their ache.

"I imagine you will provide an unlimited source of fascination." He nuzzled his lips against her neck and bracketed her hips with his long fingers, pulling her against his erection. "Shall we go to my room and see?"

"Oh yes."

He surprised her by scooping her into his arms and carrying her next door. He set her on her feet in the middle of the dark room and pushed her to arm's length.

"I'm going to turn on the fireplace so we have some light. Then I'm going to take off your clothes and spend the rest of the night pleasuring every inch of your body."

His words left her breathless and giddy. "That sounds great," she replied, reaching out to the footboard for balance. "But I demand equal time to get to know you."

White teeth flashed in the darkness as he shot her a wolfish smile. "I love a woman who knows what she wants."

While he crossed to the enormous stone fireplace, Hadley took advantage of his back being turned to strip off her sweater and shimmy out of her black stretch pants. Clad only in a pale blue camisole and bikini briefs, she shivered in anticipation. The gas fireplace lit with a *whoosh*, and Liam turned back to her as flames began to cast flickering shadows around the room. In the dimness, his eyes seemed impossibly bright as his gaze traveled over her.

"You are gorgeous."

Although his tone gave the words a sincerity she appreciated, Hadley doubted she measured up to the women he'd been with in the past. "So are you." A sudden rush of shyness made her sound flip, but Liam didn't seem to notice.

He held out his hand. "Come here."

She couldn't have resisted his command even if her feet had been glued to the floor. More than anything she wanted his hands on her.

Together they stripped off his sweater and the long-sleeve shirt beneath. Firelight highlighted the perfection of his arms, shoulders and abs as her fingers trailed along his hot, silky skin.

"You have such an amazing body," she murmured, marveling at the perfection of every hard muscle. "I'm a little worried that you'll be disappointed in me."

He chuckled. "You have nothing to fear. You are beautiful in every way."

As if to demonstrate that, his hands began to slide upward, catching the hem of her camisole and riding it from her hips to her ribs. Hadley closed her eyes to better savor the magic of his palms gliding over her skin and threw her head back as he reached her breasts, cupping them briefly before sweeping the camisole over her head.

"I was right," he murmured, dropping to his knees to press a kiss to her abdomen.

Hadley quaked as his mouth opened and he laved her skin from belly button to hip. With his head cupped in her hands, she fought to maintain her balance as his fingers hooked in her panties and rode them down her legs. With one knee he nudged her feet apart, and she shut her eyes as his fingers trailed upward, skimming the sensitive inside of her thighs until he reached the spot where she burned.

As his fingers brushed against her pubic hair, she cried out in surprise. He'd barely touched her, and her insides were tense and primed to explode.

"You like that." He wasn't asking a question. "What about this?"

With one finger he opened her and slipped into her wetness. Hadley gasped as pleasure hammered her. Her knees began to shake, threatening to topple her.

"I can't...stand."

He cupped her butt in his hands and steadied her. "I've got you, baby. Just let go."

Her knees buckled, and Liam guided her downward and just a little forward so she ended up straddling his thighs, her breasts flattened against his hard chest. He cupped her head in his hand and brought their lips together once more. This kiss, deep and hungry, held none of the gentle restraint he'd shown earlier. It was a demonstration of his passion for her, and she was enthralled by his need.

"You need to get naked," she gasped as he rolled her beneath him on the thick, fluffy throw rug.

"Soon."

His mouth trailed moisture down her neck and over the upper curve of her breast. As delicious as it was to be slowly devoured by him, the desire clawing at her was building to a painful crescendo. She writhed beneath him, her sensitive inner thighs rasping against his soft corduroy pants as she lifted her knees to shift him deeper into the cradle of her hips.

"Oh, Liam. That's so good."

He'd taken one nipple into his mouth, and the erotic tug sharpened her longing. She ached to feel him buried inside her. Her nails bit into his sides, breath coming in shallow pants as he rocked his hips and drove his erection against her.

When she slipped her hands between them and went for the button that held his trousers closed, he caught her wrists and raised her arms over her head.

"Patience," he murmured before turning his attention to her other breast.

She thrashed her head from side to side as sensation overwhelmed her. Trapped as she was beneath him, Hadley was still able to rotate her hips and grind herself against his hard length. Liam groaned and his lips trailed down her body.

It had never been this good before. Fire consumed her at Liam's every kiss. His hot breath skated across her sensitive flesh. Suddenly her hands were free. Liam continued to slide lower; his shoulders shifted between her thighs, spreading her wide. He grazed his fingertips across her nipples, ripping a moan from her.

Before she'd even registered the pleasure of his large hands cupping her breasts, he dipped his tongue into her hot wet core and sent her spiraling into orbit. Anticipation had been gnawing on her all day, and Liam's expert loving drove her fast and hard into her first orgasm. As it ripped through her, Hadley panted his name. His fingers dug into her backside, holding her tight against his mouth as she shuddered and came in what felt like endless waves of pleasure.

"Nice," she murmured. "Very, very, very nice."

Once her body lay lifeless in the aftermath of her climax, Liam dropped a light kiss on her abdomen and left her to strip off the rest of his clothes. Despite the lack of strength in her limbs, Hadley struggled up onto her elbows to better watch his gorgeous body emerge.

She was awed by his broad shoulders, bulging biceps, washboard abs, but when he stripped off his trousers and she got a glimpse of his strong thighs and the spectacular chiseling of his firm butt, she forgot how to breathe. His erection sprang out as he peeled off his underwear, and her gaze locked on its rigid length.

She licked her lips.

"Do that again and this won't last long," Liam growled as he withdrew a condom from his wallet and made quick work of sliding it on.

She raised an eyebrow. "You're prepared?"

"I've been prepared since the day you walked into my house."

His impassioned declaration made her smile. She held out her arms to him and he lowered himself onto her. Almost immediately the tip of him found where she needed him most, but he held back and framed her face with his hands.

"I don't take this next step lightly," he told her, showing way more restraint than Hadley could manage at the moment.

As much as she appreciated what he was trying to communicate about the depth of his desire for her, she shied away from letting his affirmation into her heart. If this wasn't about two people enjoying an enormous amount of sexual chemistry, she might lose herself to the fantasy that they had a future. Where Liam was concerned, she had to maintain her head.

But all perspective was lost as he kissed her. Not waiting for him to take charge, she drove her tongue into his mouth and let him taste her passion and longing. Something in her soul clicked into place as she fisted her hands in his hair and felt him slide into her in one smooth stroke.

They moaned together and broke off the kiss to pant in agitated gasps.

"Like that," she murmured, losing herself in Liam's intense gaze. She tipped her hips and urged him deeper. "Just like that."

"There's more," he promised, beginning to move, sliding out of her with delicious deliberation before thrusting home.

"That's…" She lost the words as he found the perfect rhythm.

And then it was all heat and friction and a rapidly building pressure in her loins that demanded every bit of her attention. Being crushed beneath Liam's powerful body as he surged inside her was perhaps the most amazing experience of Hadley's life. She'd never known such delirious joy. He was passionate, yet sensitive to her body in a way no one had ever been before.

The beginnings of a second orgasm caught her in its grip. Liam continued his movements, driving her further and further toward fulfillment without taking his own. In a blurry part of her mind, she recognized that and dug her fingers into his back.

"Come with me," she urged, closer now.

"Yes."

At his growl she began to break apart. "Now."

His thrusts grew more frantic. She clung to him as wave after wave of pleasure broke over her. Liam began to shudder as he reached his own climax. She thought she heard her name on his lips as a thousand pinpoints of light exploded inside her. He was everything to her, and for a long, satisfying moment, nothing else mattered.

The weather cleared after thirty-six hours, but neither Liam nor Hadley looked forward to heading back to Texas when the airports reopened. What had happened between them was too new, its metamorphosis incomplete. Liam dreaded the return to reality. The demands of the ranch were sure to overwhelm him, and he wanted more time alone with Hadley.

The wheels of the Cessna Mustang touched down on the Royal airport runway and a sense of melancholy overwhelmed Liam. He sighed as he came in sight of his hangar. The last four days had been perfect. The solitude was exactly what he'd needed to break through Hadley's shell and reach the warm, wonderful woman beneath.

She was funny and sensual. He'd loved introducing her to new foods and wines. She'd matched his ardor in bed and demonstrated a curiosity that amused him. Once she'd let loose, she'd completely mesmerized him. He hadn't been able to get enough of her. And when they were too exhausted to move, he'd held her in his arms and enjoyed the peaceful sounds of her breathing.

He'd never felt in tune with a woman like this. Part of it was likely due to the year off he'd taken to reevaluate his priorities. Hadley was the package. She captivated him both in and out of bed and let him know pretty fast that his past practices in dealing with women weren't going to work on her. He had to be original. She deserved nothing but his best.

Maggie fussed as he locked up the plane. She hadn't slept much on the way home and was probably overtired. He watched Hadley settle the baby into the car seat and sensed the change in the air. Hadley's expression had grown serious, and her eyes lost their infectious sparkle. Playtime was over. She was back on the job.

"She's going to be fine as soon as she gets home and settled into her crib," Hadley said, coaxing the baby to take her pacifier.

"Maybe you should spend the night in case she doesn't settle down."

Hadley shook her head. "I'll stay until you get back from checking in at the ranch, but I can't stay all night."

"Not even if I need you?"

"You'll do just fine without me."

He wasn't sure if she had missed his meaning or if she was pretending not to understand that he wanted her to spend the night with him. Either way, she'd put enough determination behind her declaration to let him know no amount of persuasion was going to change her mind.

"I'm going to miss you," he said, trying a different approach.

"And I'm going to miss you," she replied, her voice brisk and not the least bit romantic. "But that was Colorado and this is Texas. We had a nice time, but it's over."

To Liam's shock, he realized he was back to square one. "I think it takes two people to decide it's over."

"You're my boss. We just need to get things back to normal."

"Or we need to change what normal is."

She didn't look happy. "I'm not sure what you mean."

"We made a great start getting to know each other these last few days. I'd like to continue."

"I don't feel comfortable in that sort of arrangement."

"Then why don't you quit?" He would not fire her. She needed to choose to be with him. "If it's about the money, I'll pay you until the end of the month."

Her mouth popped open, but before she could speak, Maggie let loose a piercing wail. "Why don't we talk about this later? I really think Maggie needs to get home."

Liam agreed, but hated the idea of postponing the conversation. He wanted to batter her with arguments until she came around to his point of view. Giving her space to think would only give her space to fortify her defenses.

"Fine. But we will talk later."

Only they didn't. By the time Liam returned from the ranch offices, it was close to midnight. Hadley was half-dead on her feet, only just having gotten Maggie to sleep after a rough evening. She was in no condition to listen to his arguments for continuing what they'd begun in Colorado, and he had to watch in frustrated silence as she put Waldo in his carrier and drove away.

With disappointment buzzing in his thoughts like a pesky fly, he expected sleep to elude him. But he'd underestimated his own weariness and shortly after his head hit the pillow, he fell asleep.

When the dream came, it didn't feature Hadley, but his mother. They stood in the ranch house's entry hall and he was desperately afraid. She was leaving. He clung to her hand and begged her not to go. She tugged hard against his grip, her face a mask of disgust.

"Mommy, don't go."

"Why would I want to stay with you? I left because I couldn't bear to be trapped in this prison of a ranch in the middle of nowhere."

"But I need you."

"I never wanted to be a mother. You and your brother were a mistake."

She ripped free and strode through the front door without ever looking back. Liam followed her, but it was as if he moved through mud. His short legs couldn't propel him fast enough, and he reached the broad wraparound porch just in time to see her taillights disappear down the driveway.

Liam woke in a sweat. His throat ached and heart pounded as he recalled his mother's words. As realistic as the exchange had felt, he recalled no such event from his childhood. His subconscious had merely been reacting to Hadley's evasiveness. So why hadn't his dream featured her?

Lingering pain carved up his chest. He felt weak and unsteady. A child's fear pummeled him. Buried deep in his mind was the horror of being rejected by his mother. She was supposed to love him and care for him. Instead, she'd demonstrated no remorse when she'd abandoned her sons to pursue her real estate career.

And it was this defining fact that had caused him to never fully invest himself in romantic relationships. He couldn't bear the idea of giving his heart to a woman only to have her choose something else over him. Deep down, what he craved was lasting love.

His heart had led him to Hadley. And given the timing of his dream, his subconscious was worried that he'd made a huge mistake.

Hadley was in the nursery folding a freshly laundered basket of Maggie's clothes when Liam appeared. He'd been subdued and circumspect around her the last couple days, and she suspected she'd done too good a job convincing him that what had happened between them in Vail had been a singular event never to be repeated.

But that wasn't at all what she wanted. She was pretty

sure she'd fallen in love with him during those four days. And that left her in a quandary.

"I know it's short notice," he said. "But will you be my date for the grand reopening of Royal Memorial's west wing tomorrow night?"

The word *date* caused a spike in Hadley's heartbeat. She told herself to stop being stupid.

"Sure. What time should I have Maggie ready?"

"Not Maggie." His green eyes pierced her facade of professionalism. "You. It's a cocktail party complete with adult beverages, finger food and fancy duds." He kept his voice light, but his expression was stony.

"Of course I'll go with you." She matched his tone, kept her glee hidden. "I've heard wonderful things about the new wing. You and the other members of the Texas Cattleman's Club were instrumental in raising the funds that enabled the restoration to move forward, weren't you?"

"We felt it was important for the community to get the hospital back to one hundred percent as soon as possible." He took her hand, threaded his fingers through hers. "How about I pick you up at seven?"

Her brain short-circuited at the way he was staring at their joined hands. As if the simple contact was at once comforting and a puzzle he couldn't figure out.

"Sure." Before she recognized what she planned to do, Hadley stepped into Liam's space and lifted onto her toes to plant a kiss on his lips.

All day long she'd been thinking about how much she wanted to be in his arms. Not to feel the stirring passion of his lovemaking, but the heart-wrenching bliss of their connection, which consisted of both sexual and spiritual components. The blend was different from anything she'd ever known, and she'd begun to neglect her defenses.

Liam brought their clasped hands to his chest and slid his free hand beneath her hair to cup her head. He explored her lips with tantalizing pressure, giving her the merest taste of passion. Although she'd initiated the kiss, she was happy to let him set the pace.

When at last his lips lifted from hers, they were both breathing unsteadily.

"I've been thinking about kissing you all day," he murmured, lips trailing over her ear, making her shudder. "I can't concentrate anymore. The entire ranch staff thinks I've lost my mind."

His words excited a flurry of goose bumps. "It's that way for me, too. I forgot to put a diaper back on Maggie before I put her back in her Onesie this morning. And then I made her bottle and put it into the cupboard instead of the container of formula."

"Will you stay at the ranch tomorrow night after the party?"

She wanted to very much, but would this interfere with her determination not to get emotionally involved? "If you wish."

"I very much wish."

"Then that's what I'll do."

Nine

Liam wasn't sure how he was going to make it through the grand opening, when all he could think about was what he had to look forward to afterward. He pulled his truck into a visitor space at Hadley's apartment building and stepped out. For tonight's event he'd exchanged denim and plaid in favor of a custom-tailored charcoal suit.

Anticipation zipped along his nerve endings as he pushed the button in the entry vestibule that would let Hadley know he'd arrived. Her voice sounded distorted as she told him to come up. Her apartment was on the second floor. He stepped into the elevator, feeling the give of the cables as it adjusted to his weight. The building had obviously seen a lot of tenants, because it showed wear and tear in the carpets, layers of paint and light fixtures.

Standing before Hadley's door, Liam paused to assess his state of agitation. Had he ever been nervous going to pick up a woman for a date? Yet here he stood, palms sweating, heart thundering, mouth dry.

The door opened before he lifted his hand to knock. Hadley looked surprised to see him standing in the hallway. Waldo rushed forward to wind himself around Liam's legs.

"Hi." She gestured him in. "I thought maybe the elevator had decided to be fussy again."

He picked up the cat without taking his eyes from Hadley and stepped into her apartment. "You look beautiful."

She wore a figure-skimming sleeveless black dress with a round neckline and a half-circle cutout that bared her cleavage. Despite there being nothing overtly provocative about the style, Liam thought she looked incredibly sexy. She'd pinned her blond waves up in a complicated hairstyle that looked as if it could tumble onto her shoulders at any second. And he badly wanted to make that happen. Body alive with cravings better reserved for later that evening, he shifted his gaze to her only jewelry, a pair of long crystal earrings that swung in sassy rhythm as she tipped her head and regarded him curiously.

"Thank you." Her half smile captivated him. "You look nice, as well. I'll grab my purse and we can get going." She picked up a small black clutch and a sheer red scarf sparkling with clusters of sequins that she draped over her shoulders. It added a flamboyant touch to her otherwise monochrome black ensemble.

Realizing he was staring at her like a smitten teenager, Liam cleared his throat. His brain was having trouble summoning words. "All set?"

"Are you expecting a large crowd tonight?" she asked as she fit her key into the lock and set the dead bolt.

"About a hundred. Those responsible for coordinating the fund-raising efforts and the largest contributors."

"What a wonderful thing you've done."

Her glowing praise lightened his step. He laced his fingers through hers and lifted her hand to brush a kiss across her knuckles. "It was a group effort," he said, feeling unusually humble. "But thank you."

In truth, he was proud of the work he and the other members of the Texas Cattleman's Club had done in the aftermath of the tornado. As leaders in the community, they'd banded together during the time of crisis and although progress had been slow, they'd restored the town to its former state.

The drive from Hadley's apartment to the hospital took ten minutes. Liam filled the time with a description about an outfit his cousin Ivy had bought for Maggie that featured a chambray Onesie with three tiers of ruffles and a crocheted cowboy hat and boots.

"Complete with yarn spurs." Liam shook his head in mock dismay.

"How adorable." Hadley regarded his expression with a wry smile. "You are just going to have to get used to the fact that girls love to dress up and look pretty."

"I know," he grumbled, knowing she loved to scold him. "But is it really going to be all frilly stuff and hair bows?"

"Yes."

Liam pulled to a stop in front of the hospital's new west wing entrance, and the look he gave Hadley made her laugh. A year ago he never would have imagined himself discussing an infant's wardrobe, much less with a beautiful woman.

A valet opened the passenger door and helped Hadley out of the truck. Liam was grinning as he accepted the ticket from the uniformed attendant and caught up with Hadley, sliding his hand over her hip in a not-so-subtle show of ownership. She sent him an unguarded smile of such delight, his chest hurt. If this was heartache, bring it on.

"This is amazing," Hadley murmured as they entered the spacious lobby of the redesigned west wing, taking in the patterned marble floors and triangular glass ceiling over the entrance. In the center of the room, a bronze statue of a cowboy roping a running cow had the names of all those who'd lost their lives during the tornado etched around the base. "A wonderful tribute."

Spying Case Baxter, Liam drew Hadley toward the rancher, who had eyes only for the redhead beside him.

"Case," Liam called to gain his attention.

The president of the Cattleman's Club looked away from his fiancée and blinked as if to reorient himself. At last his gaze focused on Liam.

"Hey, Liam." His teeth flashed as he extended his hand to meet Liam's. "Mellie, you've met Liam Wade."

"Of course." A friendly smile curved her lips. Her green eyes darted toward Hadley before settling back on Liam. "At the reception when Case was elected president."

"And this is Hadley Stratton." Liam didn't explain how they knew each other. Why introduce her as Maggie's nanny when she'd become so much more? "Mellie Winslow and Case Baxter, our club president."

The two couples finished exchanging greetings and Case spoke. "Gotta hand it to you, Liam." He gestured around, his grin wide, posture relaxed. "This is one hell of a facility."

"Have you toured the neonatal unit?" Mellie asked.

"We just arrived," Hadley admitted, completely at ease tucked into the half circle of Liam's left arm. After their conversation in Vail, he'd half expected her to balk at going public with their developing relationship.

"The whole wing is really terrific," Mellie was saying, "but that unit in particular is very impressive."

Liam agreed. He'd seen the neonatal facility during his many trips to the hospital in his role as chairman of the fund-raising committee, but he was looking forward to showing it to Hadley.

"Why don't we head up now," he suggested, seeing Hadley's interest. There would be plenty of time later to catch up with Mac, Jeff Hartley and other members of the Texas Cattleman's Club. "We'll catch up with you later," he told Case.

"They seem like a nice couple," Hadley commented as they waited for the elevator that would take them to the maternity ward on the fourth floor.

"I don't know Mellie all that well, but Case is a great guy and they appear happy."

The elevator doors opened, and Liam gestured Hadley ahead of him.

Despite the crowd gathered to party in the lobby, they had the elevator to themselves. As soon as the car began to move, Liam tugged Hadley into his arms and dropped his lips to hers.

The instant Liam kissed her, Hadley wrapped her arms around his neck and yielded to his demand. Frantic to enjoy the few seconds of isolation, they feasted on each other. But all too soon, a *ding* announced that they'd reached their floor, cutting short their impassioned embrace.

"Damn these modern elevators," Liam muttered, his hands sliding off her body.

Hadley, her cheeks hot in the aftermath of the kiss, smiled foolishly. She surveyed his chiseled lips, searching for any sign that her red lipstick had rubbed off. Taking the hand Liam offered her, she stepped past a tour group that was waiting to head downstairs.

"Let's see if we can catch that tour," he said, tugging her down the hallway toward a group of well-dressed guests listening to a tall, handsome man in his late thirties.

"Next is our neonatal unit," the man said, gesturing down the hall as he started forward.

"That's Dr. Parker Reese," Liam explained, tucking Hadley's hand into the crook of his arm. "He's a neonatal specialist. Brilliant guy. We're lucky to have him."

It was hard to focus on Dr. Reese's description of the neonatal unit's state-of-the-art equipment and dedicated staff while her senses were filled with the scent, sight and feel of Liam so close beside her.

He stiffened, dragging Hadley out of her musings. She returned her attention to the speaker only to discover Dr.

Reese had passed off the tour to a slender nurse with blond hair pulled back into a bun and a brisk way of speaking.

"We call her Janey Doe," the nurse said, a hint of sadness clouding her direct green gaze. "She is holding her own, but each day is a struggle. However, thanks to Dr. Reese..." The nurse glanced up at the tall doctor, and Hadley got the impression that equal parts personal and professional admiration curved her lips.

The crowd began to follow Dr. Reese toward the birthing suites, but Liam showed no interest in continuing on. He made a beeline straight for the nurse and introduced himself.

"Hello, I'm Liam Ward. And this is Hadley Stratton."

"Clare Connelly." The nurse shook their hands. "Thank you for all your hard work on the restoration of this wing. It's such an amazing facility to work in."

"It was an important project for our town." Although his words were courteous, his tone was strained. "I was wondering if you could tell me a little bit more about Janey Doe."

Knowing that she had missed a big chunk of the story, Hadley scanned Liam's expression, noticed his tight lips, the muscle jumping in his jaw and wondered at his interest.

"She was found on the floor of a truck stop thirty miles from here..."

"No sign of her mother?" Liam's question reverberated with disgust.

Clare shook her head slowly. "None, I'm afraid."

"You mean she just left her there?" Hadley's chest tightened. "How could she do something like that?"

"She was probably young and scared. Janey was very small and obviously premature. It's possible the mother thought she was dead and freaked out."

Hadley appreciated how Clare stuck up for Baby Janey's mother but could see that none of her assumptions had eased Liam's displeasure. He was staring into the neonatal unit, his attention laser focused on the middle incubator. Was Maggie on his mind? Without knowing for certain that Maggie was related to Liam, Diane Garner had left her granddaughter in his care. Or was he thinking how his own mother had left him to be raised by his grandfather?

"What will happen to her?" Hadley asked, her own gaze drawn toward the incubator and the precious bundle. The baby was hooked up to a feeding tube, oxygen and monitors, making it impossible to get a clear look at her face.

"She'll go into foster care and eventually be adopted." Although the words were hopeful, the nurse's smile was strained.

Hadley recognized that look. She'd seen it on the faces of plenty of her fellow nannies who'd grown too attached to their charges.

"Thank you for your time." Liam glanced down at Hadley, his expression unreadable. "Shall we rejoin the party?"

All warmth had been leeched from his manner by the story of Baby Janey. Hadley nodded and strolled back toward the elevator at Liam's side. Although her hand remained tucked in his arm, the emotional distance between them was as wide as an ocean. She recognized that this had nothing to do with her. Liam had retreated behind walls she couldn't penetrate, defenses a young boy had erected to deal with his mother's abandonment.

"Why don't we get out of here," Hadley suggested as they descended in the elevator. "I don't think you're in the mood for a party anymore."

"You're right." One side of his lips kicked up. His gaze warmed as he bent down to brush a kiss across her lips. "But I should at least spend an hour here. If for no other reason than to show off my gorgeous date."

Hadley blushed at the compliment. It didn't matter what

anyone else thought of her looks; as long as she could bask in Liam's sizzling admiration, she felt flawless.

By the time the elevator doors opened, Liam seemed to have gotten past whatever had affected him in the neonatal unit. Once again the charming rascal she adored, he worked his way around the room, collecting smiles and promises of funds for several pieces of equipment the hospital still needed.

Watching him work, Hadley reveled in his charisma and marveled at his ability to strike just the right chord with everyone he met. This is what made him an astute businessman and a masterful horseman. He didn't approach every situation with the same tactic.

"I'm ready to get out of here if you are," he murmured in her ear an hour later.

"Absolutely," she replied, anticipating what awaited them back at the ranch house.

On the ride home, Liam lapsed back into silence, his public persona put aside once more. Hadley stared at his profile in concern. Her hopes for a romantic evening fled. Liam's troubled thoughts preoccupied him.

As Liam unlocked the front door, Hadley set aside her disappointment and decided to see if she could get him to open up. "How about I make some coffee and we talk about what's bothering you?"

Liam's chin dipped in ascent. "I'll get a fire started in the den."

Once she got the coffee brewing, Hadley ran upstairs to check on Maggie. She found the baby sleeping and Candace in the rocking chair, reading on her tablet. The housekeeper looked up in surprise as Hadley crossed to the crib.

"You're home early. Did you have fun?"

"It was a nice party. The facilities are wonderful." Hadley knew she hadn't directly answered Candace's question. While she'd enjoyed the company and the conversation,

Liam's mood after learning about Janey Doe had unsettled her. "Thanks for watching Maggie. Any problems?"

Candace got to her feet. "She went to sleep at eight and hasn't made a peep since."

"Good." Maggie's hair was soft beneath Hadley's fingers as she brushed a strand off the baby's forehead. "I made some coffee if you're interested in joining us for a cup."

"No, thanks. I'm almost done with this book. I'm going to head back to the carriage house and finish it."

The two women headed downstairs. Liam was in the kitchen and gave Candace a cheerful thank-you as she left. By the time the housekeeper pulled the back door shut behind her, icy air filled the space. Hadley shivered and filled the mugs Liam had fetched from the cupboard. Cradling the warm ceramic in her hands, she led the way into the den and settled on the sofa.

Liam set his mug on the mantel and chose to stand, staring into the fire. "I'm sorry I was such bad company tonight."

"You weren't bad company." Hadley was careful not to let her disappointment show. "Obviously something is bothering you. Do you feel like talking about it?"

"It was hearing about Janey Doe."

"That was a very upsetting story." She refrained from adding her own opinion on the subject, wanting Liam to share his thoughts.

"Her mother just leaving her like that. On the floor of a public bathroom. She could have died."

Hadley kept her voice neutral. "She was fortunate that someone found her."

"I thought it was bad that Maggie's grandmother left her with us. This is so much worse. How could any mother abandon her child like that?"

"Not every woman is cut out for motherhood." Hadley

thought about all the families she'd worked for in the last five years and all the stories shared by her fellow nannies. "Sometimes the responsibility is more than they can handle."

"You mean they wish they'd never given birth."

Trying her best to hide a wince, Hadley responded, "I mean that parenting can be challenging, and sometimes if a woman has to do it alone, she might not feel capable."

"Perhaps if she's young and without financial means, I could understand, but what can you say about a woman who has family and fortune and turns her back on her children so she can pursue her career?"

Not wanting to sound as if she were picking sides, Hadley chose her next words carefully. "That she acted in her best interest and not in the best interest of her children."

Liam crossed to the sofa and joined Hadley. A huge gust of air escaped his lungs as he picked up her hand and squeezed her fingers. "Maggie must never know that her grandmother left her with us the way she did. I won't have her wondering why she didn't want to keep her."

This was the true source of Liam's disquiet, Hadley realized. Whether he acknowledged it or not, being abandoned by his mother had sabotaged his ability to trust women. And where did that leave Hadley?

Liam could feel the concern rolling off Hadley as he spoke. He'd grown attuned to her moods since their days in Vail and didn't have to see her expression to know her thoughts.

Hadley covered their clasped hands with her free one and squeezed. "It's okay to be angry with your mother for not being there for you."

The knot of emotions in his chest tightened at her words. Not once as a child had he seen his grandfather demonstrate anything but understanding toward the daughter who'd run out on her children. Liam had grown up thinking that what his mother had done was acceptable, while inside him was a howling banshee of anger and hurt that was never given a voice.

"You might feel better if you talked through how it made you feel."

"I don't know how to begin." The words, long bottled up inside him, were poised to explode. "I grew up thinking it was okay that she chose to leave us with Grandfather."

"Why?"

"She had a career that she loved, and like you said earlier, she really wasn't cut out to be a mom. She got pregnant when she was seventeen. Our father was on the rodeo circuit and had no interest in settling down to raise a family. Mother felt the same way. Grandfather always said she had big dreams." Liam offered up a bitter laugh. "I guess Kyle and I are lucky she decided to have us at all."

Hadley's shocked intake of breath left Liam regretting the venomous statement.

"You don't mean that."

"No," he agreed. "Although I've thought it a hundred times, I don't think she ever considered terminating her pregnancy. In that respect, she didn't take the easy way out."

"Getting back to what you said earlier, growing up did you really think that it was okay she left you with your grandfather, or was that just a coping mechanism?"

"In my mind, I understood her decision. I can't explain to you why that made sense. Maybe because it happened when we were babies and I never knew any different. But recently I started realizing that deep down inside, I hated her for leaving us."

He'd coped by becoming a champion rider. Throwing himself into competition had preoccupied him in his teenage years. The closer he'd gotten to manhood, the less he thought about his mother's absence. The day he'd kissed a girl for the first time, he'd stopped caring.

"Grandfather wasn't exactly the most affectionate guy in the world, but he loved us in his tough-guy way. It might have been different if we were girls, but growing up on the ranch, we had more father figures than anyone could ever want."

"You sound very well adjusted." Her tone said otherwise. "Do you think not having a mother affected your relationships with women?"

"You mean because I never got married?"

"You have a well-earned reputation for being a playboy. I can't imagine you trusted your heart after what your mother did."

"I'll admit to having a wandering eye when it came to women, but that's changed."

"Just because you think you're ready to settle down doesn't mean you've learned to trust." She smiled to take the sting out of the words, but her eyes reflected wariness.

"You're the first woman I've been with in a year," he reminded her, voice rasping as frustration overcame him. "I think that proves I'm already settled down. And I trust you."

Doubt continued to shadow her eyes. He shifted on the couch, angling his body toward her. Gripped by the urgent need to kiss her, Liam dipped his head, shortening the distance between them. He would demonstrate that he was serious about her.

Before he could kiss her, Hadley set her fingertips on his lips. "Thank you for sharing how you felt about your mother not being around. I know that couldn't have been easy."

"It wasn't." And yet it had been a relief to share his anger and sense of betrayal with her. "Thank you for listening."

A moment earlier he'd had something to prove, but the mood was no longer right for seduction. Instead, he planted a friendly kiss on her cheek and held her in a tight hug.

"Let's go upstairs," she murmured, her hands sliding beneath his suit coat, fingers splaying over his back. "I want to make love to you."

At her declaration Liam took a massive hit to his solar plexus. Pulse quickening, he caught her by the hand and drew her toward the stairs. They climbed together in a breathless rush. By the time they reached his bedroom, he was light-headed and more than a little frantic to get them both naked.

Once they crossed the threshold, Hadley plucked the pins from her hair, and it tumbled around her shoulders. Liam came to stand behind her, pushing the thick mass of blond hair away from her neck so he could kiss the slender column and make her shiver. He stripped off his jacket and shirt before turning his attention to the zipper of her dress. With more urgency than finesse, he stroked the dress down her body. When it pooled at her feet, he skimmed his palms back upward, hesitating over the ticklish spot beside her hip bones and investigating each bump of her ribs. The rise and fall of her chest grew less rhythmic as he unfastened her strapless bra and tossed the scrap of fabric on to a nearby chair.

Her hand came up to the back of his head as he cupped her breasts in his palms, thumbs flicking over her tight nipples. She shuddered, her head falling back against his chest, eyes closed as she surrendered to his touch. Although the tightness in his groin demanded that he stop all the foreplay and get down to business, Liam had no intention of rushing. He'd rather savor the silken heat of her skin and bring her body as much pleasure as it could take before seeking his own release.

She turned in his arms, her soft breasts flattening

against his chest as she lifted on tiptoe and sought his mouth with hers. She cupped his face in her hands to hold him still while her tongue darted forward to toy with his. Liam crushed her to him, his fingers dipping below her black lace panties to swallow one butt cheek and lift her against his erection.

They both groaned as he rocked against her. She lifted her foot and wrapped her leg around his hips, angling the bulge behind his zipper into the warm, wet cleft between her thighs. The move unraveled all of Liam's good intentions. He plucked her off her feet and moved toward the bed. She set the soles of her feet against his calves to keep him anchored between her thighs and impatiently removed his belt. It was torture to let her undress him. Every time her fingers glanced off his erection, he ground his teeth and bit back a groan. Only by watching the play of emotions race across her beautiful features was he able to maintain his control. By the time she'd slid open his zipper and pushed the pants down his thighs, his nerves screamed with impatience.

Liam stripped off pants, shoes, socks and underwear without ever taking his eyes off Hadley. With a sensual smile she moved backward, making room for him on the mattress. He stalked onto the bed, fitting between her spread thighs, covering her torso with his before claiming her lips in a hard kiss and her body with a single deep thrust.

He loved the way her hips lifted to meet his. How she arched her back and took him all the way in. Her chest vibrated with a moan. A matching sound gathered in his lungs. For a long moment they lay without moving, lips and tongues engaged.

Framing her face in his hands, Liam lifted his lips from hers and stared into her eyes. "Thank you for being my date tonight." It wasn't what he'd intended to say, but nevertheless his words pleased her.

"Thank you for asking. I had a lovely time."

"Lovely?" He grinned. "Let's see if we can't upgrade that to fantastic."

Her eyebrows lifted, daring him to try, while her fingers stroked down his sides. "We're off to a wonderful start."

Liam nuzzled his face into her throat and began to move inside her. "We certainly are."

Ten

The night after the party at the hospital, Hadley was back on the neonatal floor she and Liam had toured. After receiving Maggie's blood work back, Dr. Stringer had determined she should undergo phototherapy treatments for her jaundice. Despite being overwhelmed with ranch business, Liam had accompanied them, wearing his concern openly, but once he discerned how straightforward the process was, he'd relaxed.

Maggie had been stripped down to her diaper and placed in an incubator equipped with a light box that directed blue fluorescent light onto her skin. The light was meant to change the bilirubin into a form that Maggie could more easily expel through her urine. While the procedure was simple, it also took time to work. Maggie would be in the hospital for a couple days while undergoing the treatment. Hadley had agreed to stay with her to let Liam focus on the ranch.

Hadley caught herself humming as she fed Maggie her late-afternoon bottle. After the party at the hospital and the night spent in Liam's arms, she'd stopped resisting what her heart wanted and let herself enjoy every moment of her time with Liam. Why fight against the inevitable? She'd fallen deeply in love with the man.

While a part of her couldn't help but compare what was between her and Liam to what she'd had with Noah, deep down, Hadley recognized the vast difference between the two relationships. With Noah she'd never enjoyed any sort of emotional security. As much as he'd gone on and on about how much he wanted her, how his kids adored her, she always got the sense that he was looking over her shoulder for someone else. It turned out that someone else had been his ex-wife.

Liam never once let her think she was second best. His focus was always completely on her, and Hadley found that both comforting and wildly exciting. For the first time in a long time, she'd stopped focusing on the future and lived quite happily in the moment. School would start when it started. Her time with Maggie would grow shorter. Already arrangements had been made for the new nanny to start at the end of the month. This freed Hadley from her professional responsibilities, and she was eager to see where her relationship with Liam led.

Maggie's eyelids started to droop before the bottle was finished. Hadley set it aside, lifted the infant onto her shoulder and patted her back to encourage a burp. A nurse stood by to test Maggie's bilirubin levels. The staff members were monitoring her every hour or so. Hadley was calling Liam with the results.

His concern for Maggie's welfare had warmed her when she thought the baby was his daughter. Now that she knew Maggie was his brother's child, Liam's commitment was just another reason Hadley found him so attractive.

She was tired of restraining her emotions. Liam made her happy, and she thought he felt the same way about her. When Maggie left the hospital, Hadley promised herself she would stop holding back.

Several days after the hospital party, Liam had an appointment with former Samson Oil lawyer Nolan Dane, who'd joined his father's family law practice. Recently,

Nolan had been accepted for membership in the Texas Cattleman's Club, and the more Liam got to know the man, the more he liked him. The idea that had begun percolating in his mind took on a whole new urgency on the trip back from Colorado. With Maggie in the hospital and Hadley staying with her, the notion had solidified into a plan that required a savvy lawyer.

Liam stepped into Nolan's office. "Looks like you're all settled in."

Nolan grinned. "It's taken longer than I figured on. I didn't expect to be so busy this early in my start-up."

"That must mean you're good. Looks like I've come to the right place."

"Can I offer you coffee or water before we get started?" Nolan gestured Liam into a chair at the round conference table.

"Thanks, but I'm good." While Nolan took a seat, Liam pulled out the paternity test as well as Maggie's birth certificate and her mother's death certificate that Diane Garner had sent at his request.

Nolan found a blank page on his yellow legal pad and met Liam's gaze. "What can I help you with?"

"I have a situation with my twin brother's baby." Liam explained how Maggie had come to Wade Ranch and showed Nolan the DNA results. "Maggie is definitely Kyle's daughter. As soon as I received the test back, I left messages for him on his cell and with the navy."

"How long ago was this?"

"About two weeks."

"And you haven't heard back?"

"Only that the message was delivered. He's a SEAL, which probably means he's on a mission overseas." Liam leaned forward. "And that's where my concerns lie. I don't know a lot about Kyle's domestic situation, but based on his past track record, I'm guessing he's not in a long-term relationship and certainly isn't in a position to take care of a baby."

"You're not in regular contact?"

"Not since he left Royal and joined the navy." Liam wasn't proud of the way he and Kyle had drifted apart, but growing up they'd been uniquely dissimilar in temperament and interests for identical twins.

"And it sounds like the child's grandmother, Diane Garner, is reluctant to be responsible for Maggie."

"She has serious medical issues that prevent her from taking care of Maggie. Which leaves Kyle." Liam paused to give his next words weight. "Or me."

"You want custody?"

While Liam's first instinct was to say yes, he intended to do what was best for Maggie. "I'd like to evaluate all the options."

One corner of Nolan's lips twitched. "You don't have to be diplomatic with me, Liam. I'm here to help you out. Now, what do you want?"

"I'd like custody, but what is most important is to do right by Maggie." Liam gathered his thoughts for a long moment. "I have concerns that while Kyle is off on missions, he'll have to rely on others to take care of her for extended periods of time. And what happens if he's hurt…" Or killed. But Liam couldn't go there. Most days he didn't give Kyle a thought, but sometimes a news report would catch his attention and Liam would wonder what his brother was up to.

"Do you know if Kyle and Margaret were in touch before she drove to Wade Ranch?" Nolan continued to jot down items on his legal pad. "I'm trying to get a sense of their relationship."

"I don't know, but I have to think if Kyle had any idea he was going to be a father that he would have let me know." Liam wanted to believe his brother would step up and do the right thing by his daughter. Yet the fact that Kyle hadn't been in contact disturbed Liam. "That leads me to believe that he didn't know. Either because she hadn't told him or she had the same trouble getting a hold of him I'm having."

Liam didn't add that it was possible Margaret had been nothing more than a weeklong fling for Kyle and he'd had no intention of keeping in touch.

"Because Margaret died in childbirth and she and Kyle weren't married, only her name appears on Maggie's birth certificate. Normally what would happen in this sort of case is that both parties would fill out an AOP. That's an Acknowledgment of Paternity. This form would normally be filled out and signed at the hospital. Or through a certified entity that would then file it with the Vital Statistics Unit. Unfortunately, without Margaret alive to concede that your brother is the child's father, this case will have to go to court. Of course, DNA evidence will prove Kyle's the father. But with you two being identical twins and no way of proving which one of you is the father…" After a long silence, broken only by the scratch of his pen across the legal pad, Nolan glanced up. His eyes gleamed. "I can see why you came to me. This situation is by no means clear-cut."

"No, it's not." But at least Liam had a clearer picture of what he wanted. Tension he didn't realize he'd been holding unwound from his shoulder muscles. "How do you suggest we proceed?"

"Let's find out what we can about Margaret and her time with Kyle in San Antonio. I have an investigator I've worked with there. If you give me the go-ahead, I'll contact him."

"Do you think I have a case for retaining custody of Maggie?" Before he let Kyle take Maggie away, Liam intended to make sure his brother was willing to fight for her. And fight hard.

"A lot will depend on how determined your brother is

to be a father. You and your brother aren't in contact. We should probably check on Kyle's current financial status and personal life as well and see what sort of environment Maggie would be going into. I think you're right that between the two situations, Wade Ranch promises the most stability for a baby. But a judge might reason that you're both single men and that Maggie should be with her father."

Her *single* father who might be activated at a moment's notice and be out of the country who knew how long.

"What if I were engaged?" Liam suggested, voicing what had been running through his head since his trip to Colorado. "Or married?"

Nolan nodded. "Might sway a judge. Are you?"

"Not yet." For a year Liam had pondered the benefits of settling down. All he'd been waiting for was the right woman. Hadley fit the bill in every way. She was smart, beautiful and great with Maggie. After Colorado he'd decided he'd be a complete idiot not to lock her down as soon as possible before she finished school and headed off to pursue a career elsewhere. "But I plan to pop the question to a special lady in the very near future."

Hadley rocked a sleepy Maggie as she checked out the photos of Liam's family on the walls of the ranch office.

"Thanks for bringing lunch," Liam said. "The day has been crazy."

With calving time a couple weeks away and a whole host of unexpected issues popping up, Liam and Ivy had decided to work through lunch. The weather had turned warmer and Hadley was feeling restless, so she'd offered to bring their meal to the barn.

As if Liam's words had the power to summon trouble, one of the hands appeared in the doorway. "Dean told me to stop by and see if you had an hour or so free. Sam is out sick," the hand said. "Barry is off visiting his kid in Tulsa. We could use some help cutting the cows who aren't pregnant."

"Sure." Liam shifted his weight in the direction of the door, but glanced at Hadley before taking a step. "Ever cut cattle?"

She shook her head, sensing what was coming and wondering why Liam, knowing what he did, would ask her to ride with him.

"Like to try?"

Hadley was surprised by her strong desire to say yes. "What about Maggie?"

"I'd be happy to watch her until you get back," Ivy offered, cooing at the infant. "You'd like to hang out with Cousin Ivy until they get back, wouldn't you?" Maggie waved her arms as if in agreement. "Or I can drive her back to the house if it gets too late."

"See?" Liam's eyes held a hard glint of challenge. "All settled. Let's go find you a mount."

While her gut clenched in happy anticipation of getting on a horse again, Hadley rationalized her agreement by telling herself it was work, not pleasure. She was doing something her employer requested. Never mind that he'd been trying to figure out a way to get her back in the saddle since she'd stepped into his home two and a half weeks ago.

Excitement built as he led her outside to the paddocks where they turned out the horses during the day. Twelve horses occupied four enclosures.

Liam nodded toward a palomino mare in the farthest right paddock. The only horse in the fenced-in area, she stood in the middle, tearing at the winter grass with strong white teeth. "Daisy could use some exercise. I don't think she's been ridden much in the last year. I'll get one of the guys to saddle her for you."

"I can saddle my own horse," Hadley retorted, insulted. "Besides, I'd like to get to know her a little before I get on."

"Okay. She's a nice mare. You shouldn't have any trouble with her on the ground."

As Liam's last three words registered, she glanced over at him, but discovered nothing in his expression to arouse her suspicions. Surely he wouldn't put her on a green horse after such a long absence from the saddle. Once upon a time her skills might have been first-rate, but a decade had passed since she'd used those particular muscles. Riding a horse wasn't the same as riding a bike.

"You said she hasn't been ridden much in the last year?" Hadley decided a little clarification might be in order. "But she has been ridden, right?"

"Oh, sure." Liam walked over to the fence and picked up the halter and lead rope hung on the gate. "We were going to breed her last year, but that didn't work out. So she's just been hanging around, waiting to become a mother." He opened the gate and handed Hadley the halter. "She's easy to catch. I'll meet you in that barn over there." He indicated the building that housed the horses in training. "You might want to do a couple circles in the indoor ring before we head out."

Sensing something was up despite Liam's neutral expression and bland tone, Hadley slipped the halter onto the mare and led her to the building Liam had indicated. He hadn't yet arrived, so Hadley got busy with currycomb and brush. She smiled as the mare leaned into the grooming. Obviously Daisy appreciated Hadley's efforts.

She would have preferred to take more time with the mare, but Liam showed up, leading a gorgeous bay stallion that was already saddled and ready to go. Hadley returned his nod before tossing the saddle onto Daisy's back, settling it in just the right spot and tightening the cinch as if she'd done it last week instead of ten years earlier. Working just as efficiently, she slipped the bit into the mare's mouth and fitted the headstall into place.

"Ready?"

All at once she became aware of Liam's attention and grew self-conscious. "I think so."

"Come on. I'll work the kinks out of Buzzard while you try out Daisy."

Leading Daisy, Hadley followed Liam and the bay into the arena. What if she made a complete hash of it and ended up getting dumped? While Hadley fussed with Daisy's girth and grappled with her nerves, Liam swung up onto the stallion's back. Buzzard took several steps sideways as Liam settled his weight, but quickly relaxed beneath the pressure of his rider's legs and the steadiness of Liam's hands on the reins.

The guy was an amazing rider, and Hadley felt a fangirl moment coming on. Embarrassed at her gawking, she set her foot in the stirrup. Daisy was a little shorter than Lolita, but she felt her muscles protest as she threw her leg up and over the mare's back. Before she'd completely found her balance, Daisy's muscles bunched beneath her and the mare crow-hopped a half dozen times while Hadley clung to the saddle horn, laughter puffing out of her with each jolt of Daisy's four hoofs hitting the ground.

At last the mare got her silliness out of her system and stood still while Hadley retrieved her breath.

"You okay?"

"Fine." Hadley could feel the broad smile on her face. "Is she going to be like this the whole time?"

"No. She just wanted to make sure you were going to stay on. You passed."

"She was testing me?" The notion struck Hadley as ludicrous. What sort of horse had Liam put her on?

"She's a smart horse." His lips kicked up. "Needs a smart rider."

Apparently Daisy wasn't the only one doing the testing. Hadley keyed the mare into a walk and then took five minutes to work through all her gaits. Whoever had trained the palomino had done a fabulous job. She was a dream to ride.

"Let's go cut some cattle," Hadley said, all too aware how closely Liam had been observing her.

Liam didn't think a woman's pleasure had ever been as important to him as Hadley's. Between their lovemaking in Vail and the joy she'd demonstrated cutting cattle today, especially when Daisy had kept a heifer from returning to the herd, he was convinced he would know true happiness only if he continued delighting Hadley.

Would he have felt the same a year ago? Remaining celibate for twelve months had given him a greater appreciation of companionship. Being with Hadley had enabled him to understand the difference between what he'd had with his former girlfriends and true intimacy. Granted, he'd only barely scratched the surface with her. Instinct told him she was rich with complex layers she didn't yet trust him to see. Moving past her defenses wasn't anything he wanted to rush. Or force.

He had a good thing going. Why make a mistake and risk losing her?

"That was amazing," Hadley crowed. Cheeks flushed, eyes dancing with excitement, she was as vibrant as he'd ever seen her. "You knew I'd love this when you suggested I ride her."

"She's a natural, boss," one of the ranch hands commented, his gaze lingering on Hadley longer than Liam liked.

"I figured she would be."

The urge to growl at the cowboy was nearly impossible to repress. Obviously, Liam wasn't the only one dazzled by the attractive Ms. Hadley Stratton. And since he hadn't yet staked a public claim, the rest of the male population assumed she was fair game. That situation was not to his liking. Time he did something to change it.

Liam nudged his stallion forward and cut Hadley off from the admiring cowboys with the ease of someone accustomed to working cattle. "It's late. We should be getting back to Maggie."

Her eyes lost none of their sparkle as she nodded. "I've probably strained enough muscles for one day." She laughed. "I can tell I'm going to be in pain tomorrow, but it was worth it."

"I'm glad you like Daisy." Liam decided to push his luck. "She could probably stand a little work if you felt inclined."

Hadley hesitated but shook her head. He was making progress since the last time he'd tried to persuade her to ride. He wanted her to talk to him, to share how she was feeling. They'd discussed her friend's accident, and Hadley had mulled his suggestion that she move past the guilt that she'd carried for years. Had something about that changed?

"I'm due to go back to school in a week. I don't know how I'd make time."

He'd found a permanent nanny for Maggie. Liam and Hadley had agreed that being together would not work if she was still his employee. But he was realizing that she would no longer be an everyday fixture in his life, and that was a situation he needed to fix.

"I don't mind sharing you with the horses," he said, keeping his voice casual. He'd never had to work so hard to keep from spooking a woman.

"Oh, you don't?" She gave him a wry smile. "What if I don't have enough time for either of you?"

Liam's grip on the reins tightened and Buzzard began trotting in place. If he thought she was flirting, he'd have shot back a provocative retort, but Liam had gotten to know Hadley well enough in the last few weeks to know she had serious concerns.

"Move in with me."

The offer was sudden, but he didn't surprise himself when he made it.

"You already have a full-time nanny moving in."

"Not as a nanny."

Her eyes widened. "Then as what?"

"The woman I'm crazy about." He'd never been in love and had no idea if that's what he felt for Hadley. But he'd been doing a lot of soul-searching these last few days.

"You're crazy about me?" The doubt in her voice wasn't unexpected.

He'd known she wouldn't accept his declaration without some vigorous convincing. Hadley wasn't one to forgive herself easily for past mistakes. She'd fallen for her first employer, only to have her heart torn up when the jerk got back together with his ex-wife. That wasn't a judgment error she would make a second time. And she was already skeptical of Liam's past romantic history.

"If we weren't on these damned horses I'd demonstrate just how crazy."

Liam ground his teeth at her surprise. What kept her from accepting how strong his feelings had become? The mildest of her saucy smiles provoked a befuddling rush of lust. He pondered what her opinion would be on a dozen decisions before lunch. Waking up alone in his big bed had become the most painful part of his day.

"This is happening too fast."

"I'm not going to bail on you."

"I know."

"You don't sound convinced." He was determined to change her mind. "What can I say to reassure you?"

"You don't need to say anything."

After regarding her for a long moment, he shook his head. "I've dated a lot of women."

"This is your way of convincing me to take a chance on you?"

He ignored her interruption. "Enough to recognize that how I feel about you is completely foreign to me." He saw he'd hit the wrong note with the word *foreign*. "And terrific. Scary. Fascinating. I've never been so twisted up by a woman before."

"And somehow you think this is a good thing?"

"You make me better. I feel more alive when I'm with you. Like anything is possible."

She blinked several times. "I think that's the most amazing thing anyone has ever said to me."

"I don't believe that. I do, however, believe that it might be one of the first times you've let yourself hear and trust one of my compliments." He was making progress if she'd stopped perceiving everything he said as a ploy.

"You might be right."

They'd drawn within sight of the ranch buildings, and Liam regretted how fast the ride had gone. He hadn't received an answer from Hadley, and the time to pursue the matter was fast coming to an end.

"I hope that means you're beginning to believe me when I tell you how important you've become to me."

"It's starting to sink in." She watched him from beneath her eyelashes. "But are you ready to have me move in?"

"Absolutely." His conviction rang in his answer. "But it's not the only thing I want."

This was something else he'd thought long and hard about. It wasn't just his feelings for Hadley that were driving him, but also his need to give Maggie a loving home and create for her the sort of stable family denied him and Kyle.

"No?"

"What I really want is for us to get married."

Eleven

While Hadley wondered if she'd heard him correctly, Liam pulled a ring box out of his coat pocket and extended it her way. She stared at it, her heart thundering in her ears. It wasn't the most romantic of proposals, but she had to bite her lower lip to keep from blurting out her acceptance. It took half a minute for her to think rationally.

"I haven't said yes or no to moving in," she reminded him, pleased that she sounded like a sensible adult instead of a giddy teenager.

"I'm afraid I've gone about this in a clumsy fashion." His confident manner belied his words. "I've never asked a woman to marry me before. Especially not one I've known less than a month."

Hadley's brain scrambled to think logically. "And the reason you're rushing into marriage?"

"I'm not rushing into marriage," he corrected her with a wily grin. "I'm rushing into an engagement."

"Semantics." She waved away his explanation. "Are you sure you don't want to live together for a while and see how it goes?"

"I've already lived with you for a while and it's been terrific. I want to keep on living with you. I need you in my life. That's not going to change if we wait to get engaged. Right now your plan is to finish school and move to Houston. I want you to make a life with me in Royal instead."

Hadley clutched her reins in a white-knuckled grip and made no move toward the tempting ring box. "Are you sure this is what you want?"

From the way the light in his eyes dimmed, it wasn't the answer he'd hoped for, but he had to know her well enough to realize she wouldn't jump aboard his runaway freight train without thinking things through. After all, her career goals were designed to carry her far from Royal. And that was something she'd have to reconsider if she married him.

"Are you questioning whether I know my mind?" He lifted the enormous diamond ring from its nest of black velvet and caught her left hand. His eyes mesmerized her as he slid the ring on her finger. "I took a year off dating and spent the time thinking through what I wanted in a woman. I wouldn't have slept with you in Vail if I hadn't already made up my mind that you were special." Liam dismounted and handed off Buzzard's reins to one of the grooms.

"But marriage?" She stared at the ring, mesmerized by the diamond's sparkle.

Here was proof that Liam's proposal wasn't something impulsive and reckless. He'd come prepared to ask her to marry him. And yet he hadn't said anything about love.

"It's been on my mind constantly since we came back from Colorado."

Hearing she hadn't been the only one who'd felt the connection they'd established that snowy weekend eased her mind somewhat. She dismounted and surrendered Daisy to the groom as well. Her feet barely touched the dirt as she walked the short distance to Liam and took the hand he held outstretched.

He tugged her to him and lifted her chin with gentle fingers until their gazes met. "You fill my thoughts when we're apart and make me mad with longing to take you in my arms when we're together."

Liam's assertion awakened a deep, profound thrumming in her heart. "I know the feeling," she said, lifting onto her toes to offer him a single kiss. "I'd better get back to Maggie."

He wrapped a strong arm around her waist and held her snug against his muscular chest. "Will you stay tonight?"

"I can't. I'm having dinner with Kori."

"Afterward?"

She laughed and danced beyond his reach. "I've been neglecting the other guy in my life so I'm going to sleep with him."

"That guy better be Waldo," he growled, but his eyes sparkled with amusement below lowered brows.

"I don't have time for anyone else."

"Bring him with you when you come back. It's time you both settled permanently at the ranch house."

Engagement. Moving in. It was all happening so fast. Her heart hammered against her ribs in a panicked rhythm. All too aware she hadn't actually agreed to marry Liam, despite accepting his ring, she opened her mouth, but her thoughts were too scattered to summon words. He might have been considering this move for a while, but for her this development was brand-new and she needed to think things through.

One of Liam's ranch hands approached, citing a problem with a mare, and Hadley took the opportunity to slip away. As she wove through the connected barns on her way back to the ranch offices, her mood shifted from giddy to concerned. She might not have said yes to marriage, but she'd accepted his ring and kept her doubts to herself.

What had happened to being practical? Falling in love with Liam for starters. How was she supposed to think straight when the man made her feel like it was the Fourth of July, Thanksgiving and Christmas all rolled into one perfect holiday?

Thank goodness she was having dinner with Kori. Talking to her best friend would help sort things out.

Kori held Hadley's engagement ring mere inches from her nose and scrutinized the diamond. "You're not seriously thinking about marrying him, are you?"

"Well, I haven't said no." Hadley wasn't sure why her friend had done such a complete turnaround. "What's changed since last week when you told me to go for it?"

"Sex, yes." Kori regarded her friend as if she'd sprouted a second head as she opened the oven and removed her famous shepherd's pie. The succulent aroma of meat and savory gravy filled the kitchen. "Marriage, no."

Hadley held the plates while Kori filled them. Her friend's unexpected reaction to Liam's proposal was disheartening. "You're right. It's moving too fast."

"For you, yes." Kori and Scott had taken about a month to decide they wanted to be together forever. But they'd spent four years planning and saving money for their wedding.

"What if it feels right?" Hadley set the plates on the table while Kori followed with the salad.

"Did Noah feel right?"

Noah had been about safety. She'd been second-guessing her decision to change careers and had been worried about money. The notion of marrying a stable man had taken that burden off her shoulders.

"At the time." Hadley had no trouble admitting the truth of her failing. In the last five years she'd done a lot of soul-searching to understand why she'd failed to see that Noah was more interested in a mother for his children than a partner for life.

Kori nodded. "You are the most practical person I know until a single guy comes along needing help with his kids and you get all wrapped up in the idea of being a family."

It was her Achilles' heel, and she was wise enough to avoid putting herself in situations like the one with Noah. Like the one with Liam. As much as Hadley needed to hear Kori's blunt summary of her shortcomings, she wanted to protest that things with Liam were different. But were they?

Kori regarded her with a sympathetic expression while she topped off their wineglasses. "I know this isn't what you want to hear."

"You aren't saying anything I haven't thought a hundred times in the last month. I don't know why I do this. It's not like I didn't have a perfectly normal childhood. My parents are happily married, rarely fight and support me in everything I do."

"Don't be so hard on yourself. You are a born caretaker and one of the most nurturing people I know. It's in your nature to get overly invested, which is why you hated teaching a class of thirty kids. You might make a difference with one or two, but it's hard to give each child the sort of attention they need." Kori hit the problem squarely on the head. "Being a guidance counselor suits you so much better."

"I know." Hadley sighed. "But none of this helps me with what to do about Liam's marriage proposal. I really do love him."

"You haven't known him very long."

Hadley couldn't believe Kori of all people would use that argument. "Not directly, but I saw a lot of him ten years ago when I was barrel racing. I had a crush on him then. He was always nice to me. Never made me feel like I was going to be his next conquest." And for Liam, that was saying something.

"Because you weren't that sort of girl," Kori reminded her. "You told me while your friends dated extensively you weren't interested in boys, only horses."

"I was interested in Liam."

"Let me guess. He didn't know you existed?"

"At first, but toward the end of my last show season, that changed. I used to compete with his on-and-off girlfriend, and he'd sometimes show up to watch her. Most of the time I beat her, and he started congratulating me on my rides. At first I thought he was doing it to make her mad, but then I realized he meant it. One thing about Liam, he was always a horseman first and everything else came after."

"So things were warming up between you. What happened?"

"Anna was my best friend at the time, and she had a huge thing for him."

"But he liked you?"

Hadley shrugged. "He was way out of my league."

"What would you have done if he'd made a play for you?"

"Freaked out in true teenage fashion." Hadley trailed off as she recalled how much more intense her emotions had been in those days. Every problem had seemed crippling. Her success had sent her straight into orbit. "I'd never had a crush on anyone before, and Liam was older by a couple years and had a lot of experience. I told myself he couldn't possibly be interested in me that way."

"But you hoped he might be?"

"Sure, but it was complicated."

"Because of Anna?"

"Yes." Hadley hadn't told anyone the story behind Anna's accident. Ashamed that her friend was paralyzed as a result of something Hadley had said in a moment of anger, she'd punished herself all these years by avoiding something she loved: horses. "It bugged her that he'd go out of his way to comment on my rides but didn't notice her at all."

"What did she expect? That you'd tell him to stop being nice to you?" At Hadley's shrug, her friend sighed. "You should've told her to go to hell."

"I did something so much worse, and as a consequence my best friend lost the use of her legs."

Kori's eyes widened. "You need to tell me the whole story."

Haley killed the last of the wine in her glass and refilled from the bottle. "It was July and Wade Ranch was throwing a huge party at their stalls in the show barn to promote one of their stallions. Anna had been flirting with Liam for a month and was convinced he was finally showing interest when he invited her to the celebration. She dragged me along because she didn't want to go alone and then promptly ditched me to go hang with Liam. I lost track of her and spent the night hanging out with some of the other barrel racers.

"It was getting late and Anna didn't want to leave, so I arranged to get a lift with someone else. A little before we took off, I went to check on Lolita for the last time to make sure she had water and because being with her calmed me down. I was mad at Anna for chasing a guy who didn't act like he was into her."

"Because if he had been into her she wouldn't have had to chase him."

"Right." Several girls at the party had poked fun at Anna for thinking Liam could possibly be interested in her. "So, there I was in the stall with Lolita and guess who appears."

"Liam?" Kori said his name with such relish that Hadley had to smile.

"Liam. At first I thought maybe Anna was looking for me and got Liam to help her, but turns out he'd just followed me."

"Where was Anna?"

"I don't know. And really, for a little while, I didn't care. Liam and I talked about my upcoming ride the next day and he offered me advice for how to take a little time off my turns. I was grateful for the feedback and when I told him that, he said that if I won, I could take him out to dinner with my prize money."

"He asked you out?"

"I guess." Even now doubt clouded Hadley's tone. Even with Liam's engagement ring on her finger, she had a hard time believing that he'd been the slightest bit interested in her. She'd been so plain and uninteresting compared with his other girlfriends.

"You guess?" Kori regarded her in bemusement. "Of course he did."

Hadley shrugged. "Like I said, he was nice to a lot of people."

"But you had to suspect he wouldn't have tracked you to Lolita's stall if he wasn't interested in you."

"I could barely hope he liked me. I was excited and terrified. His reputation was something I wasn't sure I could deal with. He dated extensively." She put air quotes around *dated*. "I was eighteen and I'd never really been kissed."

"So did you win and go to dinner with him?"

"I won, but we never went out. Anna rode after I did the next day and had her accident."

"You haven't explained how that was your fault."

"Anna overheard Liam and I talking about dinner and me agreeing to his terms. She interrupted us and told me she was leaving and if I wanted a ride I'd better come with her. Considering I'd been ready to go an hour earlier, her demand seemed pretty unreasonable. I was tempted to tell her I'd already made other arrangements, but she was obviously upset so I agreed to head out."

"She was jealous that Liam had asked you out."

"That's what I figured, but on the way to the car I tried to explain to her that he was just helping me out with my riding."

"And she didn't believe you."

"No. She'd figured out I liked him and accused me of going behind her back. When I denied it, she went ballistic. Said that the only reason he noticed me was because I beat his girlfriend and that I wasn't his type. She insisted I would be the laughingstock of the barn if I kept believing he would ever want to date me."

"Sounds like things she should have been telling herself."

While Hadley agreed with Kori, at the time, each word had struck like a fist. "I wish I hadn't been so surprised by her attack. If I'd been able to stay calm, I might have been able to reason with her. But what she was saying were the same things that had been running through my head. To hear them from my best friend... I was devastated."

"So you didn't tell her she was the one who was acting like an idiot?"

"No." And now they'd arrived at the part of the story Hadley was most ashamed of. "I told her that if Liam only noticed me because of my riding she was out of luck. The way she rode, no wonder he had no idea who she was."

"Ouch."

Hadley winced. "Not my finest moment. And for the last ten years I've regretted those words."

"But it sounds like she was asking to have the truth served up to her."

"Maybe, but she was my best friend. I should have been more understanding. And because of what I said, the next day she pushed too hard and fell badly. So, now you see. If I'd not let my temper get the best of me, Anna never would have tried to prove she was the better rider and wouldn't have fallen and broken her back."

"And you haven't ridden since."

"No." It was a small sacrifice to make for being a bad

friend. "Until today. And now I'm engaged to the guy who came between Anna and me with tragic results."

"And I can tell you still aren't guilt free over moving on. So, as your best friend of seven years, I give you permission to get on with your life and stop beating yourself up over something you said to your friend who was acting like a greedy bitch a decade ago." Kori lifted her wineglass and held it out to Hadley.

Pushing aside all reluctance, Hadley picked up her glass and gently clinked it with Kori's. The crystalline note rang in the dining nook, the sound proclaiming an end to living in the past and the beginning of her bright future.

She'd given enough time and energy to her mistakes. She deserved to be happy, and being Liam's wife, becoming a family with him and Maggie, was the perfect way to spend the rest of her life.

Liam sat on the couch in the den, using one hand to scroll through the report Nolan's investigator had sent him regarding Margaret Garner while cradling a snugly swaddled Maggie in his other arm. She'd been fussy and agitated all day, and her appetite had waned. Hadley had noticed Maggie's temperature was slightly elevated and Liam was glad she was scheduled for a follow-up visit with her pediatrician tomorrow. Maggie continued to show signs of jaundice, and this had both Liam and Hadley concerned.

As a counterpoint to Liam's agitation over Maggie's health issues, Waldo lay on the sofa back directly behind Liam's head, purring. Although he'd grown up believing that cats belonged in barns, keeping the mouse population under control, he'd grown fond of Hadley's fur ball and had to concede that the feline had a knack for reading moods and providing just the right companionship. Just yesterday Liam had been irritated by a particularly demanding client, and Waldo had spent a hilarious ten minutes playing with one of Hadley's ponytail holders, cheering him up.

The only member of his family not sitting on the den's sofa was Hadley. After dinner she'd gone upstairs to call her parents and tell them about the engagement. They'd been on a cruise several days ago when Liam had popped the question and hadn't been immediately available to receive their daughter's news. Hadley was concerned that they'd view the engagement as moving too fast, and Liam had suggested that they take Maggie to Houston this weekend so everyone could meet.

With an effort, Liam brought his attention back to the report. Despite only spending four days on the job, the investigator had built a pretty clear picture of Maggie's mom. Margaret Garner had worked at home as a freelance illustrator and had a pretty limited social life. She'd dated rarely, and her friends had husbands and children who kept them busy. So busy, in fact, that none of them had had a clue that Margaret was pregnant. Nor had there been any contact between her and Kyle after their weeklong affair. The investigator hadn't been able to determine how the two had met, but after digging into Margaret's financials, he'd figured out when the fling had happened.

Margaret's perfectionism and heavy workload explained why she hadn't gone out much, but a couple of her friends had known Margaret since college and confided that they thought Margaret might have had some depression issues. From what the investigator could determine, she'd never sought medical help for that or gone to see a doctor when she'd discovered she was pregnant.

"Well, that's done," Hadley announced, her voice heavy as she crossed the room and settled onto the couch beside him.

"How did it go with your parents?"

"They were surprised." Her head dropped onto his shoulder. She'd been anxious about how the conversation would go all through dinner. Hadley was an only child and from her description of them, Liam got the impression they didn't exactly approve of some of the choices she'd made in the last few years. Especially when she'd quit teaching and moved to Royal in order to get her master's degree.

"What are you working on?"

"I had an investigator look into Margaret Garner's background."

"You hired an investigator? Why?" She peered more closely at the report on his computer screen.

"Nolan suggested it."

"Who is Nolan?"

"Nolan Dane is a family law attorney I hired."

"You hired a lawyer?"

Liam realized he probably should have shared his plans with her regarding Maggie before this, but hadn't anticipated that she'd be surprised. "Because I'm seeking custody of Maggie."

"Have you told your brother?"

"Kyle hasn't responded to my messages about Maggie yet."

Hadley sat up and turned on the cushions to face him. "Don't you think you should talk to him before you make such a big decision regarding his daughter?"

"I think it's obvious from the fact that it's been three weeks and I haven't heard from him that he's not in a place where he can be a father. Either he's overseas and unavailable or he's choosing not to call me back. Whichever it is, Maggie deserves parents who can always be there for her." He studied her expression with a hint of concern. "I thought you'd be on board with this. After all, you love Maggie as much as I do and have to admit we make terrific parents."

Her brows came together. "I guess I thought we'd be great with kids someday. As soon as I accepted that Maggie was your brother's daughter, I guess I thought she'd end up with him."

"Are you trying to tell me you can't see yourself as Maggie's mother?"

"Not at all. I love her…" But it was obvious that Hadley was grappling with something.

"Then what's going on?"

"I was just wondering how long you'd been thinking about this." Her tone had an accusatory edge he didn't understand.

"I've been considering what's best for Maggie since Diane Garner left her on my doorstep."

"And have you thought about what's best for your brother?"

Liam struggled for patience in the face of her growing hostility. "I'm thinking about the fact that he's a navy SEAL and likely to be called to duty at any time. He's not married and lives on the East Coast, far from family. Who is going to take care of Maggie while he's gone for weeks, maybe months at a time?" Liam met Hadley's gaze and didn't care for the indictment he glimpsed in her beautiful blue eyes. "I think Maggie would be better off here with us."

"He's not married." She spoke deliberately as if determined to make a point. "So he's not the best person to raise Maggie."

"He's a career military man with no family support," Liam corrected her, unsure why she wasn't agreeing with him. "How often will he miss a school event? How likely is it he'll be around for her first steps, first words, first… everything."

"You're not married, either," Hadley pointed out, her voice barely audible.

"But I'm engaged."

"Is that why you proposed?"

"What do you mean?"

"Obviously a married couple would be a stronger candidate in a custody battle."

"Sure." Why deny it? She wasn't a fool, and she knew him well enough to suspect he'd want to put forth the strongest case for Maggie.

However, the instant the admission was out, Hadley's whole demeanor transformed. All trace of antagonism vanished. She sagged in defeat.

Liam rushed to defend his rationale. "I'd like to point out that I've never asked any woman to marry me before you," he continued, more determined than ever to convince Hadley how much he needed her. "I want us to spend the rest of our lives together. With Maggie. As a family."

"I am such an idiot."

"I don't understand." He'd missed her jump in logic. "Why do you think you're an idiot?"

"Because it's just like Noah all over again."

"Noah?" The guy who'd broken her heart? "That's absurd. I asked you to marry me. He didn't."

"He said he wanted us to be together, too." Hadley shot to her feet and backed away, but her eyes never left Liam. "Only what he wanted was someone to take care of his kids and his house. Someone to be there when he got home at the end of the day and in his bed at night."

"You don't seriously think I proposed to you simply because I wanted you to fill a role." In order to keep Maggie slumbering peacefully, Liam kept his volume low, but made sure his outrage came through loud and clear.

"Everyone is right. It happened too fast." Hadley covered her mouth with her fingertips as a single tear slid down her cheek.

The sight of it disturbed him. He was fast losing control

of this situation and had no idea how to fix it. "Everyone? You mean your parents?"

"And my best friend, Kori. Not to mention the look on Candace's face when she found out."

"So what if our engagement happened fast?" Marrying Hadley meant both she and Maggie would stay with him at Wade Ranch. "That doesn't mean my motives are anything like you're painting them to be."

She pulled off her engagement ring and extended it to him. "So if I give this back to you and say I want to wait until I'm done with school to discuss our future, you'd be okay with it."

Liam made no move to take the ring back. Gripped by dismay, he stared at her, unable to believe that she was comparing him to some loser who'd used her shamelessly and broken her heart five years earlier.

"You're overreacting."

"Am I?" She crossed her arms over her chest. "When you proposed, you never told me you loved me."

No, he hadn't. He'd known he couldn't live without her, but he'd been consumed with winning custody of Maggie and afraid that Hadley would receive a job offer in Houston that would cement her plans for the future. He hadn't been thinking about romance or love when he'd proposed.

"That was wrong of me and I'm sorry. But I did tell you that I couldn't imagine life without you."

She shook her head. "You said you needed me in your life. That should've warned me that there was more motivating you than love."

"What does it matter what motivated me when it all comes down to how much we want to be together and how committed we are to being a family?"

"I really want that," she said, coming forward to set the engagement ring on the end table. "But I can't be in a relationship with you and know that your reasons for being in it are based on something besides love."

A lifetime of suppressed heartache at his mother's abandonment kept Liam from speaking as Hadley reached past him and disengaged her cat from his snug nest. Waldo's purring hadn't ceased during their argument, and Liam felt a chill race across his skin at the loss of the cat's warmth. It wasn't until she began to leave the room that he realized his mistake.

"Don't leave." He pushed aside his laptop and pursued Hadley into the hallway. "Hadley, wait."

She'd reached the entryway and slipped her coat off the hook. "I think it will be better if Waldo and I move back to my apartment. I'll be back in the morning to take care of Maggie." She didn't point out that the new nanny was set to start work in four days, but Liam was all too aware that he was on the verge of losing her forever.

"Maybe you're right and we moved too fast," he said. "But don't think for one second that I've changed my mind about wanting to spend the rest of my life with you." He extended his hand to catch her arm and stop her from leaving, but she sidestepped him, the unresisting cat clutched to her chest.

"I think it would be better for both of us if we focused on our individual futures. I have to finish school. You have a custody case to win. Once things settle down we can reconnect and see how we feel."

"If you think I'm going to agree to not see you for the next few months you've got it wrong."

"Of course we'll see each other." But her words weren't convincing. She set down the cat. Waldo stretched and wrapped himself around her legs while she donned her coat. Then, picking up her purse and the cat, Hadley opened the front door. "But I'm going to be crazy once classes start again, and you've got a couple hundred cattle set to give birth. Let's give ourselves a couple weeks to see where we're at."

"You're not going to be able to brush me off that easily," he growled as she slipped through the front door and pulled it closed behind her, leaving him and Maggie alone in the enormous, echoing Victorian mansion.

Twelve

Hadley was still reeling from déjà vu as she let herself into her apartment and set Waldo on the floor. The silver tabby's warmth had been a comfort as she'd sped through the early-evening darkness toward her tiny apartment.

How could she have been so stupid as to let herself get blinded by love a second time? So much for being five years older and wiser. She was obviously no less desperate; otherwise she wouldn't have become Liam's convenient solution the way she'd been Noah's. Honestly, what had happened to her common sense?

With her emotions a chaotic mess, Hadley looked for something in her apartment to occupy her, but after straightening a few pillows, dusting and running the vacuum, she ran out of tasks. While water boiled for a cup of tea, she wished her classes had resumed. At least then she'd have a paper to write or a test to study for. Something to occupy her thoughts and keep her mind off Liam.

She could call Kori and pour her heart out. Hadley rejected the idea as soon as it occurred to her. She wasn't ready to tell anyone that she'd screwed up again. The injury to her pride was still too fresh. Not to mention the damage to her confidence. As for the pain in her heart, Hadley could scarcely breathe as she considered all she'd lost tonight. Not just Liam, but Maggie as well.

Would it have been so bad to marry Liam and become

Maggie's mom? The whole time she'd been falling in love with Liam, she'd thought he and Maggie were a package deal. And then came their trip to Colorado. When she'd decided to believe him about his brother being Maggie's dad, letting her heart lead for a change hadn't felt one bit scary. She'd assumed Kyle would eventually come to Wade Ranch and take responsibility for Maggie. It never occurred to her that Liam intended to fight his brother for custody and that he might propose in order to appear to be the better candidate.

Desperate for a distraction from her turbulent thoughts, Hadley carried the hot tea to her small desk and turned on the computer. Before she'd considered her actions, she cued up the internet and impulsively ventured on to a popular social media site. Her fingers tapped out Noah's name and she pushed Enter before she could change her mind.

In seconds his page appeared and her heart gave a little jump as she stared at the photo of him and his kids that he used as his profile picture. Five years had gone by. Peter and Nikki were eight and seven now. They looked happy in their father's arms. Noah's wife wasn't in the shot, and Hadley searched through some of his other photos to see if she showed up anywhere. There were pictures of her with both kids, but none of her with Noah. Were they still married? Nothing in his profile information gave her a clue.

Feeling more than a little stalkerish, Hadley searched for Anna, but found no sign of her onetime friend. She almost left the website, inclined to switch to something with less potential for heartache, when she decided to search for Anna's sister, Char. And there she found Anna. Only she wasn't Anna Johnson any more. She was Anna Bradley now. A happily married woman with two beautiful girls.

Hadley stared at the photos in numb disbelief. This is the woman she'd been feeling guilty about for ten years? Anna hadn't wallowed in her misfortune. She hadn't sat around letting life pass her by. She'd gone to college in Dallas, become an engineer, gotten married and was busy raising a two- and a four-year-old.

It was as if the universe had reached out a hand and smacked Hadley on the back of the head and yelled, *snap out of it*. Noah had moved forward with his life. He had his kids and seemed to be in a good place with his wife or ex-wife. Anna was thriving with a career and family. Apparently Hadley was the only one stuck in limbo.

With revelations pouring over her like ice water, Hadley shut down the computer and picked up a notebook and a pen. It was time for her to stop dwelling on what had happened in the past and to consider how she envisioned her future. What was her idea of a perfect career? Where did she want to live? Was the love in her heart strong enough to overcome her doubts and fears?

Liam entered the pediatrician's office and spotted Hadley seated by the wall, Maggie's carrier on the chair beside her. Overnight the baby's temperature had risen, and the concern radiating from Hadley caused a spike in his anxiety.

"How is she?" he asked as he sat beside Maggie and peered in her carrier.

"A little bit worse than she was when I arrived this morning. She wouldn't eat and seems listless. I'm glad we had this appointment scheduled today."

Hadley was obviously distraught, and Liam badly wanted to offer her the comfort of his embrace, but yesterday she hadn't believed him when he'd told her there was more to his proposal than his determination to seek custody of Maggie. What made him think that a miracle had occurred overnight to change her mind?

"Do you think the jaundice is causing this?"

"More likely the jaundice is a symptom of something more serious."

"Damn it." The curse vibrated in his chest as anxiety flared. He stared down at the sleeping baby. "I can't lose her."

"Liam, you're not going to lose her." Hadley reached across Maggie's carrier and set her fingers on his upper arm.

The light contact burned through him like a wildfire, igniting his hope for a future with her. She loved him. The proof was in her supportive tone and her desire to reassure him. But as he reached to cover her hand with his, she withdrew. When she spoke again, her voice had a professional crispness.

"She's going to be fine."

He hated the distance between them. He'd been wrong to propose to her as part of a scheme to win custody of Maggie. Even though it hadn't been his only reason for asking her to marry him, she'd been right to feel as if he'd treated her no better than Noah.

But how could he convince her to give him another chance when she'd rejected everything he'd already said and done? As with the subject of Maggie's paternity, she was either going to believe him or she wasn't. She'd been burned before, and her lack of trust demonstrated that she hadn't yet moved on. He'd have to be patient and persistent. Two things he was known for when it came to horses, but not in his personal life.

"Hadley, about what happened last night—"

A nurse appeared in the waiting room and called Maggie's name before Hadley could respond. Liam ground his teeth as he and Hadley followed the nurse into an exam room. He refocused his attention on Maggie as the nurse weighed and measured her. After it was determined that her temperature had climbed to 102, the nurse left to fetch Dr. Stringer.

Liam's tension ratcheted upward during the wait. Hadley sat beside him with Maggie cradled in her arms. She'd fixed her gaze on the door to the hall as if she could summon the doctor by sheer will.

After a wait that felt like hours but was less than ten minutes, Maggie's doctor appeared. Dr. Stringer made a quick but thorough examination of his patient, returned her to Hadley's arms and sat down, his expression solemn.

"I'm concerned that she's running a temperature and that the jaundice hasn't gone away after the phototherapy treatments," Dr. Stringer said. "I'd like to draw blood and recheck her bilirubin levels. If they continue to remain high we may want to look at the possibility of doing a blood transfusion."

Liam felt rather than heard Hadley's sharp intake of breath. She had leaned her shoulder against his as the doctor had spoken. The seriousness of Maggie's medical condition was a weight Liam was glad not to have to bear alone.

"Maggie is a rare blood type," Liam said. "AB negative. Is that going to pose a problem finding donors?"

The doctor shook his head. "Not at all. In fact, where O is the universal donor blood type, AB is the universal recipient. But let's not get ahead of ourselves. I'm going to have the nurse draw some blood and then we'll see where we're at."

Maggie's reaction to the blood draw was not as vigorous as Liam expected it to be, and he took that as a sign that she was even sicker than she appeared. This time as they sat alone in the exam room, Liam reached for Hadley's hand. Her fingers were ice cold, but they curved to hold fast to his.

Their second wait was longer, but no less silent. Liam's

heart thumped impatiently, spreading unease through every vein. Beside him, Hadley, locked in her own battle with worry, gripped his hand and stared down at Maggie. Both of them had run out of reassuring things to say.

The door opened again and Dr. Stringer entered. "Looks like it's not her bilirubin levels that are causing the problem," he said, nothing about his manner suggesting this was good news.

"Then what's going on?" Liam asked.

"We're seeing a high level of white blood cells that points to infection. Because of the jaundice and the fact that she's a preemie, I'd like you to take Maggie to the hospital for further testing. I've already contacted my partner, Dr. Davison. He's on call at the hospital today and will be waiting for you."

"The hospital?" Hadley sounded stunned. "It's that serious?"

"At this point we don't know, but I would rather err on the side of caution."

Liam nodded. "Then we'll head right over."

Hadley sat in the passenger side of Liam's Range Rover as he drove to the hospital and silently berated herself for being a terrible caregiver.

"This isn't your fault," Liam said, demonstrating an uncanny knack for knowing what she was thinking.

"You don't know that."

"She only just recently started showing signs of an infection."

"But we don't know how long this has been brewing. You heard the doctor. He said it could have been coming on slowly for a long time. What if she was sick before we went to Colorado and then we walked to town and back? Maybe that's when things started."

"We can't know for sure and you'll make yourself crazy if you keep guessing."

"I should never have…" She trailed off, biting her lip to stifle the rest of the sentence.

"Should never have what?" Liam demanded, taking his eyes off the road to glance her way.

She answered in a rush. "Slept with you."

"Why? Because by doing that you stopped being a good nanny?" He snorted derisively.

Hadley shifted away from his irritation and leaned her head against the cool window. "Maggie was my responsibility. I got distracted."

"She's my responsibility, too," he reminded her. "I'm just as much at fault if something happens to her. You know, one of these days you should stop blaming yourself for every little thing that goes wrong."

With a shock, Hadley realized that Liam was right. She'd taken responsibility for other people's decisions, believing if she'd been a better friend, Anna wouldn't have gotten hurt, and if she'd been more affectionate with Noah or acted more like a parent to his children instead of their nanny, he might not have gone back to his ex-wife.

"It's a habit I should break," she said, her annoyance diminished. "It's really not anyone's fault she's sick. Like the doctor said, her birth wasn't routine. The infection could have been caused by any number of things."

Neither spoke again, but the silence was no longer charged by antagonism. Hadley cast several glances in Liam's direction, wishing she hadn't overreacted last night after finding out Liam intended to seek custody of Maggie. But she'd gone home and filled two sheets of paper with a list of everything that made her happy. It had taken her half a page before she'd begun to break free of the mental patterns she'd fallen into. But it was the last two items that told the real story.

Horses.

Liam.

That it had taken her so long to admit what she needed in her life to be truly happy was telling.

Liam dropped her and Maggie off at the emergency entrance and went to park. Hadley checked in at reception and was directed to the waiting room. She was told someone would come down from pediatrics to get them soon.

To Hadley's relief they only had to wait ten minutes. Liam never even had a chance to sit down before they were on their way to a private room in Royal Memorial's brand-new west wing.

A nurse entered the room while Hadley lifted Maggie from her carrier. "Hello, my name is Agnes and I'll be taking care of Maggie while she's here."

"It's nice to meet you." Hadley followed Agnes's directions and placed Maggie in the bassinet. It was hard to step away from the baby and let the nurse take over, but Hadley forced herself to join Liam by the window.

Liam gave her a tight smile. "She's in good hands."

"I know." Hadley was consumed by the need for Liam's arms around her. But she'd relinquished all rights to his reassurances last night when she'd given back his engagement ring.

The nurse took Maggie's vitals and hooked her up to an IV.

"Because she's not yet four weeks," Agnes began, "we're going to start her on antibiotics right away. It may take twenty-four to forty-eight hours to get the lab results back, so we'd like to take this precaution. The good news is that it hasn't seemed to affect her lungs. That's always a concern with a premature baby." Agnes offered a reassuring smile before continuing. "Dr. Davison will be by in a little while to talk to you."

"Thank you," Liam said while Hadley crossed to Maggie.

"She looks even tinier hooked up to the IV."

Liam came to stand beside her and stared down at Maggie. A muscle jumped in his jaw. His eyes had developed a haunted look. Suddenly it was Hadley's turn to offer comfort.

"She's going to be fine."

"Thank you for being here," he said. "It's…"

She'd never know what he intended to say because a man in a white lab coat entered the room with Agnes at his heels.

"Good morning, I'm Dr. Davison. I've spoken with Dr. Stringer and he filled me in on what's been going on. I'm sure you're anxious to hear about the tests we ran on Maggie," The doctor met each of their gazes in turn before shifting his attention to the infant. "What we're looking at is a blood infection. That's what's causing the fever, her jaundice and her listlessness."

A knot formed in Hadley's chest. She gripped Liam's forearm for stability. "Is it serious?"

"It can be. But Maggie is in good hands with us here at Royal Memorial. I'm sure she'll make a full recovery. The sooner she gets treatment the better the outcome. We've already started her on antibiotics, and we're going to monitor her for the next couple days while we run a battery of tests to determine what's causing the infection."

"How long will she be here?" Liam gave Hadley's fingers a gentle squeeze.

"Probably not more than three days. If there's bacteria in her blood, she'll be on antibiotics for three weeks and you'll be bringing her in for periodic checkups."

"Thank you, Dr. Davison." Liam extended his hand to the pediatrician and appeared less overwhelmed than he had before the doctor's arrival.

"Yes, thank you." Hadley summoned a smile.

Dr. Davison turned to the nurse. "Agnes, would you prepare Maggie for a lumbar puncture?"

"Certainly, Dr. Davison." She smiled at Liam and Hadley. "We have some paperwork at the nurses' station for you to fill out," she said. "We'll need just a few minutes for the spinal tap and then you can come back and be with Maggie."

Hadley tensed, intending to resist being evicted for the procedure, but then she remembered that she was the nanny, nothing more. She'd given up her rights when she'd given Liam back his ring.

When they stepped into the hallway, Hadley turned to Liam. "I should go."

"Go?" he echoed, his expression blank, eyes unfocused. "Go where?"

"I don't really belong here." As much as that was true in a practical sense, she couldn't shake a feeling of responsibility to Maggie and to him.

Foolishness. If anyone besides Liam had hired her, she wouldn't have let herself get personally involved. She'd never slept with any of her other clients, either. Even with Noah she hadn't stepped across that line. They'd been close, but something about sleeping with him with his children down the hall hadn't sat well with her. And right before the weekend they were supposed to go away and be together for the first time was when Noah decided to go back to his ex-wife.

"Maggie needs you," Liam countered. "You can't leave her now."

"I'm her nanny." It hurt to admit it, but Hadley knew that after what had happened between her and Liam, she needed to start pulling back. "What she needs is her family. Why don't you call her grandmother?"

"You mean the woman who left her with me and hasn't demonstrated any grandmotherly concern since?"

Hadley was torn. Her presence wasn't needed while Maggie was at the hospital. The nurses would see to it that the baby was well tended. Liam could give her all the love and snuggling she required.

"I'm sorry that Maggie's mother died and her grandmother is so far away, but I can't be here for you and for her in this way. She's in good hands with the nurses and with you. I've already gotten too involved. I can't keep pretending like nothing has changed." Hadley turned in the direction of the elevator so Liam wouldn't see her tears.

He caught her arm before she could take a step. "I'm sorry, too," he murmured in her ear, his breath warm against her temple. "I never meant for any of this to hurt you."

And then he set her free. Gutted and empty, she walked away without glancing back.

Liam sat on the couch in Maggie's hospital room. A nurse had appeared half an hour ago to take Maggie's temperature and change her diaper. When she'd completed her tasks, she'd dimmed the lights and left Liam in semidarkness. It was a little past six. He'd skipped both lunch and dinner but couldn't bring himself to leave the room. He felt empty, but it wasn't because he was hungry. The hollowness was centralized in his chest. Loneliness engulfed him unlike anything he'd known before.

He hadn't felt this lost when Kyle left for the navy or when his grandfather had died. The ranch had provided abundant distractions to occupy him, and he'd thrown himself into building the business. That wasn't going to work this time.

He rarely felt sorry for himself, but in the eight hours since Hadley had taken off, he'd begun to realize the wrong turn his life had taken. The arrival of Maggie and Hadley had been the best thing that had ever happened to him. Acting as Maggie's caretaker had taught him the true meaning of the word *responsibility*. Up until now, he'd had people who did things for him. Staff, his grandfather, even the women he dated. While he didn't think of himself as selfish, he'd never had to put anyone's needs above his own.

But even as he'd patted himself on the back for championing Maggie's welfare, hadn't he ignored his brother's needs when he'd decided to seek custody of his niece? And Hadley's? How had he believed that being married to him was any sort of reward for her love and the sacrifice to her career that staying in Royal would require?

He'd played it safe, offered her an expensive ring and explained that he needed her and wanted her in his life. But he'd never once told her he was madly, passionately in love with her and that if she didn't marry him, he'd be heartbroken. Of course she'd felt underappreciated.

Liam thought about the nightmare he'd had after returning from Colorado. Sleeping alone for the first time in three nights had dragged powerful emotions from his subconscious. He could still recall the sharp pain in his chest left over by the dream, a child's hysterical panic as he'd chased his mother out of the house, pleading with her not to go.

By the time he'd awakened the next morning, there'd been nothing left of the disturbing dream but a lingering sense of uneasiness. He'd shoved the genie back into the bottle. Craving love only to have it denied him was not something he ever wanted to experience again. And so he'd only shown Hadley physical desire and made a superficial commitment without risking his heart.

She'd been right to leave him. He'd pushed her to ride again, knowing how devastated she'd been by her friend's accident. He'd badgered her to forgive herself for mistakes she'd made in the past without truly understanding how difficult that was for her. But worst of all, he'd taken her love and given nothing back.

Liam reached into his pocket and drew out the engagement ring. The diamonds winked in the dim artificial light. How many of his former girlfriends would have given it back? Probably none. But they would've been more interested in the expensive jewelry than the man who gifted it. Which explained why he'd chosen them in the first place. With women who wanted nothing more from him than pretty things and a good time, he never had to give of himself.

What an idiot he'd been. He'd stopped dating so his head would be clear when the right girl came along. And when she had, he'd thought to impress her with a trip to Vail and a big engagement ring. But Hadley was smart as well as stubborn. She was going to hold out for what really mattered: a man who loved her with all his heart and convinced her with words as well as deeds just how important she was to him.

Up until now, he hadn't been that man. And he'd lost her. But while she remained in Royal, he had a chance to show her how he truly felt. And that's exactly what he was going to do.

Thirteen

After abandoning Liam and Maggie at the hospital, Hadley took a cab home and spent the rest of the day on the couch watching a reality TV marathon. The ridiculous drama of overindulged, pampered women was a poor distraction from the guilt clawing at her for leaving Liam alone to cope with Maggie. Worry ate at her and she chided herself for not staying, but offering Liam comfort was a slippery slope. Already her emotions were far too invested.

At seven she sent Kori a text about getting a ride to Wade Ranch in the morning to pick up her car. She probably should have gone tonight, but felt too lethargic and even had a hard time getting off the couch to answer the door for the pizza delivery guy.

It took her friend an hour to respond to the text. Hadley forgot she hadn't told Kori yet about her broken engagement. Leave it to her to have the world's shortest engagement. It hadn't even lasted three days. With a resigned sigh, Hadley dialed Kori's number.

"So, what's going on that you left your car at Liam's?"

Kori's question unleashed the floodgates. Hadley began to sob. She rambled incoherently about Maggie being in the hospital and how she'd turned her back on Liam right when he needed her the most.

"I'm coming over."

"No. It's okay." Hadley blew her nose and dabbed at her eyes. "I'm fine."

"You are so not fine. Why didn't you tell me about this last night?"

"Because I wasn't ready to admit that I'd screwed up and fallen in love with the wrong man again. Honestly, why do I keep doing this to myself?"

"You didn't know he was the wrong guy until too late."

"It's because I jump in too fast. I get all caught up in his life and fall in love with the idea of being a family."

"I thought you said Liam hadn't told you that he planned to fight for custody of Maggie."

"Well…no."

"Then technically, you weren't planning on being a family with Liam and Maggie, but a couple with Liam."

"And eventually a family."

"Since eventually is in the future, I don't think that counts." Kori's voice was gentle but firm. "You love Liam. You told me you had a crush on him when you were a teenager. Isn't it possible that what you feel for him has nothing to do with seeing yourself as part of a family and everything to do with the fact that you're in love with him?"

"Sure." Did that make things better or worse? "But what about the fact that he asked me to marry him because he thought he would have a better chance to get custody if he was engaged?"

"I'm not really sure it's that straightforward," Kori said. "Liam Wade is a major catch. He's probably got dozens of women on speed dial that he's known a lot longer than you. Don't you wonder why he didn't ask one of them to marry him? I think he fell for you and is too afraid to admit it."

As tempting as it was to believe her friend's interpretation, Hadley knew it would just lead to more heartache. She couldn't spend the rest of her life wondering what if.

Kori's sigh filled Hadley's ear. "I can tell from your

silence that you don't agree. I'm sorry all this happened. You are such a wonderful person. You deserve the best guy in the world."

"And he's out there somewhere," Hadley said with what she hoped was a convincing amount of enthusiasm.

"What time do you want me to come get you tomorrow?"

"It doesn't matter." She figured Liam would stay at the hospital with Maggie until she was ready to go home, and that would give Hadley a chance to collect her things from the house without the risk of running into him.

"I'm meeting a client at eight. We can either go before or after."

"I guess I'd rather go early." The sooner she collected all her things, the sooner she could put all her mistakes behind her.

Maggie's new nanny was set to start the day after tomorrow, and Hadley doubted Dr. Davison would release her before that, so she didn't have to worry about seeing Liam ever again. The thought sent a stabbing pain through her.

"How about seven?"

"That would be perfect," Hadley said and then switched to the less emotionally charged topic of their upcoming girls' night out.

After a few more minutes, Hadley hung up. It took about ten seconds to go back to thinking about Liam. How was Maggie doing? Had her test results come back yet? Liam must be frantic waiting to hear something.

She brought up the messaging app on her phone, but stopped as she realized what she was doing. Contacting Liam would undo what little peace she'd found during the afternoon. It might be agonizing to cut ties with Liam and Maggie, but in the long run it would be better for all of them.

Yet no matter how many times she reminded herself of that fact as the evening dragged on, she wasn't able to put the baby or Liam out of her mind. Finally, she broke down and sent Liam a text around ten thirty, then shut off her phone and went to bed. But sleep eluded her. Despite having reached out to Liam, she couldn't put concern aside.

Around six, Hadley awoke. Feeling sluggish, her thoughts a jittery mess, she dragged herself out of bed and climbed into the shower. The closer it got to Kori's arrival, the more out of sorts Hadley became. Despite how unlikely it was that she'd run into Liam, she couldn't stop the anxiety that crept up her spine and sent a rush of goose bumps down her arm. By the time Hadley eased into Kori's passenger seat, she was a ball of nerves.

"You okay?" Kori asked, steering the car away from Hadley's apartment building.

"Fine. I didn't sleep very well. I couldn't stop thinking about Maggie and wondering how she's doing."

"You should call or text Liam and find out. I don't think he would have a problem with you letting him know you're worried."

"I did last night. He never got back to me." Hadley sounded as deflated as she felt. What had she expected? That Liam would fall all over himself telling her how much he missed her and that he regretted letting her go?

"Oh," Kori said, obviously stumped for an answer. "Well, then to hell with him."

That made Hadley smile. "Yeah," she agreed with fake bravado. "To hell with him."

But she didn't really mean it. She didn't even know if Liam had received her text. His focus was 100 percent fixed on Maggie, as was right. He'd answer in due time.

Twenty minutes later, Kori dropped her off at Wade Ranch. Hadley was relieved that her car was the only one in the driveway. She wouldn't have to run into Liam and make awkward conversation.

As soon as Hadley opened the front door she was assailed by the mouthwatering scent of cinnamon and sugar. She followed her nose to the kitchen and found Candace putting caramel rolls into a plastic container. Forgetting her intention had been to pack her suitcase with the few belongings she'd brought to the ranch house and get out as soon as possible, Hadley succumbed to the lure of Candace's incomparable pastries and sat down on one of the stools next to the island, fixing the housekeeper with a hopeful gaze.

"Those smell incredible."

"I thought I'd take them over to Liam at the hospital and give him a break so he could come home and clean up."

"That's really nice of you."

"But now that you're here, maybe you could take them to him instead." Candace caught Hadley's grimace and frowned. "What's wrong?"

"I don't know that Liam is going to want to see me." At Candace's puzzled expression, Hadley explained, "We broke off our engagement and I left him all alone at the hospital yesterday." *After freaking out on him*, she finished silently.

"I don't understand. Did you have a fight?"

"Not exactly. It's more that we rushed into things. I mean, we've only known each other a short time, and who gets engaged after three weeks?"

"But you two were so much in love. And it is an engagement, after all. You'll have plenty of time to get to know each other while you plan your wedding."

Hadley couldn't bring herself to explain to Candace that Liam didn't love her and only proposed so he could improve his chances of gaining custody of Maggie. "It was all just too fast," she murmured.

"But what about Maggie? I'm sure that Liam would appreciate your support with her being in the hospital."

Nothing Hadley could say would be good enough to rationalize abandoning a sick baby, so she merely hung her head and stared at the veins of silver glinting in the granite countertop. "I'll take the caramel rolls to Liam," she said at last. "And maybe some coffee as well. He's sure to be exhausted."

Candace nodded in approval. "He'll like that."

While Candace sealed up the rolls, Hadley poured coffee into a thermos, wondering how she'd let herself get talked into returning to the hospital. Then she sighed. It hadn't taken much prompting from Candace. In fact, Hadley was happy for an excuse to visit.

"If you're afraid because things between you have happened too fast," Candace began, turning away to carry the empty caramel roll pan to the sink, "I think you should know that I've never seen Liam as happy as he is with you."

"He makes me happy, as well." Had she let a past hurt blind her to everything that was true and loving about Liam?

"Whatever stands between you two can't possibly be insurmountable if you choose to work together to beat it."

What if fear of being hurt again had led to her overreacting to Liam's desire to seek custody of Maggie? Was it possible that she'd misjudged him? Attributed motives to him that didn't exist, all because she couldn't trust her own judgment?

"You're probably right."

"Then maybe you two should consider being open with each other about what it is you want and how you can achieve it."

Hadley offered Candace a wry smile. "It sounds so easy when you say it."

"Being in love isn't always easy, but in my experience, it's totally worth the ride."

"And Liam is totally worth taking that ride with," Hadley agreed. "Perhaps it's time I stopped being afraid of telling him that."

"Perhaps it is."

* * *

Liam hovered over Maggie's bassinet as the nurse took her temperature. "Her appetite was better this morning," he said.

The nurse hadn't missed his anxious tone and gave him a reassuring smile. "Her temperature is down a couple degrees. Looks like the antibiotics are doing what they're supposed to."

While it wasn't a clean bill of health, at least Maggie's situation was trending in the right direction. "That's great news." He wished he could share the update with Hadley, but she'd made it clear yesterday that she needed distance. It cut deep that he'd driven her away.

"She's sleeping now," the nurse said. "Why don't you take the opportunity to get something to eat? From what I hear, you skipped dinner last night."

"I wasn't hungry."

"Well, you're not going to do your little girl any good if you get run-down and can't take care of her once she's ready to go home." The nurse gave him a stern look.

"Sure, you're right." But he couldn't bring himself to leave Maggie alone. "I'll go down to the cafeteria in a little while."

Once the nurse left, Liam brushed a hand through his hair, suddenly aware he was practically asleep on his feet. He hadn't been able to do more than snatch a couple naps during the night and could really use a cup of coffee. It occurred to him that he wasn't going to be able to keep this pace up for long, but he would never be able to forgive himself if Maggie got worse while he was gone.

A soft female voice spoke from the doorway. "How's she doing?"

Blinking back exhaustion, Liam glanced up and spied Hadley hovering in the hallway. From her apprehensive expression, she obviously expected him to throw her out.

"A little better."

"That's great. I hope it's okay that I came by."

"Sure." After yesterday, he could barely believe she'd come back. "Of course."

"I wasn't sure…" She looked around the room as if in search of somewhere to hide. "You didn't answer my text last night."

He rubbed his face to clear some of the blurriness from his mind. "You sent a text? I didn't get it."

"Oh." She held up a rectangular container and a silver thermos. "I brought you coffee and some of Candace's caramel rolls. She was going to come herself, but I had to pick up my car and was heading back this way…" She trailed off as if unnerved by his silence. "I can just leave them and go. Or I can stay with Maggie while you go home and shower or sleep. You don't look like you got any last night."

She didn't look all that refreshed, either. Of course she'd worried. He imagined her tossing and turning in her bed, plagued by concern for Maggie. It was in her nature to care even when it wasn't in her best interest to do so.

"I'm so sorry," he told her, his voice a dry rasp. "I should never have let you leave yesterday. We should have talked."

"No." She shook her head and took two steps toward him. "I should apologize. The way I acted yesterday was unforgivable. I should never have been thinking of myself when Maggie was so sick."

Liam caught her upper arms and pulled her close. He barely noticed the container of rolls bump against his stomach as he bent his head and kissed her firmly on the lips, letting his emotions overwhelm him. The aching tightness in his chest released as she gave a little moan before yielding her lips to his demand.

He let go of her arms and stroked his palms up her shoulders and beneath her hair, cupping her head so he could feast on her mouth. Time stood still. The hospital room fell away as he showed her the emotions he'd been keeping hidden. His fear, his need, his joy. Everything she made him feel. He gave it all to her.

"Liam." She breathed his name in wonder as he nuzzled his face into her neck.

"I love you." The words came so easily to him now. Gone were his defenses, stripped away by an endless, lonely night and his elation that she'd returned. He wasn't going to let her question his devotion ever again. "No, I adore you. And will do whatever it takes for as long as it takes for you to believe you are the only woman for me."

A smile of happiness transformed her. He gazed down into her overly bright eyes and couldn't believe how close he'd come to losing her.

"I love you, too," she replied, lifting on tiptoe to kiss him lightly on the lips.

"I rushed you because I was afraid your career would take you away, and I couldn't bear to lose you." Suddenly it was easy to share his fears with her, and from the way she regarded him, she understood what he'd been going through. "This time we'll take it slow," he promised. "I'm determined that you won't feel rushed into making up your mind about spending the rest of your life with me."

She gave a light laugh. "I don't need any time. I love you and I want to marry you. Together we are going to be a family. No matter what happens with Kyle, Maggie will always be like a daughter to us and a big sister to our future children."

"In that case." He fished the ring out of his pocket and dropped to one knee. "Hadley Stratton, love of my life, would you do me the honor of becoming my wife?"

She shifted the thermos beneath her arm and held out her left hand. "Liam Wade, loving you is the most wonderful thing that has ever happened to me. I can't wait for us to get married and live happily ever after."

He slipped the ring onto her finger and got to his feet. Bending down, he kissed her reverently on the lips. One kiss turned into half a dozen and both of them were out of breath and smiling foolishly when they drew apart.

"Kissing you is always delightful," she said, handing him the coffee. "And we really must do much more of that later, but right now my mouth has been watering over these caramel rolls for the last hour."

"You're choosing food over kissing me?"

"These are Candace's caramel rolls," she reminded him, popping the top on the container and letting the sugary, cinnamon smell fill the room.

"I get your point." He nodded, his appetite returning in a flash. "Let's eat."

The morning of her wedding dawned clear and mild. The winds that had buffeted the Texas landscape for the last week had calmed, and the weather forecasters were promising nothing but pleasant temperatures for several days to come.

Today at eleven o'clock she was marrying Liam in an intimate ceremony at the Texas Cattleman's Club. Naturally Kori was her matron of honor while Liam's best man would be Mac McCallum. Because the wedding was happening so fast, Hadley had opted for a white tulle skirt and sleeveless white lace top that showed a glimpse of her midriff. Since she was marrying a man she'd reconnected with less than a month earlier, Hadley decided to kick conventional to the curb and wear something trendy rather than a traditional gown.

Kori had lent her the white silk flower and crystal headpiece she'd worn at her wedding. Her something borrowed. She wore a pair of pearl-and-diamond earrings once owned by Liam's grandmother. Her something old. For her something blue and new, Hadley purchased a pair of bright blue cowboy boots.

The shock on her mother's face validated Hadley's choice, but it was the possessive gleam in Liam's eyes as she walked down the aisle at the start of the ceremony that assured her she'd been absolutely right to break the mold and let her true self shine.

"You look gorgeous," he told her as she took the hand he held out to her.

She stepped beside him and tucked her hand into the crook of his arm. "I'm glad you think so. I thought of you when I bought everything."

He led her toward the white arch where the minister waited. A harp played in the corner, the tune something familiar to weddings, but Hadley was conscious only of the tall man at her side and the sense of peace that filled her as the minister began to speak.

Swearing to love, honor and be true to Liam until the day she died was the easiest promise she'd ever had to make. And from the sparkle in his eyes as he slid the wedding ring onto her finger, he appeared just as willing to pledge himself completely to her.

At last the minister introduced them as husband and wife, and they led their guests into the banquet room that had been set up for the reception. Draped with white lights and tulle, the room had a romantic atmosphere that stopped Hadley's breath.

Flowers of every color filled the centerpieces on the tables. Because of the limited time for the preparations, Hadley had told the florist to pull together whatever he had. She'd carried a bouquet of orange roses and pink lilies, and Liam wore a hot-pink rose on his lapel.

"I had no idea it was going to be this gorgeous," she murmured.

"The only gorgeous thing in the room is you."

Hadley lifted onto her toes and kissed him. "And that's why I love you. You always know what makes me smile."

And so ended their last intimate moment as newlyweds for the next three hours as social demands kept them occupied with their guests. At long last they collected Maggie from her circle of admirers and headed back to Wade Ranch. Together they put her to bed and stood beside the crib watching her sleep.

"I meant to give this to you earlier but didn't get the chance." Liam extended a small flat box to her.

"What is it?"

"Open it and see."

Hadley raised the lid and peered down at the engraved heart-shaped pendant in white gold. She read the inscription, "Follow your heart. Mine always leads to the barn." She laughed. "I used to have a T-shirt with that on it."

"I remember." Liam lifted the necklace from the bed of black velvet and slipped it over her head. "You were wearing it the first time I saw you."

"That was more than ten years ago." Hadley was stunned. "How could you possibly remember that?"

"You'd be surprised what I remember about you."

She threaded her fingers through his hair and pulled him down for a kiss. "It's a lovely gift, but it no longer pertains."

"I thought you'd gotten past your guilt about your friend."

"I have." She smiled up at him. "But my heart no longer leads me to the barn. It leads me to you."

He bent down and swept her off her feet. "And that, Mrs. Wade, is the way it should be."

* * * * *

MILLS & BOON®

Desire™

PASSIONATE AND DRAMATIC LOVE STORIES

'The perfect Christmas read!' - Julia Williams

Jewellery designer Skylar loves living London, but when a surprise proposal goes wrong, she finds herself fleeing home to remote Puffin Island.

Burned by a terrible divorce, TV historian Alec is dazzled by Sky's beauty and so cynical that he assumes that's a bad thing! Luckily she's on the verge of getting engaged to someone else, so she won't be a constant source of temptation... but this Christmas, can Alec and Sky realise that they are what each other was looking for all along?

Order yours today at
www.millsandboon.co.uk

MILLS & BOON®

Man of the Year

Our winning cover star will be revealed next month!

**Don't miss out on your copy
– order from millsandboon.co.uk**

Read more about Man of the Year 2016 at

www.millsandboon.co.uk/moty2016

**Have you been following our
Man of the Year 2016 campaign?**
🐦 #MOTY2016